PRAISE FOR *THE LOST FLAMINGOES OF BOMBAY*

'Siddharth Dhanvant Shanghvi's literary forebears are Somerset Maugham, Graham Greene, and E.M. Forster. He's also an original, major storyteller, who beguiles us into a world of illusion and bestows us with a sharp-eyed lens into the heart. *The Lost Flamingoes of Bombay* is a triumph'—Amy Tan, bestselling author of *The Joy Luck Club* and *The Kitchen God's Wife*

'Shanghvi's wit is exhaustingly dazzling, and more than a little provocative ... an articulate, buccaneering, confident writer ... his tale is both entertaining and thought-provoking'—Sam Miller, *India Today*

'Once in a while a book comes along that is refreshingly different in content and structure. It seeks neither to deliberately shock nor does it indulge in verbal pyrotechnics, yet the overreaching impact is such that it leaves one numb with a hundred different feelings. Emotions linger much after the book has been put aside and its characters develop tentacles that dig into the deepest recesses of the heart. *The Lost Flamingoes of Bombay* is one such book'—*Pioneer*

'Shanghvi's novel brings Bombay alive ... startlingly new ... immensely readable'—*The Hindu*

'Simply brilliant'—*Economic Times*

'There is a strangely lyrical, even operatic tenor in Siddharth Dhanvant Shanghvi's second book, *The Lost Flamingoes of Bombay*. In a style that is uniquely his, Shanghvi builds note upon note, strikes poetic image upon photographic image till he binds you into a spell you have to struggle to snap out of days after you have finished the book. The ambiguity of Shanghvi's prose contains a luscious incantory power'—*Asian Age*

'*The Lost Flamingoes of Bombay* is at once scathing and meditative. At the heart of the book lies a web of intricate relationships between Karan, Samar, Zaira and Rhea. And while Shanghvi spins out their stories in graceful, potent prose, he also holds up an unforgiving mirror to the darkness of urban India and its failings. This compelling book epitomizes how fiction can be the most powerful chronicle of a society and its unravelling'—*Elle*

'A twisted relationship between a married woman and a younger photographer forms the central plot in the story. Through the life and relationship of these two characters, the author has superbly examined modern India; its perverse fascination for celebrities; the clash between mortality and personal desires; and all that is condoned in the name of love. A captivating read'—*Platform*

'A remarkable book. What is admirable about this story, perfectly controlled by the author, is precisely what is silent or hidden'—*Le Monde*, France

'Shanghvi's novel leaves a sharp and original impression; dealing with the hidden side of modern India it exposes what lies beneath her golden surface'—*Il Tempo*, Italy

'One cannot stop reading it'—*Os Meus Livros*

THE LOST FLAMINGOES OF BOMBAY

SIDDHARTH DHANVANT SHANGHVI

HarperCollins *Publishers* India

First published in 2009

This edition published in India by HarperCollins *Publishers* 2024
4th Floor, Tower A, Building No. 10, Phase II, DLF Cyber City,
Gurugram, Haryana – 122002
www.harpercollins.co.in

2 4 6 8 10 9 7 5 3 1

P-ISBN: 978-93-5699-868-1
E-ISBN: 978-93-5699-924-4

Typeset in 11.5/16.2 Garamond Premier Pro at
Manipal Technologies Limited, Manipal

Printed and bound at
Nutech Print Services - India

FSC
www.fsc.org
MIX
Paper | Supporting responsible forestry
FSC® C195953

This book is printed on FSC® certified paper
which ensures responsible forest management.

In memory of my mother,
Padmini
(1944–2008)
Beloved Lioness

Om tat sat

that which is

Author's Note

The Lost Flamingoes of Bombay is inspired, in part, by a range of events discussed extensively in the print media, films and on television. While some of the events in the book do bear echoes of such reports, this novel remains a work of fiction.

PART 1

1

'OH GOD, IQBAL,' KARAN SETH SAID, LOOKING warily at his boss, 'you sound like you're setting me up for trouble.'

'Trouble is good for character building, Karan.'

'Character building is too much work.'

'I'm asking you to photograph a subject whom most other photographers on the team would give an arm and a leg to shoot,' Iqbal said impatiently.

Karan grinned. 'You picked me because I'm junior on your team and wouldn't have the guts to say no.'

'Well, I'm glad you see the light.'

Iqbal Syed and Karan Seth were sitting across from each other at a long cafeteria table; two glass mugs of cutting chai freed tendrils of steam between them. Copies of the magazine

they both worked for—*The India Chronicle*—were scattered over the length of the table.

'The story is on musicians who were once world famous but have now fallen off the grid,' Iqbal said. 'I want you to photograph the pianist Samar Arora.'

Karan looked blankly at Iqbal. Who was Samar Arora?

Gauging his puzzled expression, Iqbal added, 'After graduating from Juilliard, around fifteen, maybe sixteen years ago, Samar performed at his first concert. He was twelve, or some such ridiculous age. *The New York Times* declared that a new star had arrived. Samar produced many hit records and performed at countless concerts to standing ovations. And then, without a word of warning, he quit.' After a pause, Iqbal added, 'At the ripe old age of twenty-five. Three years ago.'

'Why did he do that?'

'No one knows; I doubt he himself does. But you can see why Samar would be a fantastic subject for this feature.'

'Yes, he would be perfect for the story but why do you want *me* to photograph Samar?'

'You're both in your twenties; it's likely you'll capture a side of Samar the seniors in the team may miss.'

Iqbal did not tell Karan that the real reason for his choice was that never before had he hired a junior photographer who had come to the desk almost fully formed: Karan had consistently delivered eloquent, powerful pictures, with unsaid things trembling at their corners; his work possessed the dazzling throb of permanence. Iqbal admired the oblique

humour and elegant restraint in Karan's pictures; of course, he would need time, and experience, for the raw, ferocious energy of his oeuvre to discover wholeness and patience, but fate had sent him out with a deck aflush with aces.

Although swamped with assignments, Karan figured that photographing a formerly famous pianist would be a breeze. 'I'll set up something with Samar Arora.'

'You might be getting ahead of yourself,' Iqbal cautioned. 'After retiring, Samar hasn't agreed to a single interview.'

'I could always request his agent.'

Iqbal sipped on his chai. 'He doesn't have an agent since he no longer performs.'

'What if I wrote to his record company and requested a one-off meeting? I could assure them that Samar would have the right to choose the pictures he wanted to see in print.'

'It won't make a difference. After moving to Bombay a few years ago he's been a bit of a hermit. Although, when Samar does step out, he paints the town every shade of red and people talk about it for days.'

To their shared dismay, they were assailed at this point by the fluted voice of Natasha, the magazine's fashion editor. She settled her plump, provocative derrière on the chair next to Karan; the new kid on the block had caught her eye at the water cooler the previous week.

Karan, however, had been avoiding Natasha from his first day on the job because she proudly sashayed around the office with a crocodile-skin clutch, as if announcing how she had

thoughtfully rescued a poor reptile from the terrifying obscurity of the swamp.

'I've met Samar,' she said after enquiring what the two men had been discussing. 'At a party in Bandra; he was guzzling Bellinis on the roof of the mansion, his best friend in tow.'

Karan tilted his head. 'On the roof?'

'One drink too many and he'd have come rolling down like squirrel shit.' Natasha ran her predatory fingers through her bright blonde highlights. 'Apparently, Samar claims the low temperature on the rooftop after midnight does his complexion a *world of* good. At one party he had to be rescued by firemen, ladders, the whole shebang; most Bombaywallas think he's one pretentious prick.'

'Who is his best friend?' Karan asked, in the hope that the person might provide a lead to reaching the eccentric pianist.

'Zaira, of the movies. I styled her shoot for our last issue. So beautiful she's single-handedly responsible for raising India's National Masturbation Index.'

'The nation's biggest film star is Samar's best friend.' Karan shook his head. All of a sudden, his proposed subject was not just another comet whizzing by in a distant galaxy of enigmatic failures. 'So, why was Zaira on the roof with him?'

'So they could be smug together! One is famous; the other is notorious; they're joined at the hip. Y'know how it is: birdbrains of a feather ...'

Karan sighed. He was new to Bombay—he had lived in the city only a few months—and Natasha exuded that odious,

imperious indifference sired by snarkiness. He was not immune to its discouraging effects.

'How do you propose I get hold of Samar for my assignment?'

'Why don't you try waiting outside his house?' Iqbal suggested.

'And jump him when he steps out!' Glee dripped out of Natasha like precum.

'I'm sorry I can't be more helpful.' Iqbal rose to leave. 'And since you have a deadline that *cannot* be missed, get on with it.' He strode off, winking at Karan, who looked stricken at the prospect of being left unchaperoned in Natasha's clutches.

'I will.'

Karan turned to Natasha. 'What a pity Samar no longer does the media.'

Natasha touched Karan's arm and intoned in a voice laced with suggestion, 'Luckily, I'm a firm believer in doing the media.'

'In that case,' Karan said as he picked up his camera and slung it over his shoulder, 'you should get going, too; you have a lot of ground to cover.'

The young man's sharp, watchful face, his deep-set auburn eyes, the swathe of jet-black hair and defined jawline continued to excite Natasha even after he had walked out of the line of her vision. For a little hick out of Shimla, she thought in the glowering light of his rebuff, he's got a lot of cheek. But let's see

how far it gets him in a city that'll chew him and spit him out like he's a sliver of supari.

For the next two weeks Karan tried but failed to get hold of Samar. Calls to Samar's cottage on Worli Seaface went unanswered. As Iqbal had told him, there was no agent to set up a meeting. He had to write off the Zaira lead too as it would mean he would have to cosy up to Natasha for Zaira's coordinates. As the days went by, his dejection at failing to contact Samar was compounded by fear; Iqbal repeatedly asked for the photos and Karan wasn't ready to let his mentor down.

One night, a week before the deadline, Karan was ruminating on the fact that he had come to Bombay in search of images that would reveal its most sublime, secret stories; instead, here he was, single and sleepless, busting a vein on a paparazzo job. He knew his desire to document Bombay was not wholly unique but perhaps his hunger had an original worth, an intensity powered by ravenous curiosity and a quality that was a lot like compassion but without its air of moral conceit. How many others, he thought, had come to the city with a dark, delicious dream in their pocket and four thousand rupees in the bank? And how many others had found their passion exchanged for indifference, even resentment?

His mood was darkening by the minute when Iqbal rang him to say that he had just got word that Samar Arora had been spotted at the city's most cunning joint, Gatsby. Although exhausted, Karan bolted up; it was like the moment in a rave when people are no longer dancing to or against the beat of the

music but *into* it, the currents of bass and tune raging through their body and into the spirit. Not bothering to change out of his crumpled white tee shirt and torn blue jeans, he raced down the stairs of his rental in Ban Ganga, made it to the main road, flagged a taxi and begged the driver to get him to Colaba in less than ten minutes: he didn't want to get to the restaurant only to be told that Samar Arora had left the building. As he adjusted the lens cover over his Leica he found himself secretly hoping that Samar Arora *had* left the building and was, in fact, dusting a tile on the roof and drinking to the moonlight that now cast luminous bars outside the window of his taxi. What a photo *that* would make!

A little before 2.00 a.m., Karan reached Gatsby, tucked away at the end of sleepy old Mandalik Lane.

In front of the portal, under a big rain tree, liveried chauffeurs traded flashes of filthy gossip about their bosses, and tipsy memsahibs, smelling of their husbands' abandonment, waited for valets to pull up their fancy cars.

No sooner had Karan stepped into the restaurant than he was subsumed with unease; in his shabby clothes and his unshaven, sleepy face, he was an obvious impostor. The waiters looked on with indifference and the haughty maître d' eyed him as if he was going to walk right over and ask Karan to make tracks.

Karan slunk through the bubbly horde of painted faces, negotiating a jungle of expensive perfumes, vines of vetiver, marshes of musk. So as not to drown in a whirlpool of anxiety,

he focussed all his attention on spotting his subject. Where was the piano man? He scanned the throng, but it was impossible not to be led astray. For here was a perma-tanned socialite with angry silver hair and narrow rapacious eyes, clanking her ivory bangles. A pack of icky corporate types, obese and bald, were surrounded by heroin-thin models with sepulchral expressions gouged with scorn. He recognized a famous film-maker, dressed in a stunning orange sarong, standing regally under the outrageous shield of a green cloth umbrella, his long wrist bent like the spout of a teapot. The music—a canvas for the assembled to spew their bon mots and display their neuroses—was electric tandava, and it washed over Karan, diluting all his worries. He imagined that the people here would never die: they would simply evaporate into the carnal smoke of the music, their loins wrapped around each other, self and sorrow abandoned to the roar of lust. His eyes coasted from one person to the next before zoning in on a small group under the wooden stairwell at the far end of the bar. Thrilled to see his elusive subject was very much around, Karan took a deep breath and readied himself for the decisive moment.

Clad in a berry-black suit, his short hair stylishly mussed up, Samar Arora was talking animatedly to Mantra Rai, the controversial columnist and author.

Mantra's hawkish face was framed by a blustery black mane. Her recently published first novel, *Remembrance of Bitches Past,* was the talk of the town: a tell-all-claw-all on the beau monde, which, among its many dirty divulgences, had brought to light the liaison between the city's most respected philanthropist and his fourteen-year-old niece, a fuck fest all the charity in the world could not hush up.

Leo McCormick, Samar's boyfriend, had just asked Mantra her views on the recent efforts of the right-wing government to rename the city: 'Bombay' would soon be whitewashed into 'Mumbai'.

'Mumbai is about as appealing a name for a city as Gonorrhoea,' Mantra declared. 'Besides, the change will pollute the collective public memory of "Bombay".'

Within minutes the trio had got worked up over the city's possible rechristening, and another angle was added to their debate as Priya Das, a newly elected member of Parliament, joined them.

'But Mumbai was the original name of Bombay,' Priya said stiffly, referring to the fact that the Kolis, one of the earliest communities resident in the city, had named it in honour of the goddess Mumbadevi. 'This is about claiming our past back from the colonists.'

Mantra exhaled loudly. 'Look, Priya, a woman is raped every hour in Bombay. Over half the population lives in slums. Twelve-year-olds work as whores. The trains are never on time. And my milk has funny water in it.'

'Your point being?'

'The Brits checked out some forty years ago. The past is important, but the present is crucial. Giving Bombay a new name is not going to make it any safer or cleaner.'

'But this is a resistance to authenticity!' Priya screeched.

It occurred to Mantra that Priya had a crusty librarian's voice, one that could only be relieved with a dildo. 'Authenticity?' she said. 'The Kolis called it Mumbadevi in the 1800s. If you're looking for authenticity, you'll have to dig much deeper than that. Bombay goes way back to the twelfth century.'

The heated debate was interrupted by a sudden, loud squeal of delight. 'Well, if it isn't the wonderful Samar Arora!' Editor of a fashion bible, Diya Sen, the source of the enthusiastic greeting, had long, naughty legs and a giggle as shiny as a penny in the sun. This evening she was all shimmied up in a black shift dress and a string of thick white pearls. 'My favourite pianist!' she burbled. 'Darling man, how lucky I am to cross your path.'

'I've been waiting here all my life only so you might come along,' Samar assured the slightly sloshed editor.

'I see your lovely boyfriend has graced our wicked acres ... Hello there, Mr McCormick. How's the new masterpiece coming along?'

'One page at a time,' Leo replied. 'Slow, but steady. How's your husband?'

'Oh, super!' Diya roped her arm around Samar, drawing a quizzical look from Leo. 'Except, he's no longer my husband.'

'Oh, I'm sorry ... I had no—' Leo blushed.

'Don't apologize, darling! After four years of marriage I discovered that the only thing we had in common was a mutual adoration of me—but even that wasn't enough to make me stay.' She kissed Samar on his car, and drawled, 'I have a new man.'

'Wonderful!' Samar said. 'What does he do?'

'The Boyfriend is working on a biography of Bombay.'

'How exciting. Bombay deserves a good memoirist. Have you read any of his work in progress? I enjoy reading the first draft of Leo's writing.'

'I gave the fellow a first line for his book; it's bound to be an opus, although right now it's more pus than opus.' She made a face.

'Well, I'm sure you'll whip it into shape, Diya; your mind could mend any book.'

'I doubt we'll be together that long,' the editor confessed.

'Why toss out a talented writer?' Samar said as he ruffled Leo's hair. 'Writing prowess often extends into the bedroom.'

'Not in the case of the Boyfriend,' Diya asserted. 'But then, not every fling comes with a bling quotient, and I was raised to believe that certain kinds of charity begin in bed.'

'You're not giving your boyfriend enough of a chance.'

'When you date writers, execute your own exit routes. Otherwise, before you know it, you'll be written out of the narrative. I've got too much self-disrespect to be a closed chapter in someone else's book.'

'That's a bit harsh,' Leo said. 'Writers are not calculating; they just understand early on that efficient editing can save a straggling story.'

Diya waved her hand in the air. 'The Boyfriend is not *half* as much fun as what I did last week in Goa; I got my first tattoo! Want to see it?'

Priya, ever the insecure politician, not about to be outdone by a fashion journalist, raised her voice. 'I guess the whole Mumbai vs Bombay issue boils down to one thing: the privileged class vs the working class.'

'I'm a writer, and no one gets more "working class" than starving writers,' said Mantra.

'If you're so working class, what're you doing here at Gatsby?' Priya asked snidely.

'I had the sense to marry well, Priya. And to divorce better.'

'Congratulations! With that one sentence you've pushed back the women's rights movement by a whole fifty years!'

Long immune to such Bombay-brand bitchery, Mantra serenely took another sip of her whisky. 'Some of us, Priya, might believe that your birth is one helluvan argument for the pro-contraceptive movement,' she said. 'But don't you go sweating over progressive politics so early in your career.'

Diya, meanwhile, was growing impatient. 'I want to show you my tattoo. NOW!'

'Well then ...' Samar threw his hands up in the air. 'What's stopping you?'

In one quick, smart motion Diya unzipped her black dress and let it fall to her feet, where it gathered in a desultory heap. Hiking up the succulent left cheek of her butt, encased in white lacy knickers, she said, 'It's Capricorn, my star sign.'

'Gosh! I thought Capricornians were supposed to be quite old school,' Samar said. 'But you've made some giant strides from there, doll.'

'What's insulting is how the politicians never once asked us.' Mantra was still at it, though now she was trying hard to peel her eyes away from the booty on show. 'How dare they take our votes and our money and play with the name of our city without consulting us? This is no democracy! This is a land of right-wing zealots. We chucked out the whites in 1947 but what sort of fiends did we elect in their place? The Hindu People's Party, that's what.'

'That's because the city's elite have different things on their minds,' Priya said. 'Real Bombay is not here.' She wondered if the young girl standing there like a besharam chaddi-baby was going to snap her dress back on. 'And it's really very reductive of you to write off the Hindu People's Party as right-wing zealots. You may have forgotten, I am one of their representatives.'

'Oh, puhleez! Save that Real Bombay-Fake Bombay crap. There may be six hundred and fifty million of us who live below

the poverty line but there are also three hundred and fifty million of us who're not doing too badly, thank you very much. Some of us, in fact, even find the time to grab a drink at Gatsby.' She looked pointedly at the politician. 'And really, Priya, it's a bit cheeky to make poverty your party line when you're *at* the party.'

While Priya struggled to make a comeback, Diya Sen jubilantly held court in her lingerie, like some sort of an ancient goddess of lust. 'So, my darling,' she said to Samar, 'I heard you tap dance like a dream, and when you do, sirens go off and the lights come on.'

'Don't flatter Samar in that department.' Leo tightened his grip on Samar's arm. 'You don't want to get him going after he's had a few drinks and, trust me, he's been careless with the Bellinis tonight.'

'Show me!' Diya cried. 'Let me be the judge.'

'Here?' Samar's brow creased. 'It's so damn crowded, babe; my feet would hardly hear me if I heckled them to kick up a step or two!'

'The bar top looks kinda free to me.' Diya giggled.

Samar surveyed the bar top. The gorgeous editor had a point. Besides, if she could stand around in her knockout knickers and pretty pearls, the least he could do was throw on a stomp fest at her plea.

Pulling free of Leo's grasp, Samar hoisted himself on to the narrow gleaming counter. As the pianist shuffled by to an internal accelerando, the guests hastily lifted their drinks to let him pass—and pass he did, in smart chuff and glide. A few

gasps, some scowls, two whistles and a lot of *hmmm* went up around the bar.

Karan felt he was witness to a scene that was as much theatre as circus; he half expected shrieking yellow canaries to burst out of someone's elaborate coiffure and fireworks to go off in one corner of the room. Not only was Samar's performance spectacular, but his audience comprising the film-maker in the orange sarong, the socialite with calf-length silver hair, the editor in her hot white knickers made for accidental, incredible props.

When Samar finally hit his head against one of the overhead lamps, Leo extended his hand, which the pianist accepted to execute a neat landing on the floor.

Leo smiled; his lover had one thing down pat: the perfect exit.

On his way out, past a swarm of bedazzled admirers, Diya pulled Samar to her side. 'At least now you know that inner beauty is nothing more than smart knickers.'

'I love you because you're deep enough to be shallow.' He gave her a farewell peck. 'And smart enough to know the difference between the two.'

With ample evidence of Samar's escapades in hand, Karan hurried home and slept restfully after nights of anxiety. The next morning he dashed off to the magazine's photo lab to print the shots. Although the pictures were expectedly impressive—particularly the one of Samar gliding on the bar top as the sarong-clad film-maker with his green umbrella blew an adulatory kiss in his direction—the lighting was awful.

'You mean we can't use any of them?' He paced the office.

Iqbal swivelled on his chair. 'The restaurant was so dimly lit, there's no way the resolution of the images would hold if we printed them; they'll be too grainy.'

'They were bound to be grainy; I was shooting on my fastest film.' Karan was quickly coming down with the glums. 'How the hell am I going to get printable pictures of Samar? Gatsby had been my best shot.'

'Why don't you give these pictures to Samar?' Iqbal advised. 'Write him a note saying that if he doesn't sit for you then the magazine will be forced to use these pictures and, wonderful as they might be, their quality is not up to scratch. He'll know it too. See if that works.'

'Basically, you want me to blackmail him.'

'Basically,' Iqbal said, leaning forward, 'I'm trying to save your ass.'

By noon that day, Karan had left a selection of the pictures, accompanied by a handwritten letter, with Samar Arora's maid, in the hope that the pianist would be amused enough to indulge him with a private, one-on-one sitting.

To his delight, the ploy worked. A note arrived for Karan at the *India Chronicle* office on Tuesday, the following week, inviting him over for 'a cup of chai or a Bellini or whatever'.

In the intervening days Karan caught up on assignments he had neglected while he had been preoccupied with pursuing Samar. He also took an evening off from work to shoot the dusty, sublime balustrades of falling-down mansions in Kala

Ghoda. After he had printed the shots, he showed them to Iqbal.

'Are they for your project on Bombay?' Iqbal's eyelids blinked rapidly as he scrutinized the bunch of black-and-white prints.

'Yes,' Karan said. 'In a few years these old houses won't be around.' They were the only two from the photo department still in office; it was past midnight. 'The beauty we will have lost ...' he added somewhat wistfully.

'What amazes me most is your skill. But I won't say more; I don't want your head to grow too big for your hat.' The detailing in Karan's photographs, the turbulent poetry of their gloom, took Iqbal's breath away. 'But the sheer grit! By now, you must have shot thousands of pictures of Bombay?'

'Seven thousand six hundred and forty-one shots, but I'm not counting. I told you, Iqbal; I joined *India Chronicle* for roti, kapda aur makaan but my heart is set on creating a record of this city.'

'Atget is your guru,' Iqbal said, referring to the legendary documenter of Paris. 'So, good luck to you, boy; I sure hope you worry Bombay with your Leica. Now,' he said, 'when do I see Samar Arora's pictures?'

'I am shooting him at his house in Worli on Tuesday,' he said, beaming.

'What did you make of Samar when you saw him at Gatsby?'

'A real performer, and quite a poser. But a superb subject; the camera loves him, and he loves it right back.'

On Tuesday morning a big fat sun careened through thick layers of cloud, revealing a sky the colour of joy. The same evening, on the bus to Samar's house, Karan saw the prairie-blue sky darken, opalescent grey turning to leaden silver. Traffic, which had slowed to a crawl around Cadbury House, came to a grinding halt outside Haji Ali dargah only a few pious footfalls away. Karan's bus too came to a standstill and he disembarked along with the other commuters.

Staring skywards, at the thundering shadow that was approaching, Karan felt it could herald the apocalypse. Flamingoes, thousands of them, were flying by in a giant skein: the birds had tight, spindled legs and large, serrated wings, and their graceful necks were so firmly held they looked like freshly serviced strings on a sitar. The birds were white—save for splashes of dirty pink—and the span of their wings in motion produced a sound not unlike huge, heaving bellows.

Children wept. Dogs howled.

Schoolgirls cried. Men stood open-mouthed.

Karan took out his camera from its case and furiously clicked the scene around him. He zoomed in on the bald, blind beggar in a ragged black suit. Turning around, he strode closer to the Medusa-maned monkey pedlar parked beside a trio of scruffy singing vagrants. The three scrawny roadside tenors stared at the sky, their hands reaching up to the flock in flight,

and sang, in a thick, ironic nasal castrato, a forgotten bakwaas Hindi love song.

As Karan tried to tear himself free of earthbound particulars and look again at the spectacle in the sky, his frame pulled into focus hundreds of red petals fluttering about gaily. A flower seller had dropped piles of ruby-red graveyard roses on the pavement, now quickly being crushed under the feet of the crowd. Within minutes a fierce sea wind had whipped the petals into the air, where they now whirled wildly. Standing amidst the storm of rose petals, with the flamingoes above him, Karan thought: So this is Bombay, monster muse, part witch, part clown, always absurd, often charming—my rogue ballad; this is Bombay, meri jaan.

Pausing to catch his breath, he brought his camera to his side. He looked around, surprised. Within seconds the scene had changed dramatically. The flamingoes were all but gone, the sky was flooded with light, and the passengers had hopped back on to the bus. Traffic began to move again, with a great revving of engines and slow shuffle of wheels. The singing trio on the pavement abandoned their tamasha recital. The bald, blind beggar knocked against a lamp post and landed flat on his back in a scattered pool of lush red petals. In the chaos, the monkey escaped his leash and scurried down the road, its pedlar chasing breathlessly after it.

2

'HOW LOVELY OF YOU TO STOP BY!' SAMAR emerged from the pool, water glistening on his skin. He walked toward Karan, who was sitting on a deck chair on the lawn.

Karan stood up and extended his hand. 'I hope I'm not interrupting your swim?'

'I was just winding up the last of my evening laps.' Samar wrapped a white towel around himself, concealing his tight blue swimming briefs.

'You have a fine home.' Karan turned and faced the house, a neat, square, brick structure with white-panelled windows and a narrow widow's porch on the first level; on the ground level was a green rectangle of lawn, a pool, a few scattered almond trees. 'There are hardly any homes like this left in Bombay.'

'Yes, the pool is a luxury but perhaps it'll come in handy when we fill it with champagne and drown ourselves drinking it up. Did you wait long, Mr Seth?'

'Please call me Karan. I've been here only fifteen minutes or so. Your maid left me here with a cup of chai.' Although Karan found Samar's warmth appealing, he questioned its authenticity.

'I'm glad Saku-bai was good to you. You're blessed; she's been trying forever to kill me.' Samar widened his eyes to feign a look of shock.

'I find that hard to believe.' Karan thought momentarily of the maid, dour and unfriendly; could she really be plotting Samar's death?

'Oh, Saku-bai's left soapsuds in the bath,' Samar complained, 'and stirred something spooky in the dal. For years she fed me raw papayas.'

'Raw papayas are poisonous?'

Clasping the sides of his face with his hands, Samar raised his brows in horror. 'They can cause spontaneous abortions.'

'That shouldn't worry you; you're a man.'

'And thank God for *that!* Otherwise, can you imagine all the babies I'd have lost by now?'

As Karan nodded uncertainly, Samar realized that his brand of absurd humour had whizzed over the young man's head; perhaps he was new to Bombay or perhaps he was just stupid.

When Karan appeared to wither a little, Samar reached out and squeezed his elbow. 'I invited you over to tell you, you have no bloody business being such a talented swine.'

'I'm honoured.' Karan blushed. The sight of Samar tap dancing on the bar top refused to leave his memory, and it confirmed Natasha's nasty edict on Samar: 'a pretentious prick'.

'The pictures you took at Gatsby make me look like a human being for a change.'

'Is that a compliment?'

'I don't think very much of human beings,' Samar confessed. 'I much prefer foxes and dahlias and whippets; they're beautiful, and scarce.'

Again, Karan looked on without a word.

Samar felt himself growing impatient with the fetching young man and his gauche pauses. Fortunately, the silence between them was shattered by a slender white whippet bounding toward them from the living room and hurling itself on Samar.

'And how is Mr Ward-Davies this evening?' Samar tried to hold the wriggling dog and avoid an avalanche of licks at the same time. 'Would you care to join Karan and me for a walk?'

Karan had never heard a man talk to a dog as if he were a human being; it was not the overwhelming affection in Samar's voice but the lambent dignity of the address that got him.

The whippet responded to Samar by gazing at him like a moonstruck teenager, as though in Samar's presence the world, its rancour and delusions, had ceased to exist.

'He's lovely but he looks so delicate.'

'Well, as a photographer you probably know that looks are deceptive; trust me, there's steel underneath that slim body.' Samar squatted to pet Mr Ward-Davies whose limber

little body writhed with the sweet havoc of unbearable joy. 'He was only four months old when he swallowed a big rusty nail. It got jammed in his gut. His stomach bloated up. He retched all night. I rushed him to the vet, who had to perform an emergency operation. He warned me not to get my hopes high. I got Mr Ward-Davies home with nine long stitches along the side of his belly. I had to nurse him day and night. He wouldn't eat, and I'd force-feed him baby food with a dropper. I slept beside him for three weeks. And, after all that'—Samar snapped his fingers—'Mr Ward-Davies made it! My grandma once told me: what you love, you can save. I'm not sure if there's any truth to that but it's kept me going during a flurry of bad hair days,' he said, running his fingers through a mop of wet hair.

'You fed him with a dropper?'

Samar stood up now. 'The vet said he might resist his food, so I had to keep at it. Besides, Mr Ward-Davies was a gift from my friend, Zaira; I wasn't about to let her down either.'

Karan tried not to let the astonishment he felt swim to his face. Having written off Samar Arora as a bit of a poser, it was now difficult, and annoying, to imagine him sitting up nights nursing a convalescent puppy. Besides, he thought edgily, there's only so much time for small talk; the light before gloaming was abundant, revealing, perfect for portraiture. It was time to get on with the shoot. 'Do you need to get ready?'

Samar grinned. 'I'm as ready as I'll ever be.'

'No make-up?' Karan could not bear to remind Samar he was bare-chested, clad only in a white towel, his wet hair

plastered over his head. What sort of a photograph would that make?

'I don't use make-up. Why hide the scars I've paid for with time?' Samar said. 'My only regret is that you're photographing me when I'm old and ugly; you should have seen me when I was young and ugly.'

'You *are* young! You're all of twenty-eight; you have only three years on me.' Karan undid the lens cap. 'You're just being falsely modest.'

'Never,' Samar said, his hand placed solemnly on his chest, 'I'm merely modestly false, but you shouldn't take it personally.'

Over the next twenty minutes the only audible sound was Karan's shutter release giving off staccato clicks. Looking through his viewfinder, Karan found it difficult not to admire Samar—his muscular, supple arms, the narrow, boyish waist, the melancholy neck with its classical arch. But the man's real beauty hides in unobvious places, he thought: the ear lobes, the deep, wry indent on his chin, the listening eyes. A certain quiet sense of ineffable loss danced around Samar's good looks; it gave him an unexpected, haunting dignity, an air of remorse, depth as well as peculiarity. Karan hoped to capture this elusive mood in his photographs.

In a while, Karan paused to change a filter. Samar sat by the pool with Mr Ward-Davies on his lap, his legs lazily weaving the undulating ripples of blue; he looked thoroughly bored, but he was being a mighty sport about the shoot. Karan stole an occasional glance at his curious subject and thought of the two stories Natasha had told him about Samar, unsubstantiated

and embellished, that seemed to bolster the glittering haze of scandal and enigma around the pianist.

At the age of eighteen, Samar had famously 'divorced' his mother. Mrs Arora, an ambitious, embittered widow who had pawned her jewels to put Samar through Juilliard, had been devastated by her son's rejection and in her resentment had tainted his name in the press to the point that it isolated him from the rest of his family. Initially restrained in his response, Samar had later clarified to the press that his mother had objected vehemently to the arc of his sexual longings; she had gone so far as to suggest that he undergo conversion therapy. He had disowned his mother, he revealed, not because she had suggested that he put himself through electric shocks and hormonal medication but because she had seen him as a sexual being more than as a human being, and as her son. For anyone, particularly his mother, to define him by what he did in bed was so repugnant to him that he had chosen to give her notice.

The other nugget of gossip concerning Samar was his inexplicable departure from the world of music. At a concert in Boston he had got up mid-recital and walked off the stage, leaving his audience bewildered. He later claimed to have stepped out for a bit of fresh air when 'the music had run out'. Critics, denied the right to write off Samar, never treated his retreat seriously, assuming he would make a comeback. But Samar gave up the lease on his shotgun apartment in Brooklyn, packed his bags and left for his home city, where he bought the last cottage on Worli Seaface and lived off the royalties his records aggregated each year.

Just when Karan was about to ask Samar if he was ready to recommence the shoot, he heard the French doors of the living room being thrown open and saw a woman running toward Samar, her red gypsy skirt flaring about her, green glass bangles jostling the length of her arms.

Samar jumped to his feet and walked forward briskly to receive her. She embraced him with such force that he almost lost his balance. He wrapped his arms around her and ran his hands gently down the length of her back. Then he led her away from the pool to the shade of a towering, leafy almond tree in the far corner of the lawn, where they stood as one in a tight embrace, lost even to themselves.

Taking a closer look, Karan was astonished to see that the woman in Samar's arms was his best friend, Zaira. He was tempted to click them right away, in that ineluctable moment of fragile affinity, but he knew that certain kinds of photographs were best not taken; they were a violation not of subject but of sentiment.

'Don't worry ... everything will be fine.'

Zaira, breathing in gasps through her mouth, gripped Samar tightly. 'You can't even *begin* to imagine what I've been through.'

'Well, tell me then.'

'It was awful ...' A sob caught in her throat.

'You'll be fine. You're here now. I'm with you, Zaira.' He felt her heart pulsating against his chest.

'He tried to kill me today!'

'What!'

'He went for me, Samar ... he really did ...'

'Are you talking about Malik?'

Zaira's wracking sobs came in the way of her reply, and Samar just held her in his arms. He found it difficult to believe that Zaira's stalker could have gone to such gruesome lengths. In the past when they had discussed Malik's mad love for her they had done so in jest; he had been for them the crazed cliché hanging on to the train of her gown. After all, what actress in Bollywood did not endure the undesirable privilege of being the object of a stalker's tainted attention?

'I never thought he could get down and dirty, Zaira.'

'Hasn't he flashed all the signs before?'

'I suppose you're right, but I think he's got a lot crazier after his father's landslide victory.'

Malik Prasad, the man in question, was the son of Shri Chander Prasad, Hon'ble Minister of State for Labour and Employment, a top-ticket politician with the Hindu People's Party. Malik ran an event management company, Tiranga

Inc., which specialized in taking Bollywood stars for dance performances to Canada. Many moons ago, when approached by Malik, Zaira had rejected his offer to participate in a show in Toronto and had believed, naively enough, that her demurral would end their communication. But this was not to be. Malik started calling her at odd hours of the night; she found him present at every restaurant she went to eat at; every now and again she received love poems by Ghalib, scribbled in his illegible, hick writing, tucked into the folds of her fan mail. Polite pleas, blatant disregard, rude rebuffs—nothing seemed to drive the message home.

But when Zaira found blood stains on the door of her Juhu apartment one morning, after Malik had spent the entire night rapping incessantly on the door, she knew the situation was hurtling out of hand. Sure enough, the following week, Malik got plastered and called her early one morning, spitting abuses and threatening to thrash her to an inch of her life. She appealed to the court for a restraining order. However, Malik's father was too well connected to break into sweat over a measly police complaint. The case went to trial, but Zaira lost.

The judge's dismissal of her case—on grounds of insufficient evidence—emboldened Malik. Certain that his father would cover his ass no matter what he did, Malik now went after Zaira with every card in the whacko book.

On the day Karan was at Samar's cottage for the photo shoot, Malik had scaled new heights of lunacy. For much of the day, Zaira had been filming with the sumptuous leading man of

the day, Shah Rukh. The director was wrapping up the last scene for the day: Shah Rukh and Zaira were to roll around in a bed, making out to a raunchy A.R. Rahman number. Just as the two of them had got into position on the bed, and the director was issuing his final instructions, Malik had stormed on to the set. He looked like a bull on the rampage, his eyes watery and red, his hands lunging out at whoever was in his way. He was calling out for Zaira and shouting invectives—saala, ma ki lauda—at Shah Rukh. Before long, he was caught by three security guards and deposited outside the film set. But Malik was not to be outdone. He got into his jeep and stepped on the pedal. He wanted to total the sets from which he had been so insultingly banished. Within an hour, a full report of Malik's sinister spree emerged: The gaffer who had tried to stop Malik had broken his wrist in the effort. The director's chair had been flattened like filo pastry. The dummy doors had been split in half. A gramophone, having fallen off the ledge of the coffee table on which it had been placed, lay on the ground like a plucked honeysuckle. A make-up artist had stumbled over the rubble and tangles of wires and hit her head against a broken beam.

Fortunately, Shah Rukh had lost no time in dragging his leading lady into his trailer, refusing to let her be alone while Malik was on the loose. The stars were undoubtedly in Zaira's favour, as it was later discovered that Malik had rammed her trailer so many times with the rear end of his jeep that it was left worthy only of scrap. When the director surveyed the wrecked trailer and remarked rather coarsely that 'Zaira could

have become sandwich stuffing', she had fled the set and headed straight for Samar's house.

Now, in Samar's presence and in familiar surroundings, Zaira's composure was restored, and the two of them walked toward the pool hand in hand.

But Zaira stopped in her tracks when she spotted Karan. 'Who's he?' she whispered agitatedly.

'A sweet kid who works for the *India Chronicle,'* Samar explained, turning to her.

'The same one who took those snaps of you tap dancing?'

Samar nodded in affirmation. 'Relax. Don't go off and have kittens, doll.'

'He's got his camera, Samar! And I've just had a crying jag ...' She swiped her cheeks with her palms to clean the dirty mascara stains.

'He's not going to tell on you.'

'He'll read about Malik and me tomorrow morning. D'you think he took a picture of us? Will he babble to the magazine? I'd *hate* for anyone to know that I came here and cried and ...' A jangled light shone from her eyes.

Samar stood, arms akimbo. 'Just look at him, Zaira. Does he look like he gives a shit?'

She glanced over Samar's shoulder: Karan was busy goofing around with Mr Ward-Davies. 'Maybe not,' she had to admit. 'But you never know when someone will squeal on you.'

'You're being paranoid because too many journalists have given you the short end of the stick; believe me, this boy is not one of them.'

'You talk like you've known him for years.' She frowned.

'Trust my instinct, and be quiet now because we're close enough for him to hear us.'

Karan looked up to find Zaira standing next to him, her hand extended. 'Hi, I'm Zaira.'

Karan continued to kneel beside the dog even as he introduced himself; he was sure if he stood up to shake hands with her he would betray how starstruck he was.

'I'm so sorry ... I botched up your shoot, didn't I?'

Karan nodded, now forced to get to his feet. Deserted by language, he was smiling foolishly at her. In her flare-hem gypsy skirt and appliqué camisole, she looked like a runaway princess. 'Something *aw*ful happened earlier on and I ...'

'But it's all under control now,' Samar cut in.

'I'm glad for that.' Karan lifted his camera, as if to remind Samar that he was here on an assignment.

Samar gave Karan a brief, discounted account of Malik's latest act of insanity.

'I'm sorry you had to go through that.' Karan turned to give her a sympathetic look.

Zaira examined his face, tidy and focussed. A touch of asceticism ran through his solid good looks like a vein in marble. Her heart, in his presence, felt like a dark, beautiful box whose mysterious, troubling contents she wanted to upend at his feet.

'I suppose you would like to get on with the shoot?' Samar said.

'Only if you want.'

'If we don't shoot now you won't make your deadline.'

Karan nodded. He looked at the sky; dusk giving in to night would soon leave them with little light. 'Yes.'

'Then we should get on with the job,' Samar said.

'Sooner rather than later. The light's perfect and won't be around too long.' He panicked suddenly, remembering Samar's pictures from Gatsby, rendered useless because of the lack of proper light; for these photos to suffer the same fate would be criminal.

'Yes,' Zaira said. 'I have been guilty of interrupting already. Why don't I go in and wait for you until ...' She turned toward the cottage but Samar caught her elbow.

'How about the two of us?' he asked Karan. 'Would it work?'

'Are you mad!' Zaira cried. 'Why would Mr Seth want to photograph *me* with you?'

'You're playing hard to get because your goop's a goner. Stop being a diva!'

Zaira could not help blushing. 'If I'm a diva, what does that make *you?*'

'Oh, go on, Zaira!' Samar cajoled. 'Say yes. If you do, I'll get us some fizzy water and make it all better.' He kissed her shoulder. 'Mr Seth won't mind at all ...'

Karan grinned as he loaded more film into his camera. 'I really don't mind at all.'

3

'I SHOULD GET GOING NOW,' KARAN SAID, PUTTING his camera back in its case. Evening was giving way to night. Mosquitoes danced over the privet flanking the path leading back to the cottage. 'Thanks for your time; it was a wonderful shoot. I'll make copies of the pictures and send them to you.'

'Won't you come inside for a Bellini?' Samar gestured toward his cottage.

'Yes,' Zaira said. 'Please do.'

Karan glanced curiously at the house. Perhaps Samar's house, in keeping with his persona, would be baroque, teeming with antiques and satin upholstery, decadent and lavish and extravagant. Then he looked at Zaira, and her presence made Samar's offer all the more inviting.

'I don't want to intrude—' Karan swung his camera case on to his shoulder.

'There's no need to be so formal,' Samar said sternly. 'And certainly not now, after you've seen me in my swimming trunks.'

Karan laughed. 'Well, then, I'd love to have a drink.'

Entering through the French doors, Karan stepped on to a cool cement floor of brick-red geru. Tropical palms in cane barrels shaded a large wicker chair. On one side of the rectangular room was a white couch with a marvellously battered air. Glass votives with tea lights on tables and in niches in the wall illuminated the room with a cognac hue and cast scurrying shadows on the ceiling. There was a neat, elegant pile of books on art and music on the coffee table and a clutter of silver glasses on an antique tray.

Zaira swung open the door to the kitchen.

An uneven black kadapa counter ran the length of the kitchen. A circular table of Burma teak, with a deep polish and shaky legs, stood in the centre; here, Karan positioned himself on a sturdy chair with a high bamboo back and watched his hosts go about their tasks. He was grateful for the monastic calm of the cottage, its profound simplicity; he had not expected Samar to live in such understated quarters.

'Shouldn't you report Malik?' Samar asked Zaira as he served olives and crackers on a long taupe ceramic platter.

Zaira, who was uncorking a bottle of Prosecco, glared at Samar. 'I'm not sure, after last time ...' she said

'Aw, c'mon Zaira!' He poured Cipriani peach base into three champagne flutes.

Zaira slumped into the chair next to Karan's. When Samar put the drink down before her she took a few sips and sat back, folding her hands across her chest. 'You know what they've done in the past,' she reminded him. 'Had me doing the rounds of the trial court, and then the bloody judge axed my case!'

'What makes you think it'll be the same this time?' Samar failed to understand how she could allow such a vicious attack to go unpunished.

Zaira was uneasy discussing Malik in front of Karan. What if he were to repeat the conversation verbatim to a gossip columnist at the *India Chronicle?* Or worse, inflate its inane particulars for *Mid-Day?* Hoping Samar would drop the matter, she said vaguely, 'Past experience is an indicator of future result.'

'Don't be such a quitter,' Samar scolded. He turned to Karan and noticed him lick his lower lip after tasting the drink; probably his first Bellini, he thought.

'We're talking about Minister Prasad's son here, in case you've forgotten,' Zaira said. Why did Samar ignore the fact that Malik, using his father's influence, had breezed his way out of numerous court cases already?

Presently, the door opened. A lean man with blue eyes and a tonsured skull peeked in gingerly.

Karan recognized Leo from the night at Gatsby, when he had offered his hand to Samar after the impromptu tap dancing session had come to an unceremonious end.

Leo looked uncertain about interrupting them but Samar extended his arms and murmured an affectionate welcome.

'Just caught a news flash on the idiot box,' Leo said, his eyes on Zaira. 'Is it true about Malik and you?'

'Oh, I'm fine,' she replied. 'A bit of a run-in with "my beau".'

'I hear it's more than a bit.' Leo bent and kissed Samar on the cheek, before settling down on the arm of Samar's chair, his hand on his lover's shoulder.

Zaira noticed Karan ducking his head and suspected that Leo's show of affection had made Karan squirm.

'Meet the genius who photographed me making an idiot of myself at Gatsby,' Samar said to Leo, his chin edged up in Karan's direction.

Leo nodded. 'So you're the wunderkind with the magic fingers.'

A cold feeling ran down the length of Karan's neck; Leo's praise, well meaning but cursory, was in stark contrast to Samar's genuine zest. It reminded him of a socialite kissing the air.

Zaira said, 'The pictures were clever and outrageous and they made me wish I'd been around to watch Samar in his element.'

'Oh, I'm sure you've seen Samar in his element many, *many* times before,' Leo said, an edge in his voice.

Zaira appeared to wither for a moment at Leo's remark. 'Are they making a fuss about Malik and me on TV?' she asked quickly.

'Big fuss, girl! But then,' Leo said with a wink, 'you're hot shit. All the channels are beaming it endlessly.'

Zaira could clearly imagine the chaotic horde of photographers waiting for her outside her home in Juhu. 'I just wish they'd go away and cover an issue of some *real* consequence.'

'Let's go beat up that big bully!'

'He's more than just a bully,' Samar corrected Leo. 'Malik Prasad has the makings of a certified criminal, and you're trying to pass him for a frat boy who's had two beers too many.' Turning to Zaira, he said, 'You should go to the press, at the very least. It's clear Malik Prasad is chemically imbalanced.'

'I don't want to flatter the creep by dissing him in print.'

Sitting quietly, watching the conversation whiz back and forth between the talented and the famous, Karan recognized that the real power of fame did not lie in its making someone instantly recognizable but in imposing obscurity upon others; he felt like a piece of furniture in their midst. During a brief pause in the conversation he decided to make his exit.

'Thanks for the drink. It's time I headed back to my dark room and printed the shots. I really ...'

'Don't tell me we're not good enough company for you, Mr Seth?' Zaira said, stalling him.

He blushed. 'I'm afraid the opposite is true.'

Zaira lowered her large bedroom eyes. 'C'mon now, have another drink! It's bad luck to leave on the second Bellini.'

Mesmerized by the melancholy whorls in her sensual eyes and the sultry lilt of her voice, Karan suddenly recalled something Natasha had said about Zaira: *single-handedly responsible for raising India's National Masturbation Index.*

'I don't know where you get your superstitions, but I find them very agreeable,' he said as he settled into the chair again.

After Karan was handed another drink, the conversation returned to the subject of Malik's attack on Zaira.

'Men like Malik can get away,' Leo said, 'because the Indian political climate fosters their juvenile machismo.' To evidence his point, he spread out the morning edition of the *Times of India.* The Hindu People's Party, the article said, had proposed a ban on masturbation. 'Because jerking off goes against Hindu culture!' Leo sounded exasperated.

'Which Hindu text prohibits masturbation?' Zaira asked. 'I mean, I'd seriously like to read it if it's true.'

'I heard the other day that if the bill is passed then convicted parties will face a jail sentence or a fine of five thousand rupees,' Karan said.

'But prison is the centre of Planet Jerk-Off!' Zaira covered her mouth as she chuckled. 'They'll be in good company.'

'And if they lock up every masturbator, there won't be any people left on the streets of Bombay.'

Karan thought the ripples of rowdy laughter in Samar's kitchen were like a nervous veil; there was only so much that humour could hide. 'Surely, the HPP can't be all that bad?' he asked.

Zaira shot Karan a look. His naivety would, no doubt, invite a sermon from Samar's boyfriend. She secretly called it 'Leo's Modem India 101 Lecture'. As she had feared, within moments Leo was passionately lecturing Karan about the Hindu People's Party, their advent and rise, their monopoly and rampant cruelties.

Zaira pulled Mr Ward-Davies into her arms for a cuddle, thinking to herself that in the time Leo would hold forth on Indian politics she could mentally rehearse all her lines for her next shoot or plan her wardrobe or, if it was not too callous, even shut her eyes and catch a quick nap. Nuzzling her cheek against Mr Ward-Davies's domed skull she gave Karan a brave, conspiring smile that seemed to say, Chin up, my friend.

Karan, on the other hand, who knew little about the history of politics in Bombay leaned forward to hear Leo's exposition.

After setting up operations in Bombay in the sixties, the Hindu People's Party, the HPP, had worked hard to spread their poison across the country, Leo began. In the early seventies the party racked up momentum by promising jobs to the state's 'natives', the Maharashtrians. On the pretext of safeguarding jobs for the sons of the soil, they attacked 'foreigners'. Migrants from the southern states, even if they had lived in Maharashtra for generations, distinguished by their dark complexion and

gentle features, had initially made for easy victims. Later, those from the north, were attacked for 'stealing' the jobs from the locals. There were daily reports of young Malayalis stabbed in daylight or entire families forced to 'go back to *wherever* it was they had come from' and of Biharis being beaten senseless by unruly gangs of HPP loyalists.

In the late seventies the HPP's violently bright star dimmed a notch when the nation was consumed by a far more scintillating spectacle of despotism: the emergency years during Prime Minister Indira Gandhi's regime. But the period from the mid-eighties to the early nineties turned out to be particularly fruitful for the HPP. The political mood was decidedly communal now and the HPP expanded ruthlessly, spreading their divisive propaganda on the grounds of caste and religion. To protest the alleged forceful conversion of Hindus by Christian missionaries, an Australian missionary was doused in kerosene and burnt to cinders. The flimsiest of reasons were dug up to incite communal riots in small and large towns across the country, and within hours dozens of families, Muslim and Hindu alike, were wiped out, their houses torched, their daughters raped and sons blinded.

Meanwhile, the economy was stretching its ravenous mouth for access to foreign booty. Most political parties did not have the nerve to crib about the influx of funds from the West. They did, however, find an easy target of attack: the *culture* of liberalization. The wicked West, they claimed huffily, would corrupt their children. As self-appointed emissaries of

the morality mafia, the HPP's resident rabble-rousers went on a rampage. They banned a film as it portrayed what they fancifully termed as 'lesbian tendencies' and burned down cinema halls which dared to screen it. An Indo-Pak cricket match Leo had been hoping to attend was cancelled on the grounds that Pakistanis were India's 'natural' enemies, rendering such a contest inherently anti-nationalist. A Muslim legend of the art world was forced to go into exile after his paintings were deemed blasphemous.

'In this confused cultural climate a hissy fit over the moral questions does nothing to change the status quo but it sure makes good copy,' Leo said. 'Politicians fighting to preserve India's "moral fibre" find it's a safe—if utterly useless—subject to amuse the middle class. Politicians have become publicity savvy "custodians of culture" but in terms of policymaking they're shooting blanks. The real thugs, meanwhile, go unpunished.' Leo connected his thesis to their conversation: Under such circumstances, Malik, whose father was one of the minor architects of institutionalized corruption in the nation, could be forgiven for assuming it was perfectly all right to smash up a film set or bang his fists on Zaira's door until he left bloody marks on the wood. 'After all, Malik has seen gangsters who work for his father's political party round up to kill the actress who dared to kiss a woman on screen; he's seen stores torched simply because they dared to sell greeting cards for Valentine's Day. As far as he's concerned, running down Zaira's set is all in a day's work.'

With that, Leo was done. He sat back, looking pleased with himself.

Karan, meanwhile, looked as if he was in dire need of another drink. He glanced at Zaira, who caught his eye and winked at him. Then she looked at Leo and nodded thoughtfully, feigning great interest. Karan grinned to himself, impressed with her acting skills.

'I still believe,' Samar said to Zaira, 'that you should register a complaint with the police. Malik should know you're not going to let him off.'

'The bloody Bombay police?' Zaira reminded them that just a week ago one of the constables from the Bombay police force had raped a college student in his cabin. 'Yeah, sure. I bet they'll come to my rescue.'

Leo left Samar's side, opened the fridge and pretended to rifle through the contents of the cheese drawer; he was glowering in private. No one had complimented his thoughtful analysis. No one had admired how he had connected national politics with Zaira's troubles. And this was Zaira's fault; after all, what was more distracting than the presence of a celebrity? He returned to the table with a tub of cream cheese and proceeded to spread it on a cracker.

'I have no idea,' Zaira said, turning to Karan, 'why we're torturing *you* with my sob story. You're probably ready to burst from boredom.'

'I've enjoyed sitting in and eavesdropping, actually.'

'Well, now tell us something about *you.*'

Reluctant and shy, Karan furnished a brief biography: raised and educated in Shimla he had trained as an English teacher in Delhi. 'But between classes, I'd go to the Habitat Centre to check out the photo exhibits. That's where I met Iqbal, my boss. He was having a show of his reportage on the '84 riots in Delhi. When I found he was looking for an assistant I volunteered, just to give something new a shot.'

'And it's been a consuming passion ever since?' Samar asked.

'Well, it became an obsession only after I moved to Bombay. Until then, I looked at photography as some sort of eccentric activity that could save me from the boring life of a teacher.'

'So why does Bombay inspire you?' Leo asked.

'Why do people come to Bombay, I thought, when I joined the *India Chronicle* here. After all, it is ugly and dirty; it is expensive; its charms are limited. But within weeks of living here I knew I could call no other place my home. Surely, *something* was attracting millions here, to this city. I noticed that everyone here was running away from loneliness; I saw it on the trains, on the street, in temples, at film premieres.'

'But most people are doing exactly that in any city and at any given point in time,' Samar said.

'True enough, but it occurs differently in Bombay. Without the distraction of beauty, without the consolation of art, people find respite in each other. Yet the sparks between two people do not qualify as companionship. In Bombay people don't offer each other too much talk or touch; rather, they look each other

in the eye like soldiers, wounded and brave and crazy. And lucky to be alive, if not happy. The power of this city is the mad desire it arouses in you to live an unlonely life.'

Samar popped an olive into his mouth. 'How do you propose to capture this quality in your photographs?'

'I have no idea. I can only trust that, as with any narrative, there's a point when the membrane between the listener and the story tears open, and they become one. I'm waiting for that moment of rupture; I'm waiting for my entry point. But until then I'm keeping my ear to the ground and my eyes peeled. I'm watching. I'm hanging around.'

Zaira found it hard to believe that the boy before her, in his blue jeans and white shirt, beat-up camera in tow, had thought about the city with such profound, careful attention. 'I feel the same way about acting,' she said. 'The moment I recognize my role in the story, I know I'll find my voice.'

'And voice,' Leo said, '*is* art.'

'I agree,' Karan said.

'Do you go back to Shimla often?' Samar asked.

'No. My mother, who lived there, died a few years ago. I was an only child.' He added that he wasn't in contact with his father.

Hearing this Zaira's eyebrows cocked up, but she said nothing.

'And where do you put up in the city?' Samar asked.

'I've rented a room in Ban Ganga.'

Leo, who had not seemed too impressed by Karan's story so far, sat up with interest. Ban Ganga fascinated him, he said, with its narrow, messy lanes, the ancient pond at its heart, its lazy, bucolic air completely at odds with Bombay's diabolic chaos, its mangy swelter. 'You got a view of the pond?'

'And the sea too—but only if I crane my neck by a mile or so!' Before he might be tied down with another question, Karan glanced at the clock above the kitchen door. 'Now, at the risk of breaking the future law, it's time for me to beat it.'

Leo smiled; he hadn't expected such an arch remark from the boy but perhaps the Bellini had loosened his tongue.

'Well, I hope you'll oblige us with your company again soon.'

'If I should be so lucky ...'

'If you're not in the slammer by then!'

Zaira escorted Karan to the door. Mr Ward-Davies trotted alongside them with quick, dainty steps.

At the gate, Karan crouched to pet the whippet.

'He's irresistible, ne?'

'There's something so fragile about him. Samar said he was your gift to him ...'

'He was a gift to us.' An unnamed loss glinted in her voice, struggling to be freed. 'I had a suggestion for your Bombay portfolio. Have you gone to Chor Bazaar yet?'

'Not yet; isn't it a bit of a tourist trap?'

'You can get a Bombay Fornicator in Chor Bazaar.'

'A Bombay Fornicator!' Karan was all ears now.

An impish smile swam up on Zaira's lips. 'But that's only *one of* Chor Bazaar's many charms ...' Her left hand reached out to adjust the crinkled collar of his shirt. 'Who knows what else Mr Seth will find there?'

That night, Karan lay on his bed, feeling untidy and lazy. The damp walls of his little square room gave off wet whiffs of white limestone; he could hear the rowdy children in the narrow street below as their night-time innings of gully cricket continued unabated under blinkering lamplight.

Puzzled by the day's events, he struggled to reconcile the uneven, exhilarating particulars. Each time he shut his eyes the scene of the flamingoes soaring overhead returned to him: not only could he see the darkening sky again, but the slightly demonic thwack of the birds' wings also draped over him like a dark cloak. Then he saw Samar swimming the length of the pool, and experienced again the tremulous wait and the eventual thrill of the shoot in the lazy light of the late afternoon. His mind treaded quickly toward Zaira, arriving on the grounds in her glamorous shudder of panic, and then to the moment when he had joined Samar and her for a drink. He had been reluctant to join them, assuming they had invited him out of some misplaced sense of charity. But maybe he had been wrong; maybe Zaira had offered him a drink because she did not want to be alone with Samar and Leo, and Samar had insisted on it because he was genuinely taken with Karan's work. (Here he smiled, against his will, for even though he

nursed an unexplained, mute antipathy toward Samar he could not help but be flattered by the attention.)

What had distinguished this evening for Karan was that he had been treated as an equal among people who were so obviously above him in status and achievement, if not in talent. Before surrendering to sleep, Karan told himself it was best not to assume that such freakish, fleeting moments of intimacy could ever add up to a friendship. Having spent some time around celebrities he knew they were vulnerable to sudden bursts of confession and affection only because most had neither family nor friends with whom to share and evaluate a day's happenings, and journalists often became the default recipients of their private, perplexed musings.

Touched by Zaira's obvious, unqualified loyalty to Samar, he contemplated the provenance of her feelings. Samar and she appeared to be the best of friends, and their affection for each other had the tremor of something like love but without its attendant confusions. Recalling how calm she had become around Samar, he decided that perhaps there was something to the pianist—above and beyond the theatre of the absurd he ceaselessly performed—that he had failed to notice. He was keen to dismiss Samar as a dandy, but checked the impulse when he remembered how Samar had stayed up nights nursing and feeding an ailing Mr Ward-Davies. Karan's palms had warmed from petting and cuddling the dog earlier in the day and, now, as the sensation returned to his hands, the image of Mr Ward-Davies flashed before his eyes, reaffirming fragility

and innocence on a day that had seemed to promise little of either.

Slowly, tenderly sleep came to his eyes, and drew him away.

Two weeks later, Karan met Zaira again at the premiere of her film. Iqbal, who had loved Karan's shots of Samar and Zaira, had dispatched Karan to the film premiere for more images of the actress.

Zaira had hardly stepped out of her white BMW when the photographers launched toward her like a juggernaut, snapping away hysterically, crying her name so it rebounded recklessly through the hot, humid Bombay night.

Robed in an ankle-length white dress with spaghetti straps, Zaira looked delectable but also a shade forlorn. She caught Karan's eye and smiled at him, walking purposefully closer so he could get a better shot.

Unfortunately, the photographers too careened toward Karan and in the frenzied chaos one of them tripped over a tripod and came crashing down on him. Before he knew it, Karan was on the floor, flattened under the weight of three other shutterbugs who had lost their balance in the mêlée. Zaira did not get a chance to respond or even notice what had happened to Karan as her publicist took her by the arm and swivelled her around to present her to a waiting throng of television cameras, and she was immediately caught in the vulgar vortex of pointless sound bites.

As soon as she entered the cinema house, she dragged her publicist to a corner. 'What happened to the photographer?'

'Who are you talking about?'

'The guy who was trampled. I know him.'

'Zaira, it's time you circulated. There are people I want you to meet ...'

'Hey! Don't *ever* grab me by the arm.'

'I'm sorry, but it's really important that you meet—'

'I asked you what happened to the photographer!'

'These things happen, Zaira; don't get carried away. He probably got off with a few bruises. It's a part of their job.'

'Listen, Ravi, do you want me to attend this film premiere?'

'Yes—I mean, that's why you're here.'

'Well, how would it seem if I turned around and walked away?'

'I'd say that would be mad.'

'You're right—and it would also result in the end of your career.'

'I—'

'So save the two of us a ton of trouble, please. I want you to take your tortured tush out of this gas pit and get me news of the boy and his camera. If he has as much as bruised his finger, take him to the doctor. If not, come back here. I'll call Mr Seth from the *India Chronicle*—that's who he is—tomorrow morning and confirm that I sent a rep to check on him, so don't pull a fast one on me, all right?'

Karan was a little taken aback when Zaira's publicist insisted on personally accompanying him to the doctor in the massive BMW and then, with his sprained ankle firmly

bandaged and the cuts on his left elbow disinfected, deposited him in his room in Ban Ganga. On the way from the clinic Ravi let on that he had been acting on personal instructions from Zaira.

Karan called Zaira a week later to thank her; she brushed off the gesture, claiming she had been responsible for the mêlée.

'So, did you go to Chor Bazaar, find something interesting to photograph?' she asked after enquiring how his injuries were healing.

He blushed. 'I'm afraid not.'

'Then I'll have to take you there personally.'

'And cause another stampede?'

'Perhaps. That would be a good lesson for you. You should come for a dinner party I'm hosting with Samar at my house,' she said. 'You'll enjoy it. There'll just be a dozen people.'

'When is it?' Karan gulped, dreading the thought of having to make clever small talk with the top-brass invitees at Zaira's exclusive party.

'Next Friday. But it'll start late—around eleven. Think you can make it?'

'I guess so.' What was he supposed to say? That he would take a look in his diary and get back to her?

'Great.'

'But thank you, again. For watching out for me.'

'Watching is what you do; I was just keeping an eye out.'

For the rest of the day Zaira wondered why she had so impulsively invited Karan to her party. She did not really know

him that well and the inclusion of a new, unknown male guest at the dinner table was bound to provoke a few raised eyebrows. She feared being misread; she had no romantic interest in Karan. Of course she had been swept away by the visual poetry of his work—hard, ambiguous, luscious, possessed with an incantatory power—but was this the guiding motive of her interest? She suspected she had invited him because he was so entirely unlike someone from her own milieu, untainted by either fame or wealth. The moment this thought crossed her mind, guilt subsumed her. What if she had invited Karan simply because he was not 'one of them'? She would hate herself if the basis of her invitation was his being the token 'struggling artist' at her dinner table, always a welcome distraction. No, she assured herself, that was not it. Rather, she believed her interest in him owed to the fact that he had engaged her solidarity by his discretion: after her breakdown at Samar's house she had feared reading about the incident in the papers but Karan had evidently not breathed a word to anyone. The only other reason for the invitation could be simpatico: they were both foreigners in Bombay—she had been raised in Hyderabad and Karan in Shimla—people who had come to the city in search of a dream, and both of them had found that Bombay gave them conscription with life or, at least, a temporary refuge from its hostile challenges.

Later that week, when Karan was at her house for dinner, she cornered him about the proposed reconnaissance to Chor Bazaar. In the dim light of her apartment in Juhu, when he gingerly confessed that he was yet to ankle it to the bazaar, it

invoked strident disapproval; he promised to make amends. Sitting barefoot on the floor of the balcony, sipping at a glass of red wine too many, they nursed something awkward between them, sadness and kinship; unsayable things lurked under the blustery sheath of fashionable music.

She threatened to banish him from her life if he failed to find and photograph the Bombay Fornicator.

He looked stricken.

She ruffled his hair playfully.

Only when Karan was back home did it occur to him that she must already consider him a part of her existence to talk of expelling him from it.

4

ON THE DAY KARAN FINALLY VISITED CHOR Bazaar, he was alone, his anxiety about his future as documentarian, journal keeper and photo maker of Bombay at a crescendo.

Rambling through the sweltering chaos of the bazaar, ungrazed by any inspiration, he recognized with some measure of dismay how many months of uninspiring, tiresome work had made it difficult for him to emerge out of the deep well of his torpor. Although Iqbal's various commissions gave him practice, he desperately needed time to work on his collection, to articulate his private and wounded sense of adulthood, its disquiet, innocence, amity and discord, all of which was being slowly played out against the stark, taut canvas of Bombay. He was desperate to photograph the caves in the forests

of the national park, the noisy dawn at Sassoon Dock and a smouldering evening at Scandal Point, the slum urchins spinning wooden tops on the pavement and the made-up memsahibs on Altamont Road, their eyes flashing envy and disdain like the diamonds on their nasty fingers.

There was all this. And more.

But time. Where was the time?

Not only was Karan hungry for time, he was also ravenous for talk. Now and again he did discuss his photographs with Iqbal, but his boss was generally too busy to talk at length. And Zaira knew precious little about the subject, even if her interest in his life was greatly encouraging. Conversation about his pictures would give him clarity and impetus, direction and current; he wanted to rub his mind against another, talk freely about the failed photograph, the lost moment, the catastrophic composition, the perfect picture plucked out of the wreckage of an imperfect day. But talk, the real, deep, purposeful thing, illuminating and difficult, with room for pause and uncertainty, eluded him. He had expected a big city to provide him the shelter of able, poignant companionship but Bombay had only introduced him to varying species of loneliness. There was the loneliness of the late night, when red moths beat harried wings against hot street lights and sleep was a faint, faraway music. There was the loneliness of having no family to count on, no letters to write, no phone calls to make. And, most wretched of all, there was the loneliness of being around people for whom he felt neither a sympathy of mind nor an appeal of the heart.

He wondered if a girlfriend might alleviate the situation, but feared that the onus of the relationship would come in the way of his real love—his camera and its unpredictable, incredible harvest. Could he find a woman who would return touch for touch, silence for silence, word for word? Someone with whom he could share, at eventide, the day's pointless particulars, and who would find in him the custodian of her most private aesthetic, as he would in her?

In the last two months some of his loneliness had no doubt been relieved by Zaira. After the dinner at her apartment, they had spoken on the phone on numerous occasions and met up again, only the previous week, at Samar's house. Zaira had badgered him into visiting parts of Bombay he had never even considered worth exploring and he had surfaced from his dark room with pictures that would make lasting additions to his work. In fact, his visit to Chor Bazaar had resulted from Zaira's ultimatum.

Unfortunately, his endeavour to locate a Bombay Fornicator had not met with any success. Two stall owners in the bazaar had barrelled him with all manner of lewd questions when he had asked them to show him a Bombay Fornicator; one fellow, with tombstone teeth, had promptly pointed north, in the direction of the city's red-light district. He left their side, a cloud of loud guffaws hovering over him.

As evening evaporated into a thick indigo dusk, Karan realized his chances of finding the Bombay Fornicator were shot, and dejection trampled his heart. He had stopped, as a

final attempt, to ask another shopkeeper about the Bombay Fornicator when he noticed a woman studying him from a distance; the intensity of her gaze was mesmeric, puzzling.

'Excuse me,' she said as soon as he was within earshot, 'I just overheard you ask about the Bombay Fornicator ...'

'Er ... yes ... do you know anything about it?' He walked toward her, entering the private cosmology of her unabashed curiosity.

She was sitting on a carved Chinese bench, legs crossed to her side, shoulder-length night-black hair splayed over the ridge of her shoulders; she was playing with a small figure in her hands, and her thin, delicate fingers suggested hidden purpose and solid efficiency.

'There are all kinds of fornicators in this city; which kind are you looking for?'

His cheeks reddened. 'I wish I knew.'

'Perhaps I might.' Her skin had the luxuriant polish of leaves in a tropical jungle.; her heavy-lidded eyes moved over his face. There was an unsettling calm about her, like a lake at midnight.

'You might?' His eyes gleamed. 'Can you help? I mean, asking a stranger in a bazaar to help look for a Bombay Fornicator sounds absurd even to my own ears but ...' he stuttered.

'It's not absurd.'

'My query did not surprise you?'

She put down the talisman in her hands on the bench, and Karan noticed it was a tiny brass monkey.

She stood up. 'I come to Chor Bazaar too often to be surprised.'

'I've spent close to an hour speaking to the shopkeepers here; all they've given me is the slip or a sneer, and I don't know which is worse.'

She folded her slender arms across her chest; her cream dress, a whisper of sultry elegance, came floating all the way down to her immaculate, girlish ankles. 'Why're you looking for a Bombay Fornicator?'

'I work as a photographer with the *India Chronicle.* And my friend, Zaira, has been on my case to find and photograph the Bombay Fornicator. Trouble is,' he said, scratching his chin, 'I don't even know what the damn thing is!'

'They're rare to find these days.' Moving away from his face, her eyes travelled the length of his long brown arms, the curve of muscles reminding her of a river at a bend. 'Not many dealers stock Bombay Fornicators.'

'At the very least could you tell me what it is?'

'Wouldn't you much rather see it?'

'I guess so, but won't you give me a clue?'

Her brows puckered. 'I thought I saw one a few minutes ago ... although finding it in the mess of this bazaar will be tricky.'

'Please! Just tell me what it is.'

She started to walk, her eyes scanning the shops; he followed her.

'Did you want to photograph the Bombay Fornicator for your magazine?'

'No,' he said. 'It's not for *India Chronicle.*'

'Then it must be for your friend who put you on the job.'

'Actually, it's for my private record. You see, I moved to Bombay and decided I would make this big, bold record of the city. The littlest things. The foams in the gullies of Dhobi Talao. The tail whip of a horse cantering at Mahalaxmi at dawn. Dusty balustrades in the wrecked mansions of Kala Ghoda. Everything would enter the lens and come through to a permanent place, and for that to happen if I'd have to tear down the walls and break sheets of glass I'd do it, to see everything raw and awful and perfect ... I'm hoping to create an epic record of Bombay.'

'An epic record of Bombay?' she repeated, amused.

'I meant ...' He blushed, conscious he was guilty of blabbering.

'That sounds like a lot of work. Why don't you have a drink instead?' She gave a laugh.

He smiled, the edifice of his confidence suddenly reduced to rubble. 'I guess I must sound like an idiot. This talk of immortalizing Bombay with my foolish camera.'

'Not entirely an idiot.' She smiled warmly; she found his ambition sincere, surprising, defensible. 'Not yet, in any event.'

'From the day I came to Bombay,' he said quietly, 'I felt like I was staring destiny in the eye.'

'Well, maybe you *were* meant to photograph the city, then.'

'Yes.' His eyes shone, luminous with excitement. 'I have no doubt about that. Bombay, this city, this moment in time, and,' pointing to his camera, he said, 'this camera.'

'You have terrible taste,' she said with a clap of her hands. 'I approve thoroughly.'

Her voice wrapped itself around him; it was easy to imagine that at the end of the corridor of her voice there was a little room in which a blues singer was hiding from the world, serenading emptiness.

'Now, for your friend's sake, I hope we find the Bombay Fornicator. You'll have to trust this Chor Bazaar old hand, though.'

'At this point, I'll trust *anyone.*'

'That would be wrong. Not ethically, but practically. That's something I've learned in my thirty-six years in Bombay.'

He stopped in his tracks. 'You're thirty-six!'

'I'm not sure if I ought to be flattered by your tone.'

'Well, you don't look your age at all.'

'How old are *you*?' Her eyes slitted, reminding Karan of a snake.

'Twenty-five.'

'You don't act your age at all.'

He tried not to look entirely deflated.

'Come along now.' Her fingers touched his arm ever so softly. 'While we look around tell me what you've seen in Chor Bazaar so far that could end up in your pictures.'

'There was a stone mermaid with an oriental face ...'

'Ah, probably nicked from a Mahabaleshwar mansion.'

'And there was a palanquin on the back of an elephant, home to ...'

'... three black kittens,' she completed.

'You saw that too?'

'How could *anyone* miss the kittens? They were so lovely, so abandoned ... Did you see the store selling antique glass bottles?'

'Yes, I did.' Light breaking through the clutter of countless bottles had splashed all over the vendor, an old man with a beard as white as a ghost. 'He looked like a disco ball with all that light raining down on him!'

'I never thought of that coot as a disco ball,' she said, amused by Karan's description, 'but you got the nail on its head.' The dignified Muslim vendor on a wooden stool, doused in echoes of ruby and jade, had been oblivious of the interest he had aroused in them.

The path ahead turned off into a bend. 'Let's go down this one last curve of Mutton Lane; if we don't find it here, I'm on my way home. I have a pottery studio,' she explained. 'And I've left three pitchers in the kiln. I've got to be home to save them from being overbaked.'

As they went down the narrow lane, their arms brushed against each other's; Karan felt strangely, powerfully aroused. The urge to touch her again, to seek the warmth and thrill of her skin, was overwhelming.

She looked as if she was trying to retrace her steps, to return to the place she believed she had seen the Bombay Fornicator

earlier. Halting before a furniture stall she rubbed her hands gleefully. 'You're in luck, Mr Shutterbug!'

'I am?'

She pointed ahead. 'Look past the carpenter.'

'Yes.' He craned his neck.

'At the end of the row of shelves.'

His eyes travelled the line of her extended arm.

'That chair with long arms and hexagonal netting?'

Karan's eyes moved to the gaunt carpenter sandpapering the claw foot of a chaise. 'Yeah.'

'That's it.' She patted his back, urging him forward. 'Go, have a look.'

He went into the shop.

'Comfortable!' he said, settling into the long-armed chair. 'Neat lines. Great wood, unusual shape.' Disappointment filled his face; what a lot of fuss for a chair. 'Why does it have this funny name?'

'Put your feet on the arms of the chair.'

The carpenter looked up, intrigued by her soft, commanding voice.

Karan swung his left leg on to the armrest. 'Like this?'

'Yes, and now the other leg too.'

Karan followed her instructions. Lying back, he dropped his hands to his sides.

'Spread your legs.'

'Excuse me?'

'I said: Spread your legs.'

His mouth fell open.

'Good.' She lowered her voice. 'Spread them some more.'

The carpenter paused his sandpapering and turned to look at her.

'Now throw your head back ... Excellent! Let your hands stay at your side. Perfect!'

With his crotch aloft, his legs drawn out, Karan felt completely exposed.

The carpenter gaped; he half expected her to march right over and sit on him, her pelvis over his, drawing him into the wilderness of her lust. Instead, she stood her ground, watching from afar, exuding a feral dignity.

'If you *still* don't get why this chair is called the Bombay Fornicator,' she said, 'then you should hop on to the next train bound for a monastery.'

He sat up, smiling like a baby who was being tickled on its soles. 'Nice! You told me never to trust anyone in Bombay; then why did you help a stranger?'

'You bear an uncanny resemblance to someone I know.'

'Really?' he asked, intrigued. 'Who?'

'Oh,' she said, 'someone I know well.'

'And what do we have in common?'

Her eyes roamed his face again, studying the thick, inky eyebrows, the indented chin, the thin, flat ears. 'Many things ...'

'I guess that must spook you out.'

'A bit.'

'You won't tell me who the person is?'

'He's ... someone.'

He decided not to probe any further. 'The resemblance must've been uncanny.'

'In our own ways, we're all gluttons for coincidence. What's your name?'

'Karan Seth.' He stood up.

'Well then, Rhea Dalal will watch for your pictures on the pages of the *India Chronicle.'*

Wiggling her pinky at him, she turned and walked away into the thick, noisy rush of lanes. On her way to her car, she passed a tandoor and halted to look at its coals, orange smouldering in black, ash at the peripheries. She touched her hair self-consciously.

An hour later, Rhea paused in the hallway of her apartment and gazed into the antique silver-framed mirror, wondering if she knew the person reflected in it. Was she just another south Bombay housewife? Could she think of herself as a potter? Or was she only a dilettante? And what of that odd, affected, trite title she had made up to impress Karan: 'Chor Bazaar old hand'?

Although a miscellany of identities was available at her disposal, none of them could define the person she secretly believed she was. Entering the living room, she stretched out on the sofa and gazed at the staghorn ferns suspended from the ceiling. Below the dramatic display of dangling staghorns was her husband Adi's wine cabinet; desire for him filled her with

a dull, sweet ache. She thought of calling him but he would probably be busy in some business meeting.

Rhea had known Adi since her teenage years; they had married sixteen years ago. Adi spent a fortnight each month in Singapore, managing a hedge fund. In the duration of his absence, on days like this, she longed ardently for him; if he were here, he would relieve her disquiet. She would lie with her head on his lap and tell him what she had seen in Chor Bazaar: the black kittens in the elephant howdah, the pewter vermilion holder for new brides, the brass monkey with its long tail curling in the air like a question mark. A recollection of her day would make it real to her, help her comprehend how lovers bore witness to the narrative of each other's fates. Sixteen years with Adi had taught her that marriage was a strange and marvellous organism; her own had kept her heart alert to the animating mysteries of life in addition to giving her the strength she needed to keep her solitude whole. But, much to her consternation, she had discovered that no matter how beautiful a marriage was, no matter how exhilarating and avid, it could still make room for despair, for the poignant acceptance that two people would let each other down without ever meaning to, their gravest errors passing unknown, and always unforgiven.

Adi's face floated in her head, and then it was replaced by Karan's as he had reclined on the chair in the bazaar, his legs parted, his fit, young lion's body radiating sensuality. Strangely enough, Karan's uncanny likeness to the man Rhea loved to distraction extended to certain mannerisms as well: the way

Karan stood, ramrod straight; his habit of scratching his jaw when he was anxious. If the rush of coincidental similarity had drawn her attention, then another aspect, murky but identifiable, had motivated her to help him in his hunt for the Bombay Fornicator: for Karan had reminded her of herself as a young woman, an artist preparing for her conversation with the world, ambivalent about the quality of her work but no less dedicated to its practice, serious and single-minded, ambitious and insecure, awkward and fierce. Not only was it astonishing how much Karan reminded Rhea of her youth, but she had also seen in his eyes the desire and drive that had once burnt bright in her own.

She rose from the sofa and went to the kitchen. After boiling water for a pot of peppermint tea she went up to the terrace, to her studio, with a tray bearing sugar, a white tea cup, a plate of Quality ginger biscuits. For a while she tried to work on her pottery, but she soon realized how severely her excursion to Chor Bazaar had unhinged her composure. She left the studio and stood on the terrace, gazing at the city Karan Seth had chosen to make his subject. Neat, vibrant squares of red chillies laid out to dry on her neighbour's terrace had not yet been collected and in the fading light they looked like patterns on a mythical carpet, so dark it was as if they had been dyed in blood. Bats shot in and out of the overgrown branches of a giant banyan, its thick, gangly aerial roots descending to the earth like tentacles. Lamps flickered tentatively over the sea, distant dhows bearing lean, drunk fishermen. These images

coalesced, becoming a blur of the familiar, consoling details that had parented her childhood; now, for the first time, she was wondering what these sights meant to someone who was not from Bombay. Just as poison could be drawn out of the veins of someone bitten by a lethal snake, she thought Karan too would draw out these images from the innumerable capillaries of the city, relieving it of its magnificent agony and iridescent delusion.

However, was he really any good?

She had not even seen a single photo he had clicked, yet here she was readily ascribing virtue to his work!

Afraid of relying too much on her instinct she went into Adi's library adjoining her studio, where she sat cross-legged on the floor and leafed through a few dog-eared copies of the *India Chronicle.* As she turned the pages, her eyes searched the picture credits. Each time she saw a photo credited to Karan she recognized what she had suspected on meeting him: his incendiary talent, so huge and rambunctious it bled out of him like monsoon from an August sky.

One picture, in particular, left her breathless.

Iqbal Syed had commissioned Karan to shoot pictures to accompany a reasonably long feature on the city's destitute lunatics. Karan had found his subject on Dadar Bridge. Fat and wildly regal, clothed in a torn bruise-purple satin gown, thick black curls corralling a dirt-encrusted face. With her elbows resting on the wall of the bridge, the woman was taking in the amazing chaos of the market below: marigold vendors and

onion wholesalers, teenage prostitutes with career crotches, shining heaps of green chillies and big baskets of burnished lemons. The madwoman had an enchanted smile; the irises of her large, lashless eyes spilled over into the whites, and this furthered the impression that something was, in fact, looking through her. Pressing the picture of the madwoman against her chest, Rhea bent her head, closed her eyes and rocked to and fro, fearing her life was about to change forever.

'Don't take this personally,' Rhea said into the phone, a week later, 'but I think you're ridiculously gifted. Your pictures are revolutionary; they're tender and funny and powerful. They're like folk songs, and old trees.'

'How did you get my number?' A goofy grin had captured Karan's face.

'I called the *India Chronicle* switchboard; the operator put me through. I have a proposition in mind.' The awkwardness she felt at speaking to him went undisclosed, her voice remaining impassive, controlled, regal.

'There's nothing more I like on a Monday afternoon,' he said roguishly, 'than being propositioned.'

'Would you care to photograph the flamingoes at Sewri?'

His eyes widened. 'I've heard a lot about them.'

'Been around a while now. The flock's got messier and massive and I thought they might add to the corpus of your images of the city.'

'I'd be glad to tag along.' He was thrilled by her use of *corpus;* it made what he did sound wonderfully important.

'If you give me your address I'll pick you up on Sunday, early morning. Very early.'

'Certainly ... But why are you doing this for me?'

'Because I believe in your work.'

'Others reckless enough to say that before have never offered to drive me all the way to Sewri.'

'And also, so you understand once and for all, no one in Bombay can be trusted.'

At dawn the following Sunday, the sullen silence in Rhea's car was fractured by Billie Holiday crooning 'Solitude' in a sad-bad-girl voice that summoned to mind low-lit bars and shots of single malt Scotch.

'Who told you about Chor Bazaar?' she asked him.

'Zaira.'

'You don't mean the actor?'

'Yeah.' Karan was impressed with Rhea's driving; keen and swift, like a sting ray, he thought.

'How do you know her?'

'I had photographed her best friend, Samar ...'

'The pianist.'

'Yes. I met Zaira at his place. We became friends.' He blushed, uncomfortable with what she might misread as name-dropping. 'She's real, with a terrific heart; he's over-the-top and hilarious.'

'My husband admires Leo McCormick's work. You've met him too, right?' Rhea refrained from adding that she considered

Leo's writing sterile, soulless crap. 'His approach to India is, well, unique.'

Karan paused, registering for the first time that she was a married woman. 'You don't sound like you're a big fan of Leo.'

'My husband is the one who's really into McCormick's writing,' she deflected. She noticed the mention of her husband had caused his tone to stiffen.

'What do you do?'

'On a good day, I'm a potter; I recall telling you as much in Chor Bazaar.'

'And on a bad one?'

'An artist.'

'What's the difference?'

'The degree of pretence.'

'So you think I'm all up there because I call myself a photographer.'

'I don't apply my standards to others; it protects me from being judged by theirs.'

'Well, thanks a lot.'

'Don't get so worked up.' When she slapped the back of her hand playfully against Karan's shoulder, a sharp, aching bolt of pleasure shot up his spine. He looked at her, but her face was relaxed and vague, neither confirming nor denying the voltage running between them. 'What?'

'Nothing.' He felt his ear lobes throb with white heat.

She brought the car to a halt beside an industrial unit; in the distance were the remains of abandoned ships, hulks and

anchors; an overpowering scent of salt and grease hung heavy in the air. 'Well,' she said, her eyes feasting on his face again, 'here we are, Mr Seth.'

The Sewri mudflats were like nothing Karan had seen before: the land was cratered and huge puddles of water had collected in the undulations, reminding Karan of the first pictures of the moon. In the soft light of a new day, flamingoes spread out as far as his eye could see. The birds had shallow-keeled mandibles, elongated, spindled legs, wide wings with serrated, feverishly pink feathers at the edges. Their curved, pirate-hook beaks reached industriously through the silt, pulling up crustacean algae. From time to time they rent the air with flat, unimpressive goose-like cries.

Almost as if he were under a spell, Karan left Rhea's side and marched off into the shallow, stinking water.

From a distance, Rhea admired his purposeful, agile stride, his correctly held shoulders, his narrow waist. She was drawn not so much to the high summer of Karan's body—his dark hair with its dapper shine or the tight brown ropes of his long, determined arms—as to his virility, the reckless, organic abundance of youth; she imagined him on his knees, gently bending a woman in the exquisite distress of ecstasy, his hands gripping her by her waist, pulling himself deeper within her in smooth, energetic motions.

He returned to her side about twenty minutes later, his eyes sparkling. 'Incredible! Where do they come from?'

'Who knows?' She shrugged. 'They were just wandering before they stopped here. But it couldn't have been for the view!'

'I could never imagine there would be a place for lost flamingoes in Bombay.'

'Who'd have thought, huh?'

'That lost things end up here?'

'Beautiful things, too.'

'They ought to be taken care of.'

'If they can care for their own, that's plenty.'

'Where do you reckon they'll go from here?'

'Where does anyone go from Bombay?'

'Surely Sewri was never meant to be their final destination!'

'Maybe they had no destination in mind.'

'How can they live in a swamp ... In a city of one too many millions?'

'They've learnt to hustle, settled for Sewri when they could have had more. I guess if you don't snatch what someone else needs, you're okay.' She folded her hands about herself. 'Which means they're an endangered species in more ways than one.'

'Don't they have to leave? Go some place, like their home?'

'Home?' She looked at him, then blinked slowly. 'What's that?'

'You know ...' he said, 'the place where they belong.'

'Maybe they don't know it just yet, but here's where they've always belonged.'

A loud noise in the distance—perhaps a gunshot or a burst tyre—interrupted their conversation and set off the flock: one or two of them flapped their wings anxiously, giving off a strange, piercing shriek.

'Maybe we're all lost,' Karan resumed thoughtfully.

'Maybe so,' Rhea said. 'But how terrible to be found out.'

'Look!' Karan pointed excitedly, scrambling for his camera. 'They're taking off'

The flock hurled itself against the warm, burnished sky with a thunderous flutter.

'I'm so glad I came,' he said as the birds passed overhead. 'I saw them a few months ago, when I was on my way to photograph Samar. They must be an omen.'

'An omen of what?' she asked, knowing there was no answer to her query.

He didn't answer; he was working. His silence reminded her how completely given he was to his task. She raised her head and stared at the birds with him, caught in a web of awe and loneliness. As she watched the flock rise higher into the sky, something in her lovely, frightened soul took flight, freeing her, unexpectedly and briefly, from the earth's heinous gravity.

5

THREE WEEKS AFTER THE TRIP TO SEWRI KARAN rang the doorbell outside Rhea's apartment.

She answered the door herself and looked confounded at finding Karan there.

'You forgot about our appointment?'

'Would I ever?' she lied. Flour streaked her wrists; the tails of a blue oversized man's shirt were loosely knotted at her waist, over a pair of beige cigarette pants. 'I was baking a cake for my husband. He's coming home tonight from Singapore; I'm always a little distracted when I'm cooking.'

'Are you sure we should hang out today?' Karan resembled an earnest schoolboy, clutching four folders of photos to his chest. 'If it's a bad day ...'

'Now that you're here,' Rhea said warmly as she led him inside, 'my day is bound to be excellent.'

'I got something for you.' He handed her a manila envelope.

She slipped the envelope under her arm. 'You shouldn't have, but I'm glad you did.'

'You don't even know what it is!'

'That's besides the point; knowing is always besides the point.'

On the way to the kitchen they passed her living room. Amazed by its elegance—the staghorn ferns suspended from the ceiling, the masterly paintings tastefully framed, an antique dowry chest and a tiger skin dramatically mounted on a wall—Karan stood with his mouth open wide enough to trap a few flies. His admiration made her uneasy; she loathed being reminded of the privilege she had married into. She hurried him to the kitchen, a basic, humble space, cleverly laid out, warm and snug. Saucepans were strung along an iron galley rail and a fine dust of cocoa covered the marble-top island.

'Was my place easy to locate?'

'Not difficult at all. Your apartment is at the top of a hill ... I bet you have a terrific view.'

'Well, when I say I look down on Bombay, I actually mean it.' She picked up a copper whisk and started to fluff up egg whites.

Lila-bai, fat and short, entered the kitchen. She glared at Karan.

'Lila-bai,' Rhea said, 'why don't you finish the vegetable shopping and then go on home? I'm completely out; I'd like some brinjals for lunch tomorrow.'

Lila-bai grunted in reply.

Rhea handed her a list and a small wad of cash, and packed her off. On her way out Lila-bai eyed Karan suspiciously.

As Rhea resumed work on the cake batter, adding flour and cocoa, Karan found his place by the window ledge from where he gazed out at the ugly and delicious city, the master of his curiosity. In spite of the great view, his mind was unable to shake off the disturbing privilege he had walked into: the magnificent house, the hard-working husband, the duty-bound wife. But he also knew that when everything is in place, something has to give. When he stole glances at her, he was irritated to see her profoundly absorbed in the process of baking a cake, a pedestrian task that seemed to diminish the sublime opacity of her existence. Why couldn't she just go out and buy a cake? She certainly had all the money in the world, and the Oberoi deli did a roll-call of fabulous pastries. He felt a sudden, jagged stab of contempt for her husband for shackling her to the house, to the kitchen; then he reluctantly considered that maybe *she* had chosen this life over others, and he felt inadequate and unwanted. It was unlikely he would ever own such a grand house or win the glittering, single-minded ardour of a woman like Rhea. In the places self-loathing could reach, lust trembled, and so he turned to face her after she shut the oven door and found himself craven at her elegant neglect.

'You seem a little lost,' she remarked.

He walked towards her, entered again the delicate havoc of her gaze. 'How could I be lost in a kitchen?'

'Very easily. Happens to me all the time. I'm sorry you had to wait while I was so busy being boring, but I promise to make up for it now that I'm done.'

'Do I get to see your pottery studio?'

'Yes. But after the house tour, we'll discuss your pictures; you came here for work, and I don't want to distract you from that.' Her voice was officious, solemn.

'That means a lot to me.'

'Follow me.'

She led him up a narrow, steep stairwell that opened on to the terrace. Bougainvillea, a profligate purple, was trellised over rungs of decaying bamboo; red palms, sunburnt at the ends, swayed in circular terracotta pots. Two small rooms, divided by a common wall, stood on one side of the terrace. Both the rooms had large glass-panelled doors so one could look out at the sea in the distance.

'Come into my studio.' She led him in by the hand, a gesture that had a slightly ceremonial, illicit air.

'It's like a temple,' he marvelled.

The inlay of Venetian tiles on the floor caught slabs of light filtering through the glass; a clutter of half-finished vases and sculptures added to the heavy, ruminating air of an artist's lair. Someone wounded might come here to be repaired, he thought.

'The other room,' she said, opening the wooden door in the wall dividing the two rooms, 'is Adi's library.'

Wide wooden shelves of innumerable books attested to scary scholarship. Tracing the gilded spines of all the books he would never read, Karan tried to conceal a quiver of envy so palpable he feared she might notice it. It was only inevitable, then, for him to ask about Adi Dalal.

As Rhea unspooled his story, and theirs, her face shimmered with a big and glorious feeling.

Anamika Pandit had been Adi's first girlfriend. They had started to date at the age of thirteen. Tall, curvaceous, with moss-green eyes, Anamika was also Rhea's closest friend. Anamika and Adi went out for two years, splitting up rather abruptly after a silly row at the Bombay Gymkhana. In truth, Adi had been desperate to slip out of the clutches of the bossy, selfish south Bombay girl, who would invariably grow up to be the sort of woman who slaps her maids when no one's looking. It was only a matter of days before Adi's rejection transformed Anamika into a talented insidious little shrew. Unwilling to put up with the disgrace of being dumped, she made it seem to their friends and peers that Rhea had masterminded the split.

A year later, when Adi actually started seeing Rhea, Anamika's insinuations seemed to be confirmed. Overnight, Rhea turned into the girl who had 'stolen her best friend's boyfriend'. Gentle and private, with heavy, inscrutable eyes, Rhea was easily vilified in the clumsy narrative of their youth, but in truth this cluster of friends had to count on such fiction

to shatter the chimaera of 'childhood innocence'. Rhea's purported deception thrust them into a temporary, tentative adulthood, replete with its air of ruinous betrayals and romantic havoc.

Crushed by the avalanche of Anamika's lies, Rhea withdrew from their common circle of friends, and Adi reached out to her in her seclusion, drawing her out of her shell. Rhea was elated to discover that she could tell Adi everything—her scuffles with her mother, her erratic periods, her slowly emerging interest in pottery—and amazed by how intently he listened to her, offering the balm of sensible, comforting words and respecting all the spaces that ought to remain unvandalized by language.

One night, a few weeks before Rhea's board exams, Adi showed up at her door with a present in his hands, the monsoon in his hair.

'For you,' he said, as he extended a jar of fireflies toward her.

She peered into the glass: there were insects in it, small and plump, with translucent wings and downy bellies; they were terribly unattractive.

He had picked them, he said, from the forests of the national park, hazarding physical safety as he climbed the trees where they hid underneath thick, dusty leaves.

'Why do they give off those strange bursts of light?'

He lied confidently: 'Mating ritual.'

For two nights in a row she gazed fixedly at the sublime flickers of luminosity. On the third day the fireflies died. Staring at their fat, upended, diaphanous bodies at the base of the

jam jar, she called him, panic swirling in her voice. Later that evening, after burying the fireflies on the seashore in a matchbox casket, she suspected that his theft from the forest was as close as he could come to telling her he loved her.

'Why did he give you fireflies?' Karan spoke as softly as possible, reluctant to shatter her reverie, fragile and powerful like a tarantula's web.

'I had told him I dreamt of fireflies; oddly enough, I could never sleep peacefully once I woke from those dreams. My father, who was an expert dream analyst, helped me grasp the significance of their appearance in my sleep and Adi felt left out in the volley of metaphors between father and daughter,' she said with a smile. 'The next best thing was to get me a few fireflies and see what I thought of them in real time.'

'And?'

'His gesture served two purposes: I stopped dreaming about fireflies, and slept soundly as a result. It brought me closer to Adi; not as close as I was to my father at the time, but a door opened between us ...'

'Did Adi inherit this romantic streak from his father?'

'I doubt it.'

'What did his father do?' He picked up a yellow vase from the shelf above him and studied it with admiration.

For generations, she said, the Dalals had owned mills in Parel. When the recurrent labour union strikes grew to be too much of a hassle, the senior Mr Dalal sold off his stakes and pursued his lifelong passion for collecting and exhibiting

vintage cars. Adi's mother, a former society columnist for the *Indian Express,* had abruptly left her husband and son when Adi was all of fifteen. Adi had broken up with Anamika the same year but his friendship with Rhea continued to blossom. A few months later he found that Rhea's companionship significantly defused the gloom sponsored by his parents' divorce. Rhea's robust, enterprising company consoled Adi greatly; although she refused to allow him to sentimentalize his parents' parting of ways, she heard him out patiently as he recounted their tempestuous courtship, their remarkable infidelities, their wild fights. When Adi claimed he would not repeat the mistakes his parents had made, she reminded him that the strength of a marriage was measured not only by how it was upheld but also by how people responded to its betrayal. Rhea firmly believed that love between two people was frequently betrayed because it was inherently imperfect; however, an acceptance of its imperfection could go a long way in securing its future, its vitality, perhaps even its permanence.

Karan leaned against the wall, dazzled not only by her love story but her insight into life. 'And what were your parents like?'

'I loved my father more than any man.' There was blistering conviction in her voice; her eyes followed Karan's hand as it returned the yellow vase to the shelf from which it had been moved.

Rhea's mother worked for Bank of India and her father, Dr Thacker, had been the head of the department of philosophy at

Banaras Hindu University. A book he had written, enquiring into the idea of life as a series of interconnected illusions, had come to be considered a classic.

'May I see a copy of your father's book?' Karan asked.

Rhea played with her ear lobe. 'Give me a minute.'

Sprinting down to her bedroom, she returned with a badly bound edition of *Divine Sport: Deconstructing Maya,* its pages yellowed with time. Karan gingerly admitted he knew precious little about maya, certainly not as much as he would have liked. As he read the synopsis on the back cover and turned the pages, he wondered: if life were a tapestry of interwoven illusions, then did his photographs merely add to the bulk of cosmic invention? More crucially, was life, in its illusory context, exempt from moral stipulations?

'Did your father like Adi?'

'They never had a chance to get to know each other better,' she said.

After his eighteenth birthday, Adi had left for New York to pursue a degree in finance. Rhea enrolled at Sophia College, where many of her peers had boyfriends who were artists or musicians and she would hear the women complain about their dirty rows, their passionate reconciliations, their unpredictable, fragile moods. Increasingly convinced that one artist's union with another artist, for all its tumult and tenderness, was not worth the upheaval, she felt lucky for Adi, who harboured no artistic ambitions.

Study hard, she wrote to Adi in one of her innumerable letters. *I pray for you.*

Manhattan was only Bombay's long-lost twin, Adi wrote back—it had that same slyness and bad comic timing. From a café on Spring Street, he wrote, *You remind me of jazz; you are the echo of my solitude.*

Rhea had fallen silent.

Karan gave her a few moments to gather her thoughts, but it appeared her nostalgic recollection was about to take a severe, disconsolate turn.

'In my last year at college I won a scholarship to study pottery in Berlin; I was raring to go to Germany. Besides, my graduation project, "Sight, Unseen", had got the attention of two important gallerists. They wanted to acquire the work, show it.'

'I don't know much about pottery but the stuff in your studio is pretty spectacular.'

She blushed. She never displayed on her walls the certificates of excellence she had won as a student. Rhea Thacker would, one tutor had written, elevate Indian pottery from the medium of craft it was conventionally considered to be an art form, as it was accepted in the West. Rhea was lauded for her playfulness with form. One creation was a simple blue pot, thrown on the wheel with immense verve, then matt glazed rough; when turned, it revealed the great head of Shiva. Her innovation and skill with glazing added to the feverish interest in her future as a ceramic sculptor; her name came to be

whispered with awe in Bombay's art circles; everyone wanted to know how her life would unfold.

'In those days, I had a lot of ambition.' Her expression betrayed the awkwardness she felt in disclosing her past. 'But, as with everything, that too fades.'

'Does drive have to fade?' Karan thought of Samar, who had walked away, mid-recital, from his scintillating life as a pianist.

'No. It doesn't have to. But we all make trade-offs. I knew my life could take off, but for that I'd have to keep my relationship with Adi on hold.'

'So you chose to give up on the possibility of a fantastic career.'

'Let's not assume I'd have made good on my initial promise, for what *that* had been worth.'

Karan grimaced; she was being perfunctorily modest.

'Was it worth it, sacrificing your career for your marriage?'

She sighed. 'Adi's love is a kind of personal oxygen; it can lift you, and once it's in you it becomes vital to you. I could wrap it around me like a shawl or use it like a sword against the world; I could hide with it, run with it, play with it, show it off like a badge of honour or curl up with it like a cat. It's moist and huge, pliant and energizing.' She paused, breathless. 'Around Adi, I feel lit up from some place deep inside; I feel invincible, extravagant.'

He nodded, unsure why she was extolling her husband; such rampant, exasperating praise made it hard for him to hide the frown gathering at his mouth. 'Right.'

As if reading his thoughts she said, 'I should stop ...'

'No,' he urged. 'Please go on.' He was terrified his face had disclosed his true feelings about Amazing Adi but he did not want his envy to interrupt a full account of her marriage. 'Adi sounds like, well, quite a man.'

'He is, although he doesn't allow for a lot to come in the way of him and me.'

'I see.' The word *possessive* flared in front of Karan's eyes. 'So his love comes at a price.' He was relieved to learn her utopia had a secret fretwork of landmines.

'Yes—and it was a price I was prepared to pay. I chose marriage. And I chose Adi.' She shut her eyes. When she opened them a few seconds later, Karan could not decipher if she had been fighting to hold back tears. 'At times, art can come in the way of being human and you wonder if it's worth it ...' Rhea trailed off. She knew she was telling Karan more than her discretion normally permitted; she hardly knew him, but perhaps his unfamiliarity was fostering their intimacy.

'You chose Adi, you chose marriage, and gave up your career in the process ...'

Pain seized her face. 'Sometimes I think about what would have happened if I had pursued pottery professionally. If Adi had not minded me staying with pottery masters and studying in their ateliers, my work would have had an entirely different level of finesse. There would have been exhibitions. There would have been reviews of the work. But I will never know all that.' Rhea looked out through the glass doors; the afternoon

was slipping away. She knew he had come here to talk about his photographs but she was swept away into the turbulent currents of her past. She realized that part of the fascination of telling a story was to hear it for oneself. 'When I met you in Chor Bazaar and you were out hunting for an absurdly named plantation chair I saw in your eyes the rush and rapture that had one day been mine.' Her voice roiled with sullen contempt. 'I *know* what you feel when you step out on the streets with your camera; I know what it is to be in your mood, and live under its compulsion. I know what it is to be an artist at the threshold, with possibilities that remind you only of a blue sky, its boundlessness.'

'And you know that mood because you had to give it up?'

'I chose to give it up; it's not difficult to travel through life without a ticket.'

'But what about your tutors who believed in your work?'

'You can't please everyone, Karan.'

'And the gallerists would have thought you just fell off the radar.'

'If folks mistake your silence for muteness that's *their* problem.' She swirled the wheel before her; it started up with a crank, then rotated to a slow halt. 'Why should I tell a gallerist or a tutor I lost my nerve for an altogether unexpected reason?' Her face clouded over. 'A few days after my finals at university, my parents left for an ashram near Aranangaon.'

'Is that the village near Ahmednagar?' He put his hands on the wheel between them.

'Yes, it is. And my parents never returned from the pilgrimage.'

Rhea had received a call in the middle of the afternoon from the Ahmednagar police station informing her of the accident. Just when she felt she would slip into a place where there was no light and where she could hear no sound, Adi returned from America, a brief but direly needed appearance. In the arbour of his arms, she cried with demonic strength, soundless sobs that shot up from the well of an inconsolable sorrow.

'My father often said "everything is just right". That became my mantra. Accept things. Just be.'

Before Adi left again for New York, they were engaged; a year later, they married on a barge off the Gateway of India, under the silver bangle of a December moon. 'I have no photographs of my wedding day.' A cloud of sadness obscured her voice. 'It's as if that day never happened.'

The suddenness of her parents' death and the swiftness of her marriage to Adi had resulted in Rhea's lifelong engagement with solitude. As her seclusion gradually gathered the intensity of a cyclone, it forbade friends; women, in particular, she continued to distrust, scarred as she had been by Anamika's lies. In any event, Bombay famously discouraged friendships; there was neither the time to forge meaningful affinities nor to foster a steadfast intimacy.

On their second wedding anniversary, Adi gifted her the pottery studio on their terrace.

She rose and walked toward the kiln, and opened its door. 'It's one of the first electric kilns in Bombay. Adi had it shipped in from Germany.'

'Where you had gone for further studies?'

'Oh, the scholarship?' Rhea said, her voice caressing an afterthought. 'I never followed through with it. Adi was not keen for me to give up this city and shack up with a bunch of hippie potters.'

She looked around her studio. In its dim, flattering light it was easy to forget that she had lost her parents or that she had so cruelly abandoned her friends; here, it was possible to focus so clearly on her art that she could successfully exclude the rest of the world, its rancour and flaws, its expectations and its regrets. She devoted all her spare time to transforming mounds into a certain shape of clay with her bare hands, baking it to perfection in her kiln, glazing it with the colours she had seen in her dreams. What little time she had left for herself she spent volunteering at the animal shelter in Parel.

'You must really like animals.'

'They accept pain with tremendous dignity; their suffering is plain, sincere, without noise. I admire this quality above all things.' She latched the kiln door, her mind recalling the day it had arrived from Hamburg, Adi's excited face as it had been fitted in the studio.

'Is it difficult to spend so much time away from Adi?'

'Not at all.'

When Adi was in Singapore Rhea missed his habit of playing jazz in the evenings; her ears were famished for the crumbs of an Ellington ditty. She knew that Adi thought of her with ruinous ache, relentlessly; he sometimes said that he missed the tinkle of the bangles on her wrists. But their time apart taught them to count on each other's absences, to journal the wisdom of separation. The dreamy look on Rhea's face was now slowly replaced by august composure, making Karan feel that the winding road of her reminiscence had ended at a cul-de-sac.

'That's a beautiful story; your husband sounds like a gem.' He decided to never bring Adi Dalal into their conversation again.

She did not respond.

'Are you all right?'

'I was thinking of the talisman I left behind in Chor Bazaar.' She twirled an errant curl of hair between her fingers.

'What talisman?'

'It was a little brass monkey. I'd been looking for one forever.' The store owner had told Rhea the talisman was used to protect someone you loved. 'I'd put it down somewhere in the shop when I met you ... I forgot it there.'

'I'm sorry.'

'It's not your fault.' Her mood had shifted; she was suddenly aware she had spoken too much, that she could not take back her words. Moreover, the vital, trembling attraction

between them made her resent herself. 'Anyway, I had better go and look at the cake in the oven—'

'I should be going now.'

'Well, we never had a chance to look at your pictures.'

'Next time?'

She said nothing to encourage him to believe they might meet again.

On the way down the narrow spiral staircase Rhea missed a step and Karan bucked forward to steady her. But the force of her pushed him down and she found herself on him. She hurriedly stood, turned, faced him, asked him if he was okay. Karan nodded before reaching to touch her ear lobe, the gentle, perfect thing. When his hand was on her sternum, she gasped, unsettled by his audacity. The touch was warm, assured, and she shook her head, as if to say no. But it was larger than either of them, desire as deep as a canyon.

Neither did a thing, yet it happened, effortless as a breath.

Rolling on the landing, they fought for and off each other, unhaunted by either shame or guilt.

His tongue slid over her long neck, her elegant fingers. Her hands pulled off his white tee-shirt, revealing lean, firm flesh, perfect shoulders, a flat stomach. He relieved her off her cigarette pants, leaving her only in what was so obviously one of her husband's office shirts. Parting her legs, he dove his head between her thighs. His tongue, moist and thick and interested, was like fingers parting the petals of a reluctant rose. She blamed herself for unbuttoning his jeans, but restraint seemed

impossible. Flexing her hands over his legs, she was surprised to find his thighs muscled: from walking Bombay for miles, she imagined. She lay back on the landing, his tee-shirt bunched under her head, their bodies suffused in the dusk dribbling over them through a skylight. His movements were athletic, confident, and, once in her, he moved his pelvis gently, in small circles, as if he was stirring her. Grabbing his hips, she pulled him in, then out, halting the head of his organ at the onset of her hidden thing.

She allowed him to lunge in.

Her legs, wrapped around him until now, were freed to either side of her.

She was in beautiful shock, unsure how any of this had happened. She avoided his eyes, held her face firmly down to one side. He continued to buck, her loins holding him captive, even as her mind floated over the innocuous details of her house, the painting on the wall, the useless curio on the desk, motes of dust banished under the door. When she came back, when her mind was shoved to its senses, to who she was, a married woman, he was about to climax—and she caught it expertly, the thick rain of an angry storm.

6

AFTER AN EXHAUSTING DAY OF FILMING FOR A shampoo commercial at Film City, Zaira was counting on an evening out. She was dithering over her choice of earrings when the phone rang—again.

She sounded so irritated as she answered, that Karan, who was at the other end, feared he had got the wrong number.

'Swear I was going to hang up, Zaira,' he said, wondering what had got into her.

'If *only* you could see my room right now,' she said in her defence. 'There are mountains of skirts and piles of jackets; there are four shawls and two gowns and one halter-neck top on the floor. My room looks like a football stadium. I just cannot decide what to wear; it's brought me to the conclusion that one of the finest uses for a man is having him choose what to wear for the night.'

'Most guys are awful with such things, you know.'

'Not Samar; I'd wear a sackcloth he put his fingers on.' There was silence for a moment and then she gave a long, troubled sigh.

'Something on your mind, Zaira?'

'Oh, I've been getting some cheap calls over the last hour.' She tried to press the anxiety out of her voice. 'Nothing to worry about, yaar.'

'Okay, but who was it?'

'Don't bleed over it ...'

'If you say that, it's precisely what I'm going to do.'

'I mean it, Karan. Just forget it.' She slammed a tube of mascara on the dressing table.

'Hey, Zaira, cool it.'

'I'm sorry I snapped ...' She admired Karan's decision to stand up to her; his voice was gentle but firm. 'I'm having a difficult day.'

'I'm sorry it's been a rough day; I hope it improves now.'

'It will—after I decide what I'm wearing for Samar's party tonight.'

'And I'm calling about the party; will you write me off as a total rat if I cancel on dinner plans this evening?'

'Not a total rat. But I'll certainly file you under "Mouse". What happened?'

'Some work. Came up last minute.' Iqbal had asked him to cover an awards function at the Taj.

'Come afterward,' she encouraged.

Karan considered her offer. Although he would have been happy to head home and hit the sack, the prospect of spending time with Zaira was not without its charms. He was interested by her but not in her; she felt the same way about him. Both were aware of this, and found it remarkably liberating. 'Okay if I show up around midnight?'

'Expect me to be totally toasted by midnight. But then, sobriety is so overrated.' She put down the phone and studied the lipsticks on her dressing table, her fingers carefully inspecting each tube before deciding on a dazzling shade of rogue red.

By the time Karan ankled it over to Samar's party, it was swinging despite a power cut.

The velvet, whispering darkness, punctuated by fickle-flamed candles, revealed exuberant revellers milling about on the lawn. No sooner had he entered the gate than a soft, warm hand gripped his arm, led him across the green, down the terrazzo, into the living room with its stark, white walls and up the staircase to the terrace.

Zaira lay back on the stone tiles, plonked a bottle of bubbly between them and stared at a jumble of stars without so much as a word. The crowds roiled on below.

'How're you?' He was catching his breath as he sat beside her.

'I'm overwhelmed,' she said. 'And you?'

'I'm working my way toward whelmed.'

Music, electronic, low bass, electric and gritty, rose up like a gauze of sexual memory.

'Are you hungry?'

'I ate after the awards ceremony; thanks for asking, Zaira. Why do you like to hang out on the roof?'

'That's the only way I can enjoy a party: drinking alone. All the slick chatter inaudible, and so far away. Years ago, Samar put the idea into my head and I've been hooked ever since. When Samar and I did it people said we were nutcases or fussy, but how else do you deal with the screwball jitters?'

'Parties make me nervous too. I avoid them as much as possible.'

'In that case, I owe you double thanks for coming, Karan.' She touched his shoulder. His company enlivened her; she felt safe and suddenly content. Looking up at the big, dirty sky she felt there was no place she would rather be.

'Well, being up here makes it a lot easier for me. Do Samar and you still do your rooftop rendezvous?'

'Not any longer. Leo caught us one time and said it was too dangerous. I guess,' she said without conviction, 'Leo does have a point. By the way, I'm sorry I snapped at you earlier today.'

'Who was calling you all day?'

'Have you heard the phrase "asshole's asshole"?'

Malik had been calling her repeatedly, she told him, proposing marriage. After she had slammed the phone on him for the fifth time, he had called back, sounding manic, ranting about picking out her guts with a butcher's blade.

'Aha, that's a new one,' Karan said, 'but it's custom cut for the creature at hand.' Now he knew why she had sounded so cheesed off when he had called her.

'Why doesn't Malik just give up? I've tried everything, you know.'

'You should report him to the police. Samar was right all along.'

'I've complained before ... And where has it got me? You know the police in this city. You could buy them off for a few thousand, and Minister Prasad has more than that to play with.' She said she could hear so much booze in Malik's voice that he could pass for a bar.

'That's not just booze you hear in his voice; apparently the minister's munda likes his coke by the ball.'

The hair on Zaira's neck stiffened. 'How d'you know?'

'A stringer at the magazine was going to run a story on the neta lot who get high as a kite every other night. Delhi's teeming with scumbags who get off on group sex in farmhouses, where heroin comes on the same platter as pakoras. And now this same lot has landed up in Bombay ...'

'Did *India Chronicle* ever run the story?'

'Minister Prasad got wind of the piece and got higher-ups to scrap it.'

'See what I mean? That man can do whatever he likes.' Her rage was amputated by helplessness.

'You really should tell the police, Zaira. They should have Malik on file.'

An awkward, jittery silence followed. Zaira turned toward him, her head on her elbow. 'How's your love life?'

'Excellent!' he replied. 'Non-existent. Almost.'

'You said her name was Rhea Dalal?'

'Yes—and I met her thanks to you.'

Zaira gave him a quizzical look.

'You sent me to Chor Bazaar; that's where I met her.'

'Ah.'

'Well, I doubt it's going anywhere; she's married and all that.'

'Like *that's* stopped anyone before.'

'We went up to Sewri to shoot the flamingoes. We've been around Bombay scouting subjects for my project. She's got one cunning eye.'

'Hope her eye is the only cunning thing about her. I've met one too many kaminis in a kurti, and you'd never ever guess.'

'You sound suspicious.'

'I am; don't you think it's strange that she's chosen to help you in this manner?'

'Maybe she's foolish enough to believe in my work.'

'*Any*one would believe in your work, Karan. It's singular and exceptional, and it doesn't take rocket science to figure out you're going to go places. What's with the husband?'

'He lives away for part of the month, in Singapore. He manages a hedge fund there.'

'So she's a lonely housewife ...'

'She's not lonely; she likes alone. I gather the arrangement with her husband works for both of them ...'

'Why?'

'They need time apart to stay together.'

'But if she likes to be alone then why does she want to hang out with you?'

After a minute he said, 'Because she was once an artist on the verge of something special ... But she surrendered it for domesticity.'

Zaira closed her eyes. 'So that's what's going on. She met you in the bazaar and loved your work. Her life allows her the time to take you around Bombay. A part of her believes she can fulfil through you now what she gave up in her younger days.'

'Thank you, Dr Zaira,' he said with a laugh. 'Has it occurred to you that she might be attracted to me?'

'Why does every man assume that just because a woman might enjoy his company she's wet in her panties each time she sees him?'

'Ouch!'

'I'm sure she has the hots for you,' she said warmly. 'Who wouldn't? But what I'm trying to get a handle on is, if she's happy in her marriage then why would she mess around?'

'Are you asking me to be careful?'

'I'm asking you if you know your stop. If it's a fling, treat it like one; if it's more, figure out what's *more.* And you should do it quick; you sound like you're really into her.'

Karan had grown to relish the arbitrary, opaque charms of Rhea Dalal, and the conversation made him uneasy. He decided to move on from the topic. 'Were you ever wound up around someone?'

'Like you are around Rhea?' Zaira said with a grin.

He blushed so deeply it could have shown even in the darkness.

'Yes, when I was younger,' she said. 'Sahil and I were engaged during my last year in college. He wanted me to settle down, play wife, breed like a bunny. Would you believe it if I told you I was totally game?'

'What did your folks have to say about Sahil?'

'Folks? My mother died at childbirth. When I was three my father remarried and then decided to return me to my grandmother. She was a seamstress with the nawab in Hyderabad; I grew up in this rambling old royal pad with hundreds of doves in the courtyard. When I was twenty, my grandmother died of a stroke.'

'Did you like your grandmother?'

'No, I *loved* her. She made the best biryani ever. She was there for me when I had nightmares.'

'Nightmares?'

'Nightmares plagued my adolescence; I'd wake screaming.'

'What was your scariest nightmare?'

Zaira thought for a while, then said, 'I was in a noisy, crowded room. A man was chasing me. No one seemed to notice us. I felt invisible; my screams were heard by no one.

Only *he* could see me. He cornered me and came so close I could feel his breath on my cheek. Then he said, *I am afraid of love,* and his words were loud as thunder. I would wake at this point in a cold sweat. My grandmother was always there, holding my hand when I bolted up. She was everything to me ... until Samar came along and snapped me up for four rupees and fifty paise.'

'I'd say Samar got a steal. And your grandmother sounds like an empress.'

'She was only a seamstress but her ordinary circumstances didn't prevent her heart from being extraordinary.'

'How did you cope with her passing?'

'I was with Sahil at the time. He tried to comfort me. But I needed to be alone; I left for Kashmir. An odd thing happened in Srinagar. A director spotted me in a rose garden, and he asked me if I wanted to act. I said yes, not because his offer was particularly appealing but I was ready to do anything to get the sorrow out of my head. And if it meant dancing around trees, I was sold.'

'So you said yes.'

'When I did, Sahil had a duck fit. He ordered me to call the director and back out on the acting job in Bombay. Control freak! I called off the engagement on principle; I was ready to be married but not to be owned.'

'Did the break-up take you out?'

'Not really,' she said. 'I moved to Bombay. Put up as a PG in Goregaon. My first film was such a spectacular bore even I couldn't bear to sit through it.'

'But your second film, *Murad,* more than made up.' Karan had watched *Murad* in Shimla, amid a clamour of catcalls and wolf whistles; one man was thrown out of the hall after he was caught masturbating into a popcorn bag. 'The film was, as the trade press calls it, a Super Hit. You looked like you could start a forest fire.'

'Forest fire?' she repeated, embarrassed by his compliment. 'Most days I can't even get the stove going.'

'Your life must have really taken off after *Murad.*'

'And how! I travelled the world. I attended obscure film festivals and sat through difficult, oddball French flicks. I read reviews, tossed even the most flattering ones in the bin. The film was screened in so many countries I couldn't even identify the language some of my fan mail came in.'

'I remember, at one point one couldn't drive a mile without seeing your face plastered on a billboard or pick up a magazine that didn't have you on its cover.'

'I'm sorry. When fame crosses over into ubiquity, it makes one obnoxious. And ubiquity was never my intention; it just became an occupational hazard.' She stroked her neck. 'I did seven films over the next four years and then I felt like the flashbulbs were going to bust my eyeballs. I took off for a year.'

In her gap year, Zaira travelled through Mexico, spent a month in Sienna learning how to cook, conducted a short, smutty affair with a Cuban dancer, following which she made a beeline for Bombay because there was no other place she would rather call home. In the autumn of her idleness, at a party in

Bandra, she stumbled upon a man in a roguish red turban, black tee-shirt and slim-fit indigo jeans hiding under a giant palm leaf, sipping a Bellini all by himself.

She asked the little imp if she might join him. He nodded.

'When you look at people from this angle, they all seem wonderfully unique,' Samar had observed, raising his glass to the crowd before them. 'As if God hand-picks each and every bottom.'

'I for one have never believed that eyes were the window to the soul.'

'I wouldn't call the ass a window to the soul,' he hurried to clarify. 'Although some asses are profoundly soulful in their own way.'

'I'm afraid,' she complained, 'I haven't seen one like *that* tonight.'

'I'll drink to that.'

They spent the evening conjuring up the lives of the guests before them, ascribing fictional fates to each one. The model in the slinky black dress was actually a man, he told her; he had worked as a pearl diver in Sri Lanka and had his toes bitten off by a man-eating turtle. She pointed to the painter in the head wrap, claiming he was going to die the following Thursday, collapsing face down on his last and most significant canvas; they sighed together at the loss of an extraordinary painting, destroyed by the painter's untimely, inelegant death. She added that the most attractive woman in the party had the blood of a demon in her veins. He promptly confirmed her suspicions,

saying that on full-moon nights she sported a forked tail and prowled in wait for weedy waifs on Grant Road.

The hour before dawn arrived while the city's well-heeled were still downing martinis and shooting up. He asked her if she would go for the morning prayers at the Babulnath temple. They fled in stealth, and got to the temple in time for the dawn aarti. Bells tolled; the pandit recited shlokas; devotees poured milk over an obsidian black lingam.

On the way out, Zaira's booze buzz wearing out, she burbled, 'Will you ... be my friend?'

Samar hooted aloud. 'No one's asked me that since the fourth standard!'

'You must have had bad breath a *long* time,' she retorted, thrilled she had inspired in this goofy, adorable man laughter as loud as applause.

The early days with Samar always reminded Zaira of the monsoon: moist and savage gales that burst open the bolted doors of her soul in a great and transformative ravage. She bloomed, for she had met a man who could tap dance and fry up a frittata and had arms wide enough to make her feel safe. Spending more time with him, often waking on his beat-up old couch, she found that her relief sank deep into her bones.

One morning, over coffee and eggs, she said theatrically, 'I need to tell you something.'

'You're pregnant?'

'Yes!' She laughed, tossing a Bollywood formula line: 'I'm going to be the mother of your child!'

'Oh, hon!' Samar slapped his thigh. 'I've said that to a dozen guys already and it hasn't stopped even *one* of them from leaving.'

'I'm a kleptomaniac, Samar.'

Her confession left him unfazed.

'I like to steal flowers, only flowers,' she disclosed. 'At night. From gardens, public or private.'

'Heard of Dubash House?' She stole a glance at him; he looked perfectly serious.

The giant fortress-like abode on Napean Sea Road was rumoured to have wild jasmine, an orchard of frangipani and giant gulmohars. 'I've wanted to break into their garden from the time I set foot in Bombay!'

On the night they stole flowers from Dubash House, she kissed him.

'That's really hetero-erotic,' Samar said, pulling away. 'But I'm not into that shit.'

At the door to his cottage, Samar reminded her that just because he had no boyfriend didn't mean he was looking for a girlfriend. Her face tore up like fine lace.

They were in his kitchen; on the floor lay frangipani, long, mottled branches, some of which had grazed her luscious arms.

'We can be more than lovers,' Samar said. 'If you like.'

She started to tidy the table, as if enacting gestures of domesticity might allow her to claim it.

'The price of tomatoes has gone up,' he said, watching her every move.

'What does sex have to do with the price of tomatoes?'

'Good point!' he said. 'What does sex have to do with anything?'

She threw a plate in his direction.

'I'm glad it's not my Limoges,' Samar responded calmly, although he was impossibly relieved that she had missed. 'But that *still* doesn't mean you can trash my crockery just because we won't fuck in this lifetime.'

'This is *not* about fucking!' The scream in her voice couldn't match the scream in her head.

'Actually, it is. And I'd rather have a man, as would you. We're in the same boat, sunshine: so, you can either go down shit creek with me or you can row solo.'

She left him.

She returned to acting. Her directors were frazzled to see the number of retakes she needed to get one scene right; a producer went as far as to replace her.

After the rage in her despair calmed, she recognized how she had insulted Samar.

She showed up at his place one night, so late even the moon had sunk. 'Let's go down shit creek together,' she said as he opened the door.

'Too late: I've pulled in my canoe.'

'Don't be a spoilsport.'

'I thought of stealing flowers,' Samar said, 'but it wouldn't have been the same without you.' Acknowledging it made him

realize he had missed her with a sharp, stabbing pain. 'You ever wonder why you're so hooked on to this idiot pianist?'

'Low blood sugar? Early stage dementia? Compulsive Pianist Disorder?'

'All of those can cloud your judgement, for sure.'

When he said something to the effect that perhaps she was inherently suspicious of straight men, she sat up.

Her father had walked out on her, he reminded her.

Zaira replied that she had never taken it to heart. After a moment, she added, 'Don't ever use anything I trust you with against me.'

'In the larger scheme of things,' Samar said, 'I used it against myself.'

That summer a fan showed up on the set of Zaira's film with a litter of whippets and asked her to choose one. Picking out a fragile white puppy, she took it over to Samar's.

He was overjoyed. 'I want to call him Mr Ward-Davies.'

'Cool name.'

'Mr Ward-Davies was my favourite piano teacher in New York; a Brit who introduced me to the pleasures of drinking absinthe.'

'Glad you like the pup, Samar.'

'Are you sure you don't want him with you full-time?'

'I'll borrow him on weekends. That's if he'll have me at all. I'm hardly around, so I'd rather he shack up with you.' Neither of them knew it at the time, but Mr Ward-Davies became the

love letter she sent to him and he opened the seal and read it with all his heart for all of hers.

'He's in the running for my main man.'

The same evening, over dinner at China Garden, Samar asked Zaira if she would introduce him to men.

She tried not to look upset by his request. 'Surely you've met enough boys on your own?'

'Most of them are from the city of New Dulli!'

'Not all of them are *that* boring.'

'True, true; but the ones who're not are selfish, or they split their infinitives.'

'I hardly ever meet men in Bombay who're out of the closet.'

'The few who are out and about are so ugly they should stay in their closets. In fact,' he added wickedly, 'they should be locked from the outside.'

'What a mean thing to say!'

'I'll rot in hell for that,' he said. 'But I hear the bar up in Devilsville makes a martini to murder for. Are you going to get me a guy to groove with?'

'I'll try my best.' Her voice suggested something in her had dried up forever. 'But remember what I told you: I'm going to be the mother of your child.'

'We're on, girl!'

Zaira took his request seriously because Samar never asked her for anything. Although she met several men at work, all possible candidates—costume designers, stylists, film

directors—none of the men seemed to fit the bill for Samar. She realized she had quite a task cut out for her when one ambitious architect told her that he only dated 'straight-acting' men. When she repeated the remark to Samar, he grimaced. 'How straight-acting will he be when he's got my dick in his mouth?'

Then, just when she thought she was running on empty, she met Leo at a party in Delhi.

Dumpy Roy, a literary critic with a certain distinctive presence, like mould on bread, introduced them.

'Leo writes for the *N*________. It's a magazine in America. Surely, you've heard of it?'

'Oh, yes,' Zaira assured the literary critic. 'America is south of Calcutta, right?'

'I meant the *N*_______!' Dumpy Roy had so many opinions she no longer had any room for common sense. 'It's, well, dare I say, legendary?'

'I hear the cartoons are excellent.'

For a moment, Leo felt as if she might have been talking about more than the magazine that published his work. 'I've been wanting to interview you for a long time,' he admitted.

'Do *N*________ readers watch Bollywood films?'

'I wouldn't surrender to the stereotype.'

'You're right,' she apologized. 'I'm making no sense at all; I must be hopelessly sober. Why don't we meet up in Bombay?'

When Leo and Zaira met up in Bombay, she unravelled his life story.

Leo had been drawn to India during his university days at Berkeley, not because of some corny new-age faith but because his thesis had been on contemporary Indian films. Zaira was impressed that Leo knew all about Yash Chopra's romantic opuses, Rekha's numerous lovers, the labour union the dance extras were struggling to form. He told her serious cinema was on the descending elevator in India; he knew that Bollywood posters were an art form unto themselves. Leo's first book, *Old Gullies,* which had established his credentials as a writer, had been praised by critics for authorial acuity and a spry, unaffected facility with language.

Zaira was not sure if Samar and Leo were destined for long-term bliss but she suspected they would enjoy the cocktail hour.

'He's wonderfully erudite,' she told Samar.

'He's from America!' he retorted.

'You're so rude.'

'He probably thinks the Middle East is Vermont.'

She laughed, then reached out and punched him gently. 'Stop it! His book, *Old Gullies,* was nominated for the National Book Award. He's one of the youngest recipients of a Guggenheim scholarship. His work has been translated into twelve languages!'

Samar listened intently, vaguely impressed. 'And you're sure he's not the kind of fellow who's going to tell me he loves "Indian culture" or that he's just had his chakras tuned?'

'I don't know about Leo, but you could do with some tuning. Why don't you just meet him and make up your mind for yourself?'

To Zaira's amazement, Samar took to Leo like a duck to water. In a couple of weeks Samar dropped off Mr Ward-Davies in her care for a month because he was accompanying Leo on his trek through rural Gujarat. Zaira was glad Samar was going on holiday but she worried that his impulsive affections were, in fact, inspired by an extended season of sexual loneliness. Later, on his return, Samar furnished a full account of the adventure she concluded was a honeymoon that came before the marriage that could never be. The two men had slept on charpoys in villages with outdoor lavatories and woken with roosters crowing against the taut cheek of a crimson dawn. Savouring blood-red berries with no names and arguing about books they had read in their adolescence, they formed a kinship larger than the sum of the differences between them.

'I told Zaira I didn't want to meet an American bimbo who came here in search of mantras.'

Leo grinned. 'Aren't I lucky you thought so highly of me.'

'When did you know India was your subject?' Samar asked; they were on their way to a lion reserve.

'From my early twenties. Every writer has a sense where his big book is coming from; I've always known mine would be a gift from India.'

'Will the book be travel writing, or a novel, or essays?'

'I don't know, Samar; I just know India will give me the book that will be savoured. And remembered.'

Two days later, in the forests of Gir, they huddled in a beige canvas tent, trembling in each other's arms: a lioness had killed a calf near their campsite and was devouring it noisily with her pride only inches away from them.

They spent the last week of their travels on the terrace of a lost castle, swimming at midnight in a monsoon-green pond on the rambling estate. Samar was ecstatic. How beautiful their bodies tasted, how free was the wind against their faces, how sweet the daybreak music of a brook running wild.

'Come with me to San Francisco,' Leo said on the last day of their trip.

'I'd love to,' Samar replied.

When Samar told Zaira he was going away with Leo she heard a deafening sound in her head, as if bats, thousands of them, were thundering out of a cave into a milky violet sky before nightfall.

'I'll be gone only for two months.'

'You'll miss this city.'

'And you.'

'Why are you going?'

'Leo spends much of his year in Bombay; it's only fair I go along with him when he's on his turf.'

'Mr Ward-Davies will miss you,' she said. 'He'll die without you.'

This is San Francisco, Samar wrote to Zaira from Leo's apartment. *You can smell sex in the air: the gangbangs in warehouses in Portero Hill, the fisting seminars in the Castro, three black men in nuns' habits rollerblading on Market Street 'for love', the woman who slept with all the firemen and built them a monument, a white tower I can see from my bedroom window. Hands lunge at you at parties; sex feels like someone peeling the skin over a wound. But there are also marches in this city, demonstrations, protests, vital public introspection. At the end of the day, when love and politics collide, who is left standing?*

A few days after he wrote the letter, Samar called Zaira and told her he was restless. He wanted to come back.

'Then why don't you?' Zaira's old greed for Samar twisted brightly with hope.

'I don't want to abandon Leo.'

'Doesn't he want to come back too?'

'He needs to be here right now.'

'I feel there's something you're keeping from me.'

A long sigh unfurled. 'Perhaps Leo doesn't want me around.'

'Don't be ridiculous.'

'He's lived alone all his adult life. I'm in his space, and feel like an intrusion.'

'I'm sure he'll get over it. Teething troubles are part of every relationship, Samar.'

'How is Mr Ward-Davies?'

'He misses you so much,' she said. 'He sulks in the corner. I have to force him to eat. I'm afraid he's decided to up and quit without you.'

'Then I'd better come back and see him soon.'

Samar decided to confront Leo one night, about how he felt he had gatecrashed Leo's life.

'You're right. I feel the need to be alone,' Leo said when he saw Samar sit up in bed, sleepless, grumpy.

'Then you should have told me.'

'I wasn't conscious of my need for independence myself; I didn't have reason to be.'

Four months had passed since Samar's move to San Francisco. Limerance having worn, they were weary of each other.

'But don't you like that I'm here with you?'

'Of course I do ... But you're not your usual self'

'I guess I'm missing Mr Ward-Davies.'

'Do you want to go and see him?'

'Yes. But if I leave, it would also be because I feel like I have intruded into your life, Leo.'

'I haven't lived with anyone before you; I don't know how to roll it as it plays.'

'You think I'm having a blast playing "The Couple"?'

Outside their window, thick curtains of fog were melting under the first sallow shafts of sunlight.

'I haven't spent a whole night with anyone except the tricks I used to pull; anonymity is comforting.'

'I can't sleep with someone in my bed either.' He thought of Zaira, of how she crashed on his couch, a thoughtfulness he'd always taken for granted.

'I love you, Samar.' Leo struggled with the intricate, mercurial force of his feelings: although he enjoyed Samar's company in San Francisco he liked his lair to himself.

'Don't say it unless you mean it.'

They decided it was more sensible to split up their time between San Francisco and Bombay, an amicable middle path. Early on, Leo had cut out monogamy from their relationship on the grounds that he wasn't about to go 'all hetero' on them. Samar had retorted that he really had to give breeders the benefit of the doubt, forcing Leo to admit that he just wasn't wired for fidelity. At this point Samar had decided that sometimes you took what you could get and made the best of it; after all, a man's a man, and there were any number of old queens who had waited for the whole samosa and had ended up, instead, with a collection of butt plugs they took along to heaven.

He returned to Bombay.

A few weeks later a postcard arrived, with three words on it: *I mean it.*

'I guess there are all kinds of love stories,' Karan told Zaira now.

She smiled in the liquid darkness. 'And the most important ones are also incredibly difficult.'

'I had no idea about the nature of your feelings for Samar.'

'Neither did I! But then he's a small guy with a huge heart, and his generosity makes him my hero in a one-act nonsense play I could watch every night for the rest of my life.'

'You stepped back. You let him go with Leo.'

'He was never mine for me to let go.' She felt a chill and tightened her arms around herself. 'Souls get stuck in bodies. What the soul needs is one thing and what the body desires is quite another, and what a lot of love is lost in the space between the two.'

'Did you ever look for someone after Samar?'

She lingered on Karan's words: *after Samar*. But, she wanted to tell him, she was not ahead of him, he was not behind her, she did not believe that love affairs ended simply because lovers took on other lovers. Although conventional wisdom prompted her to 'move on', she had no say in the matter: for love rushed through her like a river, touching and transforming everything in its path but keeping its eye only on its final destination. 'Samar tried hard to hook me up with all the guys he knew,' she said after a pause. 'He was happy, he said; so now it was my turn.'

'Did you meet any interesting candidates?'

'Interesting candidates?' She rolled her eyes. 'I met half the single guys in Bombay, and they sent me straight into therapy, yaar!'

Zaira told him about Leo's friend, the music composer who on their first date savaged her with a full-on six-hour session of Punjabi hip-hop compositions. Then there was Samar's friend,

the chef who assaulted Zaira with the worst pickup line: 'Baby, let's Kama Sutra!' She came home singing, *You can't curry love, no, you just can't curry love,* and declared that Samar's selection in men would put her off sex forever.

But she could not blame Samar because she had already met every kind of man in Bombay: the Bollywood producer with a belly so big he hadn't seen his wee-wee in years, who dropped his pants before every bucolic bimbette with romance-novel boobs; the hunk on the cover of *Stardust* who owned a museum-sized collection of tit clamps; the fan who inscribed her name in his blood and sent her such letters with abiding regularity. She had met men who liked to wear elegant silk saris and be called Miss Maharani and others who howled at the moon because they had been dispossessed by the women they never imagined could abandon them. Men with fake accents and big mouths; men with a strut in their walk and a shake in their voice; men with far too much moolah and men without a chavanni to their name (these men wrote poems, were often drunk, and died before turning forty, unmourned, anonymous). Men, short and thick, who reminded her of whale blubber; men so thin you could use them as bookmarks; men with eyes that seldom blinked, like geckoes in business suits. Artists, bankers, directors, spot boys, journalists, animal trainers, plumbers, intellectuals—men of every colour, stripe and odour had passed her gaze, and she had learnt to acknowledge them with both respect and aloofness, to accept their flaws and fete their transitory virtues.

And tonight Zaira lay beside Karan Seth, whose bumbling, sweet air she cherished more than his strange, lamenting photographs of Bombay.

'Did you ever see Sahil again?'

'He came to see me on a film set once,' she said, sounding bored. 'He had a wife and two kids. They looked like the people you see in mutual fund advertisements.'

'You must be glad you got away.'

'Sometimes I am.'

Clamour from the party below distracted Karan. He got up to see why people were cheering loudly and his eyes zoned in on the pool. 'Samar's cummerbund,' he remarked, 'makes for a curious bathing suit accessory.'

'I'll take your word for it.'

Below, in the evaporating crowd, a champagne flute fell to the floor. She imagined the pieces, jagged yet elegant; she knew the flute was useless now, but in her mind the shards held a peculiar, terrified beauty, scattered in the darkness, reflecting moonlight and the textured silk of dry, uneven laughter.

7

'THERE ARE SOME CHURCHES IN THE BANDRA villages I want you to see.'

'I'm not religious,' Karan said, casting admiring glances at Rhea's flowing grey dress, which accented her body's angular, stark lines.

She changed the gear, slowing down as they approached a traffic light. 'Then it's time you were converted.'

He felt she was talking about more than their visit to Bandra.

At Carter Road, she stopped outside a chapel and pointed at the ancient fretwork balconies. However, the chapel did not interest Karan. He turned around and crossed the road; he had spotted a derelict mansion with an out-of-use fire exit of arabesque beauty, a metal helix that seemed to end in the

air, abruptly. She heard the quick, excited clicks of the shutter release. When he was done, Karan turned to Rhea. 'I'm not particularly taken by beauty.'

'Then what are you after?'

'Truth.'

Gazing at the conviction in his eyes she found herself transported back to her past, to an industrious afternoon in the studio at college, where she was working on the wheel, throwing, glazing. The extravagant words of her tutor's praise reverberated in her head like the concentric swathe of music from a gong that has just been struck; she remembered the leathery-skinned Parsi gallerist who had approached her to exhibit her graduation project, 'Sight, Unseen'. Most of all, she remembered herself possessed with steely focus, with secret curiosity for the impressions of her art.

Having forsaken that determined young woman on the day she married, Rhea was now heartened to meet the echo of those qualities in Karan; secretly she wished the ingenious mayhem of art's single-minded pursuit of itself would never leave him, as it had her. Emerging from the haze of recollection, she said, 'But beauty is truth.'

'I try to see things for what they are.' He sounded defiant.

'That's impossible; nothing is what it seems.'

'Well, what about this fire exit? What else could it be but a captive to its ruin?'

'In its early years beautiful people would have thundered down its curves. Lovers would have waited below it, drenched

in rain or moonlight. Drunks could have slipped and fallen down the steps to their death.'

'But right now it is what it is,' he argued. 'And that's what I'm keen to capture in my pictures.'

She didn't know which was larger, his talent or his earnestness; the former she found admirable, the latter forgivable. 'It would be quite cricket to die in Bandra, amid the wreckage and splendour.'

'All of Bandra has an air of impermanence; I've come here before, dozens of times, but you've shown me Bandra in another light, Rhea.'

'You came alone?'

'Most of the time. But twice Zaira brought me here, late at night.'

'You have quite a soft spot for her.'

He hunted for jealousy in Rhea's voice, but worryingly found none. 'She's been a great friend.'

'She seems to trust you immensely.'

'The first time we met, she was in crisis mode. A stalker had rammed her trailer to pieces. She had come up to see Samar in a panic. Unfortunately, I was there to do a shoot with him and she was paranoid I was going to photograph her during a meltdown. No such thing happened; the media never learned of her breakdown in Samar's arms. She was grateful for my discretion.'

'But you would have been like that with anyone,' Rhea said.

'Exactly. But I was also drawn to her. Once I was caught in a mad crowd at the premiere of her film and she sent her publicist in her car to ensure I was treated by a doctor. And she's had genuine regard for my work on Bombay; if you recall, I went to Chor Bazaar because she insisted on it. Once or twice she even drove me around Bombay to suggest the places she thought would work for the project.'

'So I have a predecessor?' Now she sounded jealous.

'Yes. But she had to drive me after midnight, for reasons of anonymity. There was little I could photograph in the dark. And when I returned to the same places at daytime, I did not find them half as inspiring. Besides,' he said loyally, 'your aesthetic and hers are entirely different.'

'Shall we go and light a few candles at the shrine of Mount Mary?'

'Why not? We're in the neighbourhood, in any event.'

'I used to come to Mount Mary very often when I was in my twenties. Oh, how much I've prayed here!' She halted, her hand cupping her mouth, regret lodged in her eyes like shrapnel.

'What did you pray for, Rhea?'

She walked ahead without replying and bought a dozen candles from a bright-eyed, legless, adolescent vendor in a Coca-Cola emblazoned tee-shirt. As they ascended the steps leading to the shrine, she enquired, 'So did Samar ever come with you on the nights Zaira and you drove around Bombay?'

'No; I'm not all that chummy with him. Zaira had suggested that he come along but I wanted to do the trip only with her.'

Lighting a clutch of thin white tapers, she placed them to bum before the idol of Mother Mary. 'It's strange that you would not ask Samar to join you even though you know Zaira because of him.' She wiped her hands clean and gestured to him to light the candles she had handed to him.

'I guess ... I guess Samar and I have no common interests.'

Witch-fingers of candles burned bravely against the rapid wind, melting into sooty, gnarled heaps on a metal tray.

She said, 'Samar has a boyfriend ...'

The candles lurched out of Karan's hands and he sat on his haunches to gather them.

'Yes, I know. I have met him.'

'Does that bother you?'

'No ... no ... not at all. To each his own.'

'Are you cool with Leo?'

'Well ...' He grew red-faced. 'What are you insinuating?'

'Well, to be blunt, I think you're not comfortable with Samar because he has a boyfriend.'

'That's ridiculous!' he said, more loudly than he had intended. 'Samar is not someone I think about very much.'

'Although you don't mind going to his house for dinners?'

'That's only when Zaira invites me there; I don't hang out with him one on one.'

She looked at him, disbelieving.

He tried to explain his unease around Samar. 'He's too loud, Rhea. He's always seeking attention. When he's not tap

dancing on a bar he's standing in the pool in a tux. He's always being funny and clever; he's trying too hard.'

'Too hard to win some gold stars from you?' she asked sarcastically. 'Wow; someone should send Samar a news flash that he just doesn't make your grade.'

'Are you taking me on about something?'

'What I pity is that I've got to take you on about *this.* You probably think he squats to take a leak.'

'I didn't think you could be so coarse.' He was breathing through his mouth; rage was filling his head but he didn't want it to show on his face. 'Anyway, where shall we go next? Another village in Bandra?'

'As far as I'm concerned we've covered too much ground for one day.' It was as if she had slammed a door on his face.

'Are you pissed off with me, Rhea?'

'I'm not anything with you.'

'I don't hate Samar or anything like that.'

'And certainly not because he's got a boyfriend.'

'Are you getting a kick out of this?'

'Out of what?'

'Making me feel small about myself?'

'Am I making you feel small about yourself or are you too lazy to confront your own prejudice?'

'Whatever.'

He tried to keep calm by telling himself she had got up at dawn and taken him to Sewri; she had sat him down and talked

to him about the ways to use colour; she had introduced him to the best photo lab in Bombay.

Rhea believed that Karan's explanation for resisting Samar because he was 'too loud' was cheesy; she would much rather he own up to his prejudice than flit around it. 'Grow up,' she said. 'And make it quick: from the sound of it, you've got a lot of catching up to do.'

'Oh, please, Rhea, give it a rest,' he barked. 'You shouldn't be giving me a hard time over some flashy fag.'

'You shouldn't try so hard to prove my point.' She started to walk toward her car. 'And I will take your advice: I'll give it a rest.'

With astonishing alacrity, Karan found himself consigned to the last drawer of Rhea's memory. On several occasions, he picked up the phone to call her, but pride came in the way. Three weeks of intolerable isolation ensued. Karan resumed his work on the photographs but when he printed the shots he found the decisive link between his taking pictures and understanding them now missing; Rhea's language had come to illuminate his pictures, restrained excess and egged him forward. He felt restless and angry, like a caged animal, captive to a personal isolation even as the city continued to breathe its toxic, black fumes down his neck. Finally, desperate for chit-chat, Karan called Zaira a little after midnight.

'Am I interrupting?'

'Not at all.' Zaira was delighted to hear from Karan. 'You are only interjecting in the conversation I was having with

myself. The terrible thing about talking to yourself is not having a third person for a second opinion.'

'So we can call you schizo?' He knew he could trust Zaira to cheer him up.

'Schizophrenic? I've been in two minds about that forever.'

He laughed. Then he whispered, 'Are you alone? Can you talk?' He wanted to tell Zaira about his row with Rhea.

Zaira said Samar was meant to come for dinner but had cancelled at the last minute as Leo had plans for them to be elsewhere. 'So, sure, I can talk. Why are you up so late?'

'To keep tabs on your debauched existence.'

'I wish!' She lay down on her bed. 'You give me way too much credit.'

'Are you put off that Samar bailed on dinner at the last minute?'

'Not at all.' Her voice aimed for nonchalance but got only as far as the glums. 'I wish I'd been told in time; at least then I wouldn't have cooked a seven-course meal.'

'You cooked seven courses!'

'See what I mean? You give me *way* too much credit.' She giggled. 'Actually, it's biryani I bought and a salad I threw together but maybe that explains why Samar's been a no-show.'

'Have you eaten?'

'I was waiting for you to drop in for some nosh.'

On his way to Zaira's house, Karan found himself growing more resentful of Samar. Zaira, he thought, had moulded her life around Samar's so they could talk till dawn, steal flowers at

midnight, lunch late in the afternoon and, every now and again, come home to the profound silence of the other. However, when Samar had found love—a love sponsored by conventions of desire—he had coolly turned his back on her. Maybe Samar was not entirely to blame: for Leo, threatened by Zaira's intimacy with Samar, had kept them apart. As soon as Zaira had spotted the flicker of Leo's insecurity she had backed off. But wasn't greater allegiance expected from Samar?

Karan thought of the night Zaira had led him by the hand to the roof of Samar's house, where they had talked and talked while the pianist got drunk with his dandy buddies and then walked into the pool, standing in water all the way up to his cummerbund. He recalled her face, its banished, immaculate loveliness. In the room Zaira now occupied in his head, perhaps permanently, he worried over the embarrassed, stilted loneliness in Zaira's voice as she had disclosed to him earlier that day that she was alone at home on a Friday night. Although Zaira had the choice of allowing the city's vibrant nightlife to consume her—she had only to swirl the dial on her phone and men would materialize out of thin air, powerless slaves to her ravishing charm—she adhered to a code of dignified privacy, the kind only the very famous can truly guard. Samar should have known that, he thought; he should not have been irresponsible and let her be alone.

As his taxi went by Juhu Chowpatty, driving past a bright orgy of billboards that hacked up the tender night with neon blinkering, a part of him wished Zaira would find the loyalty of

a man who would respond to her ably, with shy intelligence and an appreciation of her solemn moods. He found it ridiculous that she was still single; she had looks, money, independence, fame, character, yet she was stuck in the dusty alcove of an almost-romance, unable to wrestle free of her past and lunge headlong into life's grand panic of possibilities.

But then love's clichéd preconditions were hardly a guarantee for its attainment.

The complications of relationships, lately exfoliated in his eyes in the light of his recent row with Rhea, made him wonder if it were better to be alone than to be wishing for aloneness. He wondered if he too would be better off without Rhea, and if a reunion was really worth the bother.

But, could he write her off so easily? Longing for Rhea came in spasms, with an almost physical acuity, and he took deep breaths to wait out the pain. He thought of the time they had stood under the flamingoes at Sewri; for days after, the advent of love had heightened the colours around him, made any music he heard more distinguished, deepened the experience of existence. Every now and again, through the window of the taxi, he looked out at the city, which seemed to be chuckling at him. The taxi's headlights finally lit up the road to Janaki Kutir, a private estate famous for housing the Prithvi Theatre, where deadbeat communists, lovelorn playwrights, aspiring actors congregated under the bamboo shade of Prithvi Café.

'End of the lane,' Karan told the taxi driver.

He emerged, and the watchman on duty at Zaira's apartment complex eyed Karan suspiciously, then buzzed the intercom to ask Zaira if she was expecting any visitors. When she said she was, the man looked crestfallen, unable to entertain the possibility of her having an affair with a complete nobody.

'You made it in one piece!' She embraced him.

'Got a taxi. Roads were empty.' He pulled away and handed her a big, bold bunch of traffic-signal roses—long-stemmed, thorny, fifty rupees to the dozen.

'You and your courtly ways! I bet that's how you won over Mrs Dalal, rascal!'

'I have an update on the Dalal Chronicles.'

'I can't wait! Wine?'

She touched his wrist lightly.

He smiled. The relief they experienced in each other's company was so pure it could manifest only as silence: food would follow, as would wine and talk, but in this moment some deep, inexpressible need had already been met.

'The salad is super,' he exulted at the dining table. 'You're a great cook, Zaira.'

'You have a thing for home-cooked meals.'

'That I do.' Miss Mango, his landlady at Ban Ganga, did not allow him to cook at home and his hankering had intensified since moving there. 'I can never forget my mother's cooking.'

'Why don't you go back and see your dad?'

'There's nothing there, Zaira, between him and me.' He paused. 'Actually, what *is* there keeps me here.'

'You've never told me about your childhood.'

'I've told no one. It was not a happy time.'

'Childhoods are messy affairs; I don't know why people talk of them as wonderful and innocent. Mine was corrupt and painful, and each day of my adulthood has been an effort to recover from its disappointment.'

After a long silence, in the course of which they ate biryani and drank wine, Karan said, 'My father was a colonel. When he walked into a landmine, his left leg had to be replaced with a Jaipur foot.'

'Oh God, Karan,' Zaira cried. 'I'm so sorry.'

'That's only the start.' Wine had loosened his tongue; he decided to tell Zaira everything.

To escape the ignominy of his war injury, Colonel Seth moved his family to Shimla, wishing for a quiet, forgettable life in a small town; instead, the embittered man unwittingly steered his wife toward sexual boredom and himself in the direction of whisky. So Karan grew up under the ugly attention of a full-blown alcoholic father and a mother who flirted greedily with the adolescent grocer.

'When I was sixteen I understood why my father yelled at my mother all the time.'

During an ugly confrontation one evening it was revealed that Karan's mother had fallen into the habit of watching him bathe through the keyhole of the bathroom door, kneeling on the floor, her hand on the jamb. Karan thought his father was a vile drunk to accuse her of such things but he was scandalized to

discover that the allegation met no refutation from his mother. 'I decided to leave Shimla; I'd never go back home. My own mother …' Tears slipped down his face and rested at the edge of his jaw.

Zaira's heart spun with pain. 'Karan …' She went to his side, put her arm around him. 'What an awful thing to live through …'

He wiped his face. 'The funny thing is, I don't blame my mother; she was bored, dissatisfied, tortured. She did what she had to although she had no right to do it.'

'You don't blame her for what she did?'

'Not any more; I try and understand her more. I left Shimla shortly after my eighteenth birthday. I decided to train as a teacher; instead, I got waylaid. I got drawn to photography. I always tell people I like photography because it's about ways of looking, but deep down, Zaira, it's about my perception of the relationship between self and surface. When I look out, I look in. But I never *ever* look back.'

Looking at his face, streaked with tears, a summary of private violations, she was overcome. How bravely he had fled home, how defiantly he refused to return, how fiercely he had given himself to his craft. It struck Zaira that Karan's fascination with Bombay and his desire to document its details was not merely an aesthetic decision but also an emotional obligation: Bombay had filled the bullet wound made in Shimla.

'I cannot forgive what my mother did,' he went on, armoured by her attention, 'but I can try and forget it.' Then

he laughed. 'Who the fuck am I kidding? I guess what keeps me going is what she wrote to me in a letter only a few weeks before she died. I was in my last year of college; she was bed-bound after a stroke.'

'What did she write, Karan?'

'People love people in such strange ways that you will need more than one lifetime to figure that one out.'

'Amen.' Zaira's mind reached to comprehend the ugly, unbearable loneliness and sexual discontent that had forced Karan's mother to commit such a heinous infringement. She felt Karan's mother had been a weak person, but honest to her weakness; this did not make her actions forgivable, but perhaps in her last days the consequence of her contravention—Karan's defection—had been transformative for her.

'The closer I get to Rhea the more I discover the truth of my mother's words.' Karan's voice was calmer; he seemed to have moved on from the heart-halting recollection of his desecrated childhood.

'I'm not sure I follow you.'

'I think it means I have to learn why Rhea is drawn to me although she is so obviously and madly in love with her husband. Although,' he added, tilting his head, 'I'm not so sure about her feelings for me any longer.'

Zaira suspected a romantic fracas. Karan's face had fallen; there were dark circles under his eyes. He was a textbook image of romantic disrepair. 'Has she chucked you?'

'I came here to tell you about our fight and that it's gutted me but I ended up telling you about Shimla ...' He shook his head. 'I'm a fool, Zaira.'

She returned to her chair and resumed eating. 'Why did you fall out with Rhea?' Her brow crinkled with curiosity.

'She got mad at me and quit on me.' He shook his head. 'Been a few weeks now.'

'Why on earth, Karan? She was hung up on you so bad, and the last time I checked you were doing pretty neat.' Zaira was glad that he was talking about Rhea; the confession about his childhood had shaken her, although her training as an actor easily allowed her to conceal the depth of her shock.

Karan's face was overcast. 'Can't you see how cut up I am now?'

'You're bleeding,' she said, immediately acting on his plea for sympathy. 'Broken bones and all. I should call paramedics, but before I do, tell me: why would she leave a lovely lad like you out in the rain?'

'Argument, et al. She was trying to be helpful; I was being pig-headed.'

He was not going to make the mistake of telling Zaira that Rhea suspected he was not cool with Samar's private life. Rhea might still get around to forgiving him, but Zaira, a Samar loyalist, would grill him on a skewer.

'She has no dil in her, Karan.' Zaira left the dinner table and Karan followed her to the living room.

A line drawing of a nude man dominated the square, cosy room: the man had thin, ungainly legs and an attractive torso; his hair came down to his neckline, and he was looking into the distance. On a couch was a fuchsia paper bag with the label, Good Earth. There was a mess of CDs on a small table between the couch and two batwing chairs.

'Well, maybe she had a good reason to vanish,' he said in Rhea's defence. 'I was too hung up on my point of view.'

'You're not sharing the small print here.'

'It's petty stuff,' he said evasively.

'It generally is; but small things add up to a ghotala so big you wouldn't believe.' Opening the window, she stood with her hands on the balcony railing, her face against the currents of a warm, sweet breeze unleashed from the seashore. She knew Karan wasn't going to give her the details of the fight and she resisted intruding further. 'Have you tried to meet up with her since then?'

'Her husband might be in town. I don't want to show up on her doorstep when he's around. If she wants to be alone,' he reasoned, 'why crowd her?'

'Are you sure your pride is not coming in the way?'

'Well, she's never said as much but I get her need for solitude. She's a bit of a solo show.'

The blurry details Karan furnished slowly coalesced into a clear picture in Zaira's head. Rhea had recognized Karan's electric talent, and she had taken him under her wing. She had driven him around the city, given his mind her alert, vigorous

and sophisticated companionship. But when Karan had grown needy—maybe even possessive—it was enough to make the feline Mrs Dalal up and go.

'You're having an affair, aren't you?'

'An affair?' He gulped uneasily.

'Yes, she's cheating on her husband with you.'

Zaira's words alarmed him. 'I don't have a name for our set-up,' he said stiffly.

'I can buy that.' Zaira was only too well versed with love that lay beyond language. 'Maybe the two of you are, as the trade press likes to say, "just good friends"?' she teased.

He shot her an exasperated look.

'Give her some time,' Zaira said. 'She's overwhelmed, but she'll come around.'

'I guess.'

She touched Karan's cheek and, in his watchful, tender eyes, glimpsed his engagement with first love, its insurgency and disrepair. Having known this love, its permanent wound, she was glad for Karan. 'What do the boys of Bandra call it? *Loveria.* Fever of the heart. Do what it takes to get you through it. Eat a peach. Go for a walk. Drink gin. Wish on falling stars. And then there's steam inhalation.' Momentarily, loneliness flared out of her, almost scalding him. 'That always works. Steam.'

Although she swiftly returned to the succour of her low-lit studio, Rhea remembered Karan with reproachful regularity, like a newly abandoned bad habit.

Before long, loneliness set in once again like a nagging toothache. Adi was away in Singapore. There were no friends to call. She missed her father. She put in an extra shift at the animal shelter, returning home after long, tiring days, counting on exhaustion to bring sleep. But that was not to be and, lying in bed, her mind relentlessly sought Karan.

She missed how he had reacquainted her with the city that had grown her up, mercurial and revolutionary, congested and irate, a city she had forgotten she had loved too greedily for too long already. If she had been looking for neither friendship nor romance, what had she hoped to derive from her association with Karan? And what question in her heart had he answered that she was still remembering him? She was furious with herself for succumbing to the gleaming coin of Karan's genius, his subtle, unhurried, engaging charm. Although she had resolved never to meet him again she no longer knew how she would cope with the inertia of her marriage.

A month after she had left Karan on the streets of Bandra and driven away, he reappeared at her doorstep. Longing had left him suddenly gorgeous.

'Is Adi in town?' he asked cautiously when she opened the door to her apartment.

'Singapore.'

'Are you busy?'

'Only occupied.'

'May I come in for a bit?'

She led him up to the studio where, minutes later, her arms thrown out in ecstasy wrecked an exquisite but flawed vase.

Karan cradled her in his arms as she wept. 'Why are you so sad, Rhea?'

'It's broken.' She pointed to the pieces of pottery. 'It was perfect.'

'I thought you were crying ... because you're cheating ...'

'Don't be so pedestrian!'

'You love Adi.'

She closed her eyes, turning away.

'Then why do you want to see me?'

'Consolation in contradiction?'

'Not to forget convenience.'

She slapped him. 'I just want love to leave me alone for a while.'

He said nothing; the ardour of her wrath excited him terribly.

Their field trips recommenced.

The road leading to Kanheri Caves was narrow, potholed. From either side of the road, green bamboos shot into the sky, forming an overhead trellis that banished almost all light, leaving them in leaf shadow. Karan found the air pungent; he heard crickets chirping in verdant places of renewal as a puzzle of shadows changed shape with the passing sun.

Rhea brought the car to a halt near a signboard warning visitors of leopards in the vicinity.

When, after an hour of meandering through second-century monastic chambers, Karan blurted impatiently, 'I'm not into this historical shit,' Rhea disappeared into the spectral gloom, craving Adi, his old-world poise, his ability to indulge her without making her feel indulged.

'Let's go and sit by the waterfall, Rhea.'

'If you don't want to take any photographs then we should leave.'

'This is a wonderful place; thank you for coming up here with me.'

'But if it's of no use to you ...'

'Everything does not have to have use, or a function, Rhea.'

She looked at him, astounded.

'Who brought *you* here?' he asked, his tone softer now.

The expression in her eyes mellowed. 'Adi. Our last year in college. He'd once stolen fireflies from the forest bordering the caves as a gift for me.'

'I remember. You told me about it one afternoon in your studio.'

She studied Karan's face; its tightness reminded her of a bowstring on which an archer has balanced a poisoned arrow.

'Would you ever tell Adi you came here with me?'

'No.'

'You should.'

'I don't tell Adi everything about my life,' she said. 'Just the interesting bits.'

'Would that include your gift of being able to fuck two men at the same time?'

'In case you haven't noticed, I've never fucked two men at the same time. But now that you've planted the idea in my head.'

Several minutes of silence passed.

A copper-winged cuckoo called out from the verdure. Screeching wildly, two monkeys flung themselves on to a branch high above them, unleashing little leaves like rain.

Her words had hurt him, she knew, and she drew him into her arms.

He shrugged off her embrace; it felt like ugly charity.

They were quiet for a while, their eyes drifting over the topography before them. Here, the wild forest had met the remnants of civilization in the caves, and they felt suspended in the collision between the two. The timeless splendour surrounding them resounded with wisdom and betrayal, and they were compelled to speak in whispers, for the landscape discouraged sound, supplying a stillness that held them both like a flag in a fist.

'My marriage is not perfect.' She dusted leaves off her hair. 'It's not what you think.'

Right after their marriage, Adi had eagerly suggested the idea of raising a family. 'I agreed. I didn't care about children one way or the other. If it made Adi happy, I was ready.' But when she didn't conceive after three years of trying, they started to frequent doctors who gradually made their lives hell with

innumerable tests, awkward questions and enterprising but impossible advice.

Finally, peacefully, she resigned herself to the bleak, cruel possibility of infertility.

'And Adi?' Karan asked. 'How did he take it?'

Her forehead crinkled. 'There must be something he's trying to forget in his bourbon. There must be some noise in his head he cannot bear to hear ... so he listens to jazz.'

'Has he been depressed for long?'

'Several years now; he's not the man I married. It's easy to feel loved by him, but also terribly lonely.' Adi's sadness was his mistress; a secret shrew she could neither confront head-on nor overcome in private. 'I would do anything to make him whole again.' Her eyes glinted. 'Anything at all.'

'Did you consider adoption?' Karan asked. He now knew what Rhea had prayed for at the shrine of Mount Mary.

'We went to several agencies,' she replied. But she had sensed Adi's reservations: he wanted children of his own. 'I refused to bring home a child only to have her feel like a second-class citizen.'

'But there's still hope?'

'I could conceive any time ...' She struck her tongue against the roof of her mouth. 'It's a matter of luck and chance, and I can't seem to wrap my head around that.'

'The last few years have been rough for you ...'

'And for Adi.'

'He must be resigned to it by now.'

'I wish ... at one time there was nothing more important for him than his own flesh and blood. It's left him so ...' she struggled for the right word, '... aloof.' She could picture him on his chocolate-coloured recliner, immured in the blues, sipping bourbon, a soft, slow melancholy waltzing between them, in the ballroom of their marriage. 'Actually, he's been very depressed. He's been treated for it. But it's not as simple as a chemical imbalance.'

'What is it then?'

'An old-fashioned melancholy. It's strange; he's such a pukka corporate guy that you'd never associate such complexity of emotion with him. But he's also got a wonderful, large heart, and it's only natural he should want to fill some of it with children.'

'And you would have his children even though you're not actively interested in them?'

'If it would make him happy, yes.'

Karan was silent. It occurred to him that she had committed some extraordinary sacrifices for Adi. She had given up her career as a potter because she didn't want to compromise on the quality of her marriage; she had tried hard to have children, although she knew that if she ever had them they would only disrupt her solitude. He thought of the first time he had gone to her house; foolishly, he had been impressed with the exquisite interiors when, in fact, the house merely curated the unholy quietness held hostage in Adi's heart. He thought of her baking a cake for Adi, and he remembered thinking that she

could just as easily have bought it; now he saw it was the depth of her love that had encouraged the selflessness with which she whisked eggs and dusted cocoa on her kitchen counter.

After a moment, he reconsidered the word he associated with her: sacrifice. Perhaps they had not been sacrifices, he thought, but choices she had exercised to live her life with the man she had fallen in love with as a young woman. The choices had driven her from the safety of her Breach Candy apartment to Chor Bazaar and into the web of their initial conversation; the choice had led her to this moment. He wondered where choice and chance intersected, and how much either he or she was responsible for anything they had done so far, and would embark on in the future.

His heart shuddered. 'I'm sorry ... for the both of you.'

If she had concealed the discontented details of her marriage—the infertility, Adi's depression, her truncated career—it was not to appear mysterious but because she despised being pitied. 'How can you say you're sorry for us?' she asked.

He didn't know what to say, or if he should say anything at all; she looked like a sky readying for a storm.

When he opened his mouth to speak she had already left his side.

He followed.

She ran through the maze of caves, darting around pillars, hiding behind a lingam.

He caught up, reached for her.

She buried her head in his chest.

Her eyes were not moist as her lips reached for his mouth; she saw then, in his eyes, the hint of a wolf, the man he would become one day.

Grabbing her by her hair, he buried his lips in the hollow at the base of her throat.

The nail of her thumb, painted the red of ox blood, tore a line along his neck.

8

ZAIRA POTTERED ABOUT IN HER KITCHEN, A PART of her conscious that Samar was by her side. They darted round each other as they got dinner ready, with the charmed, chaotic, intercepting motions of two people who had known each other for far too long.

'Thanks for getting the biryani,' she said.

'I bet you single-handedly keep Mahesh Lunch Home in business.'

'Arre, yaar, their biryani is a killer!'

'How was work today?'

'I had an interview with *Cine Blitz.*'

'Didn't you stop giving interviews?'

'They're giving me a cover, and my producer asked me to work the machine for this new film,' she said, rolling her eyes.

'Anyway, this young journalist walks into my trailer and asks me what I do in my spare time. I told her I watch films and read books. She looked at me in horror and asked, "You read?" and I was, like, "Yeah, it's not tough," and she continued to look amazed, and repeated, "You actually read," at which point something in me snapped and I said, "Well, only when I'm not masturbating fervently, you know, so I don't get a lot of reading done but you've got to keep at it ..."'

Samar laughed.

Zaira mentioned the new film she was working in, and how much she was learning from her co-star, Shabana, a childhood idol, but went on to confess abruptly that she was bored of Bollywood and was considering an extended hiatus.

'You sound harried.'

'The director's a harami,' she complained as she laid the table, 'but I can work around that.' It was the politics of her milieu she deplored, the hankering for fame, the unremitting bitchiness, the shabby, sexual treatment of women. 'It's getting to be very toxic.'

Over dinner, in the dim cast of tea lights, she spoke some more about her new film. 'I'm enjoying the role ... but one of my co-stars is a real pain in the butt.'

'Who's this unfortunate person?' Samar asked with concern.

'Bunty Oberoi.' She uttered the name with disgust.

'Why haven't I heard of him?'

'No one has. He's this two-rupee model out of Bangalore. Thinks he's a stud on the ranch but if there was ever a bigger slice of cheese in pants, then Allah help me.'

Bunty Oberoi, the supporting male lead in Zaira's film, scouted publicity at the drop of a hat: he was not a media whore as much as a one-man photo-op brothel.

'What's Bunty done to steam you up? Bollywood is all about the hustle to start with, Zaira, and you've been around the block a time or two; so why're you knocked for a whammy?'

'Maybe that's why I need a break from Tinseltown.'

'Time out?'

'More like a long leave of absence.'

'All because of Bunty?'

She opened her mouth to say something, but what she wished to say was too large and messy for words. Fame, which she had come to loathe, had broken her, cut her up, turned her into a series of cosy little codes; she was now the idea of herself. Actually, she was the idea of Zaira, whatever that had come to stand for. She did not believe fame had made her familiar; if anything, it had left her alarmingly anonymous, generic even, and she suffered ubiquity by default rather than by design. 'I want to travel for a bit.' Even to her own ears her comment sounded annoyingly lame.

'Are you sure your exit plans don't have anything to do with Malik Prasad?'

'Oh, I *wish* I could blame this phase of mine on that psycho!'

'But?'

'But Malik's been out of my screen for so long I'm almost certain he's over me.'

'You're kidding!'

'I haven't heard a squeak from that lafanga in weeks. Thanks to his dad!'

Minister Prasad had apparently ordered his son to keep out of trouble: with election season round the corner the last thing the minister needed was a ready scandal for a round of mud-slinging in Parliament.

'I'd watch out if I were you.'

'Yeah,' she said distractedly. 'I've watched out for myself long enough. Gets to you after a while, yaar.'

After dinner, they sat in the travertine balcony watching the sea being glazed by the rippled, pearly hue of moonlight, the beach almost abandoned.

She told Samar that as part of the promotion campaign for her new film she had been roped in to make an appearance at the Maya Bar, a spanking new haunt in Juhu.

'What're you going to do at Maya Bar?'

She tried to avoid answering his question. Then, hesitantly, she said, 'Don't laugh. I'm playing a celebrity shaker. I know it's ridiculous, but I can't get out of it now.'

Samar looked flabbergasted. 'Why did you agree in the first place?'

'I didn't want to let the production team down.' Besides, if she resisted, she would be written off as a stuck-up bitch. So the middle ground was to make an appearance, mix a few martinis,

hang around until the paparazzi got their shots and check out as soon as she could. 'Even so, I'll be stuck manning the bar with *Cunty* Oberoi.'

'Oh, you poor thing!'

'And he loves to ham it up in front of flashbulbs. I'm counting on you to rescue me, Samar.'

'I'm sure you'll be anything but bored at Maya; Leo said it's dandy.'

'Well, tomorrow night is the closing of the Bombay Fashion Week: so I'm expecting it to be Moron Central.'

The crowds at Maya Bar would be friends of the owners, fashion designer Tara Chopra and her mother, Nalini, a society bee. In addition to Tara's designer chums, Bunty Oberoi would invite his fellow ramp rats.

'That *certainly* doesn't sound like a fun night out.'

'Do you blame me for wanting to take a break from Bollywood?'

'Why don't you bail out of this stupid celebrity bartender shtick.'

'Well, it's too late now.'

'Just cancel.'

'I hate bailing on my commitments to my producers.'

'You don't need to feel responsible about such stupid things.'

'You're being dismissive about my work, I'll have you know.'

'So you can diss Bollywood and want to quit it, but I can't call a spade a spade?'

She was silent, sulking, and he decided to back off. 'Have you asked Karan to come too?'

'Yes, and thank God he's agreed.'

'Well, I'm surprised; I've hardly seen him since he took up with this Rhea chick.'

Zaira looked as if she had just chewed something bitter. 'That woman gives me the creeps.'

'My guess is she likes to play rough and tumble.'

'Well, she certainly sets the rules, and they seem to be going through more rough than tumble. Karan doubts she'll ever leave her husband; apparently, she's be*sott*ed with the hubby.'

'Perhaps she really is.'

'Then why fool around with our Boy in Ban Ganga?' She felt her mood lift; the huff passed.

'It could be that the steam in her marriage ran out?'

'And, I suppose, no one should underestimate the charms of an older woman. But I have to give credit where it's due: Rhea's had quite an impact on Karan's work.' Having recently viewed Karan's photographs, thuggish, mesmeric, galvanic, she was all the more convinced that Karan was going to be a star in the world of modem Indian photography. 'But no matter what she does for his art, I don't want to see him on the sidewalk, bleeding and broken.'

'Why're you so downbeat about their affair?'

'Do you *really* think Rhea is going to leave her swanky pad and her hedge-fund hubby for a struggling shutterbug?'

'I don't really get what makes them click.'

'Maybe it's a mind thing,' she said. 'Particularly since Karan tells me she's no cover girl.'

'But we both know Plain Janes work so much harder!'

They hooted aloud. Then she covered her mouth with her hand and sobered up. 'We're awful! Why are we giving the poor woman such a hard time?'

'Particularly since we haven't even met her!'

'But if I don't gossip, my blood sugar dips, yaar.'

'Likewise,' Samar said, standing up to leave. 'Thanks for dinner, hon. I had the time of my life.'

'Maya Bar, tomorrow.'

Gripping her palms in his, he said, 'I hope Karan comes through without a scratch.'

'I hope so too, Samar. No one knows what to do with this idiot heart.' She reached forward and gave him a fierce hug, then pulled back, turned him around and gently patted his back, a gesture to urge him forward.

On the ride back to Worli, Samar was almost giddy with good cheer.

No great nugget of wisdom had been uncovered, no insuperable angst resolved; they had only whispered wisecracks and gossiped mercilessly. He was seeing her after weeks and to be reunited was the acknowledgement of an affinity that was larger and far more satisfying than romantic alliance. He thought it an awful thing that friendships did not encourage fervent, undying, outrageous declarations of love. As far as he was concerned, he wanted to thrust his head out of the taxi window and let all of Bombay know he had had dinner with

his best friend. He would shout that he adored Zaira's elegance and wit, and that she was his.

However, by the time he had reached home his elation melted into a pool of sorrow. As he entered his bedroom he felt that he need not have come home, that he could just as easily have spent the night at Zaira's. A love unassaulted by desire was not a lesser love; a love strong enough to arc over petty concerns of the body—well, that was something. What filled his heart with sadness was not that he had been denied the chance of a life with Zaira but that he had decided to be sincere to his desire and chosen to honour its circumference. And because Zaira lay outside this circumference, she had eventually found her place in the centre of his life. He was glad for this, but there was something inherently unfair in his being unable to turn off one switch and turn on another. To love one. And desire another. Treading quietly so as not to wake Leo, he stood a while at their bedside, studying the shape of his lover in repose, the creases Leo's body formed under their blanket. The bed is an island, he thought; briefly, the sadness of being marooned left him when he heard the sea outside, pushing wave to shore.

When Zaira woke at three in the morning, it was with a smile on her lips and an ache in her heart. She sipped at a glass of red wine before setting off for a walk on the beach on impulse. A casual breeze, warm and lazy, moved through the coconut palms, rustling the long green fronds. She heard the odd cricket chirping in the background.

She felt heady, light, at peace at this sprawling, sacred hour.

At 4.30 a.m., under a sky unclipped by dawn, she passed a madwoman in a purple satin gown reclining on the beach. A little way from the madwoman, a lovelorn junkie stood at the edge of the sea, yelling obscenities at the amber hare reposing in the fat moon.

Like a stone sinking into the stillness of a pool, Zaira found herself slipping with involuntary force into the tender darkness of nostalgia.

Years ago, as a struggling actor, she had had to fend off directors and producers who tried to get it on with her. Their touch sickened her and she would take to the beach to erase its filth. The scene at dusk was unforgettable, a tangerine sky stretching over her: overweight housewives jogging with the menacing air of migrating wildebeest; a beggar and his more glamorously decayed consort, an armless retard blowing enormous spit bubbles, crouched in the sand; an obese Labrador barking mournfully at the surf.

Then, as now, Zaira was subsumed with an amazement for life: not her own—never—but for life, the thing in itself.

Life, the beating-fast heart of a sparrow; a new leaf in spring.

Standing at the edge of the sea she allowed the water to gather at her ankles, and the silk of shifting sand beneath her feet made her toes curl with pleasure.

You cannot ask for more, she thought as the last lengths of moonlight draped her with a feeling as light as the wings of butterflies.

No, you cannot ask for more.

PART 2

9

'SLAP YOURSELF, MADARCHOD!' MINISTER CHANDER Prasad thundered into the phone. 'Again! Harder—until you stop babbling like a madman and make some sense.'

Calls at 2.00 a.m. seldom brought good news, and the nation's Minister for Labour and Employment braced himself for what was to come.

'I have,' Malik Prasad whimpered.

'Well, do it again!' the minister roared. 'Slap yourself ten more times, you son of a bitch! Then call me!' He rose from the bed and walked to his study.

He sat at his desk, switched on a goose-neck lamp and poured himself a drink.

When the phone rang again Minister Prasad had downed two shots of Black Label and was several shades calmer for it. 'Now speak clearly. What time did you leave for Maya Bar?' He

was in his study now, sitting at his desk in very low light, his notepad and pen ready before him.

'It must've been twelve-thirty.'

'What time did you get there?'

'Around one o'clock. The place was packed, Dad. All high-flyers. Models, designers, the works ...' Malik had locked his bedroom door from inside. He sat on the marble floor in pitch darkness, his knuckles pale from dread.

The minister took another gulp. 'Why did you go in the first place?'

'I'd heard Zaira was going to be there as a bartender for the night. I was desperate to see her.'

'A bartender! Why would Zaira have to work as a bartender?'

'It was not for real, Dad,' he explained. 'It was part of a promotion campaign for her new film.'

At Maya Bar, behind the counter, in a dazzling white-and-silver strap dress that highlighted her fluted shoulder blades and hugged her curves, Zaira had looked lovely and frightened.

'Oh.' The minister had never understood the flashy set; he had never wanted to. 'Who was with you?'

Malik mentioned a friend from America who had tagged along. 'I went with Lucky.'

'Your friend from school?' The minister remembered Lucky Singh because his father had been a member of Parliament, famously gunned down a few years earlier on the steps of Parliament House. 'That tall thin boy with very long curly hair?'

'Yes.'

'But hadn't he moved to San Jose?' The minister's recollection was correct. Lucky Singh, like his father, had had a host of cases filed against him by the time he was twenty-one. Lucky had not moved to San Jose: he had been exported there.

'Lucky was in town on holiday. We decided to go out and celebrate.'

The minister wondered why on earth his son kept such shoddy company, but it came to him that perhaps the boy had no choice.

'I entered Maya. I wanted a vodka with soda.'

'All right.' Minister Prasad took notes with secretarial diligence.

'I went up to the bar and greeted Zaira. She looked right through me, Dad. Then I asked her for a drink and ...'

'And? What did she say?'

'She said the bar had closed and she couldn't serve me alcohol.' Malik was whining now. Paranoia had broken through his dread.

'And?'

'I—I took out my gun and I shot at the ceiling.'

'What? Are you mad or what?' The minister didn't really need an explanation: he could practically smell the powder his son had snorted.

'She was acting so damn pricey, Dad. She turned me down simply because she thought I was a nobody. She was treating me like I was one of the losers who hang around in a corner at a

party. She thought she could throw her star power around and ... she thought she was the ...' He paused in his hysterical rant and, a moment later, blurted out a confession.

'You *shot* her?' The minister stood up in a fit, accidentally knocking over a metal pen holder on his desk. 'You shot her!' The pens scattered across the floor and rolled about haphazardly.

'I didn't mean to!' Malik wished his father wouldn't sound so scandalized. 'I meant to shoot generally in her direction. I was upset; I thought ... I thought she would be scared. I'm *not* a nobody. She had *no* right to ignore me in front of that crowd, Dad. I had taken enough from her.' He was still reeling from her rejection; the reality of her death was yet to sink in.

'Shut up, behenchod! Do you know what you've done?'

'I shot Zaira in the head.' He collapsed in sobs. 'I shot her in the head.'

'All because she refused to serve you a drink?'

'I'm sorry, Dad. I really didn't mean to.' The vision of Zaira pleading for Samar after slumping to the floor in a ruined heap flashed before Malik's eyes. Then his father's growl broke through.

'Do you have any idea how this is going to affect *my* career?' Minister Prasad felt sick to his guts; he wanted to beat his son. 'Saala chutiya!'

'I'm sorry, Dad ... I'm so sorry ...'

Then, picturing his son in an apartment in Bombay, bawling over some Tinseltown tart, his tone softened. Although he had

no specific interest in his son's life, he could empathize with the boy's circumstances. The minister knew well what it entailed to be so blatantly rejected; he also knew of the consequences of doing something stupid and cruel in the wake of an insulting public rebuff. 'Now, now, Malik ...'

'Dad ... please save me ... I can't believe this has happened.'

'Malik, compose yourself ... stop crying ...'

'Only *you* can save me, Dad.'

In his son's voice Minister Prasad caught the traces of a humiliation he knew inside out. Decades ago, he had come to Delhi as a young man, earnest and fiery, determined to make his name in public office. Having assumed the capital to be a level playing field where only political success mattered, he was shocked to see members of established political dynasties enjoy key walk-on roles in a scene in which he had to fight for the part of a bit player. His naivety received a further jolt once he was elected member of Parliament. His new title gave him power, even wealth, but social acceptance still eluded him. He approached the India International Centre for membership but they did not even consider his application without a file of glowing references. He tried to join the Delhi Whisky Society; they said they were taking no new members, which he knew was a cover-up. When he tried to get into Über, a well-known restaurant in Greater Kailash, the door attendant stalled him and said that he could not enter because he was wearing slippers. Minister Prasad had gone to Über with a bunch of his chamchas, and to be turned away in their presence had been

the last straw. To think a bloody doorman had the guts to turn *him* away! He decided he had put up with enough snobbery, and from now on it was going to be an eye for an eye. The very next week the door attendant at Über, who had stopped Minister Prasad, was run over by a speeding truck. There were no witnesses to the accident. The police did not even consider it could have been anything other than a freak mishap.

Now, as he listened to Malik's sobs echoing in an empty flat in Bombay, his son's embarrassing rejection jolted him back to the days of his own youth, its terrible, insolent struggles. A part of him believed that someone as powerful as he ought not to feel slighted by such small society types, but another part, embittered and furious, was determined to equal the score on behalf of his son.

He swallowed. Recognizing this was no time for nostalgia, he reassigned his mind to the present situation and resolved to help his son. 'How many people were present at the bar?'

'Maybe two hundred or so.' Malik's heart was thudding so hard he could barely speak.

'Did anyone see you shoot her?'

'Of course, Dad!'

'Don't raise your voice, kutta!'

'How could someone *not* have seen me?' Blood had shot out from Zaira's temple and stained Malik's shirt.

'Was someone with Zaira when it happened?'

'Yes. Bunty Oberoi. He's her co-star in her new film.'

'Do you know this Bunty chap?'

Malik had met Bunty Oberoi in passing, and he told his father they were acquaintances.

'So Bunty saw you shoot her?'

'He was the one who raised the alarm.'

Bunty Oberoi's scream had been effete and comical, as if he was auditioning for the role of a widow in a Hindi film.

'And then you left the bar?'

'Lucky thought it was the smart thing to do; I just followed him. We ran out. Everyone was looking at me, Dad. Her blood had messed up my clothes. I desperately needed to shower.'

'Is the gun with you?'

'Yes, it is.'

As Malik had rushed out of the bar a few models, svelte and glazed-eyed, had shrieked and pranced out of his way like impalas taking on the plains of the savannah. He had just got into his car when he heard Nalini Chopra begin to shriek in panic.

'Who else was there? Did you see?'

'Samar Arora. He was out on the deck and rushed in just as Lucky and I were taking off'

'Who is Samar?'

'Zaira's best friend. He's a musician or something.'

'Did Samar see you shoot Zaira?'

'I don't think so.'

'Okay.' He sighed, scribbling again in his pad. 'That's one more thing in your favour.'

Pushing the notepad away, Minister Prasad sat back on the chair, closed his eyes and reflected on the cast of characters whose hazy figures filed in before him. There was his son, the murderer. Bunty Oberoi, the key witness. Samar Arora, an intimate of the deceased. And he, the minister, was the scribe. Slowly, other characters would latch on to the narrative, fill gaps, embellish bare patches, provide motion. But it was vital to shape the story as it unfolded, deftly manipulate it through inevitable detours and complications and lead it up to its logical conclusion. This story was not only about crime and punishment, it was also a chance to settle scores with the sort of people who had mocked him in his youth and who had now put his son through the same, classic ignominy. Those snobby scoundrels would be served their just deserts. Besides, his own political future needed to be safeguarded.

'Don't worry, son. I will handle the situation,' he assured. 'But first things first: I want you to take the gun and dispose of it in a lake or a well.' He made a note to call the forensics expert who would be sent the evidence once the police registered the case and began their investigation.

'Okay.'

'Next, burn the clothes you wore to the bar that night.'

'I will.'

'See to it that the car you drove is also out of the picture. Bum it. Lose it. But get it out of the way. Understood?'

'I'll take care of it.'

'No! You ask Lucky to junk it. Don't go close to that car until this is all wound up.'

'Okay, Dad.'

'And tell Lucky to catch the next flight back to America. He cannot be a party to this case in any way.'

'I will ask Lucky to go back; no one knows he came with me. And I doubt if anyone saw him leave with me. He was already in the car when I got in.'

'Good. And then,' the minister said, clearing his throat, 'Malik, come to Delhi ... Come home to your family, beta.'

'I'm sorry, Dad,' Malik repeated. 'To put you through all this.' 'I will ... try my best'—emotion surged up in his chest and clogged his throat—'to bring you out of this. You just come back home.'

The minister returned to his bedroom. His wife, asleep in their bed, reminded him of a beached whale. He was gripped with the desire to beat her with a stick, break the glass bangles on her wrists, leave a few dark purple bruises on her forehead. But he found age had deflated his will; besides, she would probably cry for hours and then he wouldn't be able to sleep.

He decided to jack off.

His favourite fantasy involved a day from his childhood. At the age of six the minister had been caught smelling his sister's soiled tampons. His father had thrashed him with a washerwoman's mallet; the beating had turned him off women till he was well into his twenties. In the interim, the relief of his uncontainable urges was achieved unusually. When he was

twelve years old a buffalo on his father's farm had caught his eye. Dawn was yet to break as he had tiptoed to the cattle sheds. The buffalo, whose large head was flanked by long curled horns, moaned as he had thrust into her. Quickly, furiously he worked her, his hands slapping her flesh, teeth grinding, flesh taut. As his groin smacked against her, she bellowed wildly, a sound that excited him all the more. The following morning, he walked about the farm with a strut, eyeing the peasant women with a condescending look. *I know what your pussy was made for,* his eyes said. But before long, his elation was replaced by fear. What if the buffalo were to bear his child, he thought. He was too young to know better, and the prospect of encountering progeny with two legs more than his own proved to be so scary that he returned to the stable that night and poisoned the buffalo. Once the beast was dead, he felt he could breathe again.

As on past occasions, recalling the incident never failed to excite the minister, and he rubbed his messy right hand on his wife's pillowcase. He had hoped masturbation would relieve him, but he continued to feel ill at ease. He wondered what he would have to do *this* time—now that his son had shot the nation's most famous star.

That chutiya has poisoned the buffalo, the minister contemplated bitterly. Now I'm going to have to clean up the remains.

10

'I WAS WITH HER THE NIGHT BEFORE,' SAMAR SAID, his voice quivering like a candle flame, 'at her apartment.'

Leo said, 'I know.' He noticed a half-eaten sandwich on the piano, before which Samar was seated, his feet on the rung of the stool. Mr Ward-Davies sat next to him, his head resting on the floor, tail between his legs.

'We were together until almost one in the morning.'

'Why haven't you eaten lunch?' Leo asked gently.

'She was wearing her long blue dress. She looked beautiful, wounded, a little lost.'

'Stop, baby. You can't ...'

Samar wiped his cheeks. 'She was on my lap in the ambulance, Leo. She was clutching on to my hand.'

'You were there for her.'

'And then she said something to me.'

'What did she say?' Leo leaned forward.

'She was in unbearable pain ... She was writhing as if she wanted to fling her life out of her.'

'What did she say to you, baby?'

Samar clasped and unclasped his hands. 'Who am I going to steal flowers with?' He buried his face in his palms.

'Huh?' Leo looked on helplessly, suddenly feeling excluded and small.

'Who am I going to steal flowers with?'

'What're you talking about, Samar?'

'The garden in Dubash House ...'

Leo looked at Mr Ward-Davies who had now pressed his head between his paws. Although the dog could not understand the severity of the situation Leo knew he could feel Samar's pain deep in his bones.

After a week Zaira's body was released for the last rites. Her head had been picked for the bullet. Her flesh was cold and dehydrated from the days in the morgue freezer.

Karan accompanied Samar to the morgue. Zaira was shown to Samar one last time; then her coffin was closed and carted off to the van. On the way to the burial ground Samar threw up in the car. Karan had never seen such violent retching: it was as if Samar's elemental principle, the composite of his instinct, memory and emotion, had been forced out. Karan reached for his handkerchief to clean the mess on Samar's trousers. Leo, who was driving, looked stricken, and discreetly shielded his

nose with his hand. Karan asked if they could stop for a drink of water but Samar was keen to get to the cemetery where he expected chaos.

Thousands of fans had gathered outside the cemetery.

Outdoor broadcasting vans and photographers had laid siege to the entrance to record the arrival of celebrities. An anonymous wail sporadically struck the hot air like a spear. It would take an hour, at the least, to reach the entrance to the cemetery. Much to Samar's dismay the police officer on duty asked him who he was. When he said he was Zaira's friend the police officer refused to believe him and pushed him to the side. Luckily, Karan caught the eye of the editor of *India Chronicle,* who knew enough people to get them entry into the grounds.

Karan stood next to Samar, who stared fixedly at Zaira's grave; rage had now come to occupy the dark chasm of his grief. Leo noticed an endless entourage of mourners—actors, producers, directors, editors of magazines, journalists, socialites—all nattily turned out. Most conspicuously, in a corner, clad in cool white salwar-kameezes and black shades, were Tara and Nalini Chopra, crying softly, inviting sympathy from bystanders and provoking shutterbug mania. Journalists who knew of Samar's friendship with Zaira asked him incessant, moronic questions: 'Sir, how do you feel?'; 'How're you taking her murder, sir?'; 'How did you feel when you heard she had been shot?' Samar did not utter a word and maintained an even, icy expression, though Karan could tell that he was seething inside.

'It was such an ugly burial,' Samar told Leo in the car on the way back from the funeral.

'I agree; it was too public, too noisy.'

'Journalists kept asking me how I was coping. I was tempted to say that I was fine, and that like many of the mourners I was going back to a film set. Or to a party.'

'I'm glad you maintained a dignified silence.'

'But I'm not going to maintain a "dignified silence" for long, Leo. I'm not going to let Malik get away.'

Leo could hear Samar's teeth grind against each other. 'Yes, Malik *has* to be punished. A cold-blooded murderer cannot be allowed to walk the streets.'

'I'm going to fight this case to the end.' Samar's face was tight with determination.

'I'm with you all the way.'

'You know this might mess up your schedule? You may have to stay on in India longer than you'd like to, Leo.'

'I couldn't leave you alone, Samar. We're gonna come through this. Zaira was my buddy too, remember?'

'We met because of her.'

'I remember the day she mentioned she knew you well. We were at a party in Delhi. She was eager for me to meet you ... I had no idea she was setting us up ...'

Samar's eyes filled up.

'I'll stay on with you, Samar; I'm in it for the long haul.'

'Thanks, Leo.' Samar felt angry, and he was exhausted. He had not slept properly since the murder, and when he did

sleep gruesome visions of Zaira's last moments mangled his slumber.

'You don't have to thank me, baby; I'm with you each step of the way.' Leo looked out of the window, snatched gasps of air; he was glad to be outside the stuffy cemetery, away from the crowds, the clamour. 'Karan is a decent chap,' he remarked.

Samar nodded. He would never forget the warm feel of Karan's steady hand on his back after he had thrown up, the consolation and affirmation of that simple, profound gesture; something deep had opened up between them. 'Karan will miss Zaira more than he knows now; the wound is not upon him yet.'

After the burial Karan had seen off Samar and Leo to their car and made his way straight to Rhea's. She opened the door and in her eyes he saw the smouldering pain cleaving his heart. Quietly, she took Karan up the stairs and into her studio. For almost twenty minutes they sat in silence. He looked around, picking up a pot or an urn; she studied him cautiously, concerned. She did not probe by asking about the funeral.

He leaned against the door of her kiln. 'I was with her and Samar in the ambulance.'

She came up to his side and stroked his hair.

'You know what they say about death?'

'They say a lot of things, Karan.'

'They say that you leave peacefully. That there's a glow on your face. Calm all around, angels, harps ... white light ...'

'Karan ...'

'Behenchod!'

She had never heard him swear before; the word was raw, sheathed in tremendous rage. 'Please ...'

'Zaira's death was nothing like that. It was huge and angry. Like a demon or something.' A loud, garbled sob rose from deep inside him and shook her. 'You couldn't comfort her even if you wanted to. She was staring at Samar like she was drinking him up.'

'And Samar?' she hesitated even as she asked.

'Samar ... he was ...' Karan's face said it all. *Samar was cored like an apple.* 'I couldn't bear to go with him to the morgue.'

'But you went?'

'Yes; Leo said he was too nervous. Samar just stared at Zaira's face; I could see a lifetime of memories in his eyes. He was so dignified, so contained in his grief'

'It must have been his greatest nightmare coming true—if you can have nightmares like that.'

'Until that moment in the morgue, when I saw him standing before Zaira's coffin, I had not seen him as a person. I saw him as a failed pianist, a tap dancer, a poser. But I did not see him for a man who had loved, and who could be dismantled by the loss of that love.'

'I'm glad Samar did not have to go into the morgue alone.'

'I had to see him hurt so badly to see him whole.'

Rhea was silent; she had not expected such a transformation in Karan. After a few moments, as she stroked his forehead tenderly, she asked, 'What next?'

Drawing a deep breath Karan exhaled slowly. 'The police will take over. Let's see how the investigation goes.'

'Samar is going to need all your help, Karan.'

'I know.'

'And don't forget Zaira.'

'Her, yes. But also Samar—particularly him.'

She enfolded him in her arms and together they wept, quietly, afraid of the world but united as never before.

A few days after the funeral, the investigating officer called Samar in for questioning.

An hour later Samar left the police station, disgusted.

The force with which Samar slammed the door of the car alarmed Leo. 'What's going on?'

'They asked me about her. They asked me how much blood she had lost.'

Leo looked on, unable to say anything.

'They asked me where I thought the bullet had entered her.'

'Oh God!' Leo started the car.

'They asked me if I had seen Malik on the premises.'

'You said yes, naturally.'

'I did. Then they asked me if I had seen him shoot her. But I had not.'

'You came clean.'

'Of course.'

'They asked me all manner of things.' He shook his head. 'They asked me if she and I had been having it off ... if she lost

consciousness *before* or *after* the ambulance came ... if I could have done anything to prevent her death ...'

They drove forward in silence. There were few cars on the street. At the traffic light, a man in an outlandish turban walked around selling strawberries and a leprous beggar was soliciting cash from a woman in a BMW.

'Did you speak with your editor?' Samar asked.

'Yes,' Leo said. 'I talked with Sally, and she said I could stay on in India as long as I continued to send her pieces from here.'

'I'm glad you'll be here, Leo; it means the world to me.' He caressed Leo's shoulder. 'You have been such a brick throughout.'

'Of course. I wouldn't dream of being any place else.' They were on Worli Seaface when Leo added, 'Sally also suggested I write about what we're all going through.'

'Really?' Samar cocked him a look.

'She said I could send dispatches on the murder trial.'

'She actually suggested that?'

'And as I'm on the inside—so to speak—I could write from a vantage point that nobody else would have on the subject,' he said excitedly. 'Sally said it's a subject worthy of investigation, and that my pieces could ultimately add up to a book!'

'A book.' Samar sounded incredulous.

'You know, kind of a subcontinental *In Cold Blood.'* He paused, wondering if Samar was familiar with the title he had mentioned. 'It's a book by Truman Capote,' he said helpfully.

'I read *In Cold Blood* when I was fourteen,' Samar said sharply. 'Are you just scrambling for a nice way to tell me Zaira's death is "material"?'

'I ... wouldn't phrase it quite like that.' Leo looked out of the car window; the veins on his neck throbbed. His eyes relaxed on the topography, buildings melting into each other, billboards splashing colour on the cement blur.

'I guess I'm asking you if her murder is just another book for you.'

'That's a shoddy thing to say, Samar; I take offence to that.'

'*You* take offence?' He shook his head.

'Look, I'm only trying to find my sanity in this calamity. You think this hasn't taken me apart? Writing will give me perspective on the entire incident. I want,' he said with a gulp, 'closure.'

'*Incident? Closure?*' Samar repeated. 'You sound like someone who spends all day watching talk shows.'

Leo drew the car to a halt outside the cottage. 'I'm going to let that remark pass because you've just spent four hours at the police station, Samar, and maybe that's fucked up your mind.'

'That's not true,' Samar said. 'Do you want to know what's fucked my mind?'

'Not now. I would like to go inside.'

'What's fucked my mind is that I had her blood. On my hands. And it splashes.'

'C'mon, Samar!' Leo opened the front door and they walked in. 'You're being gross.'

Samar stopped by the telephone console in the hallway. 'Gross? That's exactly what death is. Gross. Gross weight. Grossly insurmountable.'

Saku-bai appeared briefly, but seeing the two men in a heated argument she quickly turned, went back into the kitchen and shut the door behind her. Standing motionless by the stove, she watched mutton boil for Mr Ward-Davies while the voices outside rose in pitch.

'Look, don't jump on a moral high horse because ...'

'Because Zaira got shot in the head?'

Leo looked on helplessly. What could he say?

Samar took a deep breath before saying, 'I'd like her death to be private, Leo, because her life was not.'

'It was only a suggestion. I'm not bent on doing it,' Leo said irritably.

'I know you will do the right thing.'

'And what makes you think someone else is not going to write about the murder?'

'Other people *will* write about it but you knew her because of me, and that alters the equation a bit.'

'Wouldn't you prefer a more sympathetic retelling of events?'

'You mean,' Samar said with a fake, theatrical gasp, 'my very own in-house memoirist?'

'That's *so* tacky.'

'Didn't it cross your mind that this might not be an appropriate thing to ask at this time?' He turned to light a

candle in the living room. 'I'm sorry I was rude earlier on ... I didn't mean any of it.'

Leo had started to march towards the kitchen.

'Just give me open berth for a few days.'

'Yeah, sure. Whatever.'

Samar followed Leo to the kitchen. Mr Ward-Davies, sweet and lonesome, met them with gentle, enthusiastic wags of his tail. Saku-bai cleared her throat and excused herself.

'We'll get through this, Samar,' Leo said without any feeling.

'I know we will. Thank you.' Samar pulled out a bottle of cognac and two bowl glasses.

Leo was now sitting at the dinner table. 'Thank you?'

Samar poured a shot of amber liquid into his glass. 'For agreeing not to write about her death.'

'Oh, right.' Leo looked as if his wrist had been cut. 'Anything for you, love.'

11

A MONTH LATER LEO WAS RECLINING ON THE couch, browsing through the latest copy of the *India Chronicle,* when the phone rang.

It was Sally, his editor, from New York. 'What's going on?'

'Nothing much ... Just catching up on my reading.' He sat up. 'How are you holding up?' 'All right ... I guess.'

'And Samar?'

'He's okay. He's getting ready as we speak—a party we're going to in a bit. It's just down the road.' Leo could hear Samar in the shower in the adjoining room.

'Sounds like Samar is a lot more sociable since the time we last spoke.'

'His first outing since the ... It's taken a lot for him to get here.' He heard Sally click her lighter.

'And it must have drained your reserves too?'

He didn't know what to say. 'How's New York?' he asked instead.

'Cold. Relevant. Angry. Black. I'm also on my forty-second cigarette of the day.'

'It could always be worse.'

'I called to check on you.'

'This country is not letting up on the murder, and we're smack in the middle of it all.'

'Is the press going crazy?'

'The more public the trial becomes, the greater the number of photographers who park themselves outside our gate. I can barely pick up a magazine without seeing Zaira's face splashed all over it. There's mass hysteria over her death.'

'Well, you can't blame them for going after the story like sharks. I'm sorry if I sound cold, but it is a fabulous-fucking-story.'

'I guess.' He did not want to think of it as a fabulous-fucking-story, not after his row with Samar.

'And I gather media interest has only been sympathetic.'

'Well, Zaira was a superstar. Do you think the press would be filing stories of some toothless tribal raped and hacked apart in Rajasthan?'

'There's got to be more than just the bling quotient driving this.'

'Sections of the so-called liberal press want to see Malik—he's the fuckin' murderer—punished. To chalk up a few social justice brownie points.'

She coughed. 'Why do you think the guy shot her?'

'Because she refused to serve him a drink.'

'Sounds like a Man-Walks-into-a-Bar joke gone completely awry ...'

'It's not as cut and dried as that either.' Malik was part of India's newly affluent, he explained to Sally, an echelon created by rapid, rampant urbanization. 'Malik had the bucks to groove in all the right places. But once he was in, everyone treated him like a hick.' Malik's inherent gaucherie had been put to its greatest test at Maya Bar amid the lovely and the powerful; arrogance and insecurity would have been thrashing their wings inside his head. 'He must have felt wildly insulted when Zaira refused him that drink; he flashed the gun and first shot at the ceiling to scare the shit out of her.'

'But then he shot her in the head!'

'I don't know what drove him to do that. But he has a history of violence.'

'With Zaira?'

'Yes; he once rammed her trailer with his jeep.'

'Why didn't she report him to the cops for that?'

'He'd been stalking her for two years now, Sally, and the cops simply looked the other way when she asked for a restraining order.'

'Did they think it was just part of the Hot Chick Deal?'

'Well, the police, like everyone else, worship Bollywood stars and by Indian standards Zaira was royalty. But then Malik was no small beer, either. His father is the Minister for Labour

and Employment, and he knew whom to call when she went to court and asked for a restraining order against his son.'

'Why didn't she hire private security?'

'Samar and I both tried to convince her but she thought hiring security would be an intrusion on her personal space. She hated entourages of any kind; I don't think she had fully grasped the scale of her popularity either.'

'But she was huge in India.'

'There were temples built in her name.'

'Wow. That's freaky.'

'Talking of freaky ... on a TV show last night, one politician had a novel reason for her murder. He said Zaira had invited her murder by hanging out in a bar in a "sexy backless gown".'

'You're kidding!' Sally practically fell off her chair.

Leo sighed. Sally's naivety not only raised his hackles but also whetted his appetite: this was *precisely* the sort of ignorance he had hoped to confront through his book. The politician, Leo told Sally, was with the right-wing Hindu People's Party. 'He's probably been set up to save Minister Prasad's ass. The implication that Zaira's "sexy backless gown" caused her death fits in perfectly with the party's morality management agenda.'

'That's the most regressive thing I've ever heard! Even our dyed-in-the-wool Republicans are better than that.'

'This is India,' Leo told her. 'The politician doesn't mean a word. He's probably running a porn empire on the sly but on the face of things there's nothing quite like being morally outraged.'

Mr Ward-Davies padded into the room and nuzzled up against Leo's legs. Hoisting the dog under his arm, Leo walked out to the porch. The warmth of the dog's thin white coat against his body was such solace that it reminded him of his childhood, of sleeping with a teddy bear in his arms.

'Don't you think it'd help you to write about the murder then? I mean, just to get a detached point of view across,' Sally urged.

'I wish I was the man for the job, Sally.'

'Your readers would love it. The magazine will give you a fabulous layout. And, as I've said before, the pieces could add up to quite an account of contemporary India. These are the stories of modern India we never hear.'

Leo put Mr Ward-Davies down. 'You think I don't know that?'

'I'm sure you do.'

'Years ago, Sally, when I published *Old Gullies,* I knew my big book would come out of India. Some landscapes draw writers to them and ask to be written about. Leonard Woolf served Sri Lanka. Isak Dinesen did Africa. Deep in my heart I knew I would write an account of India, not the exotic, colourful version but something that throbbed with its modernity.'

'I agree; I don't know anyone who could tell India's story as well as you, Leo. So what's stopping you?'

'I ... I promised Samar I wouldn't.' He could hear her take a deep drag of her cigarette, probably the last before she would stub it out.

'Why would you do something so ridiculous, Leo?'

'Well, *he* asked me not to write about it.'

In the silence that ensued, urgent and awful things that could not be said aloud pressed against Leo's throat. Denied the right to tell a story that had gripped his mind, he had secretly grown resentful toward the man who had imposed the embargo. His immediate response had been to leave India but now the trial had forced him to stay on. His arguments with Samar were taking a toll on his writing; he had not produced a publishable page in weeks now.

'Samar asked you,' Sally repeated slowly.

'He did. And I promised him I wouldn't write a word about the murder or the trial.'

'Oh,' she said. 'I guess that's really sweet of you.'

'Sally.'

'Yes?'

'You're not talking to some kid at a lemonade stall.'

'We don't *do* lemonade stalls in New York, Leo.' A siren went off on the street outside Sally's office, briefly drowning their conversation. When they resumed she said, 'Well, ring me if you change your mind.' Then she asked offhandedly, 'What's buzzing workwise?'

'I can't seem to write about India, that's for sure.' Leo restrained himself from saying that he could not get a fix on another subject; the inertia in his creative life had suffused him with gloom. As he bit on his knuckles, Mr Ward-Davies gave a nervous yip and his own ears pricked up. He turned sharply and

saw photographers scrambling on to the boundary wall, trying to hoist a camera on the edge of the grille. He rushed indoors, keeping the panic out of his voice.

Sally said, 'Then maybe you should consider writing about America.'

'Why would I do that?' He locked the front door, leaned against it, caught his breath.

'Because you've long confronted the foreign,' she said, 'and now, perhaps, it's time to take a look at the familiar. No one could do America as well as you, Leo. And I'll publish whatever you write.'

'Thanks, Sally.'

'You sound like you've lost yourself, darling; it's understandable during such a tragedy. Come back to yourself, come back to writing.'

'I'll try my best,' he said feebly. 'That's all I have. The writing. Call you soon.'

Clicking off the phone Leo went into the bedroom.

Samar had just stepped out of the shower and said he needed a few more minutes to be ready for the party. Returning to the living room, Leo settled on the couch, wondering whether Samar, whose eyes he had noticed were red, had been crying. The lasting legacy of death, he felt, was the ambiguity of its mourning. How was one to set parameters for the time needed to recover from the loss of a loved one; how was one supposed to know when to stop? He tried to sympathize with Samar, but these days he was consumed with pure, unassailable

exhaustion and, within it, Samar's sorrow nudged and poked him, a heavy, toxic, contagious thing.

Of course, there were days when Leo was glad to be around Samar, particularly on the mornings he played the piano, nimble fingers uncoiling gilded rhymes from a few black and white keys. However, on other days, when Samar ranted endlessly about the trial, Leo found himself growing steadily impatient with his lover's notions about big, anonymous ideas like truth and justice and politics; it seemed pointless to revisit them endlessly. Luckily, Karan was often around to step in and hear out Samar, inadvertently giving Leo a much needed reprieve from endless heated tirades. Leo tried to escape the cottage and its tense, claustrophobic atmosphere but the intense media scrutiny had restricted his movements. He felt like a captive, and a captive audience to Samar's gathering wrath. The possibility of fleeing to San Francisco was only too tempting, but if he left he would be guilty of deserting a fort under attack and if he stayed he would probably not be able to write a sensible word. There was no way out of this. The only hour of calm was before dawn, when Samar went for his walk with Mr Ward-Davies, before busloads of shutterbugs arrived at their doorstep. It was a pure, restful hour, when Leo could be on his own but for the great sighing sea across the road.

Leo took a deep breath and picked up the magazine to resume his reading—yet another article on the murder, only this one featured what the guests at Maya Bar had told the cops.

I was at the bar, right beside Zaira. At around 1.00 a.m. a man wearing a white shirt and brown pants came up to the bar and asked for a drink. The bar had just been closed for the night, so Zaira said she could not give him a drink, that it was past the legal hour to serve alcohol. She was about to leave the premises. The man looked shocked and tried to persuade her, but she refused again and prepared to leave. A split second later, he pulled out a gun and shot at the ceiling. Then he pointed the gun at Zaira's forehead and pulled the trigger point blank. She collapsed. She was in great pain and she repeatedly asked for someone called Samar. She was unconscious by the time the ambulance arrived.

The man who shot Zaira was Malik Prasad.

I recognized him because he had once asked me if I wanted to be part of an entertainment programme he was putting together in Toronto for his company, Tiranga Inc.

—BUNTY OBEROI

I was present at Maya Bar on the night Zaira was shot. I was out on the deck when I heard a commotion. I rushed indoors, where I saw a crowd at the bar. Zaira was on the floor. I kneeled by her and I saw a rupture on her left temple, where the bullet had entered. She was trying very hard to speak. Then I heard a voice from behind me. Nalini Chopra was shouting at a man wearing a white shirt and brown pants. I saw him slip

a gun into his pocket as he ran out of the door. Nalini Chopra was yelling, 'He's the man who shot Zaira. Go after him! Get him!'

Zaira was in my lap at this point.

We took her to the hospital in an ambulance twenty minutes later.

—SAMAR ARORA

Although I was present at Maya Bar on that fateful night, I don't believe I saw anyone with a gun; I certainly did not see the man who shot Zaira. I was at the venue to research my new novel and was chatting with a model when I heard a shot. Later I was told the Bollywood superstar Zaira had been killed. How would I know Malik Prasad? I am sequestered in a room, writing for eight hours a day—I have no connection with the world of glamour.

—VICKY LALWANI

I was with a friend—I believe the Princess of Jaipur—when my daughter Tara rushed up to me and said something awful had happened at the bar. Since we own Maya Bar, we were both extremely worried. My daughter saw Zaira first. Blood was oozing out of her head and she was gasping for breath. My daughter, who is a sensitive person, passed out. Then I saw a man in a white shirt and brown pants put a gun in his pocket and race towards the door. Another man was with him.

> I ran after both men. At one point I caught a waiter and ordered him to help me chase the man who had shot Zaira. We made our way out through the chaos but they got into a car and drove away.
>
> —NALINI CHOPRA

'Ready?' Samar asked as he emerged from the room.

'I am,' said Leo. 'Are you?' They were going for a party Diya Sen was hosting at her apartment in Colaba.

'Yeah.'

Leo gave Samar a quick glance: he had lost most of the meat on his bones, and in his creased pants and baggy shirt now resembled a scarecrow. 'Are you sure you don't want to throw on a jacket? Maybe a nicer shirt?'

'I'm sure.' Samar took a deep breath. He was stepping out at Leo's behest; he was not going to make a fashion show out of it.

Leo flung the magazine to the floor. 'I'll get the car keys.' 'What were you reading?'

'A report on the trial. The statements the guests made to the police. It's not a pretty picture, Samar. A lot of people are backtracking.'

'So goes the rumour.' Samar tried not to look dismayed. 'Anyway, let's head out. I bet Diya is waiting for us.'

Leo was thrilled to be able to leave the house after a month-long self-imposed exile. But no sooner had they gone up to the gate than flashbulbs exploded in their faces, a riot of voices

called out their names, shouted out questions. Recoiling in horror, they rushed indoors.

'How are we going to make it past that lot?' Samar exclaimed. Photographers had laid siege to their house; their sheer number was intimidating. 'How will we ever step out?'

'Will you quit asking me questions I can't answer for you!'

Samar had no choice but to watch Leo storm off. He looked at Mr Ward-Davies, who was staring up at him curiously. 'Let's go hunt out the Arnica,' he told his dog. 'I hear it's the best thing for shock.'

12

MINISTER CHANDER PRASAD WAS FUMING. Every newspaper was on his case about the 'Zaira Murder Trial'. Television anchors were trailing him like a pack of bloodthirsty piranhas. To top it all, pressure was mounting from several leaders of the HPP. They had conveyed their collective displeasure at his involvement, not on moral grounds but from fear that the opposition would use the scandal to bring the party down. If Malik was tried and sentenced, Minister Prasad would pretty much have to kiss his career goodbye. After all, how seriously would they take him in Parliament if his son was doing time in Tihar? Perturbed by the public resentment toward Malik, he grew desperate to see his son—and himself—emerge from the tamasha without a scratch.

The minister had an astute grasp of the Indian legal machinery, a colonial beast drenched in archaic colours. The legal system was principally adversarial in nature; the prosecution had to prove the guilt of the accused beyond all reasonable doubt. The accused was innocent until proven guilty. In theory, the Indian court system was unconcerned with detecting and punishing Zaira's killer: what was at stake here was proving that Malik was *not* the guilty party. So it was vital for the defence to plant seeds of doubt wherever possible so that suspicion was diverted from the accused: to achieve this, certain steps had to be in place. Without wasting another moment the minister called Ram Dube, head of the forensics laboratory to which the evidence in Zaira's murder case had been assigned.

Over the years, Ram Dube had helped the minister out in several cases—strategic assistance that had eventually led to successful acquittals. And Ram Dube would never forget the minister's generosity: for helping out with one key acquittal a few years earlier, he had been rewarded with twenty-five acres of land in Haryana.

Minister Prasad was aware that Ram Dube's daughter, all of eighteen, aspired to attend medical school. So he followed up the initial pleasantries with the gambit of a little harmless banter on educational matters.

'So, what has come of Lata's admissions, then?'

'Lata?'

'Lata—your daughter.'

'You mean Shabnam.'

'Didn't you have a daughter called Lata?' His voice was stem, like a headmaster interrogating a particularly doltish student.

'No, I have only one daughter, Minister-saab. She is called Shabnam.'

'Are you sure?' The minister sounded exasperated.

'Absolutely.'

'Well, what about her admissions?'

'It is all very difficult, Minister-saab. She is super-brilliant, of course, but none of the universities are prepared to see this.' The minister remembered that Shabnam Dube had inherited her father's mousy appearance: dark and hirsute, with tombstone teeth and a dank, musky odour. She also had a flourishing moustache. 'These days the competition is mind-boggling.'

'What would La—, er, Shabnam like to specialize in?'

'We expect nothing fancy,' Ram Dube said bashfully. 'Just for her to be the greatest pathologist in the history of modem India.'

'Pathologist?' the minister repeated. 'Shabnam will study shit for a living?'

'She is,' Dube said in a flood of loyalty, 'clever, kind-hearted, charming, muscular'—he paused—'and a very highly exciting girl.'

The minister hiked his eyebrows. A very highly exciting girl? What did *that* mean? But he decided not to probe. 'What if she doesn't get into medical school?'

'We'll get her married off if she fails.'

'Don't lose hope so easily, Ram.'

'But if none of the good universities will ...'

'In which university do you want admission for the girl? Why haven't you called me till now?'

'It is a small matter. I feared I would be disturbing you.'

'But we have known each other for years. I am like her uncle. Now tell me, which university does she hope to attend?'

Ram Dube rattled off a list of high-ranking medical colleges, and reminded the minister again that none of them had been particularly taken with his daughter's 'super-brilliance'.

'Just send me a letter with the name of the university she wishes to attend. Let me see what I can do.'

'Sir ... you are *too* kind.' Ram Dube's pulse quickened, sweat streamed down his cheeks. He could picture his daughter on her graduation day, standing in a flowing black robe and funny hat, a scroll of papers in her hand; he could picture her bent over a microscope in a lab. Her future appeared so blazingly bright, he was tempted to shield his eyes.

'What is there, Ram,' said the minister benevolently. 'We are bum chums, no?'

'Sir, I will be forever in your debt.' Ram Dube wiped his underarm with his fist.

'Send me a letter with all the details.'

'I will.' He cleared his throat. 'Sir, is there anything I can do for you?'

'I hate to trouble you ...'

'Just tell me, sir.'

'You know this whole dead actress situation has got out of hand.'

'Of course, sir.' The news channels covered nothing other than Zaira's murder; the trial had become a national obsession.

'And you know my son has been named key accused in the matter of this dead item?'

'This is most unfortunate.'

'It is only a conspiracy of the opposition to bring me down.'

'I have been sensing it from day one.'

'They're trying to get my son because *I* am much too powerful to touch.'

'They will go to any lengths, these people.'

'And my poor boy ...'

'... is the victim of political crossfire.'

'You've really managed to take in the situation, Ram.'

'Political rivalry is full of such dirty tactics, Minister-saab. It is kalyug, the age when evil will win and good must suffer.'

'I know, I know. Such is life ...' The minister sighed. 'I don't want to fail my son.'

'You shouldn't have to. No parent should fail their children's expectations.'

'I believe the bullets found at that bar have come to your department for investigation?' The investigating teams had recovered two bullets—one from the ceiling at Maya Bar, the other from Zaira's temple—both of which had made their way to the forensics department.

'Yes sir.'

'These bullets have been traced to the gun for which my son owns a licence?'

'That is correct.'

'This is a terrible coincidence! It will only suggest that my son has shot that dirty Bollywood whore. I need help to sort out this lafda, Ram.'

'By all means, Minister-saab. It is just a set-up to sully your honour and disgrace the Hindu People's Party. That will not happen as long as I am here.'

The minister shared his scheme with Ram Dube: What if the ballistic report to be made under Ram Dube's supervision to serve as evidence in court were to imply that the bullets, although identical in model, had been shot from two different guns? Could it not be that after Malik had shot at the ceiling, someone else present at the bar, who possessed the very same model, had shot Zaira?

'Do you get what I am saying, Ram?'

'Yes, that there were two persons with two guns at Maya Bar. But, Minister-saab, where is the other man and his gun?'

'I have been wondering the same thing myself.'

'The police are taking your son for a ride, sir, because they cannot find the *real* murderer.'

'The police ...' The minister shuddered. 'The less said of those corrupt bastards, the better.'

'But it is essential to establish your point early on in the investigation.'

'I agree completely! So you shall look into this matter?'

'Consider it already looked into.'

'This is very good of you, Ram.'

'Thank you, Minister-saab. So I will send the letter of request to your house?'

'Letter?'

'For the medical college admission.'

'College admission?'

'For Shabnam.'

'Shabnam?'

'My daughter, sir. We talked about her pathology degree. She is super ...'

'Of course, of course,' the minister said distractedly as he wiped his damp palms over his trademark white kurta. 'Send it to my house.'

13

BOMBAY, MORNING.

Sunlight pushed through the silver sheath at the horizon. The hot industrial night wore off into the slothful green of the rain trees. Muscular rat trappers emerged from filthy narrow sewers, slaughtered vermin strung over their shoulders. The rattle of aluminium canisters, milkmen on their early shift, competed with the diabolic, throaty rasp of rooks perched on jacaranda trees. Little children stood in indolent clusters under leafy canopies, waiting for school buses that would come hurtling towards them like demons in the great myths. At this blessed hour, one man struggled to disengage himself from his wife, a task that was not without its sweet agony. He slid back and propped himself up against the headboard, then turned to look again at the sleeping form next to him.

Adi's eyes fell on the button of flesh on Rhea's forearm, a childhood vaccination mark, a private hieroglyph that instantly took him back to the day he had gifted his wife fireflies in a jam jar.

At fifteen, Adi was not of the legal age to drive, but one evening, when his father was out of town, he got into the family car and made a beeline for the national park. He had resolved to bring Rhea fireflies after she had complained of dreaming about the peculiar insects; she said she was unable to fall asleep afterwards. But, she added brightly, her father, Dr Thacker, had given her a meaningful analysis of her dream. When Adi asked her for the gist of Dr Thacker's analysis she refused to divulge the details. Feeling incompetent before her father's skills at unravelling the intricate knots of Rhea's inner life he decided that if he helped her confront her dream it might somehow arrest its troubling recurrence. And so he was on his way to the national park, humming along to the Ellington ditty jamming on his stereo.

When he reached the national park he parked his car by a dense grove of bamboos, then ventured into the dim, cool forest with its rarefied monsoonal air. As he walked into a grove of kadam trees near the Kanheri Caves he heard the piercing shrieks of bright parakeets soaring overhead. A little way into the forest he saw a furry brown animal, rather like a civet, snarl and then scurry for cover; the hair on his arms grew erect with dread. The burnt cobalt sky turned scarlet and, before long, the thick smoke of dusk had shrouded the day. Against such

a mysterious sylvan canvas fireflies made their appearance, shimmering like embers. Finding it tricky to capture the insects, which were soon floating all around him, Adi decided to go after the ones lurking under leaves high up on the trees. As he ascended the first tree he felt its weak branches crack under his weight, and nearly came crashing to the ground. He tried again, succeeding on this attempt. Half an hour later he returned to his car with a jar full of fireflies sparkling like the sighing of comets.

He drove up to Rhea's house.

She opened the door, a physics textbook in her hand; she looked a little flustered. 'Adi ... what a surprise.'

'This is for you.'

As Rhea extended her hands to receive the jar Adi's eyes fell on the scar on her upper arm.

'Why are your arms and legs grazed?' she asked.

'It's nothing, Rhea. I should get going.'

'And there are leaves in your hair.'

'Keep the jar by your bedside,' he suggested. 'Perhaps now the fireflies won't haunt your dreams.'

'Your hands are bleeding. Should I get some Dettol?'

But Adi was already backing away.

In the car, Adi sensed something had changed between them; she was no longer her father's daughter, she was no longer exclusive. What cemented this impression was the image of the inoculation scar on her arm—it was as if she had revealed

to him her deepest secret. Adi returned home lifted by the delectable possibility of their life together.

Now, years later, lying in bed beside Rhea, he thought of the first time he had seen the scar, how it had solidified an unspoken pact between them. He leaned to kiss her naked arm.

She woke to the touch of his lips. 'You're up early.'

'Ssh ... go back to sleep.'

'What are you doing?' Her eyes were heavy with sleep.

'Remembering the fireflies I got you.'

'How come?'

He kissed her arm again, as though anointing the scar. 'What a long way we've come from that day,' he said, so softly she could not hear him.

'What?'

'Nothing,' he said, rising. 'I should get ready.'

'I'll meet you at the breakfast table,' she said, pulling the white sheets up to her neck. 'Let me grab a few more minutes of sleep.'

'Sure,' he said before making his way to the bathroom to shower. 'Take all the time you need.'

At the table, tucking into the breakfast Lila-bai had laid out for him, Adi set about reading the *Times of India.* Presently, Rhea entered the room; before settling on the chair beside him she stretched and muffled a yawn, then glanced at the newspaper in his hand. 'Are the papers still at it about the murder?' she asked, her brow pinched.

'There have been way too many slip-ups during the investigation.' He added that the report in the *Times of India* said the dress Zaira had worn on the night she was shot dead—currently the subject of vicious censure by the Hindu People's Party—was missing from the collage of evidence. None of the officers who had been interrogated could explain where or how it had gone missing.

'Obviously Minister Prasad got to it.' She poured herself a cup of black tea.

'You think?'

'He's bent on destroying all the evidence; he'll do anything to weaken the case against his son.'

'Malik Prasad intrigues me.'

'How odd.'

'Yes, I suppose it *is* odd to not only be intrigued by a murderer but to also sympathize with him.'

'You sympathize with Malik?' A muscle in her neck tightened.

'I feel Malik has got lost in a maze of the media's glib clichés: the spoilt rich kid, the spumed lover, the bad guy.'

Rhea drank her tea without further comment.

Adi feared he had said too much. In the last few weeks he had come to feel a great deal of pity for Malik. In fact, he remembered the instance when he started to feel sorry for Malik. It was on a moonless night in Singapore, when he had been missing Rhea terribly. He had called her several times but she had not answered the phone. A thick, viscous dread had

congealed in his chest; her unavailability had implied she was either in her studio or was otherwise occupied, and it hurt him to have to explore the various venal possibilities. Where was she? Had she stepped out of the house? Had she unplugged the phone? Was she entertaining someone he did not know? Panicking, Adi's mind spiralled toward a cluster of impractical and illogical thoughts. If they were ever to be separated, he thought, he would not be able to bear the loss. Her death, if that was the cause of separation, would leave him inconsolable, but her defection from their marriage would earn his cyclonic wrath. Now, at the breakfast table, he recalled the widely public stories of Zaira spurning Malik, and he thought of Malik not simply as a murderer but also as the subject of unrequited love; his sympathy, he realized, would be deemed obscene by any standards.

Rhea said, 'Well, I hear a lot of people have been gutted by Zaira's demise.'

'Samar Arora, for starters.'

'Yes,' she said quietly, thinking of Karan in her studio, crying in her arms. 'Among others. It's a real pity ... She was an awful actress, though.'

'She was getting better with each film.'

'She was way over-hyped, Adi.'

'Her last film was pretty good. She had talent.'

'Are you joking? She was drop-dead sexy—*that* was her only talent.' Rhea shook her head and poured herself some more tea.

Adi flinched. 'Well, *I* liked her work.'

'More so after she died?'

He glared at her.

She proceeded to butter his toast idly. 'Long day?' she asked.

His day would start with an appointment at the Oberoi, he said, followed by a teleconference with the team in Singapore, and it would wind up with a board meeting back at the office. Munching on his toast, he asked what she had planned for the day.

Rhea had to be at the animal shelter at ten-thirty. 'Rekha's getting married,' she said, referring to one of her co-workers. 'I'll have to fill in for her.'

'Don't you ever get fed up of the shelter?' Adi had been to the shelter only once, when he had gone to pick her up after her car had broken down. He had never wanted to go back: the rank odour of excreta, the premises teeming with sick animals, groaning, barking, looking balefully out of their dirty cages—he had found it repugnant.

'It's mind-numbing on most mornings,' she admitted, 'heartbreaking on others. But you need to take a deep breath and chug right along.'

'You're a real trooper, you know.'

'I've got the skin of a rhino, jaan.'

'And what are you doing in the afternoon?'

'After I cover Rekha's shift, I'm back for a late lunch.'

'And then pottery?'

'Yes, although I might step out at three.'

He stood up, opened his attaché and began rummaging through it. 'What gives?'

'Oh—' For a moment she looked like someone who had missed a step on a ladder. 'I have ... I have ... to buy some clay, from Kumbharwada.'

Luckily, Adi did not notice her expression oscillate from calm to trepidation. 'You really should exhibit your work. I've been telling you for so long.'

'No one will come, Adi.'

'What bull!' he scolded. 'It would be a sell-out show. Remember the time when all the gallerists were stalking you?'

'A "show" sounds so presumptuous,' she said. 'And gallerists weren't stalking me; two of them expressed an interest in acquiring my graduation project, which was probably a charity gesture.'

He slanted his head. 'Do you ever miss not pursuing the public life of an artist?'

'Artist-shmartist,' she said dismissively. 'It's all bullshit.'

'You know you could *still* have a show. You could still contact the gallerists who admired your work in college.'

'I've lost the nerve to exhibit. And it really doesn't matter. I have a lovely studio, and I do what I like in my own time, on my own terms.'

'If it makes you happy ...'

'What time do you get home?' she asked, accompanying him to the door.

In the passageway, he pressed the elevator switch. 'Around seven-thirty in the evening.'

'You remember what we have on tonight?'

'How could I ever forget!' The Ban Ganga Music Festival, an event they attended each year, was a simple but unforgettable affair: a wooden stage was floated over the sprawling pond and renowned musicians were invited to perform. Their past experience of the concert had been sublime, lyrical, intimate, like reading a love letter from seasons past. On this particular day, Fateh Khan, the famed Sufi singer from Karachi, anticipated by all of Bombay, was scheduled to perform. 'I've been wanting to hear Fateh Khan in concert for years,' Adi said. 'His voice is sheer magic.'

It pleased her to see him so excited, like a child. She hesitated, then asked, 'Do I make you happy, Adi?'

'What do you mean?'

She fell silent and he knew immediately what she was not able to say. 'You make me ... ridiculously happy.' He nuzzled her cheek with his own. 'You're all I need, Rhea.'

'Sometimes I wonder if we would have got married if I had taken the scholarship and gone to Berlin.'

'Yes, we would have! I'd have waited for you.'

'I don't think so. Our lives would have gone on different paths.'

'Do you regret forsaking the scholarship?'

She threw her hands up in the air. 'Who's to say? Why assume that my life as an artist would have gone some place.

Why assume that Berlin would have been a transformative experience? For all you know, I could have gone there and failed.' She shrugged. 'Questions, questions ... I could ask you if you regret marrying me, and not being able to have a child.'

'I have never regretted marrying you. You are the best thing that's ever happened to me.'

'But you regret that we don't have a family.'

'I love you.' His voice trembled with emotion, and she refrained from saying anything more.

As they waited for the elevator to come up, she thought: so this is what we talk about after breakfast, in the passageway, the fork in the road of a spent, irremediable past. This is what we say. And this is what we don't. 'But I *chose* this life, didn't I?' she said quietly.

'The elevator halted behind him, and Adi stepped into it somewhat relieved. 'Work hard, you.'

'I will. See you later.'

Rhea watched the lift disappear leaving behind a dank, smoky hollow, then she took a few steps back and leaned against the wall of the foyer.

Over the years she had been with Adi, Rhea had, on innumerable times, caught him watching children—playing in a park, goofing around on the swings and the slide, trekking to school laden with bags bigger than them, clinging on to a parent's hand as they crossed the road. Each time she had felt she was trespassing on an intensely private act; his gaze had been so desperate, so hungry. As these images returned to her mind,

she wondered what their marriage would have been like if they had had children. Perhaps the taut membrane of melancholy that now existed between them would have been absent, perhaps she would never have gone to Chor Bazaar looking for talismans, never met a young photographer with his awkward questions and stunning talent. Perhaps Adi and she would have spent more time together because of the kids, perhaps they would not have gone to the concert later that day because one of their kids would have had a cold and they would have been forced to cancel at the last moment ... She sighed, returning to the present, withdrawing from the gossamer dream of the life she had been denied—or merely not lived so far.

At three-thirty that afternoon Rhea left her house. By four o'clock she was at Crawford Market.

Karan was waiting for her next to a stall selling water chestnuts. 'Hey.'

'Did I make you wait long?'

'Oh, twenty minutes or so.' He wiped the sweat on his forehead.

'You must've reached early.'

'Yes,' he said, grinning, gamely taking on the blame. 'That must have been it.'

They walked ahead, passing dusk-orange mangoes stored in bales of strewn straw and speckled quails screeching from their wire-mesh cages. Lean, cocoa-skinned hawkers volleyed obscenities. Corpulent housewives, sweating like horses, haggled for carrots and peas. A pomegranate seller was having

his ears cleaned by a professional ear cleaner. Two stray dogs were mating ecstatically in a corner, right next to a makeshift garbage dump.

'How's Samar?' Rhea asked.

Karan tried to banish the image that reappeared in his head at the mention of Samar's name. Two days ago, while walking from the pool to the cottage, Samar had suddenly fallen to his knees on the terrazzo, his hands bunched around his navel. Leo had hurried to lift him up but he continued to lie flat on the floor. Karan shook his head as he tried to describe the scene to Rhea.

'He must miss her ... terribly,' she said.

'I guess he's figuring out how much only now.'

'How's Leo taking it?' They walked by a man selling white doves roosting along the length of his arms; she wished Karan would stop and photograph the walking dovecote, but he seemed too preoccupied with Leo and Samar.

'Hard to say, Rhea. I don't know Leo well, and these days I don't want to.'

'You sound like you don't like him much.'

'Leo is not exactly Mr Likeable.' He shrugged his shoulders. 'He says he needs to move back to San Francisco; he fears that Samar and he might be attacked by a mobster from Minister Prasad's mafia.'

'But Samar has to be *here.* His presence at the trial is key.'

'Exactly!'

'Do you suspect a rift between them?'

He rolled his eyes; she was asking him the obvious. 'Everyone has acted shamefully,' he said after a moment. He mentioned the fashion designer who insisted he was out of town even though he had been chatting with Zaira at the time Malik and his buddy from San Jose had entered the bar; this same designer had risen to fame only a few years earlier for putting together Zaira's wardrobe for her appearance at Cannes.

'So how many witnesses does the prosecution have? I mean, outside of Samar.'

'Maybe two,' he said. 'Nalini Chopra and Bunty Oberoi.'

She looked shocked. 'Only two? From a crowd of two hundred?'

'Yes. The world is full of haramis. On the upside, we're lucky D.K. Mishra is with us.'

'Mishra, the investigating officer?' She had read Mishra's name earlier that day in the *Times of India* article; he had pulled up the police about Zaira's dress, missing from the evidence they were supposed to have gathered.

'That's right.'

D.K. Mishra had assured Samar that not only would he pin down more witnesses but also locate the gun registered in Malik's name. The .22 calibre bullets recovered from the crime scene tallied perfectly with the gun Malik owned.

'Does D.K. Mishra know why no one is prepared to testify?'

'Most of the witnesses are scared shitless. And, as I've learned recently myself, there's no witness protection programme in place either.'

'Have you been threatened, Karan?'

'Well, I'm not the only one.'

Her voice rippled with anxiety. 'Has someone called you and said they would attack you?' she asked directly.

'Yes.'

'Oh my God.' She cupped her mouth.

'It's okay.'

'Do you have protection?'

'No. But I'm too insignificant to matter to the case. The police said they can't give me protection.'

'Aren't you afraid for your life?'

'I find myself looking over my shoulder a lot.'

She paused, allowing the seriousness of the situation to sink in. The idea that Karan might be the subject of the minister's ire smote her heart. 'What about the famous guests?' she asked. 'The guys who are too powerful for the minister to bully around?'

'For that lot the case is just not worth the time of day,' he said bluntly. A court case could stretch for any number of years, and it was bound to hamper the lives of those who got involved. 'That leaves us with three people still willing to take the stand. And, of the three, Bunty's evidence is crucial: not only is he the key witness, but he also registered the police complaint. So if Bunty chickens out, the boat,' he said, gesturing with his thumb pointing groundward, 'goes down.'

'Has Bunty done anything to suggest he's not to be trusted?'

'Samar told me Zaira despised him; Bunty was a publicity whore. Maybe he's doing this whole Mr Key Witness number for press points.'

'Aren't you being a little pessimistic?'

'This case doesn't give any of us too much to be optimistic about.'

Perhaps he is confusing cynicism for maturity, she thought to herself; in any event, it took away from his inherent charm. She ran her fingers through her hair, freeing a knot or two; she was uncertain what had changed in Karan but he seemed so removed from the enthusiastic novice shutterbug she had first met in Chor Bazaar. 'Well, at least there's still Nalini Chopra,' she said to raise his spirits.

Karan was about to write off Nalini Chopra as a 'fly-by-night society bimbo' but refrained from doing so because he did not want Rhea to deem his comment another indicator of his deepening pessimism. 'God knows how long she's going to hang in there; at least she has a reason to backtrack.'

'Are you referring to the alcohol licence issue?'

'I am.'

In a desperate rush to usher the crowds from the Bombay Fashion Week to her new bar, Tara Chopra had bypassed the technicality of acquiring a licence to serve alcohol. This rendered both the Chopras, as the owners of Maya Bar, liable for selling booze without a permit; if found guilty, they could land in the lock-up. Although this breach was irrelevant to the

trial, everyone was aware that Minister Prasad could manipulate it to his advantage.

'But maybe Nalini will surprise everyone and stick to what she told the police.'

He laughed bitterly. 'Now let's not get carried away, Rhea.'

'You sound like you're really out of it.' She found his cynicism jarring but decided not to react.

Karan rubbed his bleary eyes. 'I've not been sleeping very well.'

'Are you sleepless because of the threats from Minister Prasad's camp?'

'Perhaps.' He shook his head. 'I still have the pictures I had taken of Zaira when I had gone to Samar's for the shoot. They seemed so happy. Safe. And invincible.'

'How's work?'

'Boring; I don't feel like touching my camera.'

'Maybe its exhaustion ...'

A swarthy hawker knocked against Karan, briefly making him lose his step. He stumbled back, bumping into Rhea, and she propped him up; he felt surprisingly heavy. When he had regained his balance he said, looking at the straw on the ground, 'I've figured out one thing in the last few days.'

'Yes?'

'I'm going to give up photography.'

'What?' She stopped him, her hand on his waist.

'I don't want to continue my work on Bombay.'

'But photographing the city is the reason you're here!'

'I'm just not cut out to be a photographer.'

She scowled. 'I hope this is only a passing phase ...'

'I'm not so sure.' He started to walk again. 'In any case, why are *you* so put off by my decision to quit?'

She gritted her teeth. How easily he had forgotten the hours they had spent discussing his photographs! How easily he had forgotten their trips around the city in search of versions of Bombay! 'Does it have to do with Zaira?'

'It might ...'

'Is it the trial?'

'Maybe.'

'Well, in either case, you can't throw away all your hard work.'

'I've tried, I really have ...'

'Try harder then.'

'Try for a kinder response, Rhea; I just told you my life's busted up.'

'I would have loved to give you a kind response,' she said, 'but I'm just not that kind of person.'

He covered his face with his hands.

They stood together in a square of noisy, hot light filtering through the stained glass pattern in the dome on the airy ceiling.

'I'm sorry.' Her voice softened; she stroked his neck. 'I know Zaira meant a great deal to you. She was a friend, true and solid and kind. So it's important for you to fight through the trial. I also know you're going to have to stand by Samar in

a way you had never anticipated. But,' she said, whispering into his ear, 'no matter *what* happens, you cannot allow the trial to disrupt your work and take over your life. How would Zaira feel if she knew you were giving up on account of *her*?'

The man with the doves on his arms advanced towards them and Rhea stepped back to let him pass. A dove shot into the air, taking off from his arms; its white wings cut the air in sharp, deft strokes.

'There's no point to my work. Nothing I do can or will make any difference.'

'Don't be so downbeat.'

'Thing is, Rhea, every time I look through the aperture ...' He was going to say, *I see Zaira. I see her as I did the first time we met, at Samar's house, as she came running down the lawn and embraced him. I see the Zaira who became my first real friend in Bombay.* But he did not complete the sentence, for Rhea was no longer listening to him. She was, in fact, examining mangoes in a wooden crate. 'I see ... nothing,' he murmured.

'It's an illusion, Karan,' she said when he touched her elbow. 'Enjoy it, fight it, know it, work around the bits that don't cut the ice for you.'

'Please don't go all philosophical on me.'

She looked at him helplessly. His decision to abandon photography had affected her profoundly, and she had retreated into herself. 'What do you think of these mangoes? Should I get a dozen?'

'Huh?' Karan stepped away from her.

The mango vendor was looking at Rhea in earnest.

'I could make a mango and cream cake.' She was thinking of Adi's love for mangoes. She turned to the mango vendor. 'How much for six?'

'Madam, three hundred rupees.'

'Don't be ridiculous! A hundred and fifty.'

'Madam, my purchase price is two hundred and seventy-five,' the vendor pleaded.

'My last offer is two hundred.' She looked at the man with narrowed eyes. He surrendered. She picked six mangoes and he gave them to her in a brown paper bag in exchange for two hundred-rupee notes.

Karan looked baffled. 'You're thinking of baking a cake when I'm telling you that Malik Prasad could walk free?'

'Yes, it's a terrible pity.' But Karan heard no pity in her voice.

'Everything is *not* an illusion. For all the illusions in this world, there are also facts.'

She folded the mouth of the paper bag. 'Oh,' she said, her tone strikingly mordant. 'Wow!'

'Because a truth is a private experience and a fact is public knowledge. Malik shot Zaira, that's a fact. Samar loved Zaira, that's the truth. You can take apart the truth but you can't argue with a fact.' He paused, wiped the sweat over his lip. 'Did you hear a word of what I just said?'

'You're very wise, Karan. And ... honourable and ...' She felt short of breath just being around him; she was not going to mother him.

'And?'

'And now,' she said, 'I have to go.'

'Already?'

'I have to be some place else.'

'Can't you stay for a bit?'

'I'm afraid not.'

'I'm going through hell, Rhea.'

'Well, I have an appointment with a clay seller in Kumbharwada at five.'

She did not flinch at her second fabrication of the day, for if she did go to Kumbharwada she would be absolved of the lie she had told Adi.

He could tell from her steely expression that she had made up her mind to leave. 'I'll walk you to your car.'

'Don't you have to be at work?'

'I'll head to the office in a while.'

Negotiating oily wheelbarrows of mud-splattered carrots and huge mounds of succulent watermelon, they returned to the parking lot without exchanging another word. As they neared her car, she turned to him, shielding her eyes with her hand over her brows, 'Well, it was good to see you.'

He was taken aback; she was talking to him as if he were just another friend. He half expected her to add something on the lines of 'Well, keep in touch' or 'Let's catch up over lunch some time'.

'I'm sorry if I bored you back there,' he said awkwardly.

'You never photographed Crawford Market, did you?' Her face was curious, but only inches beneath her curiosity scurried a tremendous regret; she could already hear his answer.

'I never did—and now, I suppose, I never will.' Karan got a sinking feeling in his stomach and he leaned against her car.

She got in.

He was consumed with the fear that they would never meet again: once he had forsaken photography what excuse would they have to meet? She would have no reason to take him to Sewri, none to visit the chapels in Bandra or the caves of Kanheri.

'If there was a storm,' he asked her, 'and I knocked on your door, would you take me in?'

Rolling down the glass she said, 'Well, storms are tricky.' In her voice he heard a train departing its station.

Several hours after her brief stop at Crawford Market and her subsequent trip to the clay vendor in Kumbharwada, Rhea sat on the stool before her dressing table trying to tighten an exasperatingly loose gold earring; she was terrified the earring, a family heirloom, would fall and get lost amid the crowd at Ban Ganga. A smart coat of mascara had made her eyelashes, already long and curled, all the more stark and feline. Priming her lips, she removed all traces of excess lipstick. She assumed she was ready, that she could face the crowds at the music festival.

She presented herself before the mirror.

Studying the reflection she experienced a familiar pang of discomfort: She did not know the woman looking back at

her. But perhaps her discomfort really stemmed from the fact that she knew the woman in the mirror only too well, and her undeclared particulars were not all that flattering. Who was she then? A wife? A potter? A traitor? She questioned the ease with which she went from wife to lover to wife, slipping in and out of the roles as if exchanging one pair of shoes for another. Guilt made her want to flee her home, its marital stipulations, the adolescent, societal impositions on the human heart. Most of all, she wanted to flee the heart itself, its intractable ability to love variously, heroically, idiotically.

She knew that to try to come to terms with what had transpired between Karan and herself was like trying to catch a fish with one's bare hands. She believed that at the onset she had been genuinely taken with his work, and so she had chosen to show him around town. But when exactly did their friendship evolve into something larger, ineluctably dangerous, beyond definition? Surely it had not started when she had slipped on the staircase and he had gripped her, and they had united on the landing, struggling in the agony of lust. Such transgressions were all too easy to commit, and they did not result in the complicated pacts formed when people engaged the unlit portion of another soul. She did not know the exact moment, the hour or the day, when her feelings for Karan had spiralled out of her control and taken her hostage. She leaned closer toward the mirror. She could not believe her eyes. The woman gazing back at her was guilty of the final betrayal in love: she had surrendered her own self.

This realization filled her with an overpowering rage.

Taking a deep breath, Rhea resolved that she would not let the tumult of her feelings interfere with the evening ahead. Composing herself, she looked into the mirror again. This time, her inspection was superficial: she cringed at her reflection. In spite of the gorgeous guava-green silk sari, the ancestral kundan necklace around her slender neck, she was plain; at most, *comely*. She stood up and surveyed herself critically. Oh, she was hopeless, she was pathetic; she was far from perfect; she had chosen the wrong sari. As if to rescue her from the eddy of her insecurities, Adi emerged from the bathroom and whistled admiringly when he saw her. She blushed, his whistle like alchemy: what the mirror had established as ordinary was now transformed, before her very own eyes, into dramatic magnetism.

'I'm going to have to keep an eye on you.' His arms enveloped her from behind and he buried his face in her neck.

'No one would give me a second glance.'

'We're going to need security to keep them from you; I'm going to have to call in the commandos!'

When Adi straightened, and stood as upright as Karan did, she felt as if both men were watching over her.

'Yeah, yeah,' she said, waving her hand before his awestruck face. 'How else will you stave off the millions of imaginary fans?'

At Ban Ganga, after locating a clean stone ledge of some vantage to sit on, they waited for the Sufi singer to take the stage. Rhea's thoughts wandered back to the concert the year

before: Hariprasad Chaurasia had played the flute, and they had been so lost in his poignant, smooth recital of Raga Desh that the night had faded, the stars had faded, the crowds had faded, and she and Adi had been left together as guardians of each other's solitude. Tonight, in her husband's company, she felt adorned, and adored—so much so that if she were to meet Karan she would find it impossible to recognize him. She was deeply involved in her role of Mrs Adi Dalal; she was like an actor on stage, completely sold to her character, running on the fuel of an imaginative sympathy that burned down the subtle but significant divide between reality and performance.

Gradually, as voices hushed and the lights dimmed, leaving only the raised platform illuminated, the faint strains of the instruments being strummed and tuned floated out over the water. Fateh Khan, who had been sitting cross-legged with his head bowed, now looked up and faced his eager audience, humming a fine, unwieldy tune to himself. Hardly had he started on a song written by Bulla Shah than Rhea found unbidden tears pressing at her eyes; her head seemed to spin with the rising fervour of the music, the mesmeric rhythm, the timeless, fire-stroked words extolling love, its madness, its retreat, and its awful wound. The singer's voice was like the wing of a bird pressed against her black heart. Rhea wondered how she—devious, impatient, made of flesh and bone, an edifice of mortality—could hold so much emotion that she feared she might burst from it. Maybe *that* was the point of having children: to distribute what might no longer be held in oneself.

In which case she was not, she would have to concede, an edifice of mortality but a sheet of music fashioned for reprise.

And Adi's desire for a child, an heir, was more than just the clamour of male vanity.

As the singer's voice opened up like the flames of a fire, she glanced at Adi's enrapt face. Briefly, she looked up, searching for Karan's room, his balcony. What if she saw him now? What she shared with Adi was rare and fundamental, a kind of oxygen, without which she simply would not exist. Karan, on the other hand, had been helium, and he had made her weightless, taken her higher, released her from the awful apathy of everyday existence. The sadness Karan had experienced at giving up his work filled her now, belatedly, making her choke. Without his camera, his world was unlit with either beauty or horror; it was in despair and pathetically mundane. Adi put his hand on her shoulder, but the tears continued to roll down her cheeks, a dark sediment of grief having broken out of her, its exodus illuminated only by the glow of music.

In the car on their way home she said, 'Why did you get me fireflies that evening, Adi?'

He was surprised; he had been remembering the fireflies when he had woken that morning, and now she was asking about them.

'Right after we started going out you kept telling me you dreamed of fireflies. You said you had talked to your father about what the dreams meant and he had connected them with some aspect of your childhood. When I asked you for details of

his analysis you clammed up. I didn't probe. But you continued to complain that you were unable to sleep when you dreamed of them. I wanted to give you some so the dreams would stop, so you would be free.'

She kept disappointment out of her expression; she had been expecting a far more cerebral reason, on the lines that the fireflies had been symbolic of something. But a few moments later, studying his face intently, she was moved by the profound simplicity of his pure and vigorous concern.

'I just wanted you to sleep deeply, Rhea.' He pressed on the pedal of the car. 'And for you to wake rested.'

She gazed out of the window.

Bombay was a different beast at midnight. She saw the stall of a paanwalla with glossy clusters of heart-shaped vein-green leaves and papyrus foils of silver; she saw a monkey pedlar goofing around with his pet. On Warden Road she turned to face Adi, whose eyes were firmly on the road; she felt unreasonably lucky and safe.

She raised her hand to her ear; the earring was loose again, and she tightened it deftly.

Family gold ought never to be lost.

14

ON THE MORNING OF HIS APPEARANCE IN COURT, Bunty Oberoi was the centre of all attention. The key witness in the trial looked dashing in his drainpipe pants and a black linen, lapelled blazer. His muscular build and cavalier smile strengthened the impression that only the truth might ever leave his lips, as if dishonesty were somehow the prerogative of ugliness.

Once he had taken oath his initial statement was read out to him, the deposition that clearly indicted Malik Prasad as Zaira's murderer. When the prosecution lawyer, Gautam Vakil, was called upon to question him, Bunty began to answer him in clumsy, half-broken Hindi.

Samar strained forward to hear Bunty, who was sounding like someone being made to speak in Hindi for the first time.

While answering the second question, Bunty paused, turned to the judge and asked if he could continue in English, a request to which the judge consented. Gautam Vakil then asked him to verify his statement to the police, which had just been read out before the court.

'But the report was recorded in Hindi,' said the actor.

'That's correct.' The lawyer tilted his head. 'What does it matter?'

'Oh, it matters—a great deal.' Bunty's tongue smacked over his lips a few times, as if they had become numb. Although he had just snorted a line of coke a few minutes earlier in the sanctuary of the stinking toilet, it had failed to put him at ease, as it usually did.

Samar, waiting for his turn to take the stand, felt his heart cave in; his fingers tightened their hold on Leo's wrist. He looked at Karan, who had got the drift of things, and was ruefully shaking his head.

Bunty said confidently, 'You see, I don't follow a word of Hindi. When the police had interrogated me on the night of the murder, they'd asked me questions in Hindi. I agreed with what they were saying because I was in shock. Also, I wasn't sure any one of *them* could speak English. So they recorded my statement in Hindi and I signed in good faith. Later, it was re-read to me. In translation, in English. That's when I knew they had recorded something I hadn't said.'

The judge rapped his gavel to hush the shocked murmurs.

Karan glanced at Samar but Samar was staring blankly at the floor, his mouth slightly open.

'Are you saying the statement you gave the police is false?' Gautam Vakil said slowly.

'Not at all,' the actor said. 'What I'm saying is that the statement the police recorded is false. They recorded my statement in Hindi. When they read it out to me, it was in Hindi. How could I verify it one way or the other since I don't understand the language?'

'In that case, why did you agree with it at the time?'

'I had no choice! The police were forceful. I was helpless. I felt cornered. I signed the statement in a state of complete shock.'

'So, Mr Oberoi,' Gautam Vakil went on, 'can you please tell the court what you *did* see on that night at Maya Bar?'

'It was very dark,' Bunty said. 'There was a crowd of about two hundred people. At around one-thirty in the morning, when the last drinks had been served, two men entered the bar. I went to get some ice from the kitchen. Although cigarette smoke had obscured my view when I returned, I could see one of the men in silhouette, dressed in a white shirt and jeans. This man shot in the air, at the ceiling. Then, someone else came up from behind him and shot Zaira. She collapsed and Nalini Chopra came running to my side. Before long, Samar Arora ran in. When Zaira lost consciousness Samar pulled her on to his lap.'

'Who was the man who shot Zaira, Mr Oberoi?'

Bunty looked at his feet. 'It was impossible to see clearly.'

'Could you identify Malik Prasad as Zaira's murderer?' Gautam Vakil pointed to Malik, seated beside his lawyer, Vijay Singh. 'That's what your police statement indicates.'

'I've already told you my statement was recorded in a language I do not understand.' Bunty looked at Malik and then at the judge. 'I've never seen Malik Prasad before.'

'Are you certain it was not Malik Prasad?'

'Objection, Your Honour.' Vijay Singh stood up now. 'The prosecution is trying to intimidate the witness.'

'Sustained.'

'Who, then, was the assailant?'

'It was too dark to identify the man in question,' repeated Bunty, his voice rising.

'We cannot hold you to the first information report you gave the police?'

'Of course not! How can you hold me to a report recorded in a language that I do not understand! I don't know a word of bloody Hindi!'

The judge glared at the model. 'Mr Oberoi, do *not* shout in my court.'

Two days after Bunty Oberoi's outrageous revelation had taken up the front-page headlines in all the leading dailies, D.K. Mishra, the investigating officer in charge of Zaira's case, lay in bed next to his wife.

'It's okay,' Rupa Mishra said. 'We don't *have* to.'

'But I *want* to.'

'You must be tired.'

'It's the weekend, Rupa!'

'Stress?' She jerked his willy, so embarrassingly limp it was like a strand of beached seaweed. 'It's the bloody case!' She sat up and covered her breasts with her sweaty fingers. 'You haven't been the same since this investigation started.'

'I'm sorry ...' He pressed a pillow over his crotch.

'When will it be over?'

'Please don't sound *so* frustrated, Rupa.'

'Do you have any idea how tough this case is getting to be on *me*?'

'You think this is a joyride for me? Do you have *any* idea how many calls I have to field every day about this bloody case?'

She asked him who was on the dial.

Calls from the press, he said; from his superiors; from Minister Prasad.

'Will they ever nail the killer?'

He threw his hands up in the air as if to say: What is there to nail?

She lay down and drew the green chequered sheet over her perspiring nakedness. 'All right then, is he going to get away?'

'Malik Prasad is not a bad sort; I don't see CRIMINAL plastered on his forehead.'

'Even if Malik is not a bad sort,' Rupa said in a tone generally reserved for castigating cocker spaniel puppies with toilet-training troubles, 'the fact that he shot a woman in the head makes him one *very* crazy man, don't you think?'

'I also get calls from the Hindu People's Party,' Mishra grumbled. 'Those rascals in Delhi are terrified this scandal will screw them in the next elections.'

A few days earlier, Ram Dube, head of the forensics department, had called Mishra and reminded him that according to the findings of his department, the bullets had been shot from two different guns. Lowering his voice, Dube asked him why he had failed to consider the possibility of two assailants being present at Maya Bar that night, thus unwittingly confirming that he was in collusion with Minister Prasad.

'They found a way to bugger the forensic report as well.'

Rupa pressed her body against her husband's. 'How much influence does the forensic report have on the case?'

Mishra said that the minister's scheme to acquit his son relied on establishing the presence of two assailants with the same gun at Maya Bar. This would beef up the defence lawyer's theory that, along with Malik, an unidentified man was at the venue—and this second man had shot Zaira.

'I see. And so the defence is trying to establish that the unidentified man is Zaira's murderer.'

'That's right.'

'What an evil little plot! This will give an entirely different twist to the case.'

'And now, even Bunty Oberoi has gone back on his original deposition.' He tugged himself free of his wife's sweaty grasp.

'Didn't he say in court there were two men at Maya Bar?'

'Yes—and that connects perfectly with the two guns-two assailants theory.'

'Why did Bunty do a turnaround in the witness box?'

'He's bought an apartment on Bandra Bandstand.'

'So?'

'Can you explain how a total nobody like Bunty Oberoi lands a sea-facing apartment worth almost four crore?' he said crossly.

She wondered just how much the minister had actually paid Bunty. 'Hmmm. But why did the judge buy Bunty Oberoi's me-no-speak-Hindi act?'

'Who knows?' Mishra yawned, wishing his wife would stop with the questions.

'But Bunty has spoken in Hindi in his films, D.K. Doesn't that go against him?'

'It can go against him *if* the judge wants it to.' He had begun to worry that the Limp Dick Syndrome was for keeps.

'He probably speaks a dozen dialects of Hindi.'

'We have records of Bunty's school education in Hindi. He studied Hindi up to the eighth standard.'

'And the judge won't take that into account?'

'I guess not.'

'But there are two other witnesses still left, ne?'

'If Malik's father managed to break Bunty what makes you think he can't take out the other two?'

'But you said Samar Arora is tough, and unlikely to crumble under pressure.'

'The minister will find a way to crack him like an egg.'

'So that leaves the socialite.'

'Nalini Chopra and her daughter did not have a liquor licence for Maya Bar. I recently got a note from higher-ups saying that I should investigate this lapse.'

She sighed. So now her husband's bosses too were in cahoots with Minister Prasad.

'The idea is to keep Nalini Chopra in line,' he added. 'They want to scare her. If she back-pedals on her statement, it throws another witness out of the ring. These are all ploys to distract from the real issue, the murder, and focus attention on the peripherals. If the defence drags the case for years, witnesses will slacken, the prosecution lawyer might lose hope, judges will get transferred. A pity, though, if Tara Chopra is thrown in prison for serving booze without a licence.' He snorted like a pig. 'What a waste of a good woman!'

'You seem to care a lot about this Tara Chopra.' Rupa Mishra suspected that if he was no longer attracted to her it was because he had been spending time with fancy folks from the fashion fraternity.

'No ... no ... It's nothing like that ...'

Earlier that week D.K. Mishra had called Tara Chopra in for questioning. After the interrogation, impressed with her tube top and fitted leggings, he had eyeballed her one moment too long and she had stormed off in a huff. He recalled now that a word—WHATEVER—had been emblazoned in tiny letters on the front of her tube top.

'How many times have you questioned Tara Chopra?' Rupa asked her husband combatively.

'A few times.'

'How many times?' she thundered.

'Cool it, Rupa. She must have come in two or three times.'

'Well, I hope you've got your answers and you don't have to call the whore in for questioning again.'

'If you think I'm being defensive about her it's only because she doesn't deserve to suffer for no real fault of her own. Picture her in some stinking jail. A butch skinhead Nigerian pedlar hissing at her: *Gimme some of that Page 3 pussy!*'

After many weeks, both of them laughed heartily. The tension in their bed lifted for a few minutes.

When they sobered down a little, D.K. Mishra turned to his wife, wiping tears from the corners of his eyes, and said, 'The minister wants me to get rid of one more piece of evidence.'

'What's that?'

'When the police questioned Malik for the first time they broke him. He had confessed to the murder.'

'So, what more do you need to nail him?'

'It's not that simple, Rupa. For any confession to hold in court it has to be recorded before a magistrate. Only then does it qualify as legal evidence.'

'Are you saying that the CD containing Malik's confession is not admissible evidence?'

'Yes—because it was not recorded before a magistrate.'

'Why didn't the police record it before a magistrate, then?'

'I think they forgot.'

'They forgot!'

He looked at her and curled his lips. Why on earth was she screaming like a witch being burnt at the stake?

'So what will this CD achieve?' Disappointment tolled through her voice like a church bell; her faith in the weird workings of Indian law was about as strong as her faith in her husband's dick.

'It could potentially sway the judge in favour of a guilty verdict—even if this CD doesn't count, per se, as evidence. Besides, can you imagine if the press ever got their hands on it?'

'Will you destroy the CD?'

'That would be wrong.'

'Then what is the right thing to do?'

The right thing to do. He thought that was the primmest thing he had ever heard. He was silent for a few minutes. He had been in talks with Minister Prasad; initially the interactions had been pleasant but when he had resisted the minister's offers, the minister had threatened to have him transferred. However, D.K. Mishra was in no mood to tell the resident nymphomaniac a word of this.

'Let's just go to bed.'

'Well, yes, of course; there's only sleep for you and me now.'

'Don't be a bitch!' he roared.

She countered in an equally loud voice: 'Then tell me you'll share the CD with the prosecution.'

'Probably not ... I'm tired now, Rupa. Let's just sleep.'

'I understand.'

'I'm not a weak man.'

'I know that.'

'By the way, Rupa, have you put on some more weight?'

'If anything, I've reduced!' She was outraged. 'Now, good night and sweet dreams!'

'Good night then,' he said dejectedly.

After ten minutes, a whisper lunged at him. 'I love you, no matter ...'

D.K. Mishra wanted to punch his wife. Instead, he pretended he was asleep. He could not stop marvelling at how easily he could go from loving her to loathing her.

15

THE INSTANT MRS PRASAD HEARD HER HUSBAND put out a call to Judge Kumar, she left the living room. An army of wild green grasshoppers had laid siege to the veranda. Dazed by the almost apocalyptic presence of the insects, she froze. The grasshoppers leapt and whirred around her, on her, leaving behind a sticky deposit on her skin.

Retreating toward the wall she closed her eyes.

Her mind slid back to the year after Malik's birth, when she had discovered she was pregnant again.

Waking one afternoon from her slumber she had found her young, ambitious husband in a terrific rage; he had lost a round of local elections. Later that day, he beat her black and blue. Early next morning the foetus, six months and nine days old, had left her body in a rush of blood and thick,

sticky brown fluid. Unable to deal with the abortion he had caused, the minister had fled the family home and hid for two months in his farmhouse in Haryana. Upon his return, he had been mellow, cajoling, attentive even, and one night, in a hysterical sobbing fit, pleaded for her forgiveness. Just when she had begun to hope her marriage could be saved, he tried to console her saying she should not feel too bad about the loss of the child: It had been a girl. His exact words—*it was just as well*—had haunted her ever after, and she had pulled back into herself like one of those exotic caged animals that possess all the characteristics for which they are duly prized, but defeated by incarceration and by their captors are no longer truly alive.

Malik's trial had brought Mrs Prasad to life again: the blatant lack of interest in her, following her son's escapade, had reconfirmed her remarkable insignificance. Not a single journalist had asked Mrs Prasad what it was like to be a murderer's mother; this was just as well because she suspected that her answer would have terrified them. Malik was innocent, she would have said. Of course, she did not think for a moment that Malik had *not* shot Zaira, but he was innocent in spite of it. A mother, after all, could be senseless with love, and what she would call innocent was a life that *could* have been chaste but for the violations inflicted upon it. She would never know how Malik would have turned out if he had not been fathered by Minister Prasad; perhaps he would have been a murderer nonetheless, but the idea that he might have had another, cleaner life saddened and thrilled her in equal measure.

During the uproar of the trial the one person she had most wanted to meet was Samar. She had no idea about Samar's private life; she had assumed him to be Zaira's lover. As she imagined Samar's rage and dejection, she was subsumed with awe, not only because he had been brave enough to love but braver still to stand up and fight for what that love *now* meant. She was desperate to meet Samar, to sit down with him and apologize for what could not be atoned for. She did not feel any less loyal to Malik; if anything, the tired wing of her being could extend over Samar and draw him into its sanctuary. After all, Samar had been vandalized by the same man who had vandalized Malik and her, and although she lacked the sophistication to convey either her guilt or an apology, her hurt was deep enough to give both men shelter.

Over the last few months Mrs Prasad had heard her husband talk to D.K. Mishra, the investigating officer, on several occasions. She had overheard one particular discussion that had started off cordially but ended in a roar and a holler: her husband had offered D.K. Mishra a 'gift', but the investigating officer had declined. The minister had got increasingly upset and as he yelled obscenities into the phone he had threatened not only to have D.K. Mishra transferred but also to get his wife raped. Mrs Prasad felt bad for D.K. Mishra: if he had embarked on the investigation believing he would have the culprit punished, then a single phone call from her husband was good enough to make him change his mind. D.K. Mishra would have gathered from the grapevine why no witness was prepared to come forward,

and also of the loot Bunty Oberoi had made for himself. It was wise to side with the minister because the evidence had been skewed from the start, the police had bungled on gathering evidence, and the witnesses had been bought over. If D.K. Mishra rallied on, he would go down alone on a sinking ship; in fact, Mrs Prasad was afraid for him, for she knew her husband well enough to believe he would make good on all his threats.

No wonder she felt she was watching two trials unfold: one public, and publicly discussed, fuelled by the media's naive fury and the public's castrated shock; the other private, and privately fought, entirely of her husband's creation and under his control. In moments of fancy she imagined that *she* had the guts to reach out to the press or ankle it over to the courthouse and reveal that her husband had rigged the case beyond recall. However, she quickly put such wild thoughts out of her head, knowing that she would pay for such indiscretion with her life.

As the insects slowly retreated from her body, as the whirring and flapping paled and passed, she overheard her husband talking to the judge.

'What a wonderful day for us to connect!' Minister Prasad assured Judge Kumar.

'Is it?' The sessions court judge, who had served as a lawyer for thirteen years before his current tenure, was not used to high-profile ministers calling him at home.

'Our families are connected, you do remember? Your sister's mother-in-law and my mother were best friends in school.'

He sighed; was there a point to this Rotary function rubbish? 'Minister Prasad, I'm about to leave for a family function. How can I help you?'

The judge's response raised the minister's hackles, but he knew it was not yet time to throw his weight around. 'Oh, Judge-saab, I'm so sorry to have caught you at a bad time.'

'It is not a bad time,' he said. 'I'm just, well, busy.'

'I completely understand.'

'You were saying?'

'Well, as you know the Congress Party has long been in contest with the Hindu People's Party.'

'Yes.'

'And they've used every dirty card in the pack to malign the HPP.'

'Mr Prasad, I really don't have the time for a lecture on the history of the antagonism between the Congress Party and the Hindu People's Party ...'

'This is *not* a lecture!'

'I'm sure it's not news to you that the Congress Party has already been blamed for the Partition riots of 1947, the rise in the price of onions, the rings of Saturn and the drought in Kutch. The party has quite a cross to bear, wouldn't you say?'

'The Congress Party is the bane of modem India,' the minister said, oblivious to the sarcasm dripping from the judge's voice. 'But we don't really need to talk about the Congress Party. I had called to tell you that I feel *aw*ful that a man of your excellent calibre should be stuck in a lowly sessions court.

However, I understand that you are busy. We shall speak on a better day.'

'No, that's quite all right,' Judge Kumar said hurriedly. The minister had sized up his situation perfectly, for few things were more depressing to the judge than the day-to-day drudgery of the trial court. 'How is it that you know how I feel about working at the trial courts?'

'Word gets around, as you know.'

'I'm sure.'

'Besides, you're also looking into the murder case of that item girl.'

'Zaira.'

'And unfortunately ...'

'I know, I know.' The judge smiled to himself; the minister's pathetic charade was coming apart, his true intention laid bare.

'But I am not calling you about the Zaira case.'

'Oh, I'm sure you're not.'

When he was nervous, Minister Chander Prasad had a habit of scratching his balls so savagely that his pubic lice experienced multiple orgasms. 'Many of us here in Delhi are concerned about your promotion to your rightful position.'

'Who are these "many" in Delhi?'

'The people in power, who make things happen,' he said mysteriously. 'Well, I'm convinced that when they get to know you're doing an excellent job, a promotion to the high court will be inevitable.' He continued to scratch himself, though his voice remained even.

'You believe that, do you?'

'I am certain of it! And from the high court, who can stop you from rising?'

'One can only hope,' the judge said shyly.

'But if you don't speed up a verdict in the Zaira case ...'

'Hmm.'

'I understand your position,' Minister Prasad consoled. 'The police are dragging their heels. The media is having a field day because some starlet had her brains blown up. But the burden is on *you* to smoothen the course of justice. Because,' he added, his voice suddenly taking on a menacing tone, 'the longer this case drags on, the longer you'll be stuck in trial court. Zaira's murder trial could turn into the millstone around your neck. And there are still two witnesses left to take the stand ...'

'Well, a logical conclusion is likely to come about in due course.'

'Before that happens I must warn you about Samar Arora.'

Judge Kumar's ears perked up. 'The pianist? Zaira's close friend. One of the witnesses. What about him?'

'Oh, he's not as innocent as he seems.'

'Is that so?'

Minister Prasad sighed. 'How can we have this conversation without compromising on our basic human decency? What I'm about to tell you, Judge-saab, is perverse ... perhaps we should let it go ...'

'No, no, do go on. Tell me.'

'It's sickening! An insult to Indian culture, an abomination of our values.'

'Please, Minister Prasad, just speak your mind!'

'Well, it's best to tell it like it is. I understand Samar Arora is having it off with a man.'

'You mean—'

'An affair.'

'Say nothing further, Minister Prasad.'

'I'm sorry to have spoiled your evening with such news.'

'But you were quite right to tell me.'

'I had to; it was my moral duty.'

In a quiet voice, the judge asked, 'But how can you be so sure that once I *do* expedite a verdict in this case, the high court bench will come through?'

'Oh, Judge Kumar!' The minister felt triumphant almost, confident that his latest victim had bitten the bait. 'Didn't I tell you we're family friends? Let me remind you that in Delhi we are admiring your progress as a judge. A great man like you, of such a high calibre, *has* to go up to the next level. Why don't you call on us when you are in town again, Judge Kumar.'

'It's unlikely I'll be in Delhi any time soon.'

'It's equally unlikely I will be in Bombay,' Minister Prasad snapped, 'but that hasn't stopped me from helping *you.*'

'You've helped me?'

'Not *yet.*'

'Let me give you my mobile number,' the judge said quickly. It seemed foolish to give grief to the man who could give his career one of its biggest boosts.

'I'd be glad to have it.'

'Next time, please call me on my mobile.'

'Discretion is my middle name, Judge Kumar. Once you are promoted to the high court, it will be a suitable occasion for me—a humble servant of the Indian masses—to come to Bombay and congratulate you in person.'

'I look forward to that very much.' The words escaped the judge's mouth involuntarily, like a premature ejaculation.

16

A WEEK BEFORE SHE WAS TO TESTIFY IN COURT, Nalini Chopra's phone rang just as she was leaving for a direly needed touch-up job to keep the blonde streaks in her hair intact.

She did not make it for her salon appointment. Instead, twenty minutes later, she was on her way to meet her daughter at the Taj Mahal Hotel's Library Bar, a hastily arranged rendezvous to confer on the latest development in her life.

'How did that slimeball get hold of you?' Tara Chopra, thin as a rail, with her mother's bedroom eyes, looked stunning in a calf-length denim skirt and a beige leather jacket.

'He was quite clever; he rang on my cellphone.' Their landlines were under police scrutiny.

Tara sipped at the double Scotch she had ordered. 'I hear he's pure *evil*.'

'He was actually quite polite, beta.'

'But he's, like, this politician. And he's from *Delhi* or something!'

Nalini Chopra gazed philosophically into her brandy snifter. The minister had said that if she denied in court that Malik had been present at Maya Bar on the night of the murder, he could help her by making the police forget about the bar's missing liquor licence.

This was no small matter. If they were convicted, mother and daughter would end up in the slammer themselves, giving a whole new twist to the term 'jailbird'.

'I can't believe the hell we're going through!' Tara twirled her hair with her fingers. 'All because some chick was shot in my bar.'

'I know, baby,' her mother purred. 'I know.'

'I mean, it was a party, for God's sake. People get drunk. Stuff happens, y'know what I mean? This is life. And life is beautiful and twisted. You gotta take the good with the bad.'

'Of course.' Nalini Chopra toyed nervously with the bead necklace around her haggard neck.

'It's so unfair for the police to go after *us*. And not one person has come forward to defend *us*!'

'Now it's you and me against the whole cruel world, Mummy!'

'These two-faced high society scumbags give brown trash a bad name! As for that scoundrel Bunty Oberoi ...'

'Oh, don't say a word about Bunty ...'

'If he'd stuck to his statement, we wouldn't be in this mess. His word would have been enough to carry the case through and we would not be in such a vulnerable position.'

'Well, maybe not ...' Tara had quite a crush on him. He had walked the ramp for one of her shows and she had gone down on him only a few months ago, during the Delhi Fashion Week. 'But he's kinda cute.'

Nalini Chopra sniffed, not quite sure what being cute had to do with any of this.

'You remember, Mummy,' her daughter was saying, 'how I passed out as soon as I saw Zaira lying dead on the floor?'

'You were in shock, beta. It was only natural; you've always been a sensitive girl.'

'And to think that now we're being treated like petty criminals! Like, HELLO!' she said, pointing her index finger in the air. 'There's no justice in this world.' Her voice was wobbly with emotion, like a hippo on stilettos. Then, suddenly, she lowered her voice. 'Mummy, I need to tell you something totally important.'

Nalini Chopra leaned forward. 'Yes?'

'Mummy ...'

'Yes, Tara?'

'*Bum* that fuckin' dress.'

Nalini Chopra looked as if she'd suffered a stroke. 'Surely, my outfit isn't all *that* last season already?

'And there's enough kohl under your eyes for an entire republic of racoons!'

'Tara!'

'I mean it.'

'I'm your mother, for God's sake.' She downed her drink. 'And you *cannot* speak to me like that under *any* circumstance.'

'Well, it's for your own good. Have you seen your pictures in the papers lately?' Tara decided to lay out her case. 'I'm a fashion designer, Mummy. And a fairly famous one, if I might say so myself. Now, if my own mother looks like some sort of thrift-store Thumbelina, d'you know how it'll screw up *my* image?'

'It's very hurtful that you think of me like that.'

'Why does everything have to be about *you*?' Tara proceeded to give her mother a fashion tip—why did she not wear a sheer tulle scarf around her head for a touch of the suffragette? She *direly* needed sympathy points from the press.

'Never mind your silly fashion tips, Tara!' Nalini scolded. 'I'm here to talk about something far more critical.'

'Oh, whatever!'

'I'm completely out of it,' she pleaded. 'Can you please go easy on me?'

'All right, all right. Talk to me about Minister Prasad.' She kicked off her mules and tapped her cigarette against the edge of the table; the ash fell on the carpet. 'Isn't he responsible for Bunty's change of heart on the witness stand?'

'I heard that Bunty's selling price was four crore.'

'Cool. A million dollars will buy him enough charlie to float for a few years.' She rapped her knuckles on the table. 'So, what have you decided to say in court?'

She said that Minister Prasad had reminded her that she and her daughter were single women, and in a city like Bombay, well, anything could happen to them. Someone, for instance, might throw acid on their faces one morning; someone could even climb into their bedrooms at night and rape them. This was a big, fat lie, but Nalini Chopra felt the need to punish her daughter for the vicious comments she had been subjected to.

'Did he actually say those things?' Tara Chopra felt her knees turn to jelly.

Nalini Chopra nodded like a woodpecker working on its nest.

'Will you tell the court you saw Malik at Maya Bar that night?'

'Should I?'

'I mean,' she said haltingly, 'that's the truth, isn't it?'

Nalini Chopra rolled her eyes. 'Truth is *such* a subjective matter. The truth, according to you, is that I'm a fashion disaster. But someone else might think of me as a fashion icon.'

Tara touched her mother's hand. 'I'm sorry. Was I being a bitch? I've had the mother of all Mondays doing business with a beastly bunch of billionaires from Bahrain.'

'That's okay, beta.' She smiled heroically. 'I've been through so much already—what makes you think I cannot bear this?'

'Well, Mummy, I've also had an equally tough life and then today this fat—and I'm talkin' baby hippo here—woman walks into my store and says that she can't fit into any of my clothes, and I just wanted to slap her. Instead, I told myself to calm

down. I told myself: she's not fat; she's two people. I guess what I'm trying to say is that there's more than one way of looking at any situation, and if I can find my inner peace that way then why can't you do the same with this stupid trial?'

'Well, the chubby boy I saw that night looked *somewhat* like Malik Prasad.'

'But then you had on that really rad pair of Gucci shades.' Tara had finally found one redeeming quality about her mother's ghastly get-up. 'At least you had one thing going for you.'

Nalini Chopra asserted they were, indeed, her favourite pair of sunglasses. 'The gorgeous Mr Gucci gave them to me in Milan.'

'Then it's possible you might've mistaken Malik for someone else—thanks to Gucci.'

'Don't you think that poor boy deserves the benefit of the doubt?'

'I guess people *are* turning Malik into some kind of a punching bag, aren't they? What if *your* evidence clinched the wrong guy?'

'Exactly! It would be *so* cruel if Malik went to jail for a crime he didn't commit.'

'That would be the height of injustice. We're all mortal, Mummy, and we all make mistakes.' Tara gestured to the waiter for a repeat of drinks before reassigning her eyes on her mother. 'You could have screwed up in the identification

parade. Besides, all boys, after you've had a few, look the same.' She gave a naughty grin.

'Yes, I guess there is a grain of truth in that.'

'Well, you might also like to know what Guru-ji says ...'

In recent times Tara had come to rely on the counsel of a spiritual leader who wore long, flowing red robes, maintained a wiry, sagacious white beard and had become renowned for helping politicians win elections by giving them secret mantras to chant at dawn in their birthday suits.

'Go on, beta, enlighten me.'

'Guru-ji says that everything is destined, it's all written in the lines of one's hands. Maybe Zaira was fated to drop her mortal coil ... It was her karmic path, really.'

'But why look at death as a limiting condition?' Nalini Chopra argued on the grounds of her newly discovered passion for theology. 'I mean, isn't she bound to be reborn?'

'No way!' Tara thumped her hand on the table. 'I had a long one-on-one session with Guru-ji and he assured me Zaira was an Advanced Soul. Her brutal murder was only a means for her to work out a big backlog of karma. But because of the shootout she's now eternally free.'

'Are you saying ...' The socialite's mouth fell open.

'You got it!' Tara declared. 'The N-word, mother. Zaira nailed it way sooner than any of us. Who'd have thunk, huh?'

'But that's fantastic news, Tara!' Nalini Chopra looked thunderstruck. *Nirvana,* she repeated to herself with a tinge of envy and awe, *Zaira has attained nirvana.*

Tara Chopra shrugged, opened her snake-skin clutch, fished out her Chanel compact and touched up a spot under her right eye. 'She went ahead of all of us, our beautiful little Zaira.'

'And death is *such* a small price to pay for salvation.'

'Not simply salvation, Mummy; I'm talkin' eternal release, moksha, freedom from the tortuous cycle of birth and death.'

'I must meet Guru-ji and thank him.'

Tara looked around impatiently. She was supposed to be at a party in an hour; the mother-daughter bonding fest had gone on way too long.

'You know what we should do after this is finito? We should go on a spiritual retreat of some sort,' said Nalini Chopra.

'Mummy!' A feverish glow came into Tara's eyes. 'You stole the words right outta my mouth!'

'Let's go to Haridwar and Rishikesh.' She could picture herself descending the holy steps of Har ki Pauri and meeting the great, churning waters of the Ganga.

'Totally, Mummy!'

'I've heard there's this *fab* little Italian ristorante in Rishikesh.'

'Yes, we should definitely go there!' Tara Chopra said as she stood up to leave. 'I hear Madonna hangs out there when she's tired of being a Kabbalah slut.'

17

IN HIS LONG INNINGS AS A POLITICIAN, MINISTER Prasad had dealt with the law on so many occasions that he was, by now, seasoned in the knowledge of the workings of the Indian legal machinery. He had breezed through charges of extortion, poll scams, vandalism, murder, embezzlement, arson. Each case had been a learning experience, teaching him how to slide through loopholes, dodge bullets, jump the highest bars. His renown for evading the law had spread beyond political circles. In fact, when the young Turk of Bollywood, Rocky Khan, had a bit of a run-in with the police, he had reached out to the minister for help. Minister Prasad was extremely proud of having saved the hunk from a slammer sentence and often recollected the day when Rocky had rung him in a panic.

Rocky Khan, a Bollywood beefcake dubbed 'Rip-Off Khan'—as he was frequently possessed by an impulse to

tear off his kit and gyrate like a pole dancer before crowds of dumbstruck admirers—had a major drinking problem. One night, Rocky got seriously smashed at a bar in Juhu and was speeding home recklessly when his jeep ran over three workers sleeping on the pavement. One worker, severed in half, performed a morbid drama: his lower section, from his toe up to the torso, rose up and raced forward before collapsing in a writhing heap. Getting out of his car, Rocky had drunkenly surveyed the damage and proceeded to offer the two surviving workers a few thousand rupees for the unfortunate turn of events. Outraged, the injured workers dragged themselves to the local police station, and on the strength of their evidence a case was registered against the errant superstar. Gripped with terror, Rocky had called Malik and requested him to bring his father on board to fix what was certain to flare up into one very ugly public affair.

To Malik this seemed a wonderful opportunity: if he could bail out Rocky now then the popular star would be obliged to perform in Tiranga Inc. shows on demand. Malik did not waste a second in ringing his father, who, having nursed acting ambitions in his college days, was thrilled to come to the actor's rescue. His first piece of advice to the Bollywood badmaash was to bribe the key witnesses; this would defuse the prosecution's case from the word go. The witnesses haggled with horrific alacrity, eager to milk the film star of all he was worth. Rocky was a charitable man; he acceded to their every request. One witness, a traffic policeman who turned down the monetary

offer, sadly, never reported for duty again. Then Minister Prasad put Rocky in touch with Vijay Singh, his lawyer. Vijay Singh was notorious for his aggressive line of questioning and a Rottweiler manner that made witnesses bungle up their testimony. The lawyer advised Rocky to take the butchered man's kin into confidence and pay them off; the last thing he wanted in the courthouse was an ugly cluster of maudlin relatives. The case went on for five years. Most hearings were adjourned. The final witness, Mrs Patel, a housewife who had seen Rocky race into the night after the accident, washed her hands off the case not because she had been paid or bullied but because the case had gone on so long that she just could not find the time to attend every hearing.

Once acquitted, Rocky flew to Delhi to personally thank the minister, whom he now considered his guru. By midnight the two men, the oddest of accomplices, had polished off a bottle of Black Label and wolfed down many platefuls of oily onion pakoras. The star expressed an almost reverential interest in how the minister had gathered such extraordinary insight into the law that he could torque it around like a piece of wire. Euphoric with the celebrity interest in his seedy life, Minister Prasad made a scholarly face as he unravelled his 'philosophy of Indian law'.

According to him, such blatant manipulation was possible only because corruption in India was endemic: it was not the pollutant in the air, it *was* the air. Years of witnessing and directing wholesale con jobs had convinced Minister Prasad

that although all countries under the sun wrangled with corruption in their system, India had gone one step further and accepted that there was actually a system in its corruption. Once fraud had got hard-wired into the national consciousness, the political machinery did not work to rectify the flaw but to embrace its ideals. Over the years Minister Prasad had perfected this art form. He knew how to rally round judges who were desperate to move from a low-level trial court to the high court. He knew how to intimidate witnesses. He knew how to bribe the investigating officers. Cruel as it was, such machinations were charged with a lustrous cosmic logic all their own: for after the dead were gone, life went on, as it was meant to.

Now, as the minister recalled the night Rocky Khan had dropped by at his house, the inherent unfairness of life reaffirmed itself: having orchestrated a complete stranger's acquittal on a murder charge, it would be ironic indeed if he failed at the same task when his own son's life and future were on the line. His thoughts turned to the afternoon Malik had been born, the doctor's ecstatic expression as she announced triumphantly the birth of a son, the heir apparent. The nurse had handed the infant to the minister. His arms had gone weak from holding the baby. He was so worried he might drop the baby that he refused to hold the child again. He remembered also that Malik didn't start speaking until the age of four; he suspected the boy was a bit of a retard but this doubt was quashed as soon as Malik uttered complete sentences a few days before his fifth birthday. He noticed an obsessive streak in his

son: Malik collected dinky cars and, at one point, had owned a collection of seven hundred and twenty-seven cars. In the tenth standard he started collecting stamps and in a matter of months had eleven thousand stamps glued carefully on sheets of parchment paper. At college, Malik had been a renowned failure; he quit a few days before his finals. It had come as no surprise to Minister Prasad that Malik had chosen to drop out.

Over the years, the minister had watched his son weed his way out of a litany of impressive failings: being expelled from several schools; acquiring the social skills of a born-again savage; thrashing a professor who dared to fail him; chasing after anything in a skirt. Under the rickety awnings of his adulthood, Malik had chosen the strobe lights and sewers of Bombay over the dignified avenues of Delhi. Initially, Minister Chander Prasad had worried about his son hacking it in a big city, and when Malik's event management company had met with *some* degree of success he had been extremely surprised. Later, he found out that Malik had always got his way because he had dropped the family name on every occasion.

More recently, their reconnection under the auspices of the murder trial had brought the boy under closer scrutiny. The minister was surprised they had so much in common: the same shape of the eyes, a lousy stomach, skin allergies. In Malik, the minister saw his own flawed mortality, its capacity for love charcoaled with lunacy and tenderness. He was slowly growing obsessed with saving Malik from a prison sentence not only because his own political future depended on emerging

unscathed from the scandal, but also because he suspected that if Malik went to prison then something in his own being would curl up and die forever. The image of his son in prison made his eyes well up, and had the phone not rung, he would have shut the door of his study and burst into tears.

'Good evening, Minister-saab. Am I calling you at a bad time?'

'Vijay Singh! You've called precisely at the right moment; I wanted to go over the case with you.' He picked up a pen from the desk he was seated at, and reached for his notepad.

They conferred for ten minutes before concluding that in spite of the case moving in the right direction Samar Arora was raining shit on them.

'Now what to do?' he moaned. 'That madarchod is not about to give up.'

'But Minister-saab, *why* are you worrying so much? Haven't we worked on umpteen cases together?' Vijay Singh, standing in his balcony, was looking out at the street below his house, at the endless stream of devotees walking barefoot towards the Siddhivinayak temple.

'That might be so ...'

'Did I not get you an acquittal in every one of them?'

'I helped you, Vijay.'

'Of *course* you did! I don't want to take away from your contribution at all. You've given me a fantastic headstart in this case too.' Vijay Singh knew that left to his own devices he

could not have turned Nalini Chopra and Bunty Oberoi into hostile witnesses.

'Honestly, tell me,' the minister asked, 'what is the chance of that lauda Samar Arora bungling this case?'

'He didn't see the key accused shoot the victim,' the lawyer assured. 'He's a secondary witness, Minister Prasad. He is entirely incidental to the legal proceedings. In fact, he is entirely incidental—full stop!'

'You know what bothers me the most? That bastard's nerve. He has a ... a hero complex.' The minister wasn't sure if there was any such psychological disorder but it sounded about right to him. 'He talks to the press so freely. Do you know the ripple-down effect bad press has on me?'

'That man should keep his trap shut.' Vijay Singh took a deep drag of his pipe, wondering why so many people frequented the Siddhivinayak temple.

'The head of the HPP called me to say the papers are going at it like piranhas. He said it was "all getting out of hand".'

'Yes, the coverage does seem to be in overdrive.'

'And what is this rubbish "Justice for Zaira" business? People die. Is death so difficult a concept to fathom in a country that breeds like roaches in a sewer?'

'Now, now, please don't take tension over Samar, Minister-saab. You've handled two of the witnesses like a pro. This chap is bound to fall in line.'

'I'm not so sure.'

'Don't be nervous.'

'Samar Arora is always on my mind.'

'You must forget him.' Vijay Singh paused. What were those noises? Was the minister crying?

'Minister-Saab ...' he ventured after a few moments, 'are you all right?'

'I'm sorry. I have ... a slight cold.'

'Shall I call you back in the morning?'

'No,' he blew his nose. 'I need to sort this out tonight; I'm in campaign meetings all day tomorrow.'

'Fine.' Vijay Singh was terribly amused by the minister's little weeping fit. What a girly man, he thought to himself with a chuckle; a low-class little power pussy.

'Do you know Samar Arora has a living arrangement with a man?'

'Living arrangement?' Vijay Singh pulled his pipe out of his mouth. 'You mean like a roommate?'

'Well, you know how some men are ...'

Vijay Singh went indoors and scribbled on his writing pad: *Homo?*

'Yes,' he said. 'I can almost imagine.' Vijay Singh frequented a park himself. 'I presume they're in some sort of a ... situation?'

'Who knows?' Minister Prasad sounded bashful, like a nun who chances upon a porn magazine. 'But I gather they are more than roommates.'

'Then we *have* to find a way to link his private life to the trial.'

'I'm sure that shouldn't be a problem. The times are so … so sensitive … And his private life is morally improper, isn't it?'

'Absolutely!' Vijay Singh confirmed.

'In olden days such men were sent to prison.'

'Or burnt at the stake.'

'I hear they were given electric shocks.'

'Well, obviously it didn't work. But my task will be to connect the impropriety of his life with the case before the eyes of the court.'

The minister touched his chin. 'Even if we don't find a way to do that, at least we can use it to shore up public support. The case is blowing out of proportion. I need the public on my side. We must prove Samar Arora is not a reliable witness.'

Vijay Singh considered the minister's suggestion. The Hindu People's Party used the morality card to come down on whatever they could lay their hands on. It could just as easily whip up a panic over Samar's relationship with Leo. Of course, this was irrelevant to the case but it would divert scrutiny from the real subject: Zaira's murder at the hands of Malik. Vijay Singh was impressed. Minister Prasad might be a hairy old piece of a girly man but he had come up in life with good reason.

'You're right. I'll find a way to use it. It could be my groundhog.'

'What else do you have on him on file, Vijay?'

'Nothing much, really. He's a failed pianist. He has a dog that he loves too much.'

'A dog?' asked Minister Prasad.

'Yes, I hear he's gaga over his dog.'

'Why is he crazy about a dog?'

'My spies tell me the dog was a gift from Zaira. Apparently, Samar loves it as if it were his own child.'

'What a stupid man! Imagine, loving a bloody dog! But in any event *you*'ve given me some information to work with, Vijay.'

'I have? How so?'

'You will know in good time,' said the minister. 'All in good time.'

18

THE TRIAL PROGRESSED.

On the witness stand, Samar not only testified to seeing Malik at Maya Bar but also mentioned Zaira's repeated complaints about his conduct.

Old police records were furnished. The judge was surprised to learn of the time Malik spent an entire night outside Zaira's house banging upon her door until his hand bled. The crazed attack on her trailer in Film City was recreated with the help of witnesses—a gaffer and the make-up artist injured in the attack. Zaira's failed effort to get a restraining order against Malik was mentioned, in addition to the police apathy toward her repeated complaints. Gautam Vakil then requested Karan to take the stand to help document Zaira's fear of Malik. Karan told the court how Malik constantly called Zaira and how she

had grown to loathe and dread the vulgar declarations of his 'love'.

Two days later, the defence cross-examined the prosecution witnesses.

Samar took the stand again.

Vijay Singh stood up and glared at him. Striding up to the box he demanded, 'Mr Arora, how would you define your relationship with Leo McCormick?'

'Objection.' Gautam Vakil had no idea where his opponent was taking the case with this and he tried to nip the line of questioning in the bud.

'Overruled.' Judge Kumar was curious as well.

Samar cleared his throat. 'He's my boyfriend.'

'Boyfriend?'

'My lover.'

Truth, its shameless clarity, spurred a baffled silence.

'What is the bearing of this on the case?' Gautam Vakil asked the judge.

Vijay Singh interjected, 'The defence is in the process of checking the credentials of the prosecution's witnesses. We would like to show the court that this man here is actually a violator of the law. And, surely, no court would entertain the testimony of *such* a man.'

Samar felt his back go cold.

'I'm not entirely certain of your area of contention,' Judge Kumar said, 'but I'm going to let you make your point.'

Vijay Singh looked at the judge gratefully. 'Now, Mr Arora, could you please tell me what is meant by the term "top"?'

'Isn't it a toy children play with?'

'I believe it is also a word used to define the dominant sexual partner in male homosexual relationships?'

'Yes, I believe that's true.'

'Would the word apply to you?'

Gautam Vakil plunged in desperately. 'Objection. Irrelevant. My client's personal life is not up for discussion here.'

'I'm *not* trying to discuss the prosecution's client's private fife, Your Honour.'

Judge Kumar shook his head. 'Overruled.'

Vijay Singh sighed and turned back to Samar. 'All right, then, Mr Arora, you've heard of the word "bottom"?'

Samar decided there was no point in volleying around. 'The sexually receptive partner.'

'That being you?'

'Objection! Irrelevant!' Gautam Vakil shot the judge an exasperated look.

'Sustained.'

'Then how would you identify yourself, Mr Arora?'

Samar said the word *versatile* applied to him—as receptive to sex as to offering it.

Gautam Vakil scowled; he didn't want Samar to fall in line with whatever Vijay Singh was setting him up for.

'In either case,' Vijay Singh said, 'that means you indulge in "buggery" with Mr McCormick, in India?'

'Objection. What connection does Mr McCormick have with this matter?'

'Overruled.'

'Perhaps.'

'Is that a yes?'

'Yes.' Then, more defiantly, Samar repeated, 'Yes.'

'Do you believe this is normal conduct?'

'I know it only as natural behaviour.'

'Are you saying you are a homosexual?'

'No—but you are, and it seems I'll have to take your word for it,' Samar said.

In seconds Vijay Singh had descended on Samar like a shark going after a seal. 'Now, Mr Arora, are you aware of IPC Section 377?'

Section 377, a colonial hangover in the books of the law, penalized 'sex against the order of nature'. Although there had been few convictions under Section 377, the police used it to shame men and threaten them with arrest before letting them go for a pay-off under the table.

'Yes, I have.'

'So you're aware that your sexual practices are illegal in India?'

'Yes.'

'You could face imprisonment if caught in the act of ... sodomy ...'

'Yes, I know.' Samar spoke coolly, in keeping with his lawyer's advice not to succumb to any provocation.

'You know?' Vijay Singh gave a horrified shudder. 'And you *still* went ahead with it?'

'Objection.'

'Overruled.'

'I did.'

'So, Mr Arora, do you practise other such behaviours that the court deems perverse and punishable under law? Lying before a judge, for instance? Giving a false testimony?'

'Objection!'

'And trying to monopolize media attention for a personal agenda ...' Vijay Singh said before the judge could speak.

'Sustained. The court will make a note of the accusation punishable under Section 377. But the defence should bear in mind that it is a different matter altogether.'

'I have no further questions, Your Honour.'

When the court met again in a couple of days, Vijay Singh presented Tony Fernandez.

'What do you do, Tony?'

'I work on the streets.' Compactly built, with smooth, pale skin and a crisp goatee, the defence's most unexpected pawn wore a tacky red shirt over jeans. He stroked his carefully pomaded hair.

'Can we call you a male prostitute?'

Tony looked offended. 'I put people in touch with other people. Besides,' he said primly, 'only a woman can be a prostitute.'

Karan squirmed uncomfortably; he had no idea what this strange man was doing in the courthouse or how he was connected to the case, but he noticed a sordid tremor ripple through the room as the man spoke.

'Well, Tony, do you know Samar Arora?' Vijay Singh pointed at Samar, and all eyes in the courtroom followed the outstretched hand.

'Yes, I do.'

Blood drained from Samar's face. He looked around desperately and noticed Karan looking fixedly at him; warmth and assurance came through like daylight.

'How do you know him?'

'I've seen Samar on the boardwalk opposite the Gateway of India.'

Samar now looked at Leo. His face was trembling with anxiety. What was going on? Who was Tony? How was he involved in the case? The panic in his head was a deep ringing sound, fear hiding at its centre.

'What is the boardwalk opposite the Gateway of India known for?' Vijay Singh asked, then paused. 'Or, should I ask, what is it *notorious* for?'

'Depends on what time of day you go there.'

'After dark?'

'Well, there's a lot you can get there after dark.'

'Including a flourishing trade in human flesh?'

'Yes.'

'In the course of your work, have you met Samar Arora on the boardwalk outside the Taj Mahal Hotel?'

'Objection, Your Honour.'

'Overruled. '

Tony Fernandez chewed his lip as he pretended to study Samar's face before returning his gaze to the defence lawyer. 'I have.'

'What did he want?'

'He asked if I could arrange a boy for him.'

'Objection!' From the corner of his eye Gautam Vakil looked at Samar. Had Samar been keeping things from him?

'Overruled.'

'Samar Arora did not ask for a "man"?' Vijay Singh gasped with shock. 'He insisted on a boy! An *under*age, innocent boy? Someone who probably goes to school and plays with toys?'

'Yes.'

'He asked for a child!' Vijay Singh's face creased with disgust. 'Did you get him one?'

'We did talk prices. Then he started to haggle.'

'What happened eventually?'

'I brought him a boy a few nights later.'

'And?'

'He said the boy was not to his liking. Not his type, he complained. He wanted a skinny lad. So I picked another kid. But then someone he knew died, and he got caught up in all that. The deal never went through. It was a lot of work for nothing.'

'So Mr Arora was soliciting boys only days before his so-called friend was killed in a bar!' Vijay Singh looked at the ceiling, as if addressing a power mightier than the court. 'I wonder, if I ask the esteemed pianist now, would he also call paedophilia "natural behaviour"?'

'Objection.'

'Sustained. The court requests the defence counsel to stick to questions for his witnesses.' Judge Kumar frowned. 'This court is not interested in your personal musings.'

'I'm sorry, Your Honour.' Shock and regret congealed in Vijay Singh's eyes. 'I spoke out of turn. But I could not believe my ears. How could the prosecution present a man of such contemptible moral standing as a witness before this court? But I see your point, and I apologize, Your Honour.'

Before Gautam Vakil could request for a cross-questioning, court hours for the day came to a close.

The judge adjourned the hearing for a week.

Following Tony Fernandez's deposition, outdoor broadcasting vans and journalists camped in droves outside Samar's cottage, hungry for quotes and pictures. Two days later, Leo had to duck for cover to avoid being lynched by the goons of the Hindu People's Party. The same week a child rights group held agitations in Samar's neighbourhood. One placard read: 'Dead Women Go to Heaven but Child Molesters go to Hell'. Another said: 'God Hates Homos!' Media coverage shifted from Zaira's murder and the goof-ups in the investigation to Samar's standing as a witness, his relationship with a man, and

indignation at his alleged solicitations of a boy. Looking out of his bedroom window at the furore outside his house, Samar felt his grief at Zaira's death replaced by a great fear for his personal well-being.

'Don't worry,' Karan said to him one evening over the phone. 'I'm sure your lawyer will thrash Tony Fernandez during the cross-examination.'

'I'm afraid I have more bad news.'

Karan remained silent.

'Apparently, Tony Fernandez has vanished.'

'What!' He stood up, covering his mouth with his hand. 'Where has he gone?'

'Rumour goes that the pimp left the city when it seemed likely he would be arrested on charges of hustling minors.'

But he *has* to be countered in court.'

'That's not going to happen. Tony Fernandez was a con job hired by the defence to take the steam out of our case.'

Pressing the phone to his ear, Karan walked to the balcony. 'I'm so terribly sorry, Samar.' A volt of pain seized his heart.

'Luckily, the judge has chosen to strike off Tony's remarks.'

'But the damage has been done, Samar.'

'You know what my lawyer asked me?'

Karan remained silent. A fleet of white geese were swimming in the Ban Ganga pond, past bright orange marigold flowers and coconut husks.

'He asked me why I hadn't told him about Tony before.'

'Samar ...'

Samar sighed. 'In any case, now Leo is so out of it he wants to go back to San Francisco.'

'I don't blame him.'

'Neither do I. I knew I was up against a vicious lot but I didn't anticipate such ugliness.'

'I wish I could do something.' Karan bit into his fist. 'Would you like me to come over?'

'I would, but I won't ask; I don't know how you'd dodge the reporters outside my door.'

'I'm sorry I can't do anything,' Karan said after a minute. 'I feel completely useless.'

'You've been a fine, fine friend, Karan; you've given me a man I can believe in when everyone and everything around me is falling like a pack of cards,' said Samar, his voice like a moth thrashing its wings against the white heat of a flame. 'You stuck up for Zaira; you showed me how it was done. Even if I'm out here alone, having you on my side is the best luck I could ask for.'

Before the closing arguments, Gautam Vakil requested his final witness to take the stand again.

'Samar Arora, you were with the victim on the night of the murder.'

'I was with Zaira.'

'I request you to piece together that last interaction.'

'Objection!' Vijay Singh leapt up. 'The prosecution counsel is asking the witness to reconstruct sentimental statements which have no bearing on this case.'

'Overruled.'

Vijay Singh threw his hands up in the air.

Samar faced the courtroom, his gaze even, unafraid. When he spoke, his voice was clear, muscled. 'I heard a commotion from the direction of the bar. On my way there, I saw Malik Prasad put a gun into his pocket and make a dash for the door. Then I heard Nalini Chopra yell to one of the waiters: "Get him! He's killed Zaira." The instant I heard this I ran to where I'd seen Zaira last and fought my way through the crowd around her.

'She was on the ground, breathing with great difficulty. Every breath was a huge and terrible effort. I didn't know what had happened until I stepped into a pool of blood. I pulled her on to my lap and asked everyone to back off because she needed all the oxygen she could get. I noticed a small dent on her temple; this was later identified as the entry point of the bullet. Every now and then she gasped, and blood spilled out of the side of her head.

'She remained in my lap as we waited for the ambulance.'

Zaira's pain had initially registered as shrill crescendos and jolting plunges; then it grew giant and furious; finally, it was blue, undulating, oceanic, and on its waves she drifted in and out of time. Her body revealed the codes of its functions: nerves corresponded to meridians, flesh was conscious of bone, veins alert to the passage of blood hurtling down innumerable narrow green chutes. Dazzled by the design of the human form, she found herself shrouded in a continuous, hollow humming,

as if the word 'Om' had been interminably stretched out. From the surging blue and the protective sheath of this warm, holy sound, Zaira briefly emerged to see the man who was peering at her. The same pair of liquid eyes she had been attracted to under the cover of a palm leaf in a wild garden.

She breathed in strained gasps, as though she were wheezing. 'I'm glad you're here.'

'It's going to be ...' Samar could not bear the feel of her fingertips tracing his jaw. 'The ambulance ... it will be here in minutes.'

'You're here.'

'Zaira.'

'Mr Ward-Davies misses you so much. He sulks in the corner.'

'I know. That's why I came back.' Tears streamed down Samar's terrorized face.

She whispered. 'I'm afraid he's decided to up and quit. Without you.'

'Tell him to wait. I'm coming for him.'

'You?'

'Yes ... Can you tell him to wait for just a little bit longer?'

A few seconds later, her hand slumped, the delicate weight of her body suddenly heavy and glum. She sank into his lap, no longer buoyed by a defiant will to draw another breath. She fell deeper into him, a pebble tossed into a canyon, and then she was in him, briefly watching the world, its horror and its glory, its frolic and warped melodies. He covered her face with

a crossbow of his arms; a dark silence took hold of him. The delicate, strained echo of her heartbeat continued to resound in his head like a whisper from the past. At the time he did not know, but when Zaira died the person he had been around her, the custodian of her deepest pain, the jester in the court of her imagination, also faded into a great, trembling nothingness; he would never be the same again.

'Can you share Zaira's last words with the court?'

'Huh?' Samar looked jolted.

The lawyer repeated himself. 'What were Zaira's last words to you?'

'She said ...' He experienced a great churning in his chest; he felt dizzy.

'What did she say to you, Mr Arora?'

For a moment, the entire courtroom tilted forward, eyes unblinking, ears peeled.

'She said nothing.'

'Are you sure?'

'I am certain of this much.' Closing his eyes, he bowed his head, his nails digging into the wooden rail around him.

Samar touched his lovers neck. 'I wish you did not have to go through all this; it will soon be over.'

Leo flinched from Samar's caress. He rose from the bed. 'Zaira would've been proud of you. Let's wait for the verdict. You were very brave.'

'This is not only about bravery.'

'I know.'

'Why's it so tough to believe that?'

'You doubt everything I say, Samar.' Leo walked up to the window and stared out at a cool, moonless night.

'I'm sorry.' He sighed. 'They made me stand in a box, Leo.'

'That was ...'

'They asked me.'

'Don't ... please, Samar.' He turned back toward the bed.

'They pointed at me.'

Leo did not want to comfort Samar; he did not want to ask him to stop crying.

'They asked me.'

'They had no right ...'

'They took my most honest thing ...'

'And they couldn't touch it.' Almost against his will, Leo was drawn back to Samar, into the orbit of his raw hurt.

'They took what was most personal ...'

'And they were scared of its power.'

'They had ...'

'Hush ...'

'You know ...'

'I do.'

The men in the courtroom had deemed them depraved, their desire diseased; they had been looked upon with pity and scorn, envy and odium; it now clung to their skin like a stain. Desperate to rinse it off, the lovers bathed each other. Carefully, quietly, they paid meticulous attention to the other's body, mindful that even if life would divide them, this

night, its stillness and longing would remain unextinguished. So they took the body and gave it spirit; they took spirit and rubbed its broken back, made it whole again. In the minutiae of anatomy hid their most urgent promise, their calm and baroque rage; they touched, smoothened, scratched, ruffled, caressed, kissed—ear, foot, navel, neck, back, shoulder, flank, toe, nape, shin, cheek. When morning arrived, unable to stand the emerging rays of light Samar shut his eyes and floated to and from everything, wrapped in the continuous, hollow sound that had shrouded Zaira in her anguished last moments, a deep blue swathe of feeling.

19

ON THE DAY OF THE VERDICT, RHEA SAT ON A bench in the packed courtroom, three rows ahead of the last. As Judge Kumar arranged his papers and the crowd shuffled its feet, her eyes fell on Karan; the two women sitting next to him were Diya Sen and Mantra Rai, whom she recognized from photographs she had seen in the papers. In the first row, ahead of Karan, Leo sat next to Samar. When Rhea tilted her head she noticed on the adjacent row of benches, across the aisle, Malik Prasad and Vijay Singh, their jaws clenched, sweat glistening at the base of their stout, bovine necks.

Rhea craned her neck to see Malik's face but could not.

As Judge Kumar was about to speak, a sparrow flew into the room, and after circling about in a delicate, fluttering loop slammed into the blades of the fan. Rhea was appalled to see the

folks sitting below perfunctorily wipe off the remains, as if the blood would indelibly stain their clothes. She had volunteered at the animal shelter for years but had never treated the death of a puppy or a kitten so lightly, as if death was catching, like a cold.

The court was restored to its dignity when the judge cleared his throat and opened the file of papers in front of him.

In the racket that attended the verdict, Rhea made a dash for the exit.

Much to her consternation, she found Karan stalling her passage, his hand extended before her. 'Please stay. Talk to me.'

'I need to go. I'm terribly sorry.'

'I can't believe the judge would let him off like this.'

'It's truly awful, Karan. You should be with Samar. He needs you right now.' Her voice was darting, afraid.

He kept his arm stretched in front of her, like a bar over a gate. 'Can we talk outside for a few minutes?'

'I told you I would come here today, but I have to go now. Adi will be getting home any minute.' She looked at her watch; she did not want anyone to see her with Karan.

'Just stay for a few minutes.'

'No!' She hit his outstretched arm. It fell to his side; his face looked like he had been knifed.

On her way out, she glanced at Samar, who was staring at the floor.

Then he looked up, their eyes locked.

She tilted her head and Samar, perhaps recognizing her from Karan's descriptions, folded his hands in acknowledgement; his pain was raw and lunged toward her in thundering waves. She nodded at him and moved through the crowd like a stingray negotiating the billowing currents of the deep sea, pushing at backs and elbows, sweat gathering on her neck. Outside, in the quad, she stopped to watch Malik Prasad and his cronies get into a black Mercedes and drive off to escape the noisy assault of flashbulbs.

She stared after Malik till something clicked in her head, like the trigger of a gun.

Two weeks later, Karan and Rhea met at the Babulnath temple, on a Monday morning; the wind was intent, wet, carrying something of the sea in its hot, uneven blast.

'Thanks for the birthday present.'

He was wearing grubby jeans and a white shirt; she wore a taupe sleeveless cotton dress. They looked incongruous in each other's company.

'I'm glad you liked it, Karan.'

She had sent him a Bombay Fornicator, a keepsake from the evening they had met in Chor Bazaar.

'I liked it a lot; but not as much as I liked your letter.'

'You inspired it. Have you not been eating well?'

'I've been a bit preoccupied.' With his dirty stubble and sunken eyes he looked a bit like a mobster. 'I've lost my appetite, mostly.'

'But the trial has come to a close. One way or another you'll have to find your motions and swim along.'

'In a way the trial has ended, but in another way it has just begun. Now we know what was *really* at stake.'

'How's Samar holding up?'

'He's furious, and damaged. And so tired, he complains that even his bones hurt.'

To escape the relentless battery from the press Samar had taken off to Sri Lanka, retreating to a house in a private forest owned by Leo's friends. 'He's rooting for a reinvestigation.'

Rhea could understand Samar's resolve. He was not the only one incensed by the verdict; all across India, in little towns and big cities, people had come together to express shock and solidarity in strong, simple ways, candlelight vigils, silent protests, letters to newspapers. The entire nation had united to demand a retrial of Zaira's case.

'But a retrial could take forever.' Her thoughts now turned to Leo. 'And the prospect of a trial that could stretch for years won't go down well with Leo.'

'The only thing Leo cares about is getting his ass back to America.'

'Aren't you giving Leo the short end of the stick? It's not been easy on either of them.'

'It's not been easy on any of us.'

She sighed. Karan sounded like a professional martyr. She said, 'Samar shouldn't let the trial mess up his private life.'

'There's a thin line between the public and the private, and it blurs easily.'

'So it's all the more important he should know how to tell the two apart.'

'Maybe you're right. Trials take years, and he really shouldn't get carried away by the possibility of a fair reinvestigation.' Much of the principal evidence had been doctored at source. Bunty Oberoi had said his initial statement had been wrongly recorded. Nalini Chopra had claimed her sunglasses had compromised her vision, and although 'someone rather like' Malik might have been present at Maya Bar, she was not sure it was him. Having recently resigned, D.K. Mishra was no longer available for questioning as he had left town and could not be traced.

Karan sighed. 'Samar might be setting himself up for another let-down.'

They ascended the stone steps of the temple, past the betel leaves arranged on every ledge holding lit wicks flickering defiantly in the wind; the strong scent of ghee was lightened by the vivid, sacred fragrance of lilies. Rhea told Karan she had seen Malik at close range right after the verdict. 'He was nothing like I had expected,' she said, a trace of amazement in her voice.

'What were you expecting?'

'I don't know, honestly. I wondered why he didn't look more like a murderer.'

He found her naivety intolerable. 'And what *exactly* is a murderer supposed to look like?'

'I know what you mean. There's no "type". But Malik really got to me.'

'Why?'

'Because he could be anyone. He looked like a college kid; he looked like my neighbour's grandson.'

'But Malik is not your regular thug; he's the son of the nation's Minister for Labour and Employment, so he's not going to pass for a petty pickpocket.'

She shook her head. 'What did my brain in was suddenly finding that he resembled someone I knew, or almost knew. When I thought about it later, I couldn't put a finger on it and it's continuing to bug me.' Her expression was that of a person searching for the last missing word that completes a crossword.

'Well, maybe Malik reminds you of a distant relative or an old friend.'

'Maybe,' she said, shaking her head. 'By the way, I saw Malik's father on television last night. He was at the shrine of Vaishno Devi, praying for his son.' In the television report, Minister Chander Prasad had claimed 'justice had been served' and that his son had 'finally been vindicated from a terrible political conspiracy'. 'He actually went so far as to warn the reporter that any further criticism of Judge Kumar's verdict would amount to contempt of court!'

'Minister Prasad is as smart as he is ruthless,' Karan said. 'It's a combination that makes him lethal.'

They reached the top of the stone stairwell.

Rhea looked at the deities, Ganesh and Hanuman, and then turned to Karan. 'I'll be right back.'

'Take your time, Rhea.'

She entered the sanctum.

Standing there, amid plump, perspiring housewives and lewd stockbrokers, haggard, toothless widows and randy new brides, she was soon absorbed in the chaos and chanting, the trampled tuberoses, the fragrant plume of incense, the pealing of bells. When she got her chance before the mammoth lingam, she pressed her palm on the black stone as cold streams of milk continued to fountain over her fingers. As she kneeled there, her hand on the lingam, the sounds surrounding her began to fade, the devotees blurred, and she could hear something invisible, primal, the heartbeat of the world, the place where rivers were born, the womb of instinct. A powerful jolt passed through her, animating her eyes with an ineluctable charge, turning her complexion devastatingly radiant. She emerged shaken, and she was eager to tell Karan what had occurred, but in the quad she had to give Karan's face just one cursory glance and his cynicism divided them like a curtain.

'Feeling better?'

She nodded shyly, disappointed that she could not share her experience with him.

'Why are your hands trembling, Rhea?'

'Are they? Let's go, shall we?'

On the way down they passed fat, mottled cows stabled in dim, squalid quarters.

An old, bearded sadhu on the landing held out some prasad for them. They accepted the prasad and walked on.

'I'm going to teach.'

'In a school?'

'Yes; I've been looking around for jobs.'

'Oh, Karan! Don't throw away your talent.' She joined her hands as though in a plea.

'Teaching is a wonderful vocation.'

She gave him a bored look. 'Teaching is perfectly valid, even noble, but it's not your bag.'

'Well, neither is photography.'

'God, Karan, snap out of it!'

'Out of what?'

'It's like I'm talking to a door or something. What the hell is wrong with you?'

He gulped. 'My life has turned around in the last few months.'

'Yeah, well ... the big bad world bit you. Get used to it.'

'Get used to it?'

She paused. 'Look, I'm sorry, Karan. Maybe I sounded a bit harsh. But I'd still urge you not to give up your work. And it will help you if you learn not to take life so personally.'

'But life *is* personal.'

'Well, you can't take it personally, Karan, because beggars at the traffic lights, cows, flamingoes, and bitches in heat at the animal shelter are all breathing, shitting, snorting and heaving

to get by. I hate to break the news to you, but there's nothing special or unique about your life—or mine.'

'You know, Rhea,' he said, 'I can always count on you for comfort.'

'I'm not here to play Mother Teresa to your leper-child number.' She flicked an errant strand of hair from her forehead.

'Hey, calm down.'

'I *am* calm. Who're you to tell me what I'm supposed to do?' Her face gleamed like a sword.

'Rhea!'

'Don't raise your voice at me!'

'You're really pushing all the wrong buttons.' He advanced toward her with his hand raised in the air. She felt rage billow out of him. She turned. The sadhu on the landing had stood up and was looking inquisitively at them.

'You wanted to hit me!' Rhea hissed, turning to Karan.

'You're overreacting, Rhea.' Karan had moved away.

'You did, didn't you? Look at me when I'm talking to you!'

'I'm ... sorry.'

She strode up to him, whipped him around, met his eyes. 'Did you want to hit me, Karan?'

'I'm sorry.' He bent his head.

'You cannot be sorry for what you intended to do but you had better be ashamed for a long time.'

'You hit my arm in the courtroom. What was *that* all about?' he countered foolishly.

'You were in my way, Karan,' she said. 'And what you were going to do right now is completely different; don't you dare compare.'

'I don't know what I was thinking.' His voice choked up. 'I don't know who I've become. I'm sorry. I'm so, so sorry, Rhea.'

Her most natural impulse then was to turn and run for her life. She was, she feared, in the distressing presence of a man capable of *any*thing. But she managed to pull herself together. 'I'm sorry about that; my prayer is for you to return to your vision of yourself. Be true to who you are, and if teaching feels true then go for it. But if you're using it to dodge a truth larger than yourself then it's bound to catch up with you quicker than you turn the corner.'

'I'll go back to photography, I promise.'

'You don't have to promise me anything. It's your life.'

'Please don't be mad at me, Rhea.' He spoke so quietly she reached forward and held him.

Overcome with fear, she started to cry.

Believing that her tears were further proof of their intimacy, he pulled her closer.

'I can't believe I was stupid enough to forget the brass monkey,' she said in between the sobs she tried to muffle.

'The brass monkey?'

She was breathing heavily as she spoke. 'The talisman I'd been looking for forever. I had it in my hand the day I met you in Chor Bazaar. I had put it down when I started talking to you but then we got so caught up in the conversation and the

search for the Bombay Fornicator that I forgot it there. I went back to look for it but the dealer said it had been sold and that he didn't have another one.'

'I will find it for you.' Karan tightened his hold around her.

'Thank you, Karan,' she said quietly. 'Can you please ... please let go of me?'

'Huh?'

'I can't breathe ...' She tugged herself free.

He looked at her; her face was still radiant but tear-streaked. 'Who did I remind you of?' he asked.

'Huh?' She started to walk away. Soon they would be on the road; soon she would board a taxi and go back to the safety of her home.

'In Chor Bazaar. You said you helped me look for the Bombay Fornicator because I reminded you of someone.'

'Maybe you imagined that.'

They were on the busy main road. There was a small temple behind them, a shrine to Shreenathji, bedecked in faded gold and intense green. A sloe-black woman reposed under a tree; a beige cow stood a few feet away from her, tethered to the tree trunk.

Karan's brow creased. 'I'm pretty sure that's what you said.'

'Did I?' Rhea cupped his cheek, a gesture to bid him farewell forever.

20

BARELY HAD A FEW DAYS PASSED SINCE MINISTER Prasad returned from his pilgrimage to Vaishno Devi when he received a call from the chief of the Hindu People's Party.

'I have been asked to bring up an issue with you. The party wants me to discuss it on their behalf.'

The minister, who had been watching a midnight broadcast of a mud-wrestling match between two beefy black women in yellow bikinis, stood up. His hands reached into his underwear; a rapid scratching motion ensued. 'It is bad news?'

'Well, it's not good news.'

The chief explained to him that since the Hindu People's Party bore the public mantle of the nation's morality manager, they felt the hoo-hah over Zaira's murder trial had given their

credentials a serious walloping. 'I mean,' the chief said, 'if the media wasn't making such a lot of noise over the verdict we would have looked the other way.'

'But ...?'

'But now the prime minister has taken a stand on this matter.'

'It makes you wonder if the prime minister has nothing better to do with his time.'

'And the press is also having a field day.'

'Our press believes their sting operations will save the country,' the minister complained. 'But for them it's really about the ratings war. Trial by media is absolutely unethical.'

'The media might be the biggest bastards in the business but no one can deny them their clout. Besides, look how that man—Zaira's friend—has been talking non-stop to every news channel about the case. He's got you in a lot of trouble.'

'That boy needs to be put in his place,' said Minister Prasad. 'He's become too big for his boots.'

The chief spelt out the bottom line. 'Don't you believe it's in your best interest to resign?'

'It could be,' the minister accepted bitterly. 'Since the only other option is for the party to *expel* me.'

'Well, we ...'

'I've been in politics far too long to suffer fools.'

'We're only giving you a choice.'

'Give me a few days to handle this.'

'You have two weeks. If the noise around the case doesn't die out ...'

Minister Prasad was not one to be cornered. '*Something* will die out!' he shouted before he banged down the phone.

Feeling a shooting pain in his guts, the minister rushed to the pot to pass motions the colour of bad bananas and a terrible burning sensation traumatized his stomach afterwards. His ulcer was back, he worried. Over many years it had made it difficult for him to eat or drink in peace; now, inflamed in the light of his imminent dismissal, his stomach needed urgent medical attention. On his way out of the house, he met his wife in the hallway. 'I'm going to see Dr Rao.'

'Are you all right?'

He did not respond to her query. He summoned the driver to get the car ready.

'Two things have brought on the ulcer,' the kindly Dr Rao said. 'Stress and alcohol.'

'I don't care what's causing it, just do something about it!' Minister Prasad snapped. Then he sat up on the inspection table. 'I'm sorry, Dr Rao. I shouldn't have yelled like that.'

'It's all right; I have treated you for thirty years, Chander; I'm used to your mood swings.' Dr Rao was as close to a father figure as the minister was likely to have.

'I just don't know what to do,' he said, looking contrite. 'I thought I'd covered all bases. Malik walked away a free man. And now there's talk of a retrial.'

'It must be awful for you and your family.'

'I can't sleep at night, Dr Rao; I keep imagining that the police are going to get Malik and put him behind bars. I wouldn't know what to do if they took him away from me ...' Before he could say another word the tears welled up and then flowed freely.

Dr Rao stood next to Minister Prasad, motionless, speechless, reminded suddenly of his seven-year-old granddaughter, who had wept inconsolably after her goldfish died.

Once the minister had dried his tears, Dr Rao said, 'Are you worried there will be a huge political backlash?'

'Who cares about the party? I never even knew I liked my son until I got to know him better over the last few months. I thought he was a sick little loser. But little things about him remind me he has come from me; he is my blood, he is mine. The shape of his eyes. The way he stammers when he is ... he is ... emotional ...'

'He has also inherited your bad stomach.'

'I know, I know.' The minister got off the inspection table and smoothened his white kurta. 'Malik is ... he is my son. I did not realize the intensity of my feelings for him, and it is awful to feel so helpless with affection.'

Dr Rao smiled. 'Then you must do everything you can to save Malik.'

'My other worry is that the party has asked me to resign. And if I don't have my post then I will be able to do little to

help Malik during the retrial.' He balled his fingers into fists. 'But I will not give up this fight. I will not lose.'

'I admire your spirit.' Dr Rao patted the minister on the back, as he would have his granddaughter. 'But you must give up alcohol.'

Minister Chander Prasad shook his head. 'How can I do that!'

'The ulcers will get worse, Chander. You have to give up booze.' Dr Rao returned to his seat behind his desk.

'I cannot do that; not right now. You must give me some medicines that will work around the Black Label because without whisky my life will be unbearable.' The minister rose to leave.

'I'm going to give you a sleeping pill for tonight. I hope you will heed my advice. I'm glad you had a good cry; that should help.'

'Cry?' the minister asked, looking shocked. 'Who cried?'

Dr Rao opened the door of his clinic as he said softly, 'No one cried, Chander, no one.'

Returning late, in a dour mood, Minister Prasad slammed the main door behind him. 'I'll show them!'

Minister Prasad's wife heard him and came out of the bedroom.

'That son of yours! He takes after *your* side of the family.'

Mrs Prasad took a deep breath. Over the last few nights she had dreamed of green grasshoppers feasting on her. She saw one

in particular, green as jealousy, sleek as satin, lowering its mouth into hers, feasting on the red flesh of her tongue.

'What will you show them?'

The minister stared at his wife. Behind her, on the blaring television set, he saw Samar talking to a reporter, saying that he had faith in a retrial. A different judge would preside; old evidence would be reconsidered.

'What will you show them?' Mrs Prasad repeated.

The minister looked at her. He did not *ever* expect her to speak to him; talking was just not part of her job description.

'They will have a new judge for the retrial,' he said aloud. 'What if I can't get my way with him as I did with Judge Kumar?'

'Then Malik will have to pay for his crime.'

He studied her face slowly, his eyes travelling from her nose to her chin to her ears. The back of his hand sliced the air before it sent her reeling to the ground in one swift motion. Malik's mother lay on the floor, her feet drawn to her chest, her right hand on her left cheek. She tasted blood as it slowly oozed out and mixed with her spittle.

21

SAMAR HAD JUST STEPPED OUT OF THE BATH WHEN he heard a terrible crash followed by the ominous tinkling of splintered glass. Then he heard Leo cry out in shock.

By the time Samar ran out to the living room Leo was sitting with his back against the couch, trying to dislodge something from his forehead.

Mr Ward-Davies was in the corner of the room looking at Leo, whining.

Samar rushed Leo to Breach Candy Hospital where, in the emergency ward, a thick, angular glass splinter was plucked out of his head; nine neat stitches closed a nasty wound. After depositing Leo at home, Samar went to the police station to register a complaint. The officer on duty asked him why he hadn't come to them sooner, right after the incident, and eyed him suspiciously, as if he had cooked up the story.

'The cops said they will look into it.'

Two days had passed since the attack on the house. Leo and Samar were finishing dinner, a light, simple meal of amti and rice, one of Saku-bai's classics. Tea lights threw careless shadows on the kitchen walls.

'That's what they assured you during the time of the investigation for Zaira's trial.' Leo spoke slowly, fighting off the searing jabs of pain in his head. 'You can't trust the cops. Remember D.K. Mishra?'

Samar stretched his hand to caress Leo's back. 'I'm sorry. You must feel sandwiched in all of this.'

'I need to tell you something, Samar. I tried not to bring it up during the trial because you had too much on your plate.'

'Can we talk in the bedroom?' Samar said, wanting Leo to be more comfortable.

'Sure.'

In ten minutes, once dinner was wrapped up, Leo followed Samar into their bedroom, Mr Ward-Davies at their heels. The room was square, clean, airy. A king-size bed, with a blue bedspread printed with marching elephants, stood in the centre; paperbacks were scattered across the slim divan along the adjacent wall; a half empty glass of red wine stood atop an oak desk in the facing corner.

Samar lit two candles and the room filled slowly with the sharp, invigorating citrus perfume of lime.

Leo sat on the bed and clasped his knees with his hands. 'I'm going back to San Francisco.'

'I've been expecting it.' Samar walked over to the divan and slumped on it. His fingers toyed with Mr Ward-Davies's ears, thin, pinched back, as delicate as rose petals.

'Please let me finish.' Leo's throat was dry, weary.

Samar sat up, surprised by the thunderbolt of gravity in Leo's voice.

'A few weeks ago, I had a blood test.' Leo steepled his fingers. 'And the results are not pretty.'

When Leo revealed the news, Samar felt like he had stepped on a landmine. 'I don't know what to say.'

Leo's face grew long; his eyes remained fixed on the wall. 'Doc said it could either take years to flare up, or it could take me out by next year. No one can say for sure. I just want to get on the meds as quickly as possible.'

Gathering all his reserves, Samar walked over to Leo. 'We'll get the best docs in the country. I know people at Breach Candy Hospital.' He squeezed Leo's shoulder gently.

'I don't want to be treated here,' he said, shrugging off Samar's hand.

'But we have some of the most competent doctors and ...'

'I want to get the hell outta here!' Anger flashed in Leo's eyes like diamonds in the raw. 'I don't want to hang on for a day longer in this savage country!'

Samar bit his lower lip.

'Do you know how they treat people like me? A guy in Goa was locked up in a sanatorium when they found out he

had it. In Kerala, they tied a widow to a tree and set her on fire. Anything could happen to me if they found out.'

'But no one will know, Leo.'

'Are you for real? There's no such thing as doctor-patient confidentiality in India.'

'We can keep things under wraps,' Samar said as they faced each other in the candlelight. 'It's not difficult.'

'Why are you so naive? Don't you get it? Nothing can be kept under wraps now, Samar. Because of the retrial the media is watching our every move; I feel like I'm trapped under a microscope. I can't even go for my evening walks without a fuckin' flash popping from behind a tree. If some smutty tabloid gets their hands on this it's bound to cause a stir.' The anger in Leo's eyes smouldered with hysteria. He added, 'And the HPP will find a way to use it against you and me during the retrial.'

Mr Ward-Davies jumped off the divan and scurried to the door; he looked terrified. Samar went up to his dog and scooped him up.

'But if you go to San Francisco who'll look after you there?'

'Oh.' Leo stood and slapped his hands on the sides of his legs. 'Oh, I'm sorry. Am I already so fucked up I assumed my boyfriend would come with me? I mean, I was there for *him* day and night these last few months but now Mr Social Conscience is asking *me* who'll look after me in San Francisco?' He waved his hands angrily. 'I guess the virus *is* chewing up my brain already!'

'There's an ongoing reinvestigation in the case, Leo ...' Samar said helplessly. 'I don't even know if I can leave the country. My passport is with the police.'

'For fuck's sake!' Leo shouted. 'I could soon be six feet under and you're married to the damn case? Drop out of all proceedings. Say you've got to be some place else.'

Samar looked at his feet.

Leo looked at Samar and felt out of breath. Samar had always been more devoted to Zaira than to him, he thought, and this was only proof of his suspicions; even in her death she exercised a sly, inveterate force over Samar. How little he had known Samar, and how much he had trusted him!

'That was the thing from the start,' Leo said, seething. 'I could never tell if you were with her or with me.'

'Please don't be upset, Leo ...'

'How d'you think I felt when you left me and ran off to Zaira? Your cosy meals together. Walks at midnight. Unending phone calls. On the night before she was taken out you were having one of your precious dinners. Do you know,' he said, jabbing his finger at his chest, 'I was at home *alone* that night?'

'I went to her place because I thought inviting her over to our place would be an intrusion for you.'

'Don't turn this into some sort of sacrifice you made for me! I was never a part of your sweet little set-up. You think I didn't know that she couldn't stand the sight of me?'

'Zaira did not hate you, Leo; you have the wrong impression.'

'Just shut up, Samar. Shut the fuck up!' Leo was pacing the room. 'She hated my guts; she hated herself for introducing me to you. As far as she was concerned, I was taking over *her* turf.'

Mr Ward-Davies looked nervously from one man to the other. He leapt off the bed and bolted again for the door.

Samar knew he could either feed the fire of this row, or he could bow and rein in the situation with grace; he chose the latter. 'Leo, I was being stupid. Of course I'll come. Nothing and no one is as important to me as you are.'

'It doesn't matter; I can take care of myself,' Leo said defiantly.

'Let me wrap up the loose ends so we can fly out together.'

'You sound like you're doing me a favour. I'm not waiting around for anybody's charity ... and I certainly don't want you to feel like you gave up on the case for *me*.'

'I want to do this for myself.' He sensed his response had been thoughtless, and this filled him with guilt. If he had to forsake the trial to look after Leo then that's what he would do; there were only so many battles he could pick, and only so many he could survive. 'I'm sorry. I'm unspeakably sorry ...'

The emotion in Samar's voice melted Leo's rage. 'Samar ...' He sat down on the bed.

'Yes?'

Burying his face in his hands, Leo sobbed from the dark, tarnished core of his being. 'What have I got myself into?'

Samar looked over his shoulder; the candle in the room had gone out.

22

A FEW DAYS AFTER LEO'S DISCLOSURE, SAMAR called Karan. 'Can you please come by?' Outside his window, dawn dipped its arms into the bowl of a scarlet sky.

'Of course.' Karan heard fear tremble in Samar's tone.

As he pulled on his jeans and his tee-shirt he remembered the time Iqbal had called him to report that Samar had been spotted at Gatsby. He could clearly picture Samar tap dancing on the bar counter, hitting his head against a suspended lamp. He remembered Diya Sen standing in her knickers, a sparkling vision of lust, and a man in an orange sarong with a dandy wrist. What a long way he had come from that night, he thought in the taxi on his way to Worli, as an indescribable sorrow clenched his heart.

Karan reached Samar's cottage at 5.00 a.m.

Samar was waiting for him by the pool, watching Mr Ward-Davies roll about on the dew-drenched grass. He rose as soon as he saw Karan part the French doors. 'Shall we go for a walk?'

'Sure.'

On the Worli promenade, under the sheath of retreating night, Karan asked him about the latest developments. 'Any news from the police?'

'Wrote it off as a vandal attack.' Samar pulled at Mr Ward-Davies's leash.

'Cowards.'

'Did I tell you I got two threat calls? The bastard on the line swore he would tear me into two if I spoke up in the retrial.'

'What did you tell him?'

'I said I wasn't going to back off, and that if he called again I'd get the police on their tail.'

'So Minister Prasad is *really* gunning for you now.'

Samar looked at Karan quietly, desperate to tell him about Leo's illness.

'Look at it from the minister's point of view,' Karan continued. 'If his son was sent to the lock-up, the HPP would kick his sorry ass. But now that Malik is walking free, they've *still* got him in a corner.'

'He's not a happy man.'

'Aren't you grateful for the media's support?'

'I guess ... but Leo believes the attack on the house was set off by my talking so much to the press.'

Karan said, 'How's he recovering?'

But before Samar could answer, Karan sneezed loudly.

'His cut is healing well; the stitches should be out next week.' Samar touched Karan's shoulder. 'You look pretty wrung out yourself'

'Rotten cold last couple of days.'

'I'm sorry I haven't called—'

'You had a lot going on, Samar.'

'Have you been to work?'

'On and off.'

'More off than on?'

'Iqbal said he might have to let me go.'

'What?'

'Well, Iqbal cut me a lot of slack during the trial because I often didn't turn up for work as I was at the courthouse. He was a brick. But now he wants me back on the saddle, and I'm just not up to it.'

'But surely he must know you'll need some time to get back into gear.'

'He suspects I've lost my nerve.' Karan bent to tickle Mr Ward-Davies and the dog's body wiggled with pleasure. 'He knows I'm not going to be able to take the kind of photographs I used to.'

When they resumed their stroll, Samar asked, 'Would it help if you took time off?'

'I doubt it. This big, bad wind came and knocked everything over inside here,' Karan said, jabbing his head with his index finger.

Samar had noticed a shift in Karan—not only the physical disrepair but also something else that was intangible and severe. It was as if the world had descended upon him in all its terrifying beauties: betrayal and disappointment threatened to wreck him. Through this wound, small sparkling things would enter Karan and shake him by his bones. The ache would pave the fat from him, leaving him with muscle and angularity. That's when the wolf in him would finally feel safe enough to emerge from its shadowy retreat.

'There's too much fuzz on the lens.' Karan rubbed his chest. Now every day in Bombay felt like walking deeper into quicksand.

'You could take brilliant photographs with blinders on.' Samar stopped as Mr Ward-Davies sniffed a lamp post. 'Besides, if things don't work out with Iqbal, any joint in this city will hire you.'

'But I don't *want* to work for another magazine. Iqbal is a dream boss. He raps my knuckles, and cheers me on. He knows when I have to pull myself together, and he knows when to let me be in my corner. I was a college kid when I joined him; he gave me his old Leica, and I still use it to do most of my work. He saved me from Delhi and got me this job in Bombay. When I decided Bombay was the subject of my study, he knew I wasn't joking.'

'He does sound like a dream boss.'

'And now I'm showing Iqbal in bad light at the headquarters. The hacks who think in headlines are going: Boss's Protégé Fucks Up Big-time.'

'I had no idea Iqbal meant so much to you.'

'We prize people in quiet, simple ways; just because we don't go on about them doesn't mean they don't mean ... the world to us.'

Samar thought to himself then that perhaps Karan was telling him how much he had come to miss Zaira. 'Have you told Rhea?'

'No. She doesn't give a shit what happens to me. She can't swallow the fact that I have given up on my camera. Our time together is now a wrap-up, I guess.'

'I guess she must feel awful that you gave up; after all, she took you around the block.'

'She took me around, and we talked pictures for miles.' Deep in Karan's eyes, a little bird thrashed against the dusty window of an abandoned room.

'She was good to you,' he said, wishing he had had a chance to know Rhea. They had met only once, in the courthouse on the day of the verdict: he had folded his hands, and she had smiled at him, and they had gone their own ways.

'We talked about Atget and his Paris ... about war photography and ethics ... of Cartier-Bresson. All those hours, those weeks, those months blur into each other ...' He looked furious when he said, 'I find it insulting to have to consider she was more interested in my work than in who I am. I never thought things would end this way.'

'End? Aren't you being a bit dramatic?' Samar arched his eyebrows.

Karan said dejectedly, 'Well, it's all headed downhill in a hurry; besides, she said that her husband suspects something's going on.'

'Well, that's got to be a bummer.'

'One time I went to see her, and she had the guts to look right through me!'

'You went to see her? But didn't you just say that her husband had smelled a rat? Isn't it best to lie low?'

Karan did not appear to heed Samar's words. 'I waited outside her apartment block for hours.'

'But she's got to cover her tracks, Karan! She's got a husband. And a marriage she might want to save.'

'I waited outside her apartment block and when she went by in her car she didn't even stop!'

'Maybe she didn't see you?'

'Maybe. But then one evening I went to the fruit sellers outside Amarsons. She was buying pomegranates. I tried to speak to her but she pretended to be busy. She didn't give me the time of day.'

'Perhaps her husband was nearby—'

'She probably thinks I'm following her around Bombay.' Karan tilted his head as he heard a car approaching them from behind, and a few seconds later the car went past them.

'And are you?'

'Well, sometimes I see her when she's out shopping or I'm hanging around Silver Oaks Estate. I have to keep an eye on her.'

'She's a grown woman; she doesn't need anyone to keep an eye on her.' Samar knew his voice sounded more strident than it needed to, but he could feel himself growing irritated on Rhea's behalf.

The sound of a car zooming away in the distance, its tyres burning up the tar, distracted Karan momentarily. He turned his head to look. 'I guess that must freak her out.'

'You know, you might be on to something here,' Samar said as discreetly as he could.

'You're saying I'm losing it?'

'You're spending too much time alone. And hanging around outside her apartment is not the right thing to do. She probably thinks you're stalking her ...'

'Stalking? Isn't that slightly extreme?'

'I'm sorry if I have offended you, Karan, but perhaps she's coming apart at the seams as a result of your attention?'

'No—maybe you have a point. Am I sounding like a loon to you?' He ruffled his thick black hair with his hands. 'Have I gone off the deep end?'

Samar sighed. 'I'm saying you need to go easy on her, Karan. Step back and try to see—not only see her as a married woman but also see yourself as the man you used to be before you met her.'

He bit his lip. 'Do you think Rhea ever loved me?'

'It's too early to swing to the past tense.'

'I'm not sure she ever did.'

'She has to have.'

'A little?'

'Who'd settle for anything less than the whole nine yards for you?'

'I spent some of the most beautiful afternoons of my life watching her work in her studio.' His mouth scrunched up with pain. 'She has such long, tender, purposeful hands, and fingernails painted the colour of ox blood.'

Samar was quiet for a few seconds. He was trying to find something to say that would comfort Karan, parent him through this smouldering agony. But words were like shadows, indecipherable and elusive. On some days love was a big bad truck cruising down a freeway, and you were only a skunk in its path: a stripped, stinking piece of aspiring road kill. 'Anything I say is futile but I hope you know that you're not in this alone.'

'Are you telling me something about Leo here?'

'I've been trying to, Karan.'

'I'm sorry; I've been a self-indulgent asshole. Tell me what's going on.'

Samar braced himself to speak when Karan had to interrupt him again. 'Did you see that car?'

'What car?'

Mr Ward-Davies lifted his head and sniffed the air.

'It was coasting in our direction before it turned the bend. It was ...'

'I didn't see it. I did hear a car racing, though, a few minutes ago.'

'Probably some rich kid rushing home after a night out at a club. Sorry to have cut you off. You were saying ...'

'About Leo ... He's going to return to San Francisco very soon.'

'But he goes back every few months ...'

'This is different. The thing is ...' As Samar steeled himself to go on, the black car that Karan had seen earlier came up to them from behind and slowed down beside them.

The driver of the car extended his hand and shoved a piece of paper, an address, into Samar's hand. Samar studied the piece of paper and gave him directions to his destination.

The driver thanked him for his help, and before Samar knew it Mr Ward-Davies's leash had been yanked out of his hand. A sharp, terrified whine punctured the air as the car sped off.

Samar and Karan tore along as the car raced and slowed and raced again.

Then they saw Mr Ward-Davies slam into a lamp post and heard a sound like a twig crackling in a fire. The dog's body became completely limp. The car zoomed down its path with Mr Ward-Davies hanging like a toy at the end of a string. As suddenly as the driver had snatched up Mr Ward-Davies, he let go. Then the car turned a corner and vanished from sight.

Samar and Karan fell on their knees, on either side of Mr Ward-Davies, their shirts, damp with perspiration, plastered on their backs.

'Something is hanging by the end of this nerve.'

'It's his eye. The blood vessels have burst.'

'What are you doing Samar?'

'Trying to put it back in its place.'

'He's breathing; we should get him to a vet. Leave his eye alone. I don't know if it can be saved.'

'I have to fix it.' Samar's hands went red again. 'Please,' he said looking up at Karan beseechingly, 'make him stop whining.'

'I'm sorry.'

'Just make him hush. Make him whole again.'

'Let me get a taxi.'

'His eye is not staying, Karan; it's not staying.'

'Please Samar, don't touch it. Let it be.'

'I can't leave it on the kerb. This is my baby.'

'Let's go to the vet. He will know what to do ... Please ... don't do anything.'

'They took my baby. Oh God, my baby.' Samar was breathless, weeping, turned inside out with pain.

'There, I see a taxi.'

'His eye is not staying in place!'

'We might be able to save him.'

'They took my baby, Karan; they took him from me ...'

23

FOLLOWING THE AFTERNOON WHEN THE VERDICT on Zaira's case was delivered, Rhea had planned never to take Karan's calls again, claiming that Adi was in town. She was furious that he had stalled her in a public place; she would have been happy to talk to him privately but the indiscretion of his actions had stoked the fire of her wrath. At the courthouse her anxiety had been compounded further when she had seen Malik entering his car; she believed she had seen something worryingly familiar in his countenance. Malik's face continued to flash before her eyes, and she struggled to locate what had unsettled her so. She had hoped to talk about it when she had met Karan at the Babulnath temple; she also hoped to convey her distress and her anger at the deceitful trial and the unfair judgement. But on the way down from the temple, Karan had

raised his hand as if to hit her and she had wanted to flee there and then. And then, over the last few days, his conduct had been shocking. She saw him lurking outside her apartment block and was forced to drive off in such haste that she almost ran over a stray cat. Then there was the time when she was shopping for fruit outside Amarsons and she suddenly felt his hand on her shoulder. Even the fruit vendor had given Karan a look that said, Keep off!

She had tried her best to keep the break as dignified as possible, hoping that her silent treatment would make him go away. But she was perplexed to discover that the reverse had happened.

'Can you *please* not call me?' she said into the phone when she heard Karan's voice at the other end for the fifth time that day.

'You haven't given me a reason why you won't see me, Rhea.'

'You want to take a different route in your life, and I wish you good luck with that.'

'You sound like you're firing me from a job.'

'Do you have *any* idea how many questions Adi asks me when you keep calling up like this?'

'That's *your* problem, Rhea.'

'Why're you being such a jerk? I don't mean to make it sound like it was a favour but I put in a lot of my time in your life, and *this* is payback?'

'Don't talk to me like that.' He took another gulp of whisky, liquid fire going down his dry throat.

'You don't have *any* right to talk to me like *that.*' She remembered again the encounter at the Babulnath temple, his impulse to strike her. A shiver ran up her spine.

'But I am. I'm furious. I can't help it.'

'You're furious with me?' Feeling nauseous, she pressed her tongue against the roof of her mouth, hoping the feeling would go away.

'You asked for it.'

'I don't believe this!'

'You led me on!'

'I took you around Bombay in good faith.'

'No. You led me on.'

'Maybe I did,' she said. 'But here's where you get off.' Rhea banged the phone down and stood by the phone console, shaking. She composed herself when Adi called out to her from the bedroom. The nausea, which had plagued her over several days, abated.

'Coming, jaan!' she said. She bit her lower lip, rubbed her eyes dry. She took a deep breath, told herself: *Everything is just right.*

'Who were you talking to?' Adi asked.

'Oh, some annoying telemarketer.'

'They call so late in the day?'

'I'm getting tired of Bombay, Adi.'

'Then why don't you come with me to Singapore? I have an assignment that's likely to keep me there. We could use it as our base for a year or so.'

'I might have to do that,' she said, suddenly energized by the proposition. 'At least these bloody telemarketers will leave me alone.'

That night, exiled from the land of sleep, Rhea clung to Adi, unable to tell him what was uppermost on her mind: that she had seen Malik Prasad for the first time and it had scared her senseless. Her fear, which briskly consumed her, was anchored in her naivety: she had expected to see some vivifying confirmation of Malik's wicked character, some nervous tic, some telling scar. But there had been nothing to indict Malik, so worryingly plain-faced, in fact, that had she seen him at a party or in a crowd she would never have suspected that he was the sort of man who could gun down a woman in cold blood.

What a poor judge of character she was!

To recover from the innocence of her convictions, she took off for their home in Alibaug. But there too Malik's face continued to flash before her eyes. She could not sleep properly, worrying constantly that anyone could jump over the boundary wall and enter the house. She wondered why they had appointed neither a doorman nor a guard. On her third evening in Alibaug, she noticed someone skulking outside the gate. Was it Karan? She rushed indoors, latched her door. Her heart bolted up to her throat. She instructed the gardener to

sleep right outside her bedroom that night and, a few hours later, before daybreak, fled back to Bombay.

A fortnight later, Adi walked into the house to find Rhea sitting on the bed amidst the pillows and sheets looking indulgendy regal.

She patted the bed. 'Come here, please.'

In his light blue shirt and silver tie Adi looked like another corporate type, but his loveliness lay in quiet places.

He sat by her, sensing she had something to tell him.

She undid his tie, admiring his classical nose, the thick line of eyebrow; *this is my territory,* she thought, *this is mine.*

Then, gently, she broke the news.

'Isn't this amazing?' she said, finally. 'After all these years ...' Adi's face froze; slowly, the muscles around his jaw relaxed. He smiled.

He held her hands, then kissed the tips of her fingers. 'I can't believe it, Rhea.' He flopped back on the bed, overwhelmed. When he shut his eyes, his life floated by in hazy, disorganized snapshots. He saw the tree he had climbed to get Rhea the fireflies; he saw himself walking down an abandoned street in midtown Manhattan; he saw himself standing next to Rhea on a barge on the day of their wedding; he saw Rhea in the animal shelter, rocking a puppy in her arms. The random images slowly coalesced into a picture of perfection, an immunity from fate's insurmountable inequity. He was reminded of a piece of baroque music: each instrument surged forward in anticipation of unity to allow the resultant counterpoint more than benign

consonance, and elevate the experience to the level of sublime lyricism.

He sat up, shaking his head. 'Are you sure?'

She walked to the desk, picked up a white envelope and opened its flap. She waved the gynaecologist's letter confirming the news. 'I double-checked.'

'You're not teasing me?'

'I wouldn't, Adi, not about something as important as this.'

'You're sure?'

'As sure as I can be right now.'

'Oh man! This is the best day of my life!'

'Adi, put me down!'

'You've made me the happiest man on this whole damn planet, Rhea Dalal.' Hoisting her over his shoulders he ran out of the bedroom and circled the living room.

'Put me down! You're crazy!' She slammed her wrists on his back repeatedly, her bangles jangling. 'Put me down! For God's sake, Adi, get a hold on yourself ...'

'I'm crazy! I am. And you, my crowned goddess, are my craziness!'

Adi was to fly out to Singapore the following afternoon. He cancelled his flight and took the week off. They spent seven blissful days in Alibaug, together, alone.

On this trip, fearing no intruder, she slept soundly.

Upon their return from Alibaug, Rhea busied herself with her everyday tasks. Adi returned from Singapore after a fortnight. On the day he returned she cooked him an elaborate

meal of the Gujarati delicacies he relished: dhokla, patra, shrikhand. Rhea was talking to Adi about a new surly but bright doctor at the animal shelter when he interrupted her. Miss Cooper, the chummy hag who lived on the floor below theirs, had asked him more than once about a man who had visited while he was in Singapore. 'Is that charming young man your nephew?' she had asked.

'Who's the guy who calls up at odd hours of the night?'

'What do you mean?' Rhea's guts bunched up.

'He hangs up when I pick up.' Adi deftly tore at a puran poli. 'Surely you know who I'm talking about, babes?'

Drawing a deep breath she looked out of the window at the thick crown of a haunted banyan, at the scarred, shining hide of the Arabian Sea. After a sip of water she faced Adi confidently, for a piece of fiction had arisen unbidden in her and she surrendered to its transformative avalanche. 'Yes, I do know who he is.'

She started off by confessing that the man who called her frequently was actually known to her. 'Around two or three months ago I got a call from my friend Meera who was with me in college, while you were in New York.'

'You had a friend?'

'It is possible, Adi, even for me,' she said dryly. 'Anyhow, Meera got married and moved to Bangalore. Earlier this year she called to say that her brother-in-law was in Bombay for work, and asked if I could help him out. I asked Meera what kind of help he was looking for. She said, basic stuff. The number of

a good doctor; recommendation for a decorator.' She paused to swallow a spoonful of shrikhand. 'Meera's an old friend. I just *had* to say yes. I met this fellow, Karan Something-or-the-Other, and answered all the questions he had ...'

Adi's mouth fell open. 'The man came to our house?'

'Yes,' she said. 'For a bit.'

'So Miss Cooper was right.'

Rhea lowered her eyes, as if trying to remember something.

'And you never even told me?' he asked, his voice quavering with suspicion.

'As far as I was concerned, jaan, he didn't really exist. All I did was answer a few queries. He was some photographer type who wanted suggestions for locations, where to shoot, etc., etc.,' she said as casually as she could. 'So I gave him tips on a few of the places I like in the city.' She ladled a dollop of shrikhand on the side of Adi's silver thali. 'I had *no* inkling he'd go all wonky on me.'

'Wonky?' Adi's eyes widened.

'I mean'—she caught her words when she saw Adi's expression—'he asked me out to lunch! Can you believe the nerve? I said no, of course. Then he sent me flowers. That's when I told him to keep away. I was tempted to call Meera and ask her to intervene.'

'Why in God's name didn't you tell me all this was going on?'

'You're in Singapore half the month, Adi. I didn't want you losing sleep over a trivial matter.'

'But you should have told me! This is not a trivial matter.'

'So you could extend some long-distance security service of your own?' Her ears pinched back. 'If you feel so strongly about my safety why do you go away in the first place?'

'I go to Singapore because you've always insisted you could never live with anyone full-time; early on, you set down the rules of our marriage, and one of them was that you needed alone time.'

'I needed time to work. In case you forgot, I gave up my career for this marriage.'

'I know that. You don't need to rub it in.'

'I gave up a scholarship to study in Berlin.'

'Aren't we veering off the subject we were discussing?'

'No, I'm just clarifying something here, Adi.'

'Well, I get your point.'

'And, if it helps, I did call my friend Meera and ask her to speak to Karan. He promptly denied ever sending me flowers! I felt humiliated. I figured he would go away ...'

'But he hasn't, obviously.'

'He still calls now and then.'

'And you try to pass this Karan off as a telemarketer?'

'He's a pain,' she said. 'I didn't want you to worry about some dopehead, darling.'

'Do you have any idea how these things can pan out?'

She looked at him, her face as blank as an author's first page, uninitiated by word.

'A girl who was in my class at NYU was butchered by her ex-boyfriend. She was sleeping in her studio in Williamsburg when he stole in and took her out with a bottle on the head. He hacked her up with a knife and fed her body parts to the piranhas in her tank.'

'That's sick!'

'These things happen *all* the time. Did you never stop to think about Zaira? Do you think she ever assumed some freak who had a crush on her would one day blow up her brains in a bar?'

'You're right.' Rhea looked appalled, as if such a thought had never crossed her mind. 'You want more kadhi with your rice?'

'No, I'm done,' he replied crossly. 'Now, shall we report this Karan fellow to the police?'

'What will it achieve?' Rhea felt out of breath. 'We're leaving Bombay in a short time anyway.'

'Is that why you suggested we move to Singapore? Because you were starting to fear this fellow?'

'What a ridiculous notion!' She stood up; the discussion was getting out of hand now.

'Well, I'd like to report him nevertheless. The police will track his calls and give him a thrashing.'

'I'm not sure if it's sensible to provoke such a man. God knows what these hot-blooded small-town sorts can do.'

'That ought to have occurred to you before you invited him over, Rhea!'

Before he could shout another word, she clutched her stomach, her mouth contorted. She fled the dining room and rushed into the bathroom where she retched into the white porcelain basin.

Adi rushed to her side. 'You okay?'

'I'm not handling the pregnancy too well, am I?' She wiped her mouth.

'You're doing fine; you'll be even better once we're in Singapore.'

'I don't know what came over me, Adi.' She was sobbing now, subsumed by an overwhelming sadness for Karan, burnt to cinders in the bright flames of her fiction.

'It's going to be fine, jaan.' Adi hugged her, chiding himself for pressing her with his questions during such a delicate time.

'Maybe I'm not cut out to be a mother. Becoming a mother changes you.'

'You'll handle it like a pro.'

'Motherhood is not a profession.'

'I mean you'll take to it like a duck to water.'

'To be a mother demands that you be a better person. A good person ...'

'You are one already. You are a good person.'

She looked confused, even exasperated. 'A good person?'

'A good woman,' he reaffirmed. 'You, my love, are a good woman.'

As his fingertips touched her cheek and he focussed his inky black eyes on her, tears left her eyes. She felt once again

the entire world bursting in upon her: rivers uncoiled, lions roared, a marigold bloomed, a mass of clouds floated over a delta, orange lava bristled, the sea churned, a cocoon split open and something with green gossamer wings emerged from it.

24

WHEN KARAN CALLED RHEA TO TELL HER ABOUT Mr Ward-Davies she decided to forgo her decision never to see him again; besides, she thought it would be better to tell him in person about her plan to relocate to Singapore.

'Right outside his house?' She sat on the love seat, the phone against her ear, dazed. 'In Worli?'

'I was with Samar.'

'Again?'

'I must be a curse.'

'Don't be absurd.'

'Can I see you, Rhea? Please.' He looked out at the dirty pond beyond his balcony; two geese floated by serenely.

'I'm not sure if it's quite kosher right now ... Adi is in town.'

'Please. I need to see you.'

'What did you do with Mr Ward-Davies?'

'Buried him in Samar's lawn. Under the almond tree. Pickaxe left calluses on my palms.'

'Six-thirty. Near your place.' She could hear a cat wailing in full-bodied agony somewhere outside his room.

'I'm so glad to see you,' he said later that evening.

'I can't stay for very long.'

'Well, I'm glad you came.'

They started down the steps toward the pond, past skeletal men in white dhotis, an indolent brown cow, scruffy kids playing a noisy game with moss-green marbles.

'Samar must feel ruined.'

'He's in San Francisco. Leo refused to stay in the country—he had been preparing to leave for a while—and Samar thought it was better to go with him. The trial had been enough hassle, and now this came along ...' Karan paused, inhaled deeply. He could not erase the sight of Mr Ward-Davies from his mind, the bloodied, whining heap on the pavement, Samar trying to fix an eyeball into a socket. 'It's not going to be okay.'

'I know.'

'I just want the pain to stop.'

'It will, Karan, it will.'

They paused as he leaned against a wall, squeezed his eyes shut to hold in the tears.

She felt helpless, unable to comfort him; his pain was entirely his own land, unmapped, private. Perhaps he should never have gone so deep into the trial. Perhaps the witnesses

who had backed off had done it with good reason. Perhaps he ought never to have opened the dark beating thing in his chest to the ravages of love. *Look too closely at life,* she thought to herself, *and it can blind you senseless. So* it was best to take it in small doses; it was best to bake cakes, glaze ums, clean cabinets, watch television, go for walks, care for sick animals, fuck a husband, read a novel: all sustainable terrors.

They started to walk again, and she asked, 'Did Samar report the attack?'

'The police had a laugh at his expense. A dog croaked it, they said. Shit happens. This is Bombay, take it on the chin. Move right along, or they'll deck you again.'

'Did such a bitter response freak him out?'

'More so Leo. When I was digging the grave for Mr Ward-Davies he was on the phone to his travel agent.'

She reflected for a moment. 'It's strange how little you can ever know anyone.'

'Even yourself, for that matter,' he said, thinking about how easily he had walked away from photography. 'But I wonder if it was sensible for Samar to take off to San Francisco ... Samar had something on his mind on the morning Mr Ward-Davies was picked up. He was trying to tell me something; that's why he had called me at dawn. And just as he was about to ...' His expression was one of inexplicable concern. The worry in Samar's eyes had been like the sound of a mouse in the attic, an eerie, scurrying presence in hiding.

'What do you suspect it was?'

'Maybe that he could no longer soldier on with the retrial? Maybe that he was tired of Leo?'

'Well, without Samar the reinvestigation will lose its steam. In some ways he had become the trial's public face.'

'But how much can you expect him to do? He stood his ground even after the defence falsely accused him of hustling little boys. He survived a vandal attack on his house. His dog was picked up and slammed into a lamp post. He was bound to bum out at some point.'

'I hope he heals in San Francisco ... perhaps he was right to leave. Sometimes,' she said, 'leaving is much more difficult than staying on. But I suppose'—she closed her palm over her navel—'it's usually wiser in the long run.'

His ears pricked up. 'Are you telling me something here?'

'I'm moving to Singapore, in a month, once the Ganesh festival is over.'

'On holiday?' He gulped.

'No. It's time to settle there with Adi. He's been wanting it for the longest time. I had to say yes this time.'

'But you *hated* Singapore.'

'People change.' Her voice trembled with uncertainty, as if she had said the words aloud so she might believe them herself. 'People *have* to change.'

'So you no longer think Singapore is some sort of a gigantic mall where they spank you for spitting on the street?'

'Oh, I do. But Adi wants me to go with him, and I don't have a choice.'

'You had a choice all these years.'

'Well, not any longer.'

'You'll live there permanently?'

'We'll keep the house here, of course. But I'll move with him for now.'

They passed a dingy store with low chuna walls and thick, uneven ledges on which glass jars stuffed with orange sweets the shape of kidneys were arranged in a neat row.

'Is there a reason why you're giving up on Bombay?' A tremble took up his leg.

'Is there ever a reason for giving up on something?' she asked. 'Was there a reason you gave up on photography?'

Karan felt she was punishing him for giving up on his passion. Disturbed by the news of her impending relocation, Karan wanted to take Rhea into himself and run down the dirty, abandoned alleyways in his mind and show her he had been living rough and without cover. Then he wanted her tranquil, able hands to work on the cuts. But perhaps it was best not to expect anything, for he remembered how she had advised him not to take life personally; life happened to everyone.

'I've got some news of my own.'

She looked at him enquiringly.

'I got fired.' As he laughed, the uneven, diabolic peals made her want to flee that very instant but she steeled herself to hear more about his dismissal from *India Chronicle.*

'Iqbal fired you?'

'Yeah. He got rid of me, too.'

'Why?'

'I was missing many appointments. I couldn't deliver.'

'You shouldn't get spooked, Karan; any magazine will take you on in a heartbeat. Your work is fierce and glorious.' She toyed with the silver bangles on her wrist. 'But why don't you take a break before you apply for another position?'

'Maybe I should come along with Adi and you to Singapore; a spot of sightseeing with the Dalals might pad up my resume.'

She ignored the jibe. Her heart brimmed over; she wanted to keep him safe. 'Promise me you'll quit the bottle?'

'I don't owe *you* any promises.'

'If you don't have a job, how will you cover rent?'

'I've got savings.'

'Enough to tide you over?'

'Maybe.'

'Do you need any money?'

'No, no. My services were for free,' he said. 'I absolutely enjoyed fucking you, Mrs Dalal.'

'Well, I'm glad one of us did.' She lowered her head. 'Look, Karan, I don't want to leave you this way.'

'You shouldn't leave, Rhea ...' He slapped the side of his thigh to lick its trembling.

'I have to.'

'Just stay a few weeks longer. I promise I'll clean up; I'll go back to photography.'

'Karan, this is not about photography.' She felt tears gather at the corner of her eyes. She could not imagine that the sweet,

bumbling boy she had met in Chor Bazaar was now a weary, incoherent wreck: but the politics of the trial had seeped into him and left him sick and mucky. She wondered, then, what had been the point of their meeting; perhaps they had merely passed through each other, like ghosts passing through flesh, to be exorcized only by the formidable poltergeist of fate. But there was something else here, and although words eluded a description of the experience, an image came to her mind: a curator was adjusting a light over a painting in a gallery, and once the curator's job was done, he simply turned and walked away, leaving the painting perfectly lit and absolutely alone. She looked at her watch. 'Anyway, enough of talk, time for dinner at home.'

'And time for me to hit the bottle.'

'Stay sober.' She paused. Was the sorrow of loving a man greater than the pain of having to leave him? 'For my sake.'

'I'll stay sober, Mrs Dalal.' A bitter laugh tumbled out of his lips. 'For *your* sake.'

'Are you threatening me?'

'I'm saying you're keeping me from the bar,' he hissed. 'So why the fuck don't you get out of my face?'

25

RHEA EXPERIENCED THE DISADVANTAGES OF moving from Bombay at the time of the Ganesh festival on multiple levels. Lila-bai had taken off for her village for a fortnight to participate in the celebrations there, leaving Rhea saddled with the household chores in addition to overseeing the packing. Adi was often irritable because of tiresome traffic jams brought on by the celebrations. She didn't blame him for his moods; in fact, she too found the frazzled atmosphere charged with revelry and chaos, and longed for Bombay to return to its routine and form. Her neighbours turned pious overnight, handing out churma laddoos and chanting day and night. On the streets there were bright, noisy pandals at every corner, and traffic across the city became completely gridlocked when rowdy processions led statues of the deity to the sea.

One evening, Adi and Rhea found themselves miles from home, surrounded by a daunting mass of devotees.

Rhea had noticed that Adi had been antsy all week; now, in the frustrating propinquity of a traffic jam, she asked him if something was chewing at him.

Adi tightened his grip on the steering wheel. 'You were very irresponsible to let that Karan guy into our house, Rhea.'

'I know.' She decided to let him vent his suspicions; if she defended herself too much, it would only confirm her guilt.

'You should've told me he was acting up.' Outside their car, a frenetic, colourful parade of devotees chanted stridently. 'Why didn't you tell me about it when it happened?'

'I'm sorry, Adi.' She looked out of the window and sought solace in the city that she had explored with Karan. An awful, insurmountable loss fluttered in the distance. She knew she would miss Karan in ways she had not yet imagined. 'I just didn't want to upset you. It seemed inconsequential at the time, and I'm quite good at handling tricky situations. Why don't you take one of the lanes where we might get less traffic?' she suggested casually.

'I know you're adept at handling most situations, Rhea, but you can never be sure with these things. I mean, look at what happened to Zaira. It would seem that a celebrity of her stature was unassailable and yet ...'

She cupped her hands around her face. 'Why're we talking about Zaira and the trial? I'm sick of it!'

'Rhea?' He looked at her with concern, but a sliver of suspicion pricked his mind. Was she deflecting from the conversation at hand with a quick crying jag? 'What's up?'

'I don't know if I'm ready to have a child,' she said, clearing her throat.

'Of course you are!'

'I don't know, Adi.'

'We've wanted to have a child forever, Rhea.'

She rolled her eyes. 'You, Adi, have been wanting to have a child. *You.*'

'Are you saying a child will make no difference to *your* life?'

'I am sure it will, and not all the differences are going to be as pleasant as you make them sound.'

'Tell me what scares you about becoming a mom. Do you worry your life is going to turn upside down? That you won't be able to attend to your pottery for a few months? That you will have to quit the animal shelter ...'

'Why would I quit the animal shelter?'

He looked at her in amazement. 'Are you kidding? You should have stopped going as soon as you knew you were pregnant. All those stray mutts in that skanky place carrying God alone knows what kind of bugs ...'

'So it's fine for *me* to hang out with bugs in "that skanky place",' she said mordantly, 'but God forbid if I expose *your* child to them!'

'That's not what I meant ...' Luckily, traffic had parted now and the road was clear all the way up to Haji Ali.

'Am I some sort of a cow? Useful only when in calf? When I can be milked?'

'Rhea!' He braked abruptly and pulled over to the side of the road. 'Do you have *any* idea how much I love you?'

'And do you have *any* idea how much I don't know if I will be able to love this child? Now,' she said impatiently, 'can we please get home?'

'This is absurd.' He started the car again.

'Is it? Why?'

'Because there isn't a single mother on this planet who would not love her own flesh and blood.'

'Oh, please, spare me that Mother Earth bakwaas!' Only a few days ago at the animal shelter a pie dog had eaten her newborn puppy; one day, she decided, she would tell Adi about the incident to inspire him to revisit his corny notions of maternal love. 'What if I bring this child into the world and can't care for it?'

'Sweetheart ...' Adi purred, 'you're asking all these deep and meaningful questions ... but the questions have no basis to them. You're not even a mother yet! Once our baby arrives, everything will change. You'll even look back on your outburst and laugh. You'll adore the baby more than you do me.' He scrunched up his face with mock envy. 'I'm going to come second place.'

'I don't know why I've been crying, why my moods are all over the place ...'

'Maybe it's because of that photographer freak. He's unhinged you. You're feeling vulnerable and insecure, that's why you're talking like this.'

'You think so?' she asked. Under ordinary circumstances, she would have reproached such a childish deduction but today she wanted to believe Adi because she was having trouble believing herself: if life were only a catalogue of illusions, why couldn't she occupy his, now that her own had failed her so fabulously?

'The dude's taken over your thoughts.'

She looked out of the window of the car and saw hundreds of pigeons soaring into the indigo heart of the late evening sky. The birds took off from the temple courtyard, circled Cadbury House, then turned back and landed in the same courtyard they had fled. Roosting birds fly the coop, she thought; but then they also fly back home.

'I wouldn't go so far as that ... But maybe you do have a point,' she said. 'That man could be mad.'

'That worries me; we might have a real psycho on our hands.'

Like a valium in whisky, at Adi's utterance of the word—*psycho*—Rhea's entire body melted into the narrative that had opened wide its devious arms to embrace her. *Karan Seth was a psycho. She was the victim of his terrible attention. But now Adi, her husband, would keep her safe.* These lines became the mantra that could keep her marriage intact. Not only did the word *psycho* possess a nimbus of insanity, but it also came with

a textbook tinge of pathology; she could forgive Karan once she accepted that he was, in fact, clinically crazy.

'Let's have a drink when we get back,' she said as they started up the banyan-shaded slope of Silver Oaks Estate.

'I don't think that would be good for you,' Adi said firmly.

'What would not be good for me?'

'Alcohol. Under the circumstances.'

'Oh, damn,' she whacked her palm on her forehead. 'I forgot. The bloody baby.'

'Darling, please—'

'Try not to work yourself into a sweat, Adi,' she snapped as the car pulled up at their entrance. She stepped out in a huff. 'I'm going to have to be a teetotaller for the next few months while you get to guest-lecture me on how I should live my life for your kid. Welcome to the party, sunshine.'

In the lift they were met by Miss Cooper, her trusty, incontinent dachshund held firmly on a leash. Miss Cooper smiled at them gingerly, unsure why both Rhea and Adi looked like they didn't want to be in the lift with her.

On the day of the visarjan, the last day of the festival, Karan stumbled into his kitchenette, plucked out the sharp steel blade his landlady used to mince lamb into a fine keema and, slipping the blade under his arm, stepped out into an evening of scintillating chaos. Thousands of men, women, children, decked in lower-order finery of their choice, were marching toward the sea. On Napean Sea Road a giant canary-yellow Ganesh with

a curved white tusk and indigo robes painted over his divine obesity, was seated on a plaster peacock, surrounded by devotees with a distinctly bovine air about them. Karan stumbled in front of a lorry; luckily, it skid to a halt inches before him.

The driver thrust his neck out of the window, 'Rand ki aulad! Can't you see where you're going?'

Picking himself up, Karan brushed off the dirt from his sweaty tee-shirt and carried on walking toward Breach Candy, to Silver Oaks Estate.

When the elevator halted on the ninth floor, he stepped out, a whirring in his head.

He rang the doorbell.

Rhea answered.

The sight of him, smothered in red dust and yellow sepals, swaying drunkenly, provoked her to panic. 'Get out!'

Rhea's urgent whisper was like acid thrown on his face.

'Adi is in the dining room. If he catches you he'll thrash you to within an inch of your life. Go!'

'*Listen* to yourself!' Karan was lurching from side to side. 'What a warm welcome from the lady of the house!'

She caught sight of the blade under his arm. 'Why're you here, Karan? What do you want?'

Right then, Adi appeared on the scene.

'I'm here to ask this man a few questions,' Karan slurred.

'Watch out, Adi!' She gripped her husband's arm. 'He has a knife.'

'Who is this?'

Karan stared at Adi. 'I want to have a word with you. You might like to know a thing or two.'

Sensing there was not a moment to waste, she cried out in horror, 'Adi! It's him, the psycho.'

'Psycho?' Before Karan might say another word, Adi's fist had decked him to the floor.

'How dare you!' Adi shouted.

'Stop it ...' Rhea yanked at Adi's shoulder. 'Just let it go. Come inside, Adi.'

But Adi was on top of Karan, delivering punch after punch.

'Adi ... let's go in, please ...' Rhea tried to haul Adi indoors but found herself powerless before his brute strength.

Although he tried to hit back, Karan could not fend off Adi successfully for the booze had left him blurry and dazed.

Slowly, each punch seemed to smash the inebriation out of him and the pain began to register with awful sincerity.

When Karan was at the edge of the stairs, Rhea flew into the scuffle. 'Leave him, Adi. Let him go!'

'You stay out of this.'

'Adi! Listen to me!'

'Rhea ... Get back inside or you'll get hurt.'

'I don't care—come in.' Rhea was holding Adi by his waist, trying to drag him back. 'Leave him be ...'

Adi paid her no mind. 'I'll break every single one of your goddamned bones ... Harami ... fucking son of a bitch.'

'Please, Adi!'

'You think you can barge into my house and …' Adi aimed another blow at Karan's face.

'Let him go, Adi!'

Karan's nostrils shot open, blood dripped out, he folded up like a smashed-up marionette.

'Motherfucker!'

The blade, slipping out of Karan's arm, went sliding down the stairwell. Adi looked at its dirty shine and looked up at Rhea. Even in his rage he felt comforted to know he had saved her from the pyscho.

'You'll rot in hell, you piece of shit,' Adi yelled as he stood up, heaving. 'Trying to go after a married woman … A *pregnant* married woman at that …'

'Please, I'm begging you, Adi …' She was crying now. *Who had Karan wanted to kill?*

Adi's final kick, on Karan's temple, knocked him out, but not before he heard Adi shout: 'You could've taken two lives, asshole!'

Retreating inside, Rhea leaned against the wall, closed her eyes and slid to the floor, as weightless as a feather floating down from the grey sky.

26

THIRTEEN HOURS AND NINE MINUTES AFTER Karan was deposited at Bombay General Hospital, with a face like the torn sole of a discarded shoe, a nurse asked him if he had any people in Bombay. In the haze of his defacement, he struck off Zaira, Samar, Rhea—which left him with only his former boss and mentor to call. Even Iqbal Syed, long hard-nosed to violence that could mangle the human form in unimaginable ways, felt his jaws slacken at the sight of Karan, marauded out of recognition by a man watching over the woman who would mother his child—a crocodile rage. In addition to the velocity of Adi's fury, sadness stirred up by Rhea's deception had swum into the ridges and ruptures of Karan's body, from where it now radiated a kind of holy, overcast beauty. At Karan's behest, Iqbal called Samar in San

Francisco, who found it impossible to believe what Rhea's husband had done to Karan: two broken ribs, a hairline fracture of the elbow, a concussion, multiple cuts.

Iqbal did not ask Samar to come to Bombay.

But once the details sank in, Samar could not help but imagine Karan's giant, unbearable loneliness. He thought of how they had partied at his cottage, the long Sunday lunches at Zaira's apartment, the terrible night at Maya Bar, the exhausting hours at the police station, the long, menacing days at the courthouse. Karan had come with him to the hospital when Zaira was on his lap, breathing her last. Karan had dug Mr Ward-Davies's grave when Samar was paralysed with grief. Samar knew that Karan's cuts would heal and his bruises would mend—but this, a personal dismantling, was an entirely different kettle of fish.

Samar had to think many times before leaving San Francisco. Leo had been through a particularly rough patch: he had spent a week in hospital fighting off a nasty bout of the shingles. But now he was home, in recovery. When Leo heard about Karan he encouraged Samar to go to Bombay; he, too, remembered how Karan had been there for them during the trial. At the airport, Leo kissed Samar and he felt as if he was kissing the man he loved goodbye forever. On the flight Samar heard a rumble in his chest, and when he tried to sleep, he saw himself on the Worli pavement, a bloodied hound at his feet, hands flailing at the relentless saffron sky.

In the languor of Karan's recuperation, when memories of Rhea took nips at him like a pack of hyenas, Samar read him fairy tales, cooked bad, *bad* lasagna, brought him bunches of tiger lilies, adjusted his bandages when the wounds were sore. They watched old films together. They took walks in the lawn of Samar's cottage and sat by Mr Ward-Davies's grave. When Karan was better, Samar took him to Gatsby one evening. The elegant guests gawked at the odd duo; they had the defiant, blessed gleam of survivors of a car crash. Between the knowledge that there was nothing a Bellini could not quite fix and few things a walk could not unknot, Karan fell a little in love with the man Zaira had loved a lot.

Late one night, Samar received a frantic phone call from Leo.

'Andrew died.'

'Lord. Was it—?'

'Pneumonia. Third attack.'

'Are you okay?'

'He was thirty-seven,' Leo said. 'His funeral is on Monday.'

Samar looked at his watch. 'I'll take the flight out tomorrow. I'll touch San Francisco late Sunday afternoon.'

'Which flight will you take?'

'British Airways, via London. It gets in at around 4.00 p.m.'

'I'll come, pick you up. Is Karan all right?'

'He'll be fine.'

'Are you sure you can come?'

'Absolutely.'

The next morning Samar told Karan he would be leaving in a couple of days for San Francisco. They were at the racecourse. It was an excellent morning. Horses were cantering in the paddock behind them, their coats glistening in the early morning sun. The fresh scent of dew-laden grass mingled with horse manure to complete the scene's bucolic charm. It was easy to forget that this green haven was located, in fact, in the midst of a concrete jungle.

'Can't you stay a while longer?'

'I'd like to do that more than anything else, but one of Leo's closest friends has died; Leo's come undone.'

'Oh, that's awful ... what happened to his friend?'

'He had AIDS.'

Karan froze.

'I'd been meaning to tell you before I left Bombay but Leo is also sick.'

'With AIDS?'

Samar nodded. 'I'm sorry to leave you like this, Karan, but I really do have to go back now. I don't think Leo can cope alone.' 'Where the hell did Leo pick up the bug?' Karan said after a moment's silence.

Samar looked as if he had been punched in the stomach. 'Pick up the bug? You make it sound like he went shopping for it.'

'I mean, *how* did he get sick?'

'That's not a good question.' Samar felt his pulse quickening.

'But only whores and drug addicts get it.'

'That's the last thing I expected to hear from a friend.'

'He could have made you sick,' Karan said. 'Are you, Samar? Are you sick?'

Samar pushed Karan. 'You're really crossing the line, Karan! Stop right there.'

Karan stumbled but caught his step. 'I'd be mad at Leo if he made you sick.'

'Just get out of here.'

'Are you sick, Samar?'

'I don't know! The only thing I do know is I'm looking forward to San Francisco more than anything else in the world.'

'You are going then?'

'I wish I had left earlier.' Samar started to march off.

'When you get back, ask Leo where he picked it up ...'

'Sure. Meanwhile, you can take a flying fuck to Mars,' Samar yelled as he neared the entry to the racecourse grounds. 'It's no wonder she dumped you.'

Karan watched Samar's back blur in the distance. He was distracted by a horse that bucked and neighed. Someone sounded a whip. When he turned, Samar was gone.

In San Francisco, Samar changed his phone number.

Within a fortnight of his return, Karan sent him a long, anxious, concerned letter. He said he had gone into shock when he heard about Leo's illness and didn't know what had come

over him. *I will never forgive myself for what I said, Samar, but I hope you will; you were always the better man.*

Samar read the letter with trembling impatience; how long were you supposed to put up with the bad manners of straight people? Once or twice, he even came close to picking up the phone and giving Karan a piece of his mind. But each time he reached for the receiver fatigue had watered his intentions. He had either spent the night rubbing a wet cloth over Leo's burning chest or he had been up reading about new diets that could help tank up the T-cells. If Leo had a few good days, they took off on long drives up the coast: for few things were as restorative as a ride by the ocean. As they drove by the powerful and healing blue, passing a temple of redwoods, Samar thought of Zaira. Wherever she was, he wanted her to answer one question: How much was one man supposed to take?

Other letters followed. And in each of his letters, Karan expressed heartfelt, vigorous regret, insisting he had acted out of character as he had never quite overcome Zaira's death. The prospect of losing another friend had driven him round the bend. He tried to say, in his own roundabout way, that he had never known what it was to love another man; the strength of their friendship had astonished him. Samar never replied. He knew he would write to Karan only when he could muster up the courage to ask Leo the question that Karan had left him with. *Where the hell did you pick up the bug?*

In one of the letters, Karan wrote that he was fine and that he had resolved to return to work; he was broke as a joke, down

to his last few hundred rupees. *Enough of this photography shit. I have a degree in teaching, and I can always brush up my skills and see if a school will take me on. I have to make ends meet.* Samar thought Karan was out of control.

About four months later he received another letter. Karan had found work with a school in Colaba. He wrote that he had taught for a couple of months at Patel International School. *On the Annual Sports Day all the teachers wore T-shirts that said 'I Love PIS'.* Samar couldn't help the smile that curved his lips.

Then the letters stopped coming.

As his jet cut through the city's smoggy cloud cover, Karan's mind remembered Bombay for its kindnesses. And what were they exactly? A stranger had once gifted him a black umbrella during a storm. His first monsoon in the city. His landlady, Miss Mango, had given him a slice of apple pie. A retired nurse had written to him to say she had cut out his photographs from the *India Chronicle* and pasted them on the pages of a scrapbook. Anonymous kindnesses coalesced around him, keeping him warm. For what lay outside its parameter pushed him to believe mercy had no stock in Bombay.

Mercy lay elsewhere. On the peripheries. Some place dark. Anywhere but here.

By the time he had landed in London, the scent of a charred arm had roughened his sleep too many times to keep count.

In the early part of the year, when Hindu-Muslim riots had broken out across Bombay, Iqbal had gone out to cover a scuffle in a lane that was a holler away from Mutton Street,

where Karan had first met Rhea. The mob had stripped Iqbal, found him circumcised, doused him with kerosene, thrown a match to his face. *Saala mussalman.*

Karan had accompanied Iqbal's mother to the morgue, left her shaking on a bench at the entrance and gone in himself.

'Is this Iqbal Syed?' the morgue inspector had asked Karan.

'Yes.'

'Are you sure? I mean ...' His face said it all. *This body is toast.* 'There have been so many such accidents. I don't want you to claim the wrong body.'

'His death was not an accident.'

'No one can say for sure if it was an accident or if he was a victim of the riots.'

'He was set on fire.'

'The police report has yet to establish that. Please keep your personal suspicions to yourself in such communally sensitive times. How can you be sure that this man is Iqbal Syed?'

Karan controlled an urge to throw up. 'I know it is Iqbal Syed because I recognize his fingers.' He examined the fingers closely, remembering the bony metacarpus, now without either skin or flesh, the ashen architecture of burned biology.

'He worked for the *India Chronicle?'* The morgue inspector was keen for Karan to leave now.

'He was my boss there.'

'Will you tell his mother? She's waiting outside, right?'

Karan had held Iqbal's mother as she fainted. Then he had taken her home.

That night, guzzling whisky under dirty starlight, he had decided it was time to leave Bombay.

A week later, an advertisement in the paper caught his eye: a school in London was looking for teachers. Once Karan had clinched the job, he gave notice to his landlady, sold all his Bombay photographs to a raddiwalla under the flyover at Kemps Corner and used the money to buy a new suitcase.

'Can you keep this chair?' he requested Miss Mango.

'Will you need it back?'

'I don't know.'

'If I'm alive when you come back, it's yours; I'm holding it for you for now.'

'Thank you.' He noticed Miss Mango stroke the wooden arm of the Bombay Fornicator. 'For the apple pie. It was delicious.'

'What apple pie?'

'Last year, in June, you gave me a slice of apple pie. Your son had brought you some and you had left me a slice.'

'Did I leave you a slice?' Her face evaporated into a fuzzy question mark.

In the taxi to the airport he stared at his ticket, cattle class, aisle seat, because he did not want to look out. He just needed to get up for a piss now and again. Or to throw up if the stink of a burnt arm came back in a hurry.

In the flight, he read again the letter Rhea had given him on his birthday.

I'm awkward with letters; I have had no one to write them to in years.

When I met you, I was bowled away by your guts; you had a will to do what I believed impossible. To tell Bombay's stories through pictures. You were mad and raffish, on the wild side of audacious. But the more I saw of your work, the more I grew convinced you had the skill and vision to do exactly that, and your pictures of Bombay celebrate its gaiety and its irony. Your gaze is hard and mesmeric, and it has been my great luck to serve it in some small way. I never thought I would meet the hero of my imagination.

I admire you. You stood by Samar. Like a rock. You weathered the storm when everyone else was asking for their coats. Zaira would be so proud; she knows you honoured her heart. Maybe that's why I feel so lucky to have met you in Chor Bazaar, hunting for a chair I hope you will sit on as you read this letter.

Above all, my time with you has been abundant fun; you were an ally to my solitude. Thank you for coming to Sewri, for standing with me under the birds. We were standing so close I could hear the beating of your heart. It was like the sound of a flag flapping in the wind.

PART 3

27

IN THE FIFTH MONTH OF HER PREGNANCY, RHEA felt strange and looked ravishing, as if something larger than her—the principle of continuity, perhaps—had taken possession of her. Walking through a lush green park in Singapore, she felt powerfully connected to the wiry arms of jacaranda trees, to the clean, crisp air, to the blue blanket of sky. Frequently tired, annoyed for no reason, she was given to incomprehensible impulses: she ate salt, cried flagrantly, scratched her arms until they were bloody. She dreamed profoundly, in troubling, precise particulars. She saw herself in a cold, barren room, redolent of a torture chamber, where she was surrounded by beings, minor deities, spirits that were mostly benevolent and unspeakably old, angels who scattered dust from their wings when no one was looking and then

sighed at the mess they had made. But the most recurrent image in her dreams was of a small brown beast, hairy, with a long, restless tail and large mad eyes, hissing feverishly at her. Waking from these horrifying visions, she craved for the clarifying genius of her father's words: If Dr Thacker had been alive, he would have cast an illuminating and deft narrative over the hazy, terrifying clutch of images that seized her mind. The sadness she had experienced at her father's death competed with the loneliness she battled following Karan's eviction from her life. She recognized that just as her father had lit the lamp of her imagination, she had done the same for Karan; now, remembering both men in private was a habit that made her sleepy with exhaustion.

But the sublime pleasures of uncomplicated sleep remained out of reach.

Almost every night, Adi, restored to the stamina of their courting days, met her with bestial lust. After a long day of nostalgic recollection Rhea relished the carnal distraction, and she asked Adi to fuck her harder, without restraint, tear her apart—for in that moment of rupture, the unlit aspect of her soul would escape and gallop back to where it had arisen.

Adi suspected she was occasionally withdrawn and given to whims because she missed her home city.

'Would you like to return to Bombay?' he asked her one day.

'You mean for the delivery?'

'Yes.'

'I'd like that very much. Adi, you don't listen to jazz these days.'

'I know.'

'Or drink bourbon.'

'Isn't that wonderful?' He smiled uncontrollably; he was counting the days and hours before the birth of his child. 'I'll arrange for us to leave shortly.'

They arrived in Bombay in March; summer heat lorded over the city like a lioness, one thick, violent paw resting on the other.

Rhea stood on the terrace at sunset as a copper-winged black cuckoo unleashed a plangent, hypnotic cry from the overladen branches of a dusty mango tree. In the distance below, a row of ugly cars looked like canker in a dog's ear. Adi came up from behind Rhea and pulled her into his arms; she caught her breath, more startled than reassured.

Ever since Adi had got to know of Rhea's pregnancy he had insisted their child should be born in the same private maternity clinic where he had been born, and his father before him.

'It's a tradition in the Dalal family,' he had explained.

'But you're not a traditional man, Adi!'

'I will have to be now. I'm going to be a father, and some traditions have to be passed from one generation to the next.'

'Does that include your ability to snore like a steam engine?'

'Laugh all you want, but our child will be born in the same clinic as I was, Rhea.'

'Fine, fine' she had said, waving her hands in the air.

Increasingly, though, Rhea had become apprehensive. 'Does the place have everything we might need, just in case ...?' she asked him now as he nuzzled her neck.

'It's perfect, Rhea. Don't worry, the delivery is going to be a cakewalk.'

'I want to go and see the clinic.' She was afraid the clinic might offer neither specialized neonatal care nor the cutting-edge medical resources a larger facility would have at hand.

'Very well. I will take you tomorrow morning.'

Tucked away in a sleepy Walkeshwar gully, the clinic was an old colonial building with a dusty metal Victorian dome, a spiral wooden staircase with a gothic banister and an inlay of Venetian tiles that ran the length of the corridor. She ascended the circular staircase like a child in a fairy tale wandering through a haunted castle. Standing outside the peaceful nursery, she was enraptured by the light perforating the giant glazed windows. 'It's lovely, but strange.' She looked out at an expansive jamun tree; something rustled in its branches, but she could not tell what it was.

'I know,' Adi said. 'It's almost frozen in time.'

Two days before she was due to deliver, Rhea sensed a stirring inside her. Before she could call out to Adi, she felt a stream of liquid running down the inside of her thigh.

'We need to get to the clinic.' She grasped his shoulder.

He looked at his watch. It was 2.00 a.m. 'Has the water bag burst?'

'I guess so,' she said anxiously. 'We should hurry.'

At four a.m., before violent spasms overtook her body, she was grateful for the safe span of her pregnancy. The birth pains resembled the description of a spiritual experience: she felt flung out of herself and she saw herself scream, sweat, draw deep breaths, time her contractions, and then watched life emerge from between her legs. As a part of her died quietly, another part was bom with a baffled cry of relief. Rhea was desperate to have the child *out* of her, not because she wanted to hold it, suckle it, rock it—or for any other maternal impulses—but because she wanted her body back, its solitude restored to its original sanctity, her womb free of the fidgety presence.

At twelve forty-four the following afternoon, she discovered that another human being, before acquiring the particularities of age, was only a composite of physical banalities.

Her son weighed eight pounds, had pink, nearly transparent toes. Wispy sprouts of black down on his soft skull.

Adi's face was delirious with joy. 'Rhea,' Adi said as he cradled his son, 'he's perfect.'

'His nose is too big.'

'How can you say that!'

'Oh, Adi ...'

The nurse looked away when Adi leaned over and kissed Rhea.

Later, when Rhea was alone with the infant, she studied it furtively, carefully. It looked very much like Adi's baby. Maybe it *was* Adi's baby ... She sighed with relief and leaned back against the headboard. Having given Adi a child, sating his

deepest desire, she felt as if she had done whatever she possibly could to restore their marriage to its original vitality. Now they could embark on that odd, annoying entity: 'family'. She pictured clutching her son's hand on his first day at school, a water bottle slung on his shoulder, his innocent face distraught at the impending abandonment. She pictured Adi taking his little boy for swimming lessons to the Bombay Gymkhana. She imagined hectic, memorable, dyspeptic holidays to Florida. A great change was sweeping over her like a typhoon, and she was almost ready for it.

'Are you happy, Rhea?' Adi asked her on the day before she was to be discharged from the clinic.

'I'm over the moon.'

'Thank you; I'm sorry if I walk around with this big goofy grin on my face but our new recruit has an uncanny effect on me.'

'It'll wear,' she warned. 'After you change the four hundredth nappy, the novelty is bound to wear off.'

'We're going home tomorrow. I can't wait to see how he'll sleep on his first night in the nursery.'

'He'll love it,' she said. 'You did such a splendid job with the nursery, Adi; it reminded me of the hard work you had put into creating the studio for me. It's my greatest refuge, and now our baby will have a shelter of his own.'

'Did you like the blue clouds I got painted on the ceiling?'

'Yes. And I love those old silver toys; I didn't even know you'd hidden them away.'

'I have silver rattles, bells, a wind chime to hang over his crib ... God, I'm so excited I don't think I'll be able to sleep tonight!'

'I hope you do, Adi. I slept badly last night.'

'Were you up for his feeds?'

'Actually, I couldn't sleep because when I took my afternoon nap I dreamt of my father. He looked straight at me and said: "Don't worry. Everything is just right."'

'But what he said was so apt, Rhea.'

'It was the expression on his face,' she said. 'I bolted up from my sleep as if an earthquake had struck.'

'Don't worry.' He kissed her forehead. 'Everything is just right.'

At dawn the next morning, before Rhea was to leave the clinic with her baby, the nurse was bringing him to her for a feed. As the nurse carried the infant in her arms and walked down the long, narrow corridor, she was unable to look away from the baby's bold, clean, wistful face. Staring into his eyes, she felt she was peering down a mysterious burrow, and that if she stared deep enough for long enough she could travel through the warrens that criss-crossed the baby's secret world. The little boy gazed up at the nurse in intense rumination, his liquid, almandine eyes gleaming with tender curiosity for all the terrible and fine things that lay beyond the parameters of his comprehension for now. So lost was the nurse in her thoughts that she did not hear the low but emphatic hiss a few metres behind her.

A monkey had entered the clinic.

With loops of spittle dribbling from its jowls, wide, red-streaked eyes and a bloodied neck, it clawed the air with wild, rabid gestures.

Scurrying after the nurse, it flung itself upon her like a curse.

Cold, sharp teeth sank into her flesh and she cried out hysterically.

From her room Rhea heard the scream and rushed for the door. Through the dawn haze of frantic shrieking, her eyes fell on her infant son, now on the edge of the staircase. She dashed forward to reach for the child, but she was too late, for he had started to whirl down the wooden spiral steps, tumbling from level to level, his thick cloth diaper unravelling, turning from white to red as his wailing evaporated with an air of frightening finality. Thundering down the stairwell, she reached her baby, picked him up and pressed him against her chest, finding it impossible, finally, not to tremble from the heft of maternal love, from which she had presumed immunity.

Looking up at the place she had left behind, she howled with such secular, focussed grief that all the minor deities and terrified angels of her dreams retreated into the sallow shafts of morning light.

For many months after the death of his son, Adi was vulnerable to sudden, intense headaches. The muscles in his arms felt raw. His back grew stiff. Small aches and pains developed spontaneously all through his body, vanishing as quickly as they had come, swiftly replaced by other quirks of physical agony. It was as if his body had stepped in to distract

his mind, to make life possible. Although he had been spending short spells in Singapore, he desired most to stay at home. Finally, unable to attend to his tasks at work with any measure of competency, he decided to take a break.

His sabbatical, entirely unanticipated, took Rhea by surprise. 'How long will you stay at home?' she asked cautiously.

'I don't know.'

'Can you just take off from work without any idea of when you'll go back?'

'The firm sees it as a sabbatical; they'd much rather I work when my head is clear than that I bungle up on an investment. Will my being on leave bother you terribly?'

'Oh, no,' she said faintly, 'not terribly, no.'

One afternoon, he noticed her draw out the umbrella from the closet. 'Are you headed somewhere?'

'I've decided to resume work at the animal shelter.'

He looked stunned. Seven months had passed since the death of their son.

'I won't be back for lunch,' she said. 'Ask Lila-bai to serve you some food when you're hungry.'

When she returned from the shelter, she locked herself in her studio.

Late in the evening he knocked on the door and poked his head in. Her wheel came to a cranking halt. 'Yes?' she said, looking up, her brow creased.

'Oh, nothing ... I was wondering if you'd like to come down for dinner.'

'Why don't you go ahead? I need to work an hour longer.'

'I get the feeling you're avoiding me.'

'Not at all, Adi.'

He exhaled loudly. 'I know things haven't been great between us. Why don't we take a small break? Let's go to Rome for a week.'

'We went there on our honeymoon.' She wiped a splodge of clay off her brow with the back of her hand.

'Exactly.'

'I don't think it's appropriate to go there; not even a year has gone by since ...' She looked away.

Adi wrung his wrists as he left the studio, convinced that nothing he did could thaw the ice between them now. Only after dinner did he realize that he was seething because of the tone of condescension that crept into her voice whenever she spoke to him now, as though he had some sort of a minor, manageable mental disorder.

A few days later, as Rhea descended the stairs after many hours of tinkering around in her studio, she saw Adi on his chocolate-coloured recliner, his legs propped up on an ottoman, a glass of bourbon on a three-legged table by his side.

'Are you ready to go?' she enquired. They were scheduled to catch a show at Regal, the latest Ram Gopal Verma film.

'Can we take a rain check?'

'Why?'

'I'm just not feeling up to it.'

'Oh Adi, I've spent the whole day in the studio and I'd like to get out for a bit.'

'Why don't you go alone?'

Anger seized her by her ankles and threatened to tilt her over.

'I think I'd rather go to bed.'

Jazz music unravelled in a soft, sweet whisper; eyes closed, Adi seemed to be drowning in the melancholic strains from a saxophone and the delicate tinkle of a voice that was like a pebble skipping across the taut skin of a lake. Rhea stood still, watching him.

Adi opened his eyes, looked into hers. 'Did you get good work done?'

'Yes,' she lied. 'Some.'

'I don't understand how you can be so brave, Rhea.'

'Me neither.' He did not know that her calm resulted from her acceptance that her son's death was punishment for her betrayal. 'I try not to take life too personally.'

'But life is anything but impersonal!'

Rhea felt like she was speaking to Karan again. 'Maybe you should get treatment for your depression, Adi. Drinking has taken a toll on you. I don't know why you started again after giving it up in the months when I was carrying.'

'You mean my drinking has taken a toll on us?' He lowered the volume of the music before he stood up and faced her.

'I can't stand to see you suffer like this.'

'Give me your hand.'

She extended her hand reluctantly; he held it against his cheek.

'I made your favourite—Devil's Food Cake. Shall I get you a slice before I go to bed?' she said.

'I'm not very hungry.'

'I spent an entire afternoon baking it for you.'

'I'll help myself later.'

'Suit yourself.'

'Do you know why this happened to us, Rhea?'

'No.'

Looking at her serene face, stark as winter, he searched for the woman he had married. 'Do you think it would have been different if we had gone to a different hospital? Perhaps I should not have insisted on going to that small clinic.'

'Perhaps we should have gone to Breach Candy Hospital.'

'Do you hold me responsible for this?'

'Don't be absurd, Adi; there's no point in playing the blame game.'

'I'm sorry, Rhea, I don't know how to deal with this.'

'Perhaps counselling will help.'

'Please don't take your hand away.'

'I'm uncomfortable, Adi.' He let go, and Rhea retreated.

He sat down on the recliner.

'Well, good night.'

'Sleep tight, Rhea.'

'Will you be long?'

'I want to finish this last drink.'

'Remember to turn off the bathroom light.'

She was barely within earshot when he murmured, 'I miss you, Rhea.'

'I miss you too,' she said, turning around. She went back to him and took his hand in hers, kissed the teal tributaries on his wrist. After drying her tears, and his too, she left him in the custody of unhurried piano bars picking up a tune, an elegiac, intoxicating composition that reminded her of the crushed petals of moonlight.

Adi continued to listen to music well into the night. Bats glided outside the window. City lights burned bright and brutal. He remembered one evening, years ago, when he had gone to fetch Rhea from the animal shelter. He had found the howling of the stray dogs and mewing of dirty kittens revolting, and he had been desperate to leave as soon as possible. The young veterinarian, who directed him to the shed where Rhea was sequestered with a litter of puppies, had neglected to add that the puppies had been administered a lethal injection. When Adi neared the tin shed, the strains of a lullaby sung with tender feeling made him pause and turn around. But Rhea had heard him shuffle his feet and looked up, glaring so violently he felt chastised. In the car, neither spoke about the incident, but months later Rhea had admitted the puppies were dying and a lullaby was the least she could have offered them.

But today, he thought, she looks indestructible, unfathomable, stoic.

She was no longer the woman he had married one December on a barge they had hired outside the Taj Mahal Hotel.

In the weeks that followed, Rhea's impatience intensified the longer Adi stayed at home. 'I really wish you would play your music on your headphones.'

'I had no idea it was bothering you; I thought you enjoyed jazz.'

'I do,' she said, 'but not first thing in the morning.'

'I'm sorry we're not both coping with your kind of cool.'

'What do you want me to do, Adi? I've offered to come with you to the psychiatrist. I've asked you repeatedly if you wanted to go to Alibaug for the weekend. I bake cakes for you and ensure there are flowers on your bedside table ... and you make me out to be some kind of a bitch ...'

'You're not a bitch.'

She frowned; his tone was so flat it was as if he was mocking her.

She decided to try harder. She took him to dinner at the Thai Pavilion the next evening. The following day she ordered tickets for the new Naseeruddin Shah flick. From Rhythm House she bought newly issued Billie Holiday records. They took a walk in Priyadarshini Park.

'Thank you, Rhea,' he said to her at the end of the week. 'I feel so much better.'

They were in bed. He had not had a drink.

'I'm glad. I've got tickets to the play you wanted to see.'

'Next Friday, right? At Rang Sharda?'

'Yes.' She kissed him on the lips. 'It's an Urdu adaptation of *Love Letters* starring Farouque Shaikh and Shabana Azmi.' She slid her hand down his chest and played with his nipples.

He drew back. 'I just don't feel ...'

She remembered how he would make love to her when she had been pregnant, the exquisite and brutal force, the dexterity of his motions, the diabolic greed of his body for hers. 'It's been many months now, Adi. I miss it.'

'I don't believe I can ... not yet.'

She longed for his touch, its excitement and gentleness, but he had closed himself to all physical affinities, and she now felt ugly in his company.

On Friday night Adi said he had misplaced the theatre tickets.

'Where did you put them?' she asked, waving her hands angrily.

'They were in the top drawer.' He felt her rage lunge toward him like a javelin.

'Then they should be right there. Maybe Lila-bai put them somewhere?' She yelled out for Lila-bai but the maid had left for the day.

'Why're you so crabby, Rhea? It's only a play.'

'But I've been wanting to see it with you.' She tugged at her hair.

'I'm sorry I lost the tickets, but we can always go another time.'

'And what shall we do this evening? Listen to enough jazz to make me feel like a saxophone's been shoved up my pussy?' she spat.

Unexpectedly, Adi started to cry.

'Oh, for fuck's sake, Adi!' she shouted. 'Now you've *really* turned into a girl.'

She left him on the chaise below the tiger skin, a weeping heap.

She went up to her studio and broke everything in sight, bowls of slip, bottles of glaze, vases and plates.

Two days later she apologized profusely. 'I had no business behaving the way I did. What can I say or do for you to forgive me?'

'Please leave me alone.'

'I'm deeply, deeply sorry.' She reached for his hand, placed it against her cheek.

He yanked his hand away. 'Leave me alone, Rhea.'

'Look, I'm prepared to do anything you say if you will let me off the hook this time. I just want to ...'

But his face was stony and cold, and she felt she could bear it no longer. Rage swelled within her like a sleeper wave and she blurted out, 'Get over it, Adi. I'm not even sure the baby was yours.'

She turned to abandon the room but he grabbed her roughly by the arm and swivelled her around so she faced him.

'Aargh!' she cried. 'Please ... please don't do that, Adi!'

A peculiar, impudent strength animated his touch. 'Did you mean what you just said, Rhea?'

The words had left her mouth; now there was nothing for her to do but tell Adi about Karan.

He did not ask for details, but she gave them anyway.

She told him how she had taken Karan under her wing because she admired his brilliant work, lit with wry humour and a daring, mordant vision. She told him Karan was thoughtful, with powerful arms, a quiet, ferocious intelligence—a far cry from the cliché of the crazed stalker she had earlier made him out to be.

She tried to assure Adi that Karan was no longer a part of her life.

He heard her out in complete silence.

Finally he said, 'You've hurt me to the quick, Rhea.'

'Well, I'm sorry.' Her apology sounded so amazingly incompetent to her own ears that she feared uttering another word.

'What's hurt me most is the extent to which you went to cover up your betrayal. Every lie you've spoken over the last few months to cover your tracks, to keep this from me, will haunt me for as long as I live.' He rubbed his chest with his left hand.

'There are certain things you do for love that seem to be the work of evil.'

'You're being arcane again, Rhea, and I'm afraid its charm is lost on me now.'

'I never loved Karan the way I have loved you.'

'Which only means that you *did* love him.'

'Adi ...' She had been expecting him to explode; instead, he had drawn back into himself like a snail.

'How will I ever trust you again? Why'd you do it?'

She sighed. 'We were both unhappy. There were no children; the marriage felt deserted.'

'I was sad that we couldn't have children but that was *my* sadness. I don't believe I ever imposed it on you.' He stood erect now, scratching his chin, a gesture that reminded her again of Karan.

'Not knowingly. Not all the time.'

'And so what if I did? We're allowed to share our sorrows; that's part and parcel of a marriage.'

'I was only trying to make you happy ...'

'By sleeping with some random guy you picked up from the streets of Bombay?'

She stood by the window sill and took a great gulp of dirty air.

'A marriage ends when one person betrays the trust of the other.'

'Please!' She turned, raised her hand firmly in the air. 'Save me that selfhelp manual mush.'

'Rhea!'

She bit her lower lip. He looked like he was ready to punch her. Her voice was an awkward whisper when she said, 'I need more time to explain things to you.'

'You will only end up serving me more of your dirty lies. What a fool I was to fall for your wiles in the first place!'

Her cheeks burned.

'I can't believe you brought Karan in here.'

She put her thumb between her teeth.

'In my house. On our bed ...'

She felt her throat go dry.

'On our bed ...'

She covered her face.

'You took what was at the core of us and you mangled it out of recognition.'

He came up beside her.

She was gripped by an impulse to run, but she stayed her ground. 'A marriage is not based only on trust, Adi; there is something to be said of love.'

'That makes for great copy,' he said, looking into her eyes, 'but it's doing *nothing* for me in real time.'

When he twisted her arm and yanked her toward him, the savage fury in his eyes took her back to the day of the verdict on Zaira's trial. She thought again of Malik, and whom he had reminded her of.

'I'm going to Alibaug.' She jerked her arm free of his grip.

'As far as I'm concerned,' he shouted, 'you can go to hell.'

Before she could say a word Adi had left the room, and its emptiness crowded in on her.

In Alibaug, a week of turmoil passed in a devastatingly slow rhythm.

For the first time Rhea regretted the absence of women friends in her life. She regretted she had no one to whom she could confide the tumultuous events of recent vintage. After all, only another woman could truly understand the initial heady rush of pregnancy followed by the emotional disarray that shadowed the last few days preceding childbirth; only another woman would understand the rapier pain of losing a newborn son, the scathing bewilderment, the violent pathos, the sense of being peeled and exposed, the loud, solemn wailing that resounded in her head even in her sleep.

She imagined she had one close friend, someone affectionate and thoughtful but also a little tormented, and that she had arranged to meet this friend at Willingdon Clubhouse where they would sit around a quiet table by the golf course, order a vegetarian club sandwich and cold coffee before she would reveal, in a low, defeated tone, that her marriage was failing. She would confess that her own infidelity had taken her by surprise, although she was fully conscious of its consequence. She would hold back her tears as she told her friend that what pained her more than losing her child was that the accidental disclosure of her affair had irrevocably wounded Adi. She would look at her friend ruefully and admit she wanted her marriage to survive, wanted it to flourish, discover again the excitement and depth of the initial years, and if that were no longer possible she would settle for Adi being whole again. At this point her friend would lean forward and touch her hand, and something indefinable and soothing would be exchanged between them. She would

return home thinking what a stalwart her friend had been, how lucky she was to have had an honest, difficult conversation over lunch: the load on her mind now known, and divided.

Instead, here she was, all alone in Alibaug as sea winds hammered against the windows like lovelorn, miscreant spectres formlessly floating about. Reaching for a diary, she tore out a piece of paper and scribbled on it: *I want to cry.* She wrote it repeatedly till the paper tore to shreds.

Lying on an antique four-poster bed, she plotted her return, and her confession.

She had bumped into Karan at Chor Bazaar, she would tell Adi. Karan bore such a remarkable resemblance to Adi that she had stared at him insolently, unsure if she was looking at a stranger or at Adi in his younger years. She worried over her words, their punishing inadequacy to convey the agony and purity of her twisted intentions. How would she convince Adi that she had planned the affair with Karan only to have a baby? Was that too weird—or too wicked—to be believed? Surely, if she could persuade Adi she was desperate to have a child to save their marriage, he would have to sympathize with her. But how would she explain what had happened between Karan and her; how an innocent, selfish seduction had turned into a game in which the cards were stacked against her—for she had fallen for Karan?

No, she told herself; she would not disclose to Adi her descent into the ravine principally because she herself did not know why her attraction for Karan had been so potent, organic,

rarefied, with a fate of its own, outside of the destiny of love she shared with Adi. There was no logical or reasonable way to tell Adi that Karan and she had merely become a venue for love to find itself, revel in itself; that love had been exchanged in the presence of each other, and like the very best of hurricanes it had been entirely out of their control. She struggled for the correct way to phrase her words, to make herself sound neither desperate nor indifferent. Adi would have to believe her once she told him that she had got rid of Karan as soon as she was pregnant, she told herself; there lay the proof that her affair had had only one specific purpose.

Convinced that she had achieved a logical, credible arc to her confessional narrative, her mind tried to rest. But at midnight she sat up in bed, filled with a formidable, exhausting urge to cry, her face buried in the web of her fingers. *I want to cry,* she repeated to herself, then woke the next morning, as dry-eyed as when she had slept.

The moment Rhea set foot in her apartment, its graveyard silence enfolded her, pulling her into an anxious vortex. Had Adi gone for a walk? Where was Lila-bai? Why was there no music rolling softly around the house like a bolt of aural silk? She went up to the library and waited there for Adi. In the evening she went into her studio, where, kneeling on the floor, she bent her head and took great gasps of air. The shards of what she had broken, pieces of glass and pottery, lay scattered around her like a jigsaw in which she was only another piece.

Forever unwhole.

Forever shattered.

The most crucial piece—the one that would make her marriage whole—was nowhere to be seen or heard.

Once the levee broke, the waters showed no sign of stopping. She cried until dawn flapped its burnished wing against the tall glass doors. A new day was upon her. She went downstairs and slept for two hours. When she rose she called Adi's colleagues and friends, spoke to the neighbours, the durwan, the liftman. After two days, when it was apparent that Adi was not coming back and she had made no headway in locating him, she went to the police to do what she believed was her moral duty: report a missing man. As she sat before the inspector, she was restless with frustration. She had been allowed to report Adi's physical absence, but to whom was she supposed to report the glaring, septic absence she had lived with for the last few years?

'What is your relation to the missing party, madam?' The inspector, Subhash Rajan, looked her up and down.

'The missing party?' She wondered if he was trying to be funny. When he looked at her unfazed, she said, 'He's my husband.'

Inspector Rajan smiled benevolently at her. He had already decided that Rhea's husband was either road kill on some nameless highway or had taken off with some tasty little firecracker half his age, leaving behind a hapless, middle-aged wife. 'So, tell me what happened, madam.'

'Can you please not call me "madam"?'

The inspector was surprised by the tenacity in her voice, and then he smiled again, the flat, spooky smile with its dash of empathy and scorn.

She proceeded to tell him the particulars, the argument, her defection to Alibaug, the return to an empty house.

'Are you sure there was no note?'

'A suicide note?'

'Any kind of note,' he said generously.

She said she had found nothing. He gave her a form to fill, and she handed it back, completed, with Adi's picture.

Inspector Rajan asked her if Adi had had a history of mental illness.

He had always been prone to depression, she said, and this became particularly pronounced after the death of their infant son.

'How did your son die?'

She sighed. She told him.

'A monkey!' For the first time he looked genuinely interested in her. 'Wow!'

She said nothing. He was perturbed by her blank expression; it was as if she were staring up at him from an abyss. 'Are you okay?'

'I'm fine,' she said after a moment. She thought Inspector Rajan had the slightly glandular, fatigued air of someone who masturbated for a living and moonlighted as a policeman.

'Do you have any idea why your husband might have left home?'

'I've told you everything I know, inspector.'

'Everything?' he asked her doubtfully. Leaning forward, he conjectured in a conspiratorial whisper, 'Do you think he was having an affair?'

'I don't know.'

'Because middle-aged men often take off when they are cheating on their wives.'

'An affair ...' She considered the word desolately.

'I don't mean to upset you, of course.'

'Not at all.'

'But who knows what goes on behind our backs?'

'That's correct. We don't ever know anyone at all.'

'I often tell my wife—trust no one! Not even me.'

'That's a very sound piece of advice,' she said. 'For your wife.'

To Rhea's right, two boys in handcuffs, dressed in jeans and tee-shirts, were being accosted by policemen; she overheard a policeman addressing one of them as 'saala pickpocket'. She felt the wooden sleeve of the chair she was sitting on; it was moist with her perspiration.

'But fear not!' the inspector said enthusiastically. 'This is life. This is fate. Anything can happen. But we must do our best and leave the rest in the hands of the Almighty.'

Rhea resisted a disturbingly violent urge to slap the inspector. 'Well, if there's anything else you need to know, feel free to call me and I will come by.'

'Mumbai Police is at your service. We are the custodians of your trust. We will find your husband, Mrs Dalal.'

'You will find him,' she repeated as she got up to leave. Her tongue rolled over 'Mumbai', and came away with a distasteful coating.

The inspector also stood up to say something but she could not catch a single word because one of the pickpockets had started to wail at a high, hysterical pitch.

28

KARAN HAD BEEN IN LONDON THREE YEARS WHEN he met Claire Soames.

He had taught her daughter, Sibyl, the previous year at the school where he worked.

Karan was in the green room as a performance ensued in the auditorium. Parents milled around furnishing food and providing assistance with the costumes. Several enthusiastic sorts had festooned the foyer of the auditorium with balloons, ribbons and streamers. From the green room Karan heard laughter, then faint, broken applause followed by loud jeering; he suspected that one of the performances had not gone down too well with the kids.

A few seconds later, Claire stormed into the green room, clad in a ghastly outfit of a hedgehog. At first Karan was taken aback by her dramatic arrival and oddball ensemble. Then it

occurred to him that she had dressed as Mrs Tiggy-Winkle for the amusement of the children, but had met with a round of snarky booing.

'Brutes!' she cried. 'Bloody brutes. You spend a week working hard on a look, and all they toss you is a sodding tomato; I'd have been so much better off coming as a dildo-juggling crack whore.' She yanked angrily at her dirty brown spiky wig.

'They're only children,' he said to calm her. 'They probably thought it was cool to be boorish, although I can assure you that you look wonderful ...'

'In a hedgehoggy sort of way?' Her face was taut with sarcasm.

Her spirited invulnerability and his tentative intrigue were like the opposite ends of two wires, and when they touched the sparks dazzled both briefly and privately.

'Well ...'

'You're not from England, are you?' she asked as he gaped at her helplessly. She had a voluptuous presence; a face like an open book, and small, perfect breasts.

'Why do you ask?' He worried that his accent had been a dead giveaway.

'Because you give the humans on our little island too much credit.'

As she started to disassemble the rest of her outfit, Karan turned away. She continued talking to him, asking rapid, personal questions, which he answered simply because no one else he had met in England had been so upfront.

'So, where are you from?' She was sitting on an ottoman, a few inches away from him, rolling down her stockings.

'Shimla, India.' His eyes fell on the crumpled heap of beige nylon at her feet, and he felt an obscene, hot rush of blood in his loins. 'And Bombay.'

'My great-grandfather was posted in the Punjab. When did you come to London?'

'Three years ago.' He fiddled with a pen even as he stole glances at her long legs and ballerina toes.

'To teach?' she asked, raising her eyebrows.

'Yes.'

'My God.'

'Excuse me?'

'Is that all you ever did?'

'What does that mean?'

'Sorry, that must have sounded awfully condescending. But surely teaching is not all you ever did?' In her everyday clothes now she was elegant and regal, like a cat that has fallen from a great height and landed on its feet.

'I worked as a photographer in Bombay.'

She beamed. 'I'd love to know more about your photographs—but tonight you have your hands full with our nation's bright young arsonists. So I will call you and quiz you another day, if you allow.' Claire looked at him again, a little smitten by his hangdog charm, his slightly damaged demeanour. 'Watch out for the tomatoes,' she warned on her way out.

'I've learned to watch out for more than just tomatoes.'

'I guess that's what they call a bumper crop,' she said so softly that he did not hear her.

Two weeks later, Claire asked Karan to a Henri Cartier-Bresson retrospective at the Victoria and Albert Museum.

In the carefully lit gallery smart men in suits and young women in gowns strolled with an alluring, indolent air; plummy whispers bounced around like excitable debutantes.

Claire and Karan exchanged innocuous details about their lives. Growing up in the Home Counties, with a pony and three greyhounds, Claire had never imagined she would swap the indolence of the countryside for the hysterical eccentricities of London's cocky, useless art world ('A load of bollocks but still ...'). She drove around her neighbourhood, Primrose Hill, on her ex-husband's battered Vespa, and took the train to the ICA, where she had been a curator for nine years.

'Let's go to Soho. There's this little café I know,' she said as soon as they stepped out of the museum. 'Their strawberry gateau is positively nirvanic!'

'Yes, let's.' Karan was slightly amused by the idea that dessert could confer salvation.

'You said you live in East London?' she asked in the cab.

'New Road.'

'The hipster's new paradise. I can't keep up with you young lot,' she said, although Karan was older than her by a year or two.

'When I moved there, it was sweatshop central.'

'But didn't you like the pubs around Old Street?'

'I haven't been to them. I generally keep to my studio apartment.'

'Ah, the great indoors!'

'When I do go out it's to the parks of Richmond or Hampstead.' By Karan's present socializing standards, the outing with Claire was a minor adventure.

'Do you enjoy teaching?'

'I don't know how on earth I got the job, but I'm grateful to be here.'

'You said you'd worked as a photographer. Why did you quit?'

'I fell out of love.' His tone made her disinclined to question him any further.

'And you went smack into a teaching career?'

'I have a university degree in education.'

'But that's not reason enough to savage yourself.'

'I got a lot of practice at being savaged in Bombay.'

'Ah,' she said with a smile. 'So teaching our bright young arsonists is your higher education.'

'Emphasis on higher.'

'I'm glad you're here but they say London can be quite lonely if you don't have people you know.' The cab halted outside the café; she paid, and they disembarked.

'And cold to boot.'

'Do you miss Bombay?' she asked as they climbed to the second level of the café.

He did not reply.

A waiter seated them around a circular table laid with red gingham cloth and shoddy cutlery. He glanced out at the street below: clusters of attractive men with buzz cuts walked hand in hand emitting wiry sparks of synthetic love; their eyes restless.

She motioned the waiter and asked for two strawberry gateaux.

The desserts arrived. 'Bon appetit,' she said.

'Well, here's to nirvana.'

'Don't get carried away now.' She waved the spoon before him like a little sword.

'I do,' he said, scooping a piece of the gateau. 'I do miss Bombay.' He noticed only now that she was wearing a dramatic black mink coat; when his hand accidentally touched it the luxury it broadcast fled and its softness, he felt, had a seductive voltage all its own.

They went to a bar after dessert, drank plenty; he enjoyed her glittering levity, her polished performances of enthralling diffidence. Claire made him feel indispensable, irresistible even. But he noticed she was like that with most people; her charm was an equal opportunities employer. Later, when he looked back on that evening, he could not remember whether she had pushed him against the wall and tasted his mouth with a shameless, voracious hunger, or if he had stroked her smooth, delectable thigh as she ordered her fourth glass of merlot. In the morning, sunlight streaming in through her bedroom window revealed her naughty, luscious body wrapped around him like a

smooth white scarf, the scent of their bodies intermingling like secret, wild herbs in a witch potion.

After a long season of seclusion, tender curiosity for a woman made him pull her closer.

When he joined her at the breakfast table Claire was playing with her daughter. She warmed him a scone and served it with marmalade and Valencia oranges. He drank two cups of tea, then rose to leave.

At the door, Claire clasped his unshaven cheeks and put her thumb into the dimple on his chin, as if assessing the indent.

The station was only a few minutes' walk from her house. An hour later Karan got off at Whitechapel feeling sated and bright. He could not get Claire out of his mind, her fine elbows, the musky scent of her pussy, the rain-like softness behind her shins. Tabloids billowed in a wet, wet wind. He crossed a busy street, passed grungy artists, musicians with guitars, Sylheti women in silky black jellabas. Outside Royal London Hospital, he glanced at the fat, pink, grubby bums gathered on a dirty wooden bench, surrounded by a swarm of grey and white pigeons. He sighed. This sight always evoked his sympathy; he had come to nurse the vague, corrosive possibility that he too might end up either as a wayside drunk or like the madwoman he had once photographed on Dadar Bridge, so enraptured by private pain that she seemed to be free of it. But this time he told himself that he would not end up on the streets.

The loneliness he had struggled with in the last few years in London had initially seemed insurmountable; like the cold, it

cut right to the bone. He had been perturbed to find that unlike the loneliness of Bombay, which could be shared with others, cut up like bread and sung away like a dirge, the loneliness of London held him hostage to its peculiar, unfamiliar rules. He had spent one night too many looking out of the window of his room at the young Bangla boys zooming around in little red cars blasting the latest craze in the Asian underground circuit; he had looked at people in London and found that they were protective of their own loneliness, which they polished and wore like a shield against the world. So when Claire sauntered on to the scene, a membrane tore open between him and the foreign city. Claire did for Karan in London what Rhea had done in Bombay: helped him forge a relationship with a great metropolis in the guise of a personal affinity.

'Would you like to go for a walk?' he called to ask two days later.

'You mean in Hampstead Heath?' she bit on her tongue.

'Actually, I mean Old Street.'

Claire took him everywhere. To parties where skinny women looked as if they'd fled the perfumed pages of splashy magazines, to private screenings of Pedro Almodovar's movies, to installations where artists of no distinguishable gender, age, or for that matter even talent floundered glamorously, to sit-down dinners in Bloomsbury, where dignified academics spoke with courteous scholarship about the Renaissance before they went home and begged their young lovers for golden showers.

They went on a holiday to Rome, strolled through the Villa Borghese, where, unknown to Karan, Adi and Rhea had sat years ago by an ancient mossy fountain and prayed for children. They went to Scotland, to tiny towns where the roads were so narrow only one car could navigate them and all the hotels had colossal, maudlin stag heads mounted in the hallway. Claire liked to make love in public, and he indulged her: hurried, energetic, almost violent encounters occurred on a cold gravestone in Harrow, in the last aisle of a bookstore in Bloomsbury, on the front seat of night bus No. 19. Afterward, she did not like to talk, preferring to feel wrecked open by his swift, furious dives of passion, his virile indiscretion; she never dwelt on the fact that she had asked him to violate her because it would have diluted the thrill of the experience and her subsequent sense of disrepair.

If Karan went right along, a pebble swallowed by the surf, it was because she had seduced his trust on two grounds. Unlike Rhea, who had kept their affair hidden like a mothball in a closet, Claire celebrated Karan, sharing him with her unending retinue of admirers and acquaintances. Little did he know that most of her friends were too suave to let on that they considered Karan docile and subcontinental, attractive but with a vaguely destitute air, wonderfully exportable in case of romantic malfunction; the shy schoolteacher, they all agreed, was the perfect conquest for Claire Soames.

Claire feigned no interest in India, never oohed and aahed over its history, culture or its colours. So Karan never had to

tell her about his father, the false foot, his mother, her bruised shins; he never had to tell her about Zaira and the poignant vigour of their friendship; about Samar, missing now and missed so much. If Claire was smitten with his guilty, soulful face, she never attributed his pain to an inheritance of affairs past: it was who he was, she believed, it was in the grain of his character. Karan found it easy, even exciting, to be around her, a woman with the presence of lightning, who could play a man like a harmonica tune, who wanted to devour his body with such ravenous gusto that they often found themselves in broom closets, phone boxes, ditches in Hampstead Heath, absolving themselves of some common pain in the clamour of a lust that surprised them with its force.

Rhea slipped beneath the creaking floorboards of Karan's memory, but like a loyal and enterprising ghost continued to haunt him with her flamboyant absence.

The following year, at Christmas time, Claire invited Karan to accompany Sibyl and her to her parents' home. In the four years he had been in England, no one had asked him over to their house; Karan was grateful, but nervous.

They had hardly hit the motorway when it started to rain, thin, pointless drops that gave the landscape a maudlin, incompetent air. Driving down the narrow, circuitous lanes of the English countryside she pointed to a spire jutting through a spectral cluster of leafless elms—the church Claire had attended as a child. She showed him her riding school; the clubhouse. He was amazed by the landscape, an exotic, glistening green; ravens

called out from their perches on fence posts or in leafy oaks, sooty omens of some distant doom. Periodically Claire slowed the car and pointed out an architectural quirk, a farm known for its organic produce, a parking lot where her best friend had been arrested for dogging.

By the time they reached her parents' home, the rain had cleared and the sky, the of old steel, covered them like a stern, cold sheet of canvas.

'Don't mind the dogs,' Claire said. Sibyl had already run indoors, to be greeted by a pair of shaggy, ungainly greyhounds, with posh, hollow woofs, clamouring for her attention.

'I like dogs,' he said, remembering Mr Ward-Davies.

'Oh, good; these two can be a bit much.'

'Are you sure your parents are okay having me over?'

'Of course! They've been wanting to meet you forever.'

Karan's face looked stilted; he wanted to return to the refuge of his studio apartment in London.

'They'll love you,' she promised with a peck on his cheek, and added 'Especially me mum,' in an accent generally associated with wags.

They entered through the kitchen door, where Claire's mother was stirring a pot on the fire. After the introduction, Karan said, 'Thank you for having me over.' He handed her a bottle of wine and she thanked him and said, 'We're delighted to have you! Can I get you a slice of fruit cake?' Her voice was a bright ball of enthusiasm with streaks of undisguised emotion; it made him warm to her instantly.

'I'd love some.' Karan turned to Claire, who was busy fixing herself a drink. As he ate the cake and made small talk with Mrs Soames, Claire went off with her drink to the drawing room and sat by the fire on a chair so large she almost vanished into it.

Lunch on Boxing Day turned out to be a civil, wonderfully elaborate affair.

Mrs Soames had cooked variously, efficiently, baking a thick scaled fish in an unaromatic, viscous white sauce, adorned with the leaves of a strange green herb with serrated leaves.

Claire's father, genteel and unassuming, sat across from Karan and asked polite questions.

Karan replied briefly, correctly; he felt that saying too much would not only indicate his own intelligence—or the lack thereof—but also establish that he was an awful, stammering ambassador of his nation.

Claire, wildly drunk by midday, was twirling her hair between her fingers, eyes glazed with sexual hunger. At one point, when Karan reached forward to refill her glass, she placed her hand on the rim of her glass and slurred, 'Girls from good English families like to be asked,' before dissolving into a fit of giggles that made Mrs Soames blush. Before a gawky silence might set between them like aspic, Claire's father quickly embarked on the topic of Indian novels; much to his disappointment, he discovered that his daughter's inamorata was hardly an expert on the subject.

To summon a shard of opinion, Karan's mind rifled back to a past conversation.

On a hot summer day, at Zaira's house, Leo, Samar and Karan had been reclining on a cream rug in the travertine balcony, below which an old laburnum bloomed audaciously. Samar chanced to mention a novel, *The Ochre Remains,* which had recently been awarded an important British prize. Written by a curly-haired siren from Hyderabad, the novel traced a Muslim family's breakdown following the dissolution of the Raj. The book had excited inconsequential cliques of embittered Bengali critics and intrigued legions of readers.

Opinion on the novel, among the jury of four in Juhu, was divided.

Leo complained that the prose was lurid and self-conscious. 'It's a creative-writing workshop in overdrive.'

Zaira commented that the writer was exploitative, having relearned the alphabet during a crash course in Exotica 101. *A* for Arranged Marriage. *B* for Battered Wife. *C* for Colonization.

Samar, suddenly animated, remarked sweepingly that Indian novels were no good. 'It's like they've come gushing from the almost-a-pussy of a drag queen called Lady Epic.'

Leo added his own thoughts to Samar's dismissive remark, but Zaira was quick to disregard Leo's point that such literary tomes on ethnicity, multiculturalism and colonization went so far as to mollify that dubious entity: white guilt.

'You need to explain yourself,' Leo told her, a hint of confrontation in his voice.

In her defence, Zaira said she did not believe that the colonizers really gave a rat's ass about what their ancestors had raped, pillaged or burnt to cinders. 'So, to assume that they give a shit *now* is only a flattering self-delusion.'

Karan had had nothing to add as he had not read the book, and also because he secretly regarded novels as quaint, irrelevant oddities—complex, imaginative enterprises produced by people who needed to dignify the interminability of their idleness.

As the conversation replayed in his head, Karan was struck not only by the almost magical safety of the afternoon—those languid times never failed to convince him that they could go on forever—but also by his inability to articulate its essence to Claire's father. After all this time he was unable to speak of what he had once known intimately; this was how the trial's failure had eventually registered in him, vandalizing his facility with language, forcing him back to the world of images, to the colour of Zaira's hair and the way Samar had laughed when he had said Lady Epic. He nodded politely in the direction of Mr Soames, and even laughed a little when the old man winked and said that English novels were such sodding failures it was damned good they could be 'outsourced to India'. Karan had lived long enough in the white country to recognize that such a show of self-effacement was only a parade of modesty.

In that great, gabled country home with its Flemish brick façade and trimmed privet, Karan lay on a giant, soft bed beside Claire, agitated and sleepless. His fingertips explored the distinguished line of her neck; her chin; her nose; her eyes. He

kissed her hair, remembering a word he had come across in an American yoga magazine to which Claire subscribed: *closure.* He gathered it meant the conclusion to a worrying situation or a peaceable resolution of the past. The infinite possibilities of the word enthralled him, but its reality, difficult and gangly, left him disappointed. He had abandoned Shimla and come to Bombay to be rid of the past. In the big city, he had fallen in love, and in friendship. When the world had exploded in his face, he had fled to England, to grow anew a skin that had been peeled by what he had secretly come to think of as 'those strange events in Bombay'. Now he lay listening to the glacial wind hammer the leafless fretwork of ivy against the window and the greyhounds snore outside the bedroom door. This life was entirely unlike that which he had known, but its unfamiliarity did not divest him of the affinity he continued to feel for Bombay; in fact, if anything, it seemed to solidify his resolve to return.

He tilted himself on his side, closer toward Claire, moved a strand of hair off her face, unable still to feel for this angular-minded, lissome woman the emotion he knew as love. Knowing this broke his heart. Shutting his eyes, he could see the flamingoes beating their great, stoic wings against the Sewri smog, he could see the Ban Ganga pond, marigolds and terracotta lanterns floating upon its dirty, chartreuse waters; he could hear aluminium canisters rattle on Atlas cycles manned by absurdly athletic milkmen; he could see a piebald horse at the racecourse buckle and swish its frothy tail throwing angry

curlicues of brown dust into the air. He believed he could now go back to Bombay although it was nothing more than a catalogue of his failures in art and amity. Because some people were meant to shepherd you to different shores, and some people brought you back to familiar ones. He kissed Claire's neck, feeling grateful; her skin had the sharp, fresh scent of citrus, and he thought of the big oval soap made from pomelo skin lying on a dish in her bath. He felt lucky that she had been his shelter in the cold country.

Claire woke with daybreak and nuzzled him.

He kissed her mouth, she responded—sleepily at first, till fervour lit her touch. Her tongue moved from his mouth to his neck, travelling down his chest, his navel, hipbone, seeking scholarship of his body. But if she knew he was thinking of leaving her, of returning to India, to Bombay, what would she say? Would she strangle him? Would she turn away and pull the blanket between them? Or would she laugh and then fall back to sleep?

Perhaps Rhea had been the same way, committing treacheries within kisses, and so now he passed on the deceptions he had received.

Karan lay on his back, his legs spreadeagled. Claire's lips were around his penis. Desire obscured the past, and Karan felt himself oscillate back to the present moment, excited, alert.

Outside, Mr Soames was cleaning the head of his rifle with a square of cream muslin. Rabbits frolicked in the garden, innocent flashes of white in the mist.

She licked under the head, in the place where the pleats of skin parted, tongue flicking along the ridges.

Mr Soames opened his bedroom window and positioned the rifle on the ledge at the same moment that Karan turned Claire so she was on all fours. She looked out at the garden, at the rabbits in the mist. When Karan entered her predictably, she pulled away.

Girls from good English families. It was unusual for him, a mysterious pleasure, like the rooks crying out from their perch of fence posts. *Like to be.* Tightness, a certain forbidden fruit, and the knowledge that nobody could banish either Claire or him from the garden. They were *of* the garden. But the little rabbits on the green were not, and as Claire wiggled her hips in pain, as she felt herself relax and let him enter all the way, he grunted and held her down. *Assed.* The shot was clean and the rabbit writhed briefly before one of the greyhounds went racing for it.

Claire's muscles clenched around Karan as the dark, slender beast picked up the rabbit. Red, red beads dripped from its neck, a glazed eye stared at her through the icy morning haze, from the far side of death.

And Karan felt free, as never before.

29

AFTER KARAN QUIT LONDON, HE RETURNED TO Bombay, put up in a dingy hostel in Irla and worked as a schoolteacher in Juhu.

Mrs Pal, the school's principal, was a crafty woman with a dignified, scowling face, and an ass that looked as if it had been blown up with a cycle pump. The first time they met she remarked he had extremely long fingers; the strict, ambivalent tone of her voice was such that he felt she was telling him to prune their length. On a lavatory wall in the school, Mrs Pal had been depicted by a rather creative student as a dominatrix, an elephant-sized woman clad in oily black spandex lashing a mean black whip across the ass of a helpless man on all fours. When he first noticed it, Karan smiled at the rough, strident sketch because the mockery identified correctly what it disdained, and the identification was more cruel than the mockery itself.

The principal harassed the children with devious zeal. Two boys with hair longer than what she deemed the correct length were forced to stand on stools as coconut oil was poured all over them and their hair tied up in thin, sticky plaits. Another victim was made to wash the toilet bowls with his bare hands. Eventually, when Mrs Pal caned a twelve-year-old girl until the poor thing bled, Karan reported the principal to the police. The parents were brought in for interrogation. They denied the incident altogether, fearing their child would be expelled from the school described in a glossy brochure as 'a prestigious learning institution'.

A few weeks later, Karan resigned. There was no point in standing up for anything; he should have learned his lesson years ago, he told himself. Mrs Pal refused him a reference letter. Smugness blasted out of her face like a fart as Karan collected his papers on his last day at work.

Over the next few days Karan scoured the newspapers.

In the *Indian Express* he spotted advertisements for call centre operators. Recent graduates were encouraged to apply, but Karan gave it a shot nonetheless. He was picked for the job because, his interviewer said in an impressed tone, he spoke 'pitch-perfect English'. Before he could join work, however, Karan's twenty-two-year-old boss insisted on an accent neutralization course. 'We don't want to give our clients the wrong impression,' he said. Karan agreed.

Course complete, he joined work. He felt like a fish being scaled before being sliced, out of his depth in more ways than

one. With the money from his new job Karan moved out of the roach-ridden hostel and rented a small, tidy room in a decrepit house in Juhu Gaothan, close to where Zaira's apartment had been. He worked the graveyard shift, sleeping through the day and rising at 5.00 p.m. to attend to household chores. At six, he went to the beach for a long, brisk walk, passing en route the Mukteshwar temple, the slightly seedy Anand Hotel, an ancient Jain stepwell, a row of flashy buildings guarded by durwans with haggard, lifeless expressions.

On the beach, after his walk, he sometimes sat under a coconut tree after checking the soft beige sand for secret deposits of oil or random shards of glass; he would never feel completely at ease in the city. The sea breeze felt warm against his skin; he took a deep breath. He could see Bollywood stunt extras performing their dives and chops at the end of the beach. A football game was in progress right outside the Sun-n-Sand Hotel. A few old men sat on red plastic chairs, sipping fresh coconut water. Young, perspiring lovers wrestled lust and shame as they sat with their backs against a crumbling embankment.

Bombay was going through a rough patch. The name of the city had been changed. The HPP continued to wield its own brand of institutionalized despotism. Karan had witnessed fresh attacks on 'foreigners'—not South Indians, as it had been in the sixties, but those from the northern states. Ram Babu Kamat, the Bihari shopkeeper from whom Karan bought his groceries, had been beaten up one night. Ram Babu had fractured his arm

and fled the city. A new law too had been put in place, forcing businesses to display signage in the local Devanagari script.

But when he was at the beach Karan tried not to think of the political mess the city was embroiled in. He did not think of Ram Babu's face on the morning after he had been attacked by HPP workers. He refused to consider the signage of his local dairy in Devanagari. Instead, he focussed on the immediate particulars, a perfect seashell, the warm taste of salty peanuts on sale on Juhu beach. In spite of the crowds, in spite of the mess and the whirring heat, the mean and the hustle, he was never happier than when audacious slabs of golden light unevenly lit the sky and silver waves paused over a winter sea. Once the sun retreated from the horizon and into a strengthening night, the hurt of the world boldly invaded him through the wound in him, scaring away his loneliness.

This hurt shimmered in his eyes, animating him briefly.

Sitting under the arc of the wind-bent coconut tree, Karan sometimes remembered Claire. He had ended things, giving her vague reasons, perhaps because he had been anticipating the end of their union from the hour of its commencement. Claire's absence from his life neither stoked longing nor aroused regret; if anything, it widened the rift that Rhea had originally made. The wound of first love was lasting; it raked so deep that its repair felt impossible, and the anticipation of its recurrence—its sublime and vivifying charge—rendered subsequent collisions with love devoid of its lightness, its mitigation. Karan slipped his hand into the soft, soft sand

and thousands of grains cascaded through the spaces between his fingers. Nothing stayed. Every grain passed through. He stood and walked toward the water, toward the sun that was now slipping behind the stark line of the horizon, leaving an extravagant orange spray over a flat indigo sky.

One day he rang Miss Mango, formerly his landlady at Ban Ganga.

A woman answered. 'Miss Mango died two years ago. Her son sold her place to us. Can I help you?'

'Oh, I'm one of her former paying guests. I'd given her a plantation chair to keep in holding while I was in London. I was wondering if I could come and collect it.'

'I believe her son sold all her furniture to a dealer in Chor Bazaar,' the woman said.

Karan decided to venture out to Chor Bazaar, once again in search of a Bombay Fornicator.

He found the old market changed. Its noise was frenetic and ugly; the antiques looked new; he saw tourist guides accompanying rich Indian families who hoped to take back an exotic slice of the motherland for their four-bedroom houses in Hounslow and Journal Square. They shopped avidly, bargaining on cue, returning home with prized junk.

He walked on, surprised by some of the stores, unchanged from his last visit years ago; it was as if they had been waiting for him. He went up to the store where he had first met Rhea: it was still the same. He could almost see the talisman she had laid down on the carved Chinese bench; he could see her watching

him with that quiet, devouring gaze of infinite cunning. He paused before a familiar piece, an ancient armoire, gazed at the silvered mirror, afraid that in the reflection he would see her standing behind him. A black cat emerged from behind the armoire, brushed against his leg, then vanished. He wondered if Rhea had known then what he did now: that love was largely a matter of luck. Maybe that's why she had been out hunting for talismans, the brass monkey. He looked around for the Bombay Fornicator but there were none on display. He saw a man talking to his pet rooster with a pronounced red wattle. He asked a dealer about the brass monkey; the dealer showed him, instead, a faded silver amulet created in honour of Chekkh Mata, the Goddess of Sneezes. 'If you wear it,' the dealer assured Karan, 'you will never sneeze again.'

On the bus back to Juhu, he thought about his earlier agonizing assumption that Rhea had seduced him, abandoned him, and then gone on with her life. But he reflected now that her offence, in the grand scheme of things, was inconsequential. Malik Prasad had killed a woman, and got on with his life just fabulously; such violations were not as uncommon as believed though their pain might be uncommonly experienced.

One evening Karan was sitting under a coconut tree on the beach reading the *Hindustan Times,* when his eyes landed on an article on famous trials that had been botched up due to some reason or the other. Zaira's figured prominently in it. The article outlined the course her murder trial had taken—and the subsequent reinvestigation—and bemoaned the fact that

all efforts to get justice had come to naught. The journalist mentioned that Minister Prasad had won another election but was now forced to consider retirement because of failing health. Malik Prasad, the key accused, had recently got married. D.K. Mishra had constructed a palatial, centrally air-conditioned home in Gurgaon, and his last vacation had been spent in Thailand. At the bottom of the page were photographs of Nalini and Tara Chopra, at a party to celebrate the arrival of the first Armani store in Bombay; their teeth were picket-fence white and their hair had a strained, artificial luxuriance. There was a small, sober mention of Samar who, the journalist admitted, could not be traced. Karan's own name was fleetingly stated as a witness. He put down the paper, his hands trembling with a feeling of sorrow shot through with disbelief. The wind chose this moment to pick up the paper and it was gone before he could make a grab for it to read the last few lines that remained.

Rising, Karan started to walk. He was angry, but the anger was mute, terrified of its own might, and it soon turned inward. The murder, the trial, the verdict—all of it had coalesced into a big, burly blur in Karan's head, or perhaps he was the blur in them all. He was not yet ready to 'forgive' Malik but he sensed that what lay beyond the bitterness he harboured for the criminal could be deeply affecting, and toward this mythic port his ship now steered. Seeking neither redress nor truth, Karan wanted only to be touched briefly by the unhappiness that had made Malik so inanely cruel; if he could know this unhappiness and its root, then he might see the way out of the

maze of questions he often found himself wandering through like the last soldier on the battlefield. In the end, he thought, the only justice we seek is justice for ourselves. As he walked further down the shore, the waves came up at his calves. He laughed silently. For epiphanies were only plastic trophies, handed out for winning the race that all but busted your legs.

Oh, how he'd much rather experience a full-on apocalypse now.

Standing in the warm, soothing water, he turned and noticed the building where Zaira had lived, in Janaki Kutir. Memories of pleasant, spontaneous dinners flooded him. He thought of the Sunday afternoons spent in her balcony, looking out at the string of hand-rowed boats. He missed Zaira with an ache that rang through him like an aria. She would know exactly why he had left Claire and returned to Bombay, why he had agreed to go through with the accent neutralization course for his new job. She had known his idiot heart better than anyone else. They had never walked on the beach together—the threat of being mobbed was persistent with Zaira around. But if they had gone for a stroll, he was sure she, like him, would have searched for the silence under the din, and on finding none return home all the richer with disappointment. He had no way of knowing she had stood in the same sea only hours before she had been killed.

He thought of the time she had tried to explain the disorder and profusion of her love for Samar; she had said that souls got caught in bodies, that the body wanted one thing and the soul

quite another, and ultimately this strife had left her feeling small and disembodied. As he pictured her perfect, discerning forehead, the abrupt, frazzled beauty of her eyes, he felt that the strife had now left her and she would never be pulled one way or another again. He could sense, somehow, that her bold, eccentric soul had found its place, that her tenderness for ideas and curiosity about love, which had been larger than her, were now here, safe from all men, safe from the gods.

The water pulled away, the sand started to slip from below his feet, drawing him in.

But no, he told himself, he would not go in, not yet, not here.

On his way home, Karan stopped outside the Jain stepwell on the road near his house. Turtles swam through its dark emerald waters, unleashing ripples as their ugly conical heads jutted up for air. Samar had once come here with him, and they had stood here, looking into the water, at a thick clutch of white aromatic flowers that had bloomed defiantly on the callused boughs of a dwarf frangipani. He thought of Samar walking Mr Ward-Davies on the promenade in Worli; he thought of Samar swimming, his long arms executing precise, powerful strokes. Where was Samar now, Karan wondered. He had read about the new medicines available now to manage AIDS. Perhaps this would have allowed both Leo and Samar to tide through safely.

Invariably, his thoughts returned to Zaira. If he missed her with such shooting, livid pain, then it was likely that Samar had grown almost incoherent with longing. Karan found that over

time he had not come to forget Zaira, as conventional wisdom would have him believe; rather, he had come to remember her better. Her particulars were now sharp and resplendent, like the head of a spear. Countless details fretted in the air like disturbed motes before they slowly congealed to form something composite and solid, a thing that stood in direct, cavalier opposition to the haze of memory.

Reluctantly, sadly, he had come to accept that a human being was composed not only of everything that he possessed but also of all that he had lost.

30

TWO YEARS PASSED.

Karan often visited Chor Bazaar, but he did not find either the plantation chair Rhea had given him or the brass monkey she had forgotten there.

One lazy Sunday evening, he had spread out the papers on the floor to catch up on the news; the light in his room was wavering, the light of an aquarium. An odd little item in the gossip column of the *Bombay Times* caught his eye.

Remember Samar Arora? The snippet began. *The pianist who was also a witness in the murder trial of the late actor Zaira? Well, guess what, kids? The old floozy is back in town, looking like a meth addict. Rumour goes he left America after he got no mileage in San Francisco. So now the has-been who never was is back in our social circuit. He's busy ringing up every society hostess*

in town, but no one seems to be taking his calls. Maybe someone should tell the poor thing that in Bombay out of sight is out of mind, and out of mind is history.

Karan put down the paper; reading further would have been like bathing in vomit.

The next morning, he showed up at Samar's cottage. Sakubai, leaner now, opened the door. She saw Karan and wept instantly, freely.

When she took him up to Samar's room, he understood the pain in her eyes.

'Samar ... It's me, Karan.'

The man in the bed, all bones and a rag of a spirit, lay tucked under a maroon patchwork quilt. 'Karan?'

'Yes.'

The bed was littered with paperbacks, pencils, a hardbound journal, a cowhide spectacle case. Samar sat up with great difficulty. 'Karan Seth?'

'That's right.'

'Oh, doll,' he whispered. 'Where've you been all this while?'

'Working in London.' Almost involuntarily, Karan started to tremble as he looked at Samar, slim enough to slide into an envelope: his bones protruded awkwardly from his body, his skin was creased and of a leathery texture, and the hair on his bony skull was wispy and dull.

'When'd you get back?'

'A few years ago. I work at a call centre now.'

'That's got to be rough.' Samar's eyes sparkled with anguish.

'I had to take an accent neutralization course.'

'Ouch!' He smiled and patted his bed, gesturing Karan to his side.

Karan sat beside Samar. 'You okay?'

'I'm super,' he said, before adding, 'I don't dress for dinner, that's all ... I was thinking of you, just today.'

'You were?'

'I found an old photo you had taken of Zaira and me. She'd given it to me saying it was her favourite picture.' Slowly turning on to his side, Samar pulled out a photograph from between the pages of one of the books on his bed. Zaira was sitting by the poolside, her head on Samar's shoulder: the photograph had been cropped to an uneven close-up, making it difficult to tell who they were. In itself the photograph was regular but the depth of its intimacy was startling. Karan picked it up, a misleading memento from a past that had been nearly perfect; its splintered excellence ridiculed the present moment with a distant, hyena laughter. He gulped. 'Why did she say it was her favourite?'

'She never explained. But ... turn it around.'

On the back of the picture Zaira had scribbled, *I know I'm only a matinee but you make me feel like a sold-out show.*

Karan put the photograph aside.

'Why'd you stop by after such a long spell?' Samar asked.

'I read in the papers you were back in Bombay.' Karan rested his hand delicately on Samar's lap; he was afraid his hand would go through Samar and reach the mattress. Samar

reminded him of a cut flower, blooming disobediently long after it had been plucked. 'And I couldn't forget what you had promised years ago.'

'What was that?'

'That you'd get us some fizzy water and make it all better.'

Later that week, Karan dropped by for dinner.

As he was relishing Saku-bai's classic amti and rice, he found that the house was suffused with a heavy, holy quietness, a cold, ruminating light, and the peace was volatile and resentful of itself. Outside, on Worli Seaface, the city remained embattled and heroic, wrapped in a dark smog of noise and neurosis; growling and screeching with supreme honesty.

'You like living in Juhu?' Samar asked.

'It's nice. I'm just down the road from Zaira's place.'

'Ah.'

'The beach is a short walk away. There's a vegetable market outside. All that noise!' Karan said, waving his hand. 'Keeps you company after a while.'

'And all this silence,' Samar said dejectedly. 'So large it could only ever be empty.'

Karan noticed that Saku-bai had left the kitchen; a strong scent of mixed spices wafted out from a saucepan on the stove. The room had grown hot, and he remembered that the first time he had come here it had been cool, tropical, like an orchid farm.

He said, 'I wrote to you.'

'I kept all your letters, Karan.' Samar ladled another spoon of amti over an uneven mound of rice.

'I shouldn't have said what I did.'

'I'm sure you never meant it.'

Karan took a deep breath. He made a fist of his right hand and then rolled it over his chest in even circles. 'I even learned it in sign language.'

'What?'

'Sorry.'

'Oh, don't apologize.'

'Have to, Samar, have to.'

'I should have written back, but those days in San Francisco, well, funeral season was never quite done.'

'I can't even imagine what that was like.'

'Those days were ahead of my imagination, but not of reality.' Samar's mind whirled back to the first few months in San Francisco, settling into Leo's little apartment on Telegraph Hill, nailing down the good local delis, getting a library membership, walking through Golden Gate Park on a cold Sunday afternoon, a captive bison gazing at him in stunted, diabolic rage. Running alongside such pedestrian nostalgia was the insurmountable horror of rushing Leo in a cab to San Francisco General Hospital, of waiting endlessly for blood reports in cold, ugly clinics, of cleaning soiled sheets. 'I will never forget those days.'

At the fourth memorial service Samar had attended, pelting rain could not keep away a feeble band of protesters. AIDS

TURNS A FRUIT INTO A VEGETABLE. DIE. DIE. DIE. Placards throbbed with hatred. The protesters' faces came alive with loathing.

Inside the church, bathed in light filtered through large stained-glass windows, it was impossible not to be swept away by the affettuoso churn of the chorus, alert with sadness, thick with rage. Leo's friend, Lance, an investment banker, had died, purple and crazy, in his bed. Lance was survived by his boyfriend, a poet of irredeemable mediocrity, and by a father who had refused to attend the service; his absence stood in between the pews like a plinth. An extravagance of drag queens—in long satin gowns and with enough paint on their faces for all of Bollywood—stood like gangly, exotic foxgloves in the wind; not only did they diminish any unnecessary gravitas, they also exposed death as the last word in camp. There was talk outside the church about medicines, soon to be released, which could turn the condition from Death Warrant to Long-Term Nightmare.

Samar had seen Lance's gravestone. *Lance Nichols: Who Saw Heaven in a Wildflower.* Samar had turned to Leo and said, 'What a load of shit!'

'I agree.' Both men knew Lance had never cared for flowers, wild or otherwise, and heaven, from all conventional opinion, had no room for men like him. 'I guess death turns every drama queen into an opera star.'

Respite, during a season of unending calamities, came softly and suddenly. One morning, wild parrots, a shrill, audacious lot

of feathered hooligans, stopped by on the wooden ledge of their balcony. Leo told him that years ago a flock of South American parrots had escaped a crazy collector's aviary. They had bred in Golden Gate Park, and the subsequent generations were now perfectly at home in San Francisco. Samar was excited to feed the birds each morning, and no sooner had he placed a salver of chopped guavas or kumquats than the pack would emerge in broad, flamboyant sweeps.

A few weeks later the birds could be seen hanging about on the railing, scratching their dainty feathers, squawking in protest; no food had been put out for them. The night before, Leo had been rushed to hospital, shivering so that his gums bled. Three bedsheets soaked up his sweat, almost convincing Samar that the human body was composed entirely of water. Having battled the shingles, diarrhoea and a lung infection, Leo was petrified by this new face-off with hell. But Dr Smith at the hospital was optimistic, setting him off on a promising regimen of drugs, one that would eventually lower the agonizing screech of plague to a barely discernible hum. Leo returned home that week, feeling better, finding it possible to stash aside dreams of gravestones and imagine that his life had gone on almost uninterrupted.

'How did you cope, Samar?' Karan asked, his voice tinged with awe.

'Badly. I thought of writing to you.'

'You should have called me.'

'Well, I did call you once,' he said. 'But the operator at the *India Chronicle* office said you'd left work, moved out, with no forwarding address to speak of'

'I had moved to London by then, I suspect.'

'Then I tried to get your details from Iqbal, but they wouldn't put me through to him either.'

'Iqbal was taken out during the riots, Samar,' Karan said, his cheeks burning.

'He was killed?' Samar's mouth fell open with shock.

A wave of nausea swept through Karan as he remembered his visit to the morgue to identify his mentor's remains. 'Stripped, then doused with kerosene. Set on fire. A naked man in flames.' Karan looked at his feet. 'I went to get his body. His left arm was a heap of ash. His mother passed out in the morgue.'

'Is that why you left for London?'

'Perhaps,' Karan said. He added after a moment, 'Actually, I wanted a killer tan, and East London came highly recommended.' A whorled, crazed laughter followed. 'And your stay in San Francisco? What happened after Leo started to feel better?'

'Pretty times,' he said. 'I learned to trade when the market rallied.'

One summer, Samar and Leo had rented a cottage in a little town on the coast, regarded for its uninterrupted views of the ocean. The cottage, set on a hill, had a thick grove of timeless redwoods. Deer roamed about in the unruly garden, feeding

on dew-struck grass; a hummingbird whirred in mid-air, like a dream caught in tender panic, peeking into honeysuckle the colour of butter. On the second night, they heard a bear pawing at the back door, then raiding the garbage bin. At daybreak, Leo made coffee for them both and they laughed over the bear attack. Samar noticed that Leo was looking better than ever before. After breakfast they trekked up to the top of a hill and sat under a redwood, gazing out at the view below: a majestic spread of blue water, fine, faint sky flecked with oyster-coloured clouds. The local homes, made almost entirely from timber and glass, were camouflaged against the topography; now and again, between patches of serrated black rocks, were velvet carpets of purple flowers, with thick, glossy leaves which, when crushed, gave off the refreshing scent of fennel.

After a week in the country, Leo and Samar started back for the city.

Leo fell asleep within half an hour of the journey back, leaving Samar to enjoy the sights. He saw a derelict white shed overrun by a trailer of profuse red blossoms; a family of young seals frolicking in the bay; a beach, flat, smooth, beige, almost abandoned. The wind was swift but balmy and ocean-rinsed, and a vein of sulphurous scent ran through it. Fragments from this clean, magnificent vista played out against the music filling the car. Some songs were from a soundtrack to the film in which Zaira had acted. In solitary, opaque moments Samar recalled her with a jarring flash of pain. Her last moments often replayed in his mind, and he could see her in his lap, blood oozing out

of the bullet wound in her temple, her sultry eyes straining to remain open, the trembling words that had left her mouth. Running under the sheath of this anguished memory was the delirium of his longing. He thought of how he had always been free to call her and rant about politics or gush over a film or run down a book; he had stolen flowers with her at midnight and downed Bellinis on the rooftop; they had grown to become the fearless arbiters of each other's eccentricities. And Zaira had encouraged Samar to believe that his life, which had always possessed an elusive, surreal quality, was real and blazing, not a sly, ethereal figment of his prolific imagination. Without her, the laughter had gone out of the evening; he was forced to accept that time was how one spent love, and everything else was only scenery.

'It was odd how *much* I came to miss Zaira,' Samar said after dinner. His tongue rested on her name like a mother's palm over a sleeping baby's brow.

'How did you get over her?'

'I didn't. Do you remember her often?'

'Early on, she believed in my work so implicitly it allowed me to believe in myself. That's a fine gift for a young man whose self-doubt is big enough to eat him up. I never had to wear a face around her; she was open to my gallows humour and my useless tirades against love. She was funny and clear-minded and out there.' There was a catch in his voice. 'Not only do you have to bear her loss but you have to cope with Leo's death too.'

'His life, actually.'

Karan sat up on the dining chair. He had assumed the disease had slowly and cruelly destroyed Leo. 'I don't follow you, Samar.'

'Leo didn't kick the bucket; he just moved east.' Not only was Leo alive, he was busy working on a biography of New York in a fine brownstone in Brooklyn. 'Loving someone,' Samar said quietly, 'does not insure against their leaving you.' Samar and Leo had met for the last time on the wooden steps of Grace's Garden, near the house they had shared for almost five years. Leo had said, 'I'm bad at death,' and Samar had said, 'I'm bad at life, but that never stopped me from trying.' Then Leo had looked away, unsayable things oscillating between irony and fury.

'Leo had wanted to write a book about Zaira's death.'

'He did?'

'Yes. And I asked him not to write about her, the murder, the trial.'

'You never told me.' Karan suddenly had a better picture of why Leo had made tracks. 'Is that why he moved to New York?'

'He feared being owned, above all things. He didn't want to be told what to write.'

'So he resented you for forcing him not to write about Zaira,' Karan surmised.

'We need the most irrelevant of things to remind us we are not in love any longer, and his exit clause was in small print.'

'I always had a doubt ... he was jealous of Zaira ... she had a hold over you.'

'You could be right.'

Karan looked at him with a dazed expression. 'I don't know how you survived the last few years in San Francisco.'

'With a little practice, you get used to any sort of hell.' Samar yawned, cupping his right hand over his mouth. 'Love is bizarre, I'll give you that. Some days I get nosebleeds missing Leo and on other days I'd like him fisted by a gorilla. But then, knowing him, he'd probably like a bit of animal kink. That's the awful thing,' he said, 'knowing someone, all that bloody knowing. When they up and quit, you're left with a whole heap of information you just don't know how to shelve.'

Karan assumed that Samar meant the gracious minutiae of his shared times with Leo, vivid, witty snatches of arbitrary conversation, amorous walks on a foggy pier, extravagant meals in restaurants where candles hoisted atop empty bottles of cognac melted to resemble an octopus. But Karan was mistaken. What Leo had said to Samar could never be repeated, for such accusations did not fall within the parameters of intimacy, and the phrase *professional moralizer* had stuck to Samar like a stain.

'So once he felt better he took off for Brooklyn. He did say, before he left, that our relationship had come to have the stink of death.'

Karan curled his lips in disgust. 'I'm sure he didn't mean that.'

'I wanted to ask him whose death he was referring to.'

'Why didn't you stay on in San Francisco?'

'Most of our friends had died, and hanging out by the pretty little gravestones loses its shine after a while. Everywhere I looked I was reminded of Leo. Not only his love but also his anger. Mostly, though, I was hankering for Saku-bai's meals. I wanted homemade dal-chawal. Aloo paratha. Cucumber raita. I wanted it all, and I wanted out.'

'I'm glad you came back. Are you?'

'I suppose,' Samar said. 'But there were photographs of Zaira on my piano. Photographs you'd taken on the first day we had met. And I had forgotten to get rid of Mr Ward-Davies's leash.'

In the first few days of his return to Bombay, Samar was shocked by how the past had risen from the stillness of the house and punched him cold in the face.

'Bombay felt far lonelier than San Francisco, where I'd come to count on wild parrots.'

Karan looked surprised: how could Samar, who had known so many folks in Bombay, feel lonely?

Samar touched his chin with his index finger. 'I came back slim and bruised, so I wasn't exactly an oil painting. Besides, my tap dancing was rusty on rhythm, and there was nobody to go out to steal flowers with.'

'But you have friends here.'

'I never confused my drinking buddies for friends, although there were exceptions. But Diya had hitched up with a painter and taken off for the countryside up north. And Mantra was teaching writing at a university in London. So I'd come home

to a ghost town.' Hesitantly he admitted that some people had swung by a time or two before they had drifted, afraid the bug was catching or because a sparkling, raucous shindig, somewhere out in the muggy lanes of Colaba, was calling out their name. 'As you can imagine, I'm real glad you showed up. I hope dinner made the grade?'

'Wish I'd known earlier, I'd have come sooner. Dinner was super, as always, thanks.'

Both men rose from the table; they were grateful for each other's company but reluctant to squeeze the evening dry of its shambling charm. Saku-bai was duly, extravagantly complimented on the sumptuous meal. Creamy scoops of chiku ice cream from Naturals made for a quick, quiet dessert. As Samar accompanied Karan to the door, they paused in the living room. Karan's eyes fell on the beat-up white couch, the wicker chair, the tropical palms, the tea lights throwing shadows on the ceding; the room felt warm and familiar, but the familiarity was distrustful and brittle.

'You remember I had said to you once: what you love you can save,' Samar told Karan at the door.

'Yes. Didn't your grandmother tell you that?'

Samar opened the door. 'She did. But,' he said, his face falling, 'I think she was horribly off the mark.'

'Please don't believe that, Samar.'

'All my beliefs—'

Karan's finger gripped the edge of the front door. 'Don't let them take that away from you.'

'What did they add up to anyway?'

'Samar—'

The wind shook the raat ki rani creeping up the wall beside the door, freeing a mutiny of tiny, dry leaves, some of which drifted past Karan and his host. A car honked on the road outside. After a moment, Samar said brightly, 'I'd like very much to go and sit by the sea in the evenings. Will you come with me?'

'Anything for you, champ; anything at all.'

Neither Karan nor Samar would hazard Worli Seaface ever again, so the next option was Marine Drive. Before long, a routine was set. Karan would pick Samar up every Saturday evening and the taxi would deposit the two men on the noisy promenade. Corncob sellers roasted heads of pale yellow maize on a black furnace; each time they fanned the coals, embers whooshed out, cloudy crumbs with smouldering orange hearts. Amid a swirl of gossiping housewives, muscular athletes, lovers walking arm in arm and peanut sellers, the two of them sat on a bench, audience to a mundane but deeply moving play that seemed to convey the meaning of their lives but fell short of capturing the common, unknown errors that had maimed them. The success of this play depended on its portrayal of life as a bearable thing, as something that happened to other people, like a harelip or a lottery bounty.

'Sir, you want?' A peanut seller extended a paper cone topped with warm peanuts.

'What for?' Samar asked with an amused look on his face.

The peanut seller wore a serious look. 'Timepass, sir.'

As Samar chewed on a deliciously warm peanut before he handed the paper cone to Karan, he felt glad for the present company; he also regretted having walked out on their friendship many years ago at the racecourse. In San Francisco, Karan's absence in his life had registered in vital, delicate corner; grudges were not only a waste of time, Samar had come to accept, but they also discouraged love from blooming in illicit, unpredictable ways.

'Thank you for coming here with me, Karan.'

'I'm having the time of my life,' Karan said, and meant every word.

Their evenings on Marine Drive did not signal the resumption of an old friendship—both men were big enough to recognize what had passed. But the loss of what had once been deep and peculiar did not dishearten them from starting anew, buoyed by the simple fact that a life without friends was possible but not entirely elegant.

While returning to Worli one evening, Karan broached the subject of Samar's health. What could they do to make him better?

'I should've been more careful,' Samar told him. 'I never took my pills on time. I was careless.'

'Well, now you're in Bombay. We should go and see a doctor.'

They were in a taxi at Mahalaxmi. They had passed a plush showroom of imported cars, and a temple where hundreds of pigeons crowded a chaotic courtyard.

'You want me to see a doctor?' Samar asked in a serious tone.

'Yes, I ...'

'But I'm not looking to date anyone these days.' He thumped his thighs, laughing freely.

The taxi driver turned to glare at the defiant, chuckling skeleton in the back seat.

Adamant on getting a professional opinion, Karan made an appointment with a specialist at Breach Candy Hospital.

'What's the damn point?' Samar said even as they walked down the hospital's colourless corridor.

'There's no point.' Karan stepped back to make way for a nurse with a face as featureless as a boiled egg and an insolent stride. 'We're here for the scenery.'

'Well, the scenery stinks.'

'Sshhh!'

They sat on a rexine sofa in the dreary waiting room.

After a brief, polite consultation, Dr Taraporevala, who had a jockey's slight, windswept build, offered her prognosis. Trying her best to sweep the despair out of her voice she told them that by failing to take the medicines that could have extended his life, possibly indefinitely, Samar had scuppered the chances of his survival.

The muscles on Karan's neck tightened.

Samar smiled blandly; the doctor's verdict, its polite vernacular of futility, was not new to him, but to be reminded of his mortality so plainly was like being slapped on the face.

'I'm afraid for your liver,' Dr Taraporevala said. She had a kind, perfect face; it was obvious that it had once been devastatingly attractive.

'My liver is afraid for me, too.'

Dr Taraporevala looked intently at Samar. 'Mr Arora,' she said, 'I have heard you play the piano. I attended a recital of yours quite by chance. You were playing in Santa Barbara; I was finishing a course there at the time, and I had gone for your recital with my cousin. I think you were fourteen years old at the time.' The doctor added that she had forgotten the performance despite its almost impudent virtuosity, but had returned to his music years later—after losing her five-year-old daughter to cancer. Nothing had prepared her for the tragedy, and she had retreated into a graveyard silence. She lost her appetite. Her haemoglobin had fallen so low she had to be administered a blood transfusion. She turned into a melancholy insomniac. That's when she had reached out for Samar's music, its molten dexterity. Its fine shadows had not solved her grief, but it had been an able, shy companion of her solitude. An unanticipated solace. Dr Taraporevala rose, walked to the window and stood by it. Resuming her seat after a few seconds, she cleared her throat. 'I'm sorry. I wish I could have been of greater help. I'm terribly sorry.'

But Samar had not heard the doctor's heartfelt words; his face was fixed on Karan, whose eyes had a trembling gleam. A vein had been cut, and it occurred to him that perhaps there was no point to art, political or otherwise, and perhaps its point

was its pointlessnes. But to extend to a lamenting mother a few fractured, imperfect moments of consolation was reason enough to put beauty to the service of truth. All that was corporal, photographs and statues and paintings—they could magnify sorrow in order to exorcize it and illuminate ecstasy, so it might be experienced in its entirety.

'Please call me if you have any further questions.' The doctor stood up to bid them farewell. 'The card has my mobile number on it.'

All the things they could not say came up to the surface, where they struggled for release.

'Thank you, doctor,' Karan said, trying to dislodge the stone weighing down in his throat.

'I just wish there was something I could have done.'

'You have done more than I would have expected from you, doctor.' Samar shook Dr Taraporevala's hand. 'You have told us the ride has been worth it.'

Dr Taraporevala looked puzzled.

Samar said warmly, 'Thank you again.'

The doctor removed her glasses. 'Your music, Mr Arora, I have really enjoyed it.'

'Oddly enough,' Samar said, reaching to embrace the doctor, 'so have I.'

On the way back Karan asked the taxi driver to pause outside Silver Oaks Estate. 'This is where Rhea used to live.'

'At the end of this lane?'

'Yes. She and her husband occupied the penthouse. There was a terrace with two rooms; her studio, his library.'

'I saw her only once. On the day of the verdict. She reminded me of a bird; she had mysterious, heavy-lidded eyes, as if she had just woken from a dream of something tender and imperceptible. I wish I'd had a chance to meet her,' he said, knowing he never would now. 'Thank you for taking me to meet Dr Taraporevala.'

Karan's hand was on the door handle of the taxi, as if he wanted to open it and rush out into the simmering heat of the city. 'You should have taken the medicines when you knew, Samar; you shouldn't have been so careless.'

'I hope you can forgive me. My regret is that dying will take the fun out of missing you. I know you wonder why I give up on things, be it music, or our friendship, or cities. I no longer have the strength to tell you everything. But a few things will not leave me unless you know them. When I felt I was putting on a performance of being myself on stage, I walked away from the piano; it was like I was auditioning to be somebody else. The Pianist. I might be crazy and pretentious but I'm no phoney, Karan,' he said. 'I don't know how to say all this without sounding vague or disorderly.'

'Did you abandon the medicines because Leo left you?' A wave of anger churned through Karan; his hand continued to remain on the door handle, pushing down ever so slightly.

'I blame no one except myself. One morning, after I'd fed the wild parrots, I sat on a bench. It was frightfully cold, fog was

reeling off the pine tops, and I was beat. Leo had left for good by then. I did not miss him although his conduct had astounded me; instead, I was relieved at his absence.

'But the space Leo's leaving had left in me slowly filled up with the awful, belated realization that the only person I ever truly cared about was someone else entirely. Early on, Zaira had recognized something permanent, not in me but in us. I'd grown up believing sexual honesty was more important than anything else; I chucked my mother when she tried to "cure" me. In my conviction, I failed to hear something that cut deep and stayed quiet: the heart adheres to the calling of neither body nor age. The arrow swivels on its own compass. What cut me in half and laid me down was my inability to recognize a love affair in its bloom.'

He sighed and adjusted his collar. 'I told you the first time we met after we came back to Bombay. I knew I wasn't going to win a lottery in this lifetime but, doll, I never even made the bloody raffle. Or maybe I did. Maybe they even called out my number. I just never heard, and now my meter's running out and I'm all out of dimes.' His voice was like a drop at the end of an icicle right before it falls to the ground. 'I guess it's what I told you the time you came to see me: My grandmother was wrong. *What you love, you can save.* I couldn't and, what's worse, it wasn't the only belief that failed. Or, perhaps, I failed them all.' He stroked his neck as he looked away.

'I don't know what to say to make you feel better about Zaira,' Karan said quietly. 'She had once told me she believed

that when it came to love she was card sharp but out of case money. I told her she was wrong, and she had laughed.

'I guess the trouble with an almost-romance is not knowing when it starts and knowing that it will never end. Perhaps it's true what my mother wrote to me in a letter before she died: People love people in such strange ways that it will take you more than a lifetime to figure that one out.'

Samar looked out of the window. A woman was selling strawberries at the traffic light. A crow sat on the telephone pylon, a sinister silhouette against a brazenly blue sky. He thought he wanted nothing more now than to be home, in his room, tucked in his bed.

31

ONE NIGHT, AFTER DINNER, SAMAR AND KARAN took a walk through the garden in the cottage. The pool was a mess; leaves and small twigs twirled about in the rippling blue nets of balmy water. A rat had drowned in the pool. Its fat brown body floated on the surface, the tail distended, tiny, menacing white teeth visible.

The two men walked up to Mr Ward-Davies's grave; it was easy to miss as there was neither marker nor stone, and grass had grown all over it. Yet both knew exactly where it was, the imperfect, wretched rectangle.

'After I moved back I wanted to know what happened to all the others in the trial,' Samar said.

'Did you find out?'

'At the end of my first month here I accidentally caught Bunty Oberoi on the telly. It was on a repeat telecast of a fashion show that closed the Delhi Fashion Week.' Handsome as ever, his face pared to a glossy gauntness by years of charlie, Bunty Oberoi was working the ramp after his acting career had failed to go anywhere. He strutted down the runway with a look of studied ennui, gazing blandly at the same set of posh, painted faces that had been with him at Maya Bar one summer night, many moons ago.

'But I don't really blame him for getting on with things.' Samar sat on the grass cross-legged, his hands on his lap.

'You don't?' Karan was puzzled by the detachment in Samar's voice.

'God, no. Sure he was a stinker to start with, but he was only a bit player in an amazingly twisted galaxy.'

'Well, what do you know about Malik?'

'He's given up his event management company.'

'So what does he do now?'

'He runs a production studio called Shree Durga Telefilms; he produces soap operas.' Samar could not help smiling.

Malik's production house churned out a glossy series of hugely successful soap operas, soppy sari sagas with housewives who were adorned like Christmas trees and had more affairs than their orifices might realistically accommodate. Malik had been dubbed the 'TRP Maharaja' after several of his shows on Zee and Star TV shot up to the top of the ratings charts. Television was an unexpected foray, and he had done splendidly

for himself; he came up with the storylines and his flock of writers developed them for him, complete with flimsy, filmy dialogue.

Malik had married a sloe-eyed pilot from Chandigarh and gone on to father a plump, plucky daughter. For a fancy dress competition recently held at her school, Malik had wanted his daughter to dress as Snow White. The poor girl, dark as petroleum, had valiantly dipped her face in a can of white flour before setting out to perform her number. She won the second prize, which was really an appreciation of her terrifying tenacity, her complete lack of self-consciousness, her devastating focus. Once her face had been whitened, she saw no discrepancy between who she was and who she was impersonating and, like her grandfather, believed that you became what you believed you were. The parents in the auditorium had given Malik the double take, unsure if he was a criminal or a celebrity, the distinctions between the two fast blurring in India's tabloid imagination.

'I also caught Tara Chopra's show on the same programme. The broadcaster said that the Chopra line now retails all over the Middle East; she's got quite a career.'

Samar did not know that Tara Chopra had struck a false note when she had showed, a few years back, the infamous 'Z Line'. *Couture inspired by a dear and beloved leading lady of yesteryear,* said the show catalogue. The clothes—copper-sheeted dresses, embroidered strapless tent dresses, organza evening robes with matted yokes—were difficult to fault, and

the stunning reproduction of the backless silver gown Zaira had worn on the night she had been murdered was particularly accurate. But perhaps the music had been inappropriate: a hip, tormented remix of the song 'I Just Died in Your Arms Tonight'; the music was like an imp that had come out of the trunk and hidden in a corner, chuckling contemptuously. Fashion editor Diya Sen, wearing tributaries of silver earrings that flashed arcs of fury, caused a bit of a stir when she stormed out of the showing even as it was in progress. As a result of Sen's public denunciation of Tara Chopra's show, applause had been vague and arbitrary. Recognizing the error of her ways, Tara had jumped into damage control mode, breathlessly telling the *Indian Express's* fashion correspondent that her collection was only a means 'to come to terms' with Zaira's murder, which, she added, had affected her profoundly, destabilizing her faith in the world forever. After a lot of work with my Guru-ji, she said in a muted tone, I am finally ready to put it all behind me. The press lapped up her repentant rampster number and she landed herself acres of column inches in the fashion press. Tara Chopra managed to do what her mother had achieved with an altogether different kind of finesse, entirely unexpected from the kohl-lined Maharani of Racoons.

Meanwhile, Tara's mother, Nalini Chopra had carved herself a niche in the media as a national martyr.

On talk show after talk show, she repeated that she had been the only witness in the trial who had had the guts to tell the police that she had seen Malik Prasad at Maya Bar that

night. No one asked her why she could not have said this clearly when she was in the witness box, perhaps because she managed to leak a little emotionally manipulative teardrop before an accusation could well up in anyone's throat. She also wore a scarf around her head, like a woman who had emerged from some distant repressive regime, hazarding mine fields and polygamous ass-humping men, simply to speak the truth. In very careful whispers, enunciating each vowel perfectly, Nalini Chopra let on that she had now dedicated her life to the uplift of women and the education of street children and, in her spare time, was chairing the first Indian Commission on Global Warming. After spending two years in Pondicherry, in relative isolation, she had recently emerged with an inspirational memoir, *The Truth Shall Set You Free,* which her literary agent at the William Morris Agency in New York was shopping around with top editors at big publishing houses.

'It's amazing how the media never took her to task. She had hosted a party without a liquor licence. She never even hired a bouncer,' Karan said. 'And I read the other day that she's now hustling a memoir.'

'The media needed a spokesperson. They needed a face. A professional suffragette. They needed someone who was out there that night, in the thick of Zaira's blood. But I wish she'd picked a better title for her book. Perhaps, *Every Woman's Handbook to Looking like a Drag Queen.*'

Karan laughed. 'You know, I read the other day that Minister Chander Prasad had a heart attack.'

'Yes, his third one! And I bet he could take three more, and chug right along. He's built like a brick shithouse.' They walked around the pool; the rat continued to float on the water amid a maudlin wreath of dry leaves. The beautiful pool was now a glorified sewer. 'Nothing shakes him.'

After retiring from politics, Malik's father had sequestered himself in his farmhouse in his native Haryana, the family acreage, where he had won his manhood from a buffalo. The HPP had all but forgotten him. Politics had a short memory, and politicians none at all; besides, the corrupt in India had so many heirs it was difficult to keep tabs on dethroned emperors.

Minister Prasad's wife had left him. The minister had no idea where she was but, at times, he missed her like a bad tooth. The heart formed alliances with the darnedest things. The minister often thought of visiting his son in Bombay, specifically to see his granddaughter, but Malik had no time for him, refusing to take his calls. Minister Prasad hated the fact that he had morphed into a sentimental old grandfather, but managed to convince himself that he was only desperate to see his granddaughter because Malik was denying him the right to do so. But he continued to send her extravagant presents on her birthday—gold necklaces, a lavish doll's house—and displayed her photographs on the desk in his study.

When, in private, he reflected on how he had masterminded his son's acquittal, he registered no conceit; he had done what he had to out of love, and that was a lot more than others could say. As a young man, Minister Prasad had come to terms with

the fact that the world was not his oyster; actually, it wasn't even his clamshell. But that didn't deter him from turning the world into the best little whorehouse in Delhi. And everyone who had done time at his joint, Bunty Oberoi, D.K. Mishra, Judge Kumar, had come through rapping to the tune of '*Who's your bhadva, baby?*'

All he wanted now was to spend some time with his granddaughter.

'But it wasn't all bad.' The two men sat under the almond tree, leaning against the trunk. 'There was also goodness, which I came to hoard like jewels.'

Mrs Prasad—Malik's mother, Minister Prasad's AWOL wife—had come to see Samar soon after she had read of his sickness.

'She had left her husband, she said. She'd had enough. He had kicked her and smashed her up. She had miscarried one time. He had broken her teeth, thumped her head against the wall. He called her mother a whore and her father a wild pig. She knew that her leaving her husband did not affect him in the least, but a whole new world had opened up for her; it was as if she had been reborn. She cried for what her son had done. Her own flesh and blood, she said, how could he have done what he had?

'She would visit me sometimes, bringing with her a tiffin of dal and chawal, and sit quietly at the foot of the bed. She gave me talismans to ward off the evil eye. She prayed for me, this old, beat-up wife, this mother, this woman. I think she veiled

her face with her pallu to hide her horror at my state; she felt she was looking at the road kill her son and husband had left for her to watch over. She'd assumed Zaira and I had been lovers, and treated me like I was her surviving kin, the widowed one. I don't know from where she got this notion, but somehow I allowed her to believe it, and then believed it myself. She cried so purely sometimes that she released the pain in my heart with her tears. She pressed my feet. She said that she went to the temple and prayed for my health.' Powered by the memory, Samar leaned forward. 'She was simple, true. And brave as hell. There are all kinds of bravery, Karan, and what we knew was the least of it.

Mrs Prasad returned to Delhi, only a month before you showed up. She works as a sales clerk at the Metropolitan Mall in Gurgaon. She knows me, Karan, and although it probably means nothing, she also knows the score.'

32

'IS THIS TABLE TO YOUR SATISFACTION, SIR?' THE maître d' at Gatsby had seen Samar on several occasions before but never so startlingly skeletal. He added, 'No smoking, as requested.'

'It's perfect!' Samar said, settling into his chair. There was a painting on the wall of pears in a wooden bowl; there were lilies in small square vases of clear glass. 'It's always been perfect here.'

'Thank you, sir; we're always delighted to have you here.'

'Oh, just one will be fine,' Samar said, resisting when he was handed a copy of the menu.

'You won't be eating, then, sir?'

'My friend here,' he said, 'will more than make up for me; he's a closet glutton.'

Karan looked around the restaurant, nearly empty so early in the evening; the big-assed small fry of south Bombay were still on their goop call. The dinner plans, entirely spontaneous, had been hatched after an evening on the promenade by the sea; although shabbily incongruous in such refined environs, they had about them a slightly spooky, banished allure. He thought of the first time he had come here, on Iqbal's urging, to photograph Samar, who had proceeded to tap dance on the bar top to an audience that had included an orange sarong-clad film-maker and a fashion editor standing in hot white knickers and pearls. The evening was from a distant past, he thought, but then the terrible thing about a photographic memory was the burden of scrupulous recall.

'I've decided to love myself a bit,' Samar said as he sipped on a glass of water. 'Chiefly because no one else will. Tell me, who will do a better job than moi?'

'You could be off the mark there.'

'Anything on the menu catches your eye?' His shins hurt; his chest was stuffy. 'They've turned around the menu, I see.'

Karan's eyes darted over the listing, going from the lobster risotto and the asparagus and fennel salad, to the grilled chicken, unsure if it was kosher to eat when Samar could barely hold down a bowl of soup. However, on Samar's insistence and selection, the food appeared on the table within twenty minutes, exquisitely presented and drool-worthy.

'Your nosh any good?'

'Nothing to write home about.'

'Salad makes the grade?'

'B-plus.'

'You're a bitch master; tell me about the risotto.'

'I guess you could eat it and live.'

'Living is not really the point of tonight's dinner.'

'I guess it never was the point of anything.'

'They say the prospect of death turns you around, grows you up, makes you profound. I'm afraid,' he continued with a twinkle in his eye, 'it's only made me shallower. Not only do I no longer worry about power and justice, or fate and mortality, I also find myself dreaming about the food I will never eat. The list grows longer by the hour, and I'm not counting on an epiphany to sit in for kick-ass pasta, so there we are. I wonder,' he said, almost to himself now, 'if I stuck it out with Zaira. Before and after, if you catch my drift.'

'You went further than anyone else.'

'You think?'

'You fought the case. Rallied around. And by the end of it, everyone knew they were dealing with steel.'

'They knew I was steel?'

'Yes.'

'But that never stopped them from snatching up my baby.'

Karan gulped. 'You were a good friend to Zaira.'

'I'm telling you they snatched *him* up. They took *him.*'

From the corner of his eye, the maître d' looked at Samar; why was he speaking so agitatedly?

'She could not have asked for anything more.'

'They dragged him along the street.'

Karan picked at the food on his plate.

'And his left eye was in my hand!'

'Samar.' Karan bowed his head.

Another song came on then, and in it was the DJ's rousing, taut, unrealized lust; he had put his jism into it. Into semen music entered a woman in an off-shoulder pewter gown with a daring side slit, her shoulder blades like the outstretched wings of a bird; her lips were red, the red of pomegranate. Tilting her head, she regarded the crowd disdainfully. It was just as well, the hauteur of her face said, just as well. Having recorded her arrival, supremely aloof, at once diabolic and seraphic, the restaurant enveloped the woman into its sophisticated hurly-burly, and on it went.

Samar was busy making a boat out of his napkin, folding and refolding the stiff cloth, creating a cloth origami of a sailboat. After a few minutes he placed the boat on the table, between Karan and himself.

Karan took the boat in his hand. 'You ever wish Leo was still around ... by your side?'

'I've never wanted anyone to hang around me for a second longer than they want,' he said. 'But I do wish I knew then what I've found out only recently: love no one so much that it seriously imperils your happiness.'

'He was not a bad man, but perhaps he was afraid of death.'

'Actually, I believe he was afraid of life.'

'I'm sorry he made you so unhappy in the end.'

'Am I unhappy?' Samar rapped his fingers on the table. 'Some days. Most days, the pain in my body seems to wipe everything out of my head—and maybe that's why we fall sick; so we start to loathe the life we crave so much. The older I grow, the less sure I am about anything at all. I don't mean the validity of things like fate and love. I don't mean the big things. I'm just not sure if buses will come on time, or if the flowers will bloom when they're meant to, if my horoscope for the day will come true, and perhaps that's something to surrender to.' A smile lit up his face. 'The odd thing about having these minor, meaningless arguments with yourself is never knowing which side to take.'

'I've stopped taking sides; the only sides I stand up for are the ones around bread.'

Samar dismantled the boat, folding the napkin along its original folds. 'But I owe Leo. He let me love him, and that's a lot. I guess what I got out of it was knowing that the more you fall apart, the less you fall apart. Now, would you like some dessert?' he asked briskly.

Karan said that he was quite full already. Samar insisted that he eat and for a moment Karan felt as if he was being asked to eat for the both of them. The waiter collected their dishes and presented the dessert menu. As he inspected the menu, Karan said that when they had first met he had never expected they would end up such good friends. Samar laughed and said that so many breeder boys had filed him under homo and junked

him he had become immune to rejection. Karan looked at him with regret and said that he had not known better at the time.

Samar took another sip of water. 'You're too hard on yourself; if I didn't have my prejudices to hold on to, I'd fall off the ship too. You'd never have stayed for a Bellini if I had asked, so I'm real glad Zaira told you to hang on for a drink.'

'I stayed that evening because Zaira asked, but I doubt if I'd have come back for dinner if it were only her.'

Samar looked up from the menu and his eyes smiled. 'Apple and rosemary pie looks kind of neat.'

'Yes, it does; I'll order a slice.'

As Karan dug into his pudding, the restaurant came alive. Samar's eyes moved from the usual suspects—the theatre artist with her big bold red bindi; ruddy expats clutching gin-and-tonics—to a small, noisy cluster of confident men seated around a circular table, exuding an energy that was flirtatious, wired, pulsating with the obscene confidence of a hard-on. It seemed as if they were from a different realm, untouched by either spite or contempt, held chaste in their worldly innocence, dumb with a privilege they never paid for. They reminded Samar of wildebeest crossing the river, the lot that safely makes it to the other side, with the plains before them in all their monsoonal luxuriance. There would be other rivers to cross, other plains to roam, but for now they had made it over. To the other side.

He turned to Karan. 'Have you met Mrs Dalal since you got back?'

'She lives in Singapore now. With her husband and child.'

'So she has a family.' Samar tiptoed around the subject; in the last few months Karan had spoken of her sparingly, reluctantly. In contrast, his affection for Claire had been luminous with ardour.

'Yeah, I guess. That's what she always wanted.'

'Did you hear from her when you were in London?'

'What do you think, Samar?'

Samar noticed Karan had clammed up at the mention of Rhea. 'I doubt if you would have lasted in London as long as you did if it weren't for Claire.'

Karan was silent for a moment. He believed he had been slow in recognizing his feelings for Claire, mistaking his general indifference to love for a specific inability to love her; his handicap was certainly private but not personal. 'She was a wild one. With vroom—six cylinders, all charged. Her cosmos, London's art scene, was education for me; I learned what my life could have been were I working as a photographer, and I found I wasn't missing a lot.' His face grew tense; his ears alert, as if he had heard a faraway sound. Then he leaned forward. 'It also showed me how art works here. In India. We don't go looking for it in a museum; we don't always call it by a name.' Art was the fretwork of henna on a bride's palm. A raga freed at dawn. Rangoli at the threshold. 'At one point, I was with her at a party in Belgravia, when it occurred to me that I wasn't interested in photography, but I wanted to look at things for a while.' The long gaze, he had discovered to his delight, was a restful thing. 'I did not want more than that.'

'Seems like you got a lot out of Claire, which has me wondering why you gave up a good thing.'

Karan folded his hands and settled back in his chair. He glanced to his right; a young couple was sitting with a bottle of wine between them. Their inexperienced, smiling faces were flat with pleasure; they looked like a pair of romantic fillets on a night out. His mind turned to the woman he had left behind in England.

Karan and Claire had parted company at a Greek restaurant in Hoxton.

They had been out for dinner with Claire's friend Aly Khan, who ran an art institute on Brick Lane, and Aly's assistant, Sara. Aly had talked passionately about an artist whose work he was exhibiting, Shazia Alam. He said she was 'smack out of Damien Hirst's Southall hellhole'. Claire asked him to tell them a bit more about his show, which Aly had seemed desperate to do. He rubbed his palms gleefully and began. Shazia's installation, he told them, involved women of varying ethnicities standing in wooden cubicles, almost entirely hidden save for a peephole at their crotch. Visitors at the exhibition would be invited to poke their noses into the peephole and guess the woman's nationality—Pakistani, American, Ukrainian, and so forth—from the scent. The idea, Aly said, was to propose an 'exploration of multicultural Britain through the pussy'. Karan had tried to keep himself out of the conversation, having quite often come across the word 'multicultural', used as it was with blustery awe by newspapers

and magazines. Brown people, outside of running corner shops, nursed rages, wrestled insanity, talked to mirrors, ate in silence, cheated on their lovers, danced like you wouldn't believe and sang silly on the sixth octave: this information had been recently released with fantastic velocity, startling British minds blanched over innumerable generations by bad weather, tepid tea and freezing water on all sides. The conversation had soon started to nosedive into a search for names for the exhibit and as Claire and Sara gave their suggestions Karan felt himself blacking out, floating away. Emerging from himself, his physical being looked down at the table he was seated at, playacting the humble brown schoolteacher, socially inept, privately outraged, seduced by the dazzling white curator. It occurred to him that every role in his life came with its modest particulars and its vulgar banalities, and what was deemed daringly authentic at one moment was proved false in the next, subject to scrutiny or revision—all because time had picked up her skirt and run forward.

Karan was drawn out of his musings when Aly and Sara applauded the name Claire had suggested for the installation: *The Bush Empire.* Karan had excused himself to use the restroom and when he returned to the table he did not take his seat, saying he was feeling unwell and wished to go home. Claire stood then, and they looked at each other like leopards in the delta, unsure if they should tear each other apart or pass by regally, without a second look.

When Karan had called her the following week, they chatted like old friends, each recognizing that the shape of their relationship had changed inexplicably, irrevocably. They decided to meet at Hampstead Heath, where he told her he was going back to Bombay; he could not be a photographer in London.

She reminded him that he was not a photographer in London; he was, by his own choice, a schoolteacher.

He smiled and said that she might have missed his point.

A giant oak, devastated by lightning, lay gravely in their path and a blackbird had perched on its last living branch. After a moment, Claire turned to him and said that he was really leaving London because the food had got to him in the end. He smiled and told her she was right, that he had been found out. Authenticity, she remarked, could be terribly pretentious, and he had to agree with her. Then it had started to rain and they had taken shelter under a tree, standing away from each other, shivering a little.

'Will you come back?'

'I don't know, Claire, but you should come and visit me in India.'

She did not respond to his offer; she felt her heart cave.

The shower soon passed. Instinctively, she reached forward to dry his hair with her hanky. 'Thank you,' he said, touched.

In the end, as they went their own ways, she expressed regret: 'The terrible thing about an English romance is there's just no accounting for the weather.'

'She was good to you, right?' Samar asked him.

'In ways I'm discovering only now.'

'I guess just as we never understand why we fall in love, we never know why we leave someone.' Samar's mind swung back to the evening he had met Leo on the steps in Grace's Garden, for the last time. Samar was asking Karan why he had split with Claire because he was trying to figure out what had gone all pear-shaped in his own life. Yet, part of his journey had been the process of accepting that there were always reasons for such unexpected, drastic departures, but the reasons did not add up to anything concrete.

'Artistic differences. Is that ground enough for breaking up?'

'If you want it to be,' Samar said quietly. 'Will you go back to photography now?'

'I don't know.'

'You had told Claire that you couldn't work on your stuff in London, so it's been on your mind; surely, now that you're back, you're going to give it another shot?'

Slowly, tediously, Karan explained that after returning to Bombay, and particularly after quitting work at the school in Juhu, he had tried to pick up his Leica again. But some sort of nameless, terrific inertia had chewed at him. He said he did not want to put the blame for the failure of his will on anything or anyone; it had nothing to do with Zaira's death, or Rhea, or the murder trial, or his time in London. At this point, Samar's eyes started to glaze with disinterest. 'Should I order some cheese?'

'Cheese? Why?' Karan asked.

'I thought it'll go wonderfully with the whine.'

Karan blushed. 'I don't know what I'm talking about but sometimes a photograph is not just a photograph.'

'I didn't mean to be flippant.' Samar straightened his posture. 'But one day you will discover that only the end of the world is the end of the world.'

Karan put down his fork and looked hard at Samar, memorizing his face, the crow's feet on the sides of his eyes, delicate and wise, like the lines on a map detailing a minor arm of a great river—now, the most beautiful thing he had ever beheld.

The waiter presented the bill.

They stood up to leave after putting down a generous tip. Gatsby was throbbing by now. They had to squeeze through the crowd at the bar to make it to the doorway where Samar paused for one last glance. The woman in the off-shoulder pewter gown with her electric presence was now flanked by two debonair, muscular men. One of the men was visibly drunk: he was threatening to pour champagne over the fashionable mess of her hair and she was urging him to stop, her expression as scandalized as it was wicked, her hands in the air, trying to stave off his rakish excess.

Samar turned. He did not want to see the beautiful woman bathed in champagne. 'They've still got those lamps. Someone could knock his head against them and that might mess him up for life.'

The image of Samar tap dancing on the bar top soared up in Karan's mind.

'You were wearing a grungy white tee-shirt that night, Karan.'

'I was?'

'And blue jeans. I don't think you know this, but I'd been watching you long before you ever laid eyes on me.'

As they were leaving the restaurant, Samar stopped on the last wooden step; he said that it had not occurred to him, until now, that the marvellous perfume inside had belonged to the lilies.

Karan looked up at the moon, a sliver of itself. It was tricky to tell if it was waxing or waning. But, oh, what a pretty little moon it was.

33

2001

THE WEEK RHEA TURNED FIFTY, THE CITY WAS agog with excitement over an exhibition of photographs. The series of black-and-white images of Bombay had been commended by the *Times of India* as 'technically flawless, emotionally compelling, sharp and tender, underscored by a vision honed over years'. A few of the images were printed alongside the review; she thought they were like a beautiful sadness thrown to the great blue skies. A black cat walked elegantly over an open, untidy crate of mangoes, a feline ballet dancer, the alfonso connoisseur of Crawford Market. A dead body—a track accident fatality—lay on the platform of Andheri station, a white sheet drawn up to its neck, while a black dog with a predatory look in its eyes sniffed at it with

interest. Rhea smiled as she saw the photograph of an ageing potter in Kumbharwada, his face creased by the sun, his eyes yellow and wraith-like, a hard, fine man, perfectly at home with his mortality. She tried to remember if she had seen the potter during her own jaunts to Kumbharwada, and wondered what had sent Karan to her old ilaka.

The show, which opened at the National Gallery of Modern Art, was critically admired and widely discussed, more so because of the media's acute interest in the photographer. Rumours smouldered like coals on fire. Some said the photographer was a bright young drifter with a drinking problem. The *Bombay Times* quoted 'a source' who had stated that Karan Seth was a former lover of a once-famous pianist. Preeti Modi, a prominent socialite and art collector, insisted that Karan had hit pay dirt thanks to the backing of a powerful curator in London. The most scandalous nugget of all revealed that the photographer had once worked in a call centre. The *Mumbai Mirror* had interviewed Karan's ex-colleagues who described him as 'A bit of a shy bugger' and, most tellingly, 'He, like, didn't know how to send a text message!'

Rhea visited the gallery twice, ascending the steps, only to reel on both occasions from the force of an invisible fist striking her. Over a decade had passed since she had met Karan, and her desperation to meet him again was so intense it forbade their reunion. When she finally mustered up the courage to enter the gallery, it was shut; the exhibition was being moved for a show in Tokyo. She stood outside, looking in through

the glass windows with famished eyes and a black heart, at the large frames wrapped in sheets of wax paper, tied with rattan, secured with duct tape. A single picture lingered on the wall; she could see it only a few minutes before it too was set aside, to be readied for shipping.

The photograph was of a rat trapper who had emerged from the sewers of Bombay, a battalion of bloodied bandicoots hanging lifelessly over his blood-streaked shoulder. The trapper's lean arms were grazed, probably from the bandicoots biting him in resistance and dread, and he stood erect in the plum dawn, staring at a milk van. His expression was not so much one of exhaustion as of acceptance, one that seemed to convey that, sometimes, life came down to killing rats for five bucks apiece, and that was that. Rhea's heart thrilled in the knowledge that, finally, Karan had got it. What she had tried to tell him when they had first met had now unravelled in him organically; he had, in fact, skipped backwards, fallen sideways, and stormed way ahead.

Some months later she came across a book of Karan's photographs at the Crossword Book Store at Kemps Corner. It was titled *The Brass Monkey*. The brief prologue explained the title of the book rather than setting into context any of the images splashed on its pages.

Many years ago, he wrote in the prologue, he had gone to Chor Bazaar where a friend had found an antique brass talisman shaped like a monkey. The talisman was meant to protect what one loved. However, they had been so caught up

in conversation at the time that his friend had forgotten the talisman in Chor Bazaar. Later, when she had expressed regret at losing the brass monkey, he had promised to find it for her again. He had then moved to England for a few years and, upon his return, had visited Chor Bazaar on numerous occasions and asked every dealer about the talisman, but had returned home empty-handed. *Sadly, I never found my friend's brass monkey. But these are some of the photographs I took as I searched for it,* he wrote in conclusion. *I'm still looking for the talisman. This is what I found in the meantime.*

Laying the book on her lap, Rhea splayed the pages open, touched each photograph slowly, gently, as if she were touching Karan, his face and neck and wrist. Within the pointillist brilliance of the images was a dismantled man. The splash of blood. A sigh of regret. In spite of how telling each picture was, she knew the images for what was missing in them: for Karan had painted around empty spaces, not in them. Reassigning her attention to the first few pages, she saw the dedication—*For Samar Arora*—and her mind harked back to the rumours of their coupling, which she had found impossible to believe. As she paid for her copy of the book, she recalled the serene, neat mound of her baby's grave, she could hear the music in which Adi had tried to lose himself, a labyrinth whose secret, central chamber, when located, could have freed him forever. She stepped out of the bookstore into the big, brawny arms of the city: the hard rays of the sun came down in lustrous shafts from a pearly grey sky, making her dizzy.

In her heart she heard Karan's footsteps, walking toward her, and she knew she would have to wait for him.

As she made her way up to the Sai Baba mandir on Forjett Street she thought about how foolish she had been, for failing to anticipate the hugeness of life, its detours, its cul-de-sacs. She turned a corner and went up a narrow, dirty slope where she stopped abruptly and rested her head against a moulded wall plastered with thick, peeling layers of gaudy film posters. An old woman with large holes in her ear lobes stopped to enquire if she was all right. But Rhea could not answer. She continued to cry helplessly, as if something were weeping through her. If only she could calm down she would tell the baffled old woman that if she was still here, browsing through bookstores and visiting temples, bargaining for fruit and attending concerts, it was because she wanted to meet Karan Seth, to tell him she was sorry; insanely, enormously, indisputably sorry for what she had done. If she had kept it at bay, the abomination of her losses, if she hadn't been gulped down, chewed up, spat out on the same side of the street as Mr Ward-Davies with his cracked ribs and popping eye, it was because she was waiting for Karan Seth, a fellow soldier against the same angry and heinous night.

Back home, after taking a hot shower, Rhea wore a thin off-shoulder black dress and lounged in bed. Her nails, painted earlier that same week a colour as dark as ox blood, had a grim allure. Lying on her bed, under a spell of music, she thought of the roses Adi gave her on her birthday; she thought of the concerts they had attended; she thought of his face lighting up

as he dug into a slice of the cake she had baked to welcome him home after a fortnight in Singapore. Those were the charmed days, even without talismans. Love, she thought, is *good luck.* Her eyes now fell on the photograph Karan had given her the first time he had come over to her house. Mounted and framed, it now hung above her bed. The birds in the picture were in flight, shunning the sky and the sun, dazzling the two of them beneath; there was a powerful, ineffable sense of the infinite about their movement. On the back of the photograph was Karan's lazy scrawl, *The lost flamingoes of Bombay,* words that had flagged off the beginning of the end of their lives as they had known it.

34

2005

ONE FINE MORNING IN JULY, KARAN WAS OUT ON Marine Drive making his way toward a particular bench when the figure approaching him made his heart stall.

'There you are!'

'Rhea?'

'What a wonderful morning it is.'

'What are you doing here?'

'I could ask you the same thing.'

'I'm looking for a bench.'

'The one that you had got installed for Samar?'

'How do you know about it?'

'I chanced upon it many months ago.' Rhea had noticed the metal plaque behind it, bearing Samar's name, and she

remembered Samar's obituary, written by Diya Sen. It had read like a vein, freshly cut. 'I always loved how you remembered people.'

'And I always envied how you forgot them.'

'More than ten years have passed since we last met; I'm not counting on a brass band but do I have to settle for a putdown?'

'You never asked anyone before deciding on what you would settle for ... Why bother now?'

'I decided to give civility a chance.'

He thought he heard a hint of nocturnal regret in the familiar, dangerous laughter. 'Ah, well, civility doesn't suit your personality one bit.'

'The perils of ageing, I suppose. Won't you sit for a bit? We might have words to share.'

As he walked toward her, he noticed a hint of aluminium in her raven-black hair. 'Words to share?'

'Yes. In fact, I wanted to ask you why you chose to install a bench for Samar. Here, of all places.'

'This was the place ... This was where he was happy.' He looked out at the sea, surprised by his unhesitating disclosure.

'And you came here with him?' She thought his face, its youthful angularity, had been sandpapered by time; a river stone now, smooth, timeless.

'Many, many times.'

Karan had only to shut his eyes to go back to the days when Samar and he came to Marine Drive at dusk.

One Thursday evening, after a long walk, they had sat on a bench, gazing at the serene sky veined with smouldering

orange; the sea had been inexplicably calm. Joggers panted past hunchbacked old men on cement benches. A one-eyed woman was selling a cluster of balloons. A gaggle of housewives, flesh oozing out on their sides, marched with alarming confidence. Cars, ugly metal ribbons, streamed down the main road. With only double-digit T-cells to his name, Samar was so thin a gusty wind could fling him over. Sitting next to Karan, his voice soft but broken, he had said, 'I could bear everything. Everything. Save for the loneliness. I couldn't rock it away or pray it down or scare it off. I don't know when it grew larger than me.' He paused, rubbed his shins; his mouth was open, as if the pain were smoking the words out of him. 'Because I have known Bombay, the tolling bells of Babulnath, the tigerish dawns and monsoon's ravage, because I have shopped in its bazaars, left its parties unsteady on my feet and walked at sundown by the sea, I wonder if it's too much to ask to be remembered in some small way. No, not a gravestone; that's too much fuss. Something quiet. And simple. A heap of stones. Far from all things.'

A few days later Samar had passed away in his sleep, the red patchwork quilt tucked around his neck.

Karan was living at Samar's house at the time. At 7.00 a.m., he went up to Samar's room. Even before he entered it, Karan felt an electric jolt reach up from his calves to the very top of his head; he knew, then, he would never hear Samar's voice again. When he stepped into the room he felt trapped in its sepulchral hush; there was a strange, cold, forbidding odour. He went up to the bed and stood by it. Samar's eyes were closed; he was so thin, even the quilt seemed to have more body than

him. Karan pulled off the quilt and sat by Samar, studying the tragic wasteland of his body. An inexplicable desire impelled him to touch every part of his friend's inert body. Softly, slowly, his fingers caressed Samar's eyelids first before travelling down to his toes, passing along the way his collarbone, ribs, hipbone, kneecaps, the pronounced bone at his ankle. *This is Samar,* he thought. *This is where he begins. And here is where he ends.* Then he touched himself. *This is me.* The cartography of remembrance. He looked out of the window and saw a gleaming rectangle of sea, the dusty branches of an almond tree. After a few minutes he rose to go downstairs to inform Saku-bai but before he reached the landing, he fell to his knees and doubled over. *This is not me.* The strange racking and hollow sound sent Saku-bai racing up the stairs and she found Karan there, on the landing, in a gasping, ruined, inconsolable heap.

'Let's go up to the bench.'

'It's not important, really. Besides, it's a bit of a walk from here.'

'I can leave, if you'd much rather be alone.'

'No,' he said. And again: 'No.' He was disappointed to experience no fury toward Rhea; the affinity between them had only ripened over time, its devastating power undiminished. 'Let's go and see it. You took me to see so many places in this city, it's now my turn to return the favour.'

Walking side by side along the promenade, Rhea was immutably consoled by Karan's presence, as though he were an apparition summoned by the demented force of her terrific

longing. Sunlight spilled through the thick, smog-suffused clouds, smothering them in a smooth and buttery light. Wind, swift and strong, concealed the accumulating anger of the bruise-blue sky: the monsoon, which had unravelled this season with erratic, gritty strength, was preparing to burst upon the earth with catastrophic force.

'I see it!' He crinkled his eyes.

The bench was at the end of the promenade, battered by sunlight, bloated with rain, scratched and spat on; it was perfect. 'Here it is.' When he extended his arms, pride and sadness came through.

'What a good place to rest. Samar must have suffered terribly.'

'His liver had failed. His last bout with tuberculosis was nasty; I would put a napkin to his mouth and it would come away red.'

'Didn't he take the medicines to manage the infection?'

'He wasn't careful when he first found out. When Leo left him he couldn't hang on in San Francisco alone. He came back to Bombay, to his cottage, to Zaira's photographs, to Mr Ward-Davies's leash.' Karan sighed. 'He complained that his beliefs had failed him, that his conviction had not been worth rickshaw change. But I wanted him to live long enough to see one thing.' He looked at her, head tilted. 'Even if he couldn't save what he had loved, loving them had saved him.'

She placed her hand on the bench. 'Was it a good death?'

Karan shook his head. 'But he dreamed of flamingoes. He spoke of them all the time, though he'd never seen them. I promised to take him to Sewri but then I never got around to it. Before I knew it, he was gone.'

'We should go and see them, then.' Her whisper was as quiet as a little fish coming up for a gulp of air. 'For Samar's sake.'

'A day doesn't go by when I don't think of him.' He covered his mouth lightly with his palms.

'You stayed with him all the way to the end?'

He drew his hand back. 'I carried him around the house. I'd show him his piano, the roof, the terrace. I'd show him the sea. He loved the sea, Rhea, he just loved the sea. He was so ...' Grief slammed against his voice, and her eyes filled up. 'I cleaned his crap. He threw up on me. I sang to him and held him close. We went for walks on Marine Drive and for dinner to Gatsby.'

'You cleaned his sheets too?'

'I cleaned his sheets.'

'And you held him?'

'As hard as he asked.'

'And you rocked him?'

'I rocked him.' His voice broke into so many little pieces it seemed impossible that it would be whole again. 'He was my friend.' Locking his arms around himself, Karan swayed back and forth. 'He was my friend. He was ... my friend.'

35

FOR SEVERAL DAYS AFTER MEETING KARAN AT Marine Drive, Rhea drifted in the dark, still pond of Karan's remembering gaze, imagining what he had seen: svelte black kittens in a dusty howdah, an abandoned stone mermaid, wizened faces of old women, midnight squares in an old city, the gossamer wings of night insects whirring rapidly with an eerie fever. Her visions soon grew bolder, macabre; she felt a great flapping against the darkness and she rose out of it to meet the ghosts he had summoned by name. She saw a raven on a fence post; she saw a spire; she saw a cold, wet street; she saw the deep, resplendent green of a moonlit pasture. In bed, recalling the comfort of walking down the promenade with Karan, she felt his quiet, destroyed voice conflate and cover her like a mantilla.

Toward the end of July, after a particularly fierce shower of rain had calmed, she called him. Her offer to drive him to Sewri to see the flamingoes threw him.

To ward off any suspicion about her intentions, she added that the venture was in Samar's memory.

He relented, not under any ruse of sentimentality—this was not to be a stroll down memory lane—but because he had questions to ask her.

'When should I pick you up?' She looked out of the window, at the thick, glowering sky.

'I live in Juhu now—so I'll take the train up.'

'The famous photographer does not have a chauffeur?'

'I rarely ever step out of my room in Juhu. I've been there so long I'm set like jelly.'

'Very well, then, I'll pick you up from the station.'

'Thanks.'

'If the need arises, I can always drop you back.'

'I might take you up on your offer if the rain doesn't let up.'

'See you on Tuesday.' As she put the phone down, the exhilarating anxiety that enveloped her was almost adolescent, though her experience of it was solemn.

No sooner had the train deposited Karan at the station than an announcement blared through the sodden air—all trains had been cancelled due to incessant flooding in the northern suburbs. Karan was caught off guard. When he had boarded, the rain was only the uncut diamond of a whisper, but within an hour the tracks had got flooded. Karan could

not make up his mind whether to carry on or take a taxi back to Juhu.

As he stepped out of the station now, his black umbrella blown back by the unruly gale, he saw Rhea's car pull up. He studied her profile, severe and elegant; it made him feel like he was walking on lit coals, and he recalled the first time she had come to fetch him at Ban Ganga, their subsequent drive to Sewri. The repeat of such an enterprise would not only insult the sorcery of the past, it would also mean that he had failed to gamer the lessons fate had delivered at his doorstep. But his curiosity was larger than the memory of past scalding; he had to ask her about her child. And whether he was the father.

He opened the door and climbed in. 'All the tracks in the suburbs are flooded. The trains have been called off'

She looked at him, puzzled. 'It hasn't been raining so wildly here.'

'When I left Juhu the storm was in the distance; I gather by the time I got here everything back north was swamped.'

'That's yet another reason to not live beyond Bandra.'

'You're such a south Bombay snob!'

'I'm joking, Karan.' Her face, rinsed in pain and age, held an angular, sombre quietness, like the last pew in a cathedral.

'I should not have come today,' he said. 'How will I go back now?'

'I'll take you back. I had told you I would.' She started to drive.

'What if the roads are also flooded, as they most likely will be? How will you drive through so much water and then back again?' He saw commuters tumble out of the station, looking lost and harried, unsure how they would reach home.

'Rough waters and Rhea Dalal,' she said, looping her middle finger over her index finger, 'we go back a long way.'

He sat back as she drove on. 'If the city has been so rude and cruel why did you stay on?'

'Do you know why you came back?'

'I'm a glutton for punishment but I expected you to know better.'

Rhea considered Karan's question for a few minutes. There had been any number of times she had thought of leaving the city. She had considered moving to Pondicherry and working on her pottery amid the seaside town's large community of potters; she had thought of moving to her house in Alibaug. But her heart could not free itself from Bombay.

She said, 'A few years ago I was working the morning shift at the animal hospital when a Parsi woman in a black polka-dotted dress stopped by. She was around seventy. She had knotted a navy blue scarf around her thinning white hair and she was holding a cane basket.' The woman explained to Rhea that she had been walking outside the Parsi colony in Dadar when she had seen a snake. A car had run over it, and it was writhing in pain when she had rescued it. She said she had no choice but to bring it to the animal shelter in the hope that it might be saved. Giving Rhea the snake in the basket, she said she had to

leave as her husband was critically ill and she had to schlep it all the way to Bhatia Hospital, at the other end of town. Rhea peeked into the cane basket. The snake was already dead. She looked at the woman and assured her she would do her best to save the creature. 'Promise me you will make it better,' the old woman had said with uncommon solemnity and Rhea had taken her hand in her own and said, 'I promise,' before turning and walking away toward the dispensary. Filled with awe and revulsion, a strange humming in her head, she had stood in the dispensary where a veterinarian was injecting a stray puppy. If this toothless old woman in her black polka-dotted dress and navy blue scarf could leave her husband in a hospital to come to Parel to deliver a road kill of a snake, then something was all right about Bombay, she had thought. On the days the city smarted and ached, when it jabbed and sulked, Rhea had only to shut her eyes and picture the woman with a cane basket in her hand.

'Did the woman ever come back to enquire after the snake?'

'No, but she called me.'

'What did you tell her?'

'I said the snake had been saved. She told me her husband had died.'

'Why did you tell her the snake survived?'

Rhea did not reply.

In the silence between them, he saw her more clearly than ever before, understanding that what attracted him to her was her temperament: the temperament of an artist, endlessly

curious, frighteningly detached, essentially unfathomable, brooding yet childlike, transient, abstract, of ample, generous spirit. He knew her better now because he finally knew himself; perhaps that was why they had met, to be revealed to each other in the silvered mirror of their souls.

As she navigated through deadly sheets of rain, he asked her about her child.

'The monkey, it was rabid. It got into the clinic through an open window. The nurse carrying my son was the beast's third victim. She dropped my baby.'

'Dropped?' His expression was like a page ripped in half.

'On the edge of a stairwell. He tumbled down six floors.' The sight of her son, wrapped in a white cloth, tumbling down the stairwell, sprung to her mind; she felt a tightening in her throat.

Karan closed his eyes. 'I don't know what to say.'

'I'd always assumed you needed to know someone before you might care for them,' she said, pausing to marvel at the intensity of her longing for her infant son. 'For the life of me I didn't know that certain kinds of love are a knowledge unto themselves.'

She spoke of the days after the baby's death; Adi's depression, her icy reserve, their confrontation. But she kept one key question of the narrative unanswered: the identity of the baby's father.

'Adi must have had a fit when he found out about you and me.'

'He was quite calm. On the face of it.'

'Poor chap. How is he now?'

She told him about her final fight with Adi. 'I left for Alibaug to gather my thoughts. I had decided to tell him everything on my return. I spent the week thinking of how to break the news to him. I worried over words. I drove back believing I would find a way to make things all right. But I came back,' she said, her sigh like the final breath escaping a slaughtered bird, 'to an empty house.'

'Where did he go?'

'I don't know.'

'After so many years?'

'He just,' she said, slicing the air with her hand, 'took off.' Although years had passed since she had seen Adi, as she talked about him now love flooded up the back of her mouth like a taste.

'Did you look for him?'

She nodded her head. 'Sometimes in the late evenings, when I'm not expecting anyone and the doorbell rings, my heart jumps.' Human memory, its scalding recall, terrorized her: the darnedest little flashbacks, the broken, masculine hum of an Ellington ditty, an untidily squeezed tube of Tom's of Maine, could dismantle her. 'But it's never him. He's never at the door.'

Karan felt suddenly that the well of Rhea's loneliness was deep enough to drown him.

'I thought he had left because I had cheated on him,' she said under her breath. 'But perhaps he left because he felt as if he had not loved me enough to keep me to himself.'

'You're hard, Rhea.'

'Soft is for sponge cakes ... so what's your point?'

'You haven't come undone.'

'Actually, they put the stitches in so small that you can't see them at all.'

After Adi's disappearance, Rhea had employed a private detective agency to trace him. The investigators had combed all of Bombay, then the rest of the state and, eventually, much of the country. Every few months she would receive a call saying that a man 'just like Adi' had been spotted and she would fly out to wherever it was. The fifth false alarm had sent her to Delhi, but she had returned disappointed.

In the flight back she had reflected on the fact that the man who had been spotted at Khan Market had been mad and homeless; why had he been mistaken for Adi?

'Then, four years ago,' she said, 'I got a call saying he was seen at Shirdi.'

She had got into her car, driven maniacally, devouring distance with dangerous haste. She arrived before dawn and waited outside the fortress-like enclosure around Sai Baba's crypt. In the thickening swell of flower sellers, limbless devotees, fakir impersonators, cobblers and sundry politicians, she had stood in anticipation, sweating profusely in the bestial heat of the plateau. At dusk, after scanning almost every face present, she went up to the shrine, prayed, then made her way out. She was walking down the noisy lane outside the temple when she suddenly felt helpless with rage; she wanted to grab her life and

tear out its hair, punch it in the guts, gouge out its eyes, throw it to the floor and sit on its chest till the darned monster let her be. Instead, she fell on her knees, then drew them up to her chest, curling up like an alarmed centipede. Devotees who saw her thought she had been seized by a divine presence; in fact, she was motionless with an anger too large for her.

Unfit to drive back to Bombay she checked into the Sun-n-Sand Hotel.

Lying on the double bed, she surveyed the room: the chairs were upholstered in green chintz; the curtains were thick; a sketch of Sai Baba was pegged on the wall. Although there was nothing particularly repugnant about the room, she felt it was exactly the sort of place one might choose to die in, a room without any redeeming detail or aspiration for beauty that might tempt one to stay back, to hold on. My *entire life has failed me,* she thought. *Everyone is gone.*

In a while, her despair dissipating, Rhea sat up in bed. She drew the curtains to allow the dying night to tumble around her room like a kitten playing with a ball of wool. She saw a maize field ripple under the sigh of a wind; she heard bells tolling in the foreground, the kakad aarti. Her thoughts turned to Karan, the last in the quartet, without a role as neat as of the other three, the only one who was still around, somewhere. Light emerged on the horizon and bounced boldly into the featureless hotel room, making her shudder in anticipation. The belief that she would meet Karan again gave her the resolve to return to Bombay; she would meet him, then ask him for forgiveness. She would tell

him how much she missed their conversations, she would thank him for the photograph, a sweet scribble on its flip side.

'You knew we would meet again?'

'I did.'

'How?'

'Mother's instinct?' She gave a bitter laugh. 'I don't know. I just did. I was looking for you long before I ever met you in Chor Bazaar.'

'I hope Adi is safe.' His tight whorl of anger for Adi melted, vanished; kindness and respect took its place. 'I hope he's all right.'

She gulped. 'I liked to hear him hear me; his listening was like being held by a strong pair of arms.'

He looked at her face; she was still in love with the man. But his envy rolled aside; there was no fire in it. She could sense him withdrawing, but also his indifference; she remained silent. Twenty minutes passed before she said, 'Well, here we are, back at Sewri.'

'Lost, lovely birds.' A flamingo flew into the air, squawking; its dull pink wings thrashed about.

'It's been a while.'

The same sickening stench of mudflats. Old factories in the backdrop. A shiny city in the foreground.

'Have you noticed how the birds are almost all gone?'

'Most of them leave as early as April,' Rhea said. Their shoulders touched under her huge, sturdy umbrella. 'I hear they fly to Africa.'

'The last time we came here there were at least fifty thousand birds. Aren't you amazed that this lot'—he pointed to the skimpy cluster of a thousand-odd birds—'is still around?'

This flock did not possess the dramatic presence of the one seen years ago, but their tentative tranquillity had a certain dignified strength.

'You're right. They could have left.' A wet, desultory wind rippled the hem of her widow-black dress. 'But they're still here. I guess we always underestimate staying power.'

The wind picked up intensity. Sporadic trellises of lightning streaked the sky. They turned, strode urgently to the car as rain of uncommon might approached in the distance like a miasma. 'We should get back to the car.'

'I read in the papers that Samar and you took up in the end.'

'It was nothing like that.'

'Why didn't you rubbish the rumours?'

'They were so flattering!' He held the door open for her to climb in, he smiled. 'I'm susceptible to certain kinds of vanity.'

She started the car. 'What made you return to photography?'

'Samar asked me to.' He looked around her car. A trinket was suspended from the rear-view mirror. There were old copies of *Art India* and *Tehelka* on the back seat.

'He asked you?'

'Not in so many words.' Karan recounted his visit with Samar to Dr Taraporevala, who had found in Samar's recitals salve for personal loss. The subtle, startling ways art could repair

an individual. The solitary pursuit of one artist could serve a stranger with companionship, knowledge, truth. He told Rhea what Samar had said to him at Gatsby: *One day you will discover only the end of the world is the end of the world.* 'What he left unsaid saw me through.'

'That's why *The Brass Monkey* is dedicated to him.' Her face was like a key that has finally found the lock it fits into.

'I miss him so much,' he said. 'So much.' He shook his head.

There was no consolation for such longing, she knew from experience. Her eyes briefly examined the daunting sky. 'It'll take us ages to get to Juhu; would you care to sleep over at my place?'

'Thanks for the offer, but I don't want to overstay my welcome.'

'It's obnoxious,' she said, heading north. 'To have to be so polite.' Tightening the grip on her steering wheel, she added, 'Do you have any idea how much I loved your photographs?'

'You saw them?'

'I missed the exhibition in Bombay. A year later, I caught it in a gallery in Los Angeles. I have a copy of *The Brass Monkey.*'

'The photographs must seem like familiar ground to you.'

'Not at all. You see things differently now. Will there be more?'

'I really don't know.' He had come to believe his work was concerned less with extracting meaning out of life and more with keeping the whole intact; art was not what he took away but what he left untouched, as it were, complete in itself. 'I'm

still unsure if the pictures were a result of an old ambition or a freak occurrence. Have you ever sat by a lake and seen a series of bubbles rise to the surface and pop? The pictures were a little like that, I guess.'

'The prologue was generous.'

'Was there a photograph you liked in particular?'

'The one of an old man standing in a balcony with his hands on the railing. Right in front of him is an underwear hung out to dry.'

'Yes.'

'And the underwear has a little hole.'

'I took that picture in Kurla, where I worked at the call centre.'

'It was as if he was gazing out at the world through a hole in an underwear on the washing line outside his window. You took what was wounded and forgotten, and you made it almost joyous. But,' she said, 'it was never trite.'

'I watched him every day. He was always there. An odd little sentinel. My running mate in an election for Men Going Nowhere.'

She waited for the rumbles of thunder to clear. 'You took him and made his loneliness so real it was like a river or a tree, and you took the pain away just enough for me to see it. And to see him.'

In the seclusion of the car, Rhea spoke to him of the last few years of her life, serene, without incident, unmaimed by the glamour of public success, the sort that had vandalized Karan,

driven him underground. Lila-bai, her maid, had left two years ago. Miss Cooper, the neighbour on the floor below hers, had relocated to Toronto after a psychic had told her all of India would be destroyed in an earthquake. She had tried to embark on a few tentative friendships but had retraced her steps from the periphery of meaningful intimacy; there was so much of her past she could not explain to herself that the task of explaining it to someone else seemed cumbersome. The animal shelter had a new dispensary, built in part with a donation she had made. She felt the need to explain how she continued to live her life uninterrupted, although her husband was no longer around. 'Adi left me enough. Once a month I meet this wonderful person, my "financial adviser", who manages my funds and plans how to reinvest my dividends or lock my profits. It's only catching up with me now, how far ahead Adi had thought for me. Oh,' she touched her forehead, 'and I removed the tiger skin in the living room. I had it burnt.'

'But it was a sight to behold!'

'Yes, it was. But all life had gone out of it. When I used to sit on the chaise below it I often felt it was going to come crashing down on me. It was beautiful but empty, and dead.'

The Alibaug house, whose walls she had recently got painted a pale pistachio green, continued to bring her renewal, and she returned there every month. In the house by the sea, she would read voraciously the novels Adi had enjoyed, finding companionship in their pages, silken ruminations, tragic detours, the sullen, aching resonance of an imagined life. She

would pause during certain scenes, finding that something of Adi was revealed in the reading of the novel, a particular passage he would have re-read, a line that would have seduced his admiration.

She looked gingerly at Karan. Almost everything she had said was utterly mundane. Yet, she found him enrapt, as if he had heard the most fascinating story ever. His own life, altered dramatically after his return to Bombay, to photography, paled before the story of hers.

After they passed Worli, when it seemed as if Juhu was not an impossibility in spite of the deluge, he asked her casually what was uppermost on his mind; the identity of her son's father. The muscles in her jaw clenched, she said nothing, and he pressed on. 'I wish you would tell me.'

'Is this why you agreed to meet me?' Her tone was one of extreme disappointment.

'I need to know my losses, if only to let go of them.'

'A child died, Karan, does it matter if it was yours or Adi's?'

'Yes.'

Her face chalked up with a sorrow too wide to be wept.

'I guess the north of the city took a nasty blow.'

An hour passed.

At Mahim, greeted by the daunting sight of flooded roads and traffic jams, he suggested, 'We'd be better off taking the gullies of Bandra.'

'But the gullies are bound to be flooded.'

'The main road will have massive back-ups.'

'I suppose the lanes will be less crowded.'

In the lanes of Bandra, water had risen ankle-high. Rhea's car soldiered forward, past big-boughed trees that had snapped like cocktail picks. The lightning in the sky was like the flashing mane of a runaway stallion. Frequently, thunder reverberated so loudly they had to repeat themselves.

'Why don't you turn around and go back, Rhea? I'll just walk it to Juhu.'

'No!' There was something crazed in her need to reach him home, as if the gesture was a means of restoring his trust in her or to express a kindness she had been incapable of in the past.

'There has to have been a cloudburst here,' he said, astounded by the volume of water outside the car.

'I'll keep driving until I can.'

'And when you no longer can?'

'We will walk. Or swim. But I will get you home. You will drink a cup of tea. Tomorrow morning, you will read the paper. You will be all right.'

The last of the lovely cottages was swamped; cane chairs and dictionaries and paintings and lamps and books and paintings churned together in an indecipherable mass in the thick and furious rivulets of water. Plump, dark women hurried to salvage their belongings, white ovens and love seats, silk saris and potted ferns, great old gramophones too.

'I'm sorry,' he said as they drove slowly past, 'I behaved badly in the end. I kept calling you. I followed you. Showed

up at your doorstep, wrangled with Adi. My conduct was appalling.'

'Oh,' she said, her brow crinkling, 'I wish I were man enough to apologize for what I did to you, Karan.'

He was grateful that she had not, directly, asked him for his forgiveness; that would have made him feel incredibly awkward. 'Something changed in you after the verdict, didn't it?' he asked.

'You're right.' His perspicacity impressed her.

'Was it the verdict?'

'No. Outside, in the quad, I saw Malik briefly, right before he got in his car with his lawyers.'

'Yes, I remember. You had told me you felt that he didn't look to you like a murderer.'

'I never understood why his face had upset me. And I've thought about that moment for years. A few weeks back, I was in the kitchen making tea when I realized something inside me had changed forever because,' she said, her hand on his shoulder, 'when I looked at Malik's face I saw something of myself in it.'

Rain continued to hammer on the roof of the car.

Rhea said that all the men she had ever loved were now recognized only by their absence in her life. Her father had perished in a horrific car accident. Forbidden the dignity of a proper farewell, she continued to long for Dr Thacker, his patience, his acuity, his ability to read her dreams. Although there had never been the time to forge a meaningful attachment with her son, allegiances formed in the womb were hard to

overcome. Adi, she had accepted in Shirdi, would never come back to her, and it was her greatest regret that she had failed to tell him that loving someone was not only a moral act but also an instinct for life. 'The loneliness I live with today is so large that it billows out of me; occasionally, when I wake at night, I find myself walking into it. I don't have it in me, any longer, to fight it, the emptiness. So I've been wondering, in the meantime—if we can do dinner now and again, or perhaps a walk in the morning, if you don't mind very much.'

The request threw Karan.

Rhea, so ferociously protective of her solitude, was asking for his help to alleviate the loneliness in her life. Karan smiled inwardly, without enacting the gesture. The word *irony* could not accurately be applied in the context, but its spirit was engaging, democratic, broad enough to encompass all the things that darted around language but never within it. Malik's mother, Mrs Prasad, had confirmed to Samar the suspicion he could never identify: that his loss was of a widower, and through his anger rang a lover's dirge. Zaira, once infallibly ubiquitous, was now a footnote in public memory, hostage only to private remembrance. Adi, whom Rhea had trusted with and for her heart, had vanished without a word, defeating forever her faith in a loyalty she had once assumed invincible. Leo, who everyone had expected would perish without a trace, a statistical casualty, was at his desk in Brooklyn, writing away, dotting a sentence before he embarked on a fresh one. Likewise, Malik Prasad, former stalker, murderer, loon, was now a producer of

soap operas, happily married, with a pretty, ambitious pilot for a wife and a daughter he doted on. Karan's photography, which he believed had been soiled by the tar of politics, was now free to be itself, stupendous and light, witty and authentic. And now here was Rhea, muse, madness, subject of his lunatic love, asking for his hand in friendship.

'The car's battery has died.'

'Oh.' He appeared jolted by her pronouncement.

'Are your feet also wet, Karan?'

'Yes, the water's come through.'

'We should get out.'

'May I look at your hands before that?'

She held them out to him.

He studied her veins, the elegant criss-crossing on her wrists.

She held her breath.

When he let go of her hands, she felt like an anchor crashing to the bed of the sea. *I want love to leave me alone for a while.*

'I don't know if I will last long in Bombay,' he said, palming off his unavailability on geography. 'I might move. Travel. Bombay has lost me, Rhea.'

'The glitter wears, I suppose.'

'There's no open space. Buildings everywhere. I don't know where to look, except at the sky.'

She was amazed; a few years ago the same man had sat at the end of her lane to catch a glimpse of her, had fought her husband to the ground, and here he was today, looking for exit

routes. What could attract a man could, eventually, revolt him; she knew this from experience that was not restricted to Karan. 'Where does your wagon head after that?'

'Shimla, perhaps.'

'Ah,' she cried. 'So Karan Seth comes full circle.'

'Is there any other way?' he asked. 'My father died, left me the house. I might fix it up and hang out there for a bit.'

'I can see you living in the mountains, Karan. I think you'll be happy there. But what will you do there?'

'Prepare to become an unmotivational speaker; I believe there's a market out there,' he said with a smile.

'Whatever you do, in the end, you will be fine, and things will work out. Perhaps not as you had wanted, but they will.'

'Oddly enough, I've come to believe in that more than ever before. But you, Rhea, what will you do? Where will you go?'

'Here is where I've been headed all along.' She knew Karan had his entire life ahead of him, extravagant with possibilities; her life, in stark contrast, reminded her of a train that had gone off its tracks. 'Even if I never knew it, even if I was lost all along, Bombay is where I belong.'

I'm glad you think so.'

'If you believe that,' she said, her husky laugh flashing like a rapier, 'then you'll believe anything.' She turned the key in the ignition, but the car would not start. 'Thing is, when you fell, you did it with all your strength. I, on the other hand, crashed without fanfare. And the downside of being a car wreck is there's no entertainment value in it after a while.'

His heart bolted. Did she really feel like a car wreck? But an act of tenderness he committed now would be misleading, he knew. 'You are a brave woman.'

'Not a good one, though. But I suppose bravery will see me through the long rains.'

'We're going to have to leave the car here,' he observed. But why was he finding it so impossible to open the door and jump out?

'Yes. We'll have to walk.' She too found herself holding on to the steering wheel. *Let me wait a few minutes longer,* she thought. *Perhaps he will change his mind.*

'I'll walk to Juhu. You don't need to take me back.'

'I'm sorry I failed you. I had promised to get you home.'

'It was not in your hands, Rhea. You never failed me.'

Silver arrows of rain struck the earth with sinister anger. They saw a calf floating away helplessly in the torrent.

'You will have to wade through the water all the way to Juhu. Swim, even.'

'As will you, back to Breach Candy.' He marvelled. 'How far we live from each other.'

'In the storm it doesn't matter where you live. It's about getting back safely. I'd promised to get you back home.'

'You told me once that storms were tricky.'

'But I didn't say they were impossible.'

'Well, I never knew whether to believe you.'

'That might have been a problem in more ways than one.'

'You'll make it back home safely.'

'It'll be one hell of a trek,' she said, 'and I'll make it home. But there are worse things than that.' She jumped out of the car like a cat.

He opened the door, stepped into the water.

Joining thousands of others, they entered the monsoon, its delirium and purgatory. There were women in saris and girls in jeans; bankers in suits and dabbawallas in dhotis; there were rowdy boys and baffled old men; there were dogs, mice, a white cow. Some faces were scared; others were undaunted, almost thrilled; everyone seemed intent only on surviving the storm. Karan held Rhea's hand briefly but the rain would not allow them to stay together for very long; they were soon separated by daggers of water. They managed to walk into a cul-de-sac which, oddly enough, was more or less abandoned. He turned and walked back to the crowd of people he had left behind. She waited where she was. Over the din, she shouted, 'It never meant anything.' The water came up to her hips now and she struggled to stand upright in its currents. 'The kindness. And the cruelties.'

'Then what was true, Rhea?' His hand was shielding his eyes when he turned to look at her. 'What was true in all of it?'

'Years ago, in Dadar market, the madwoman you had photographed.'

'Purple satin gown,' he said without missing a beat. 'Wild, matted hair. I remember her perfectly.'

'She wasn't insane, not at all. She knew that none of this ever happened.'

'Not even this?' He spread out his hand to underscore the tempest, its theatre of upheaval.

'Not even this.'

'Something in all of this must be true, Rhea.'

'Only the moment is true.' Her reply was so strained that perhaps he never heard it. 'Everything else is false.'

'Rhea ...' His eyes trailed after the doomed, defiant blur.

A cloud had burst over her, and sent her reeling into its foliage. She sensed, as she felt herself go under, that it was everywhere, it was everything. Love. It was this city, its ghastly buildings and the sea. Dark petals of red roses dancing in the wind and the roofs of crumbling cottages. A shell on the beach and the hum of a blind beggar. The amber cast of the street light and a dog howling at the moon. Everything was made out of it. Everything had come forth from it, as it would one day return into it. *Love.*

With her hair streaming open, arms spread out, legs caught in wreaths of water, she came up once, and through the rippled curtains of rain looked up at the sky. The world, in spite of its disquiet, or perhaps because of it, was what it was, and now this world was neither threatening nor ugly, and she was glad to know that, after all, everything was just right.

Acknowledgements

BECAUSE OF YOUR FRIENDSHIP—A.A., ADAM, ALAN, Ambika, Anjali, Bhavesh, David, DT, Elnora, Erico, Flaviano, Heather, Hemali, John, Kalyani, Kanika, Kaushik, Laura, Lorenzo, Meenu, Namrita, Nehal, NG, Nina, Nonita, Parul, Paolo, Raman, Rashmi, Sandip, Saraswathi Devi, Satya, Siddhartha, Sooni, Pico, Tinu, Tushar, Urvashi—I could write a little book about big love.

This book took a bit of spit and polish from two extraordinary editors, Poulomi Chatterjee and Danielle Durkin.

My book's agents, Jonny Geller and Lisa Bankoff, have been singular, terrific models of allegiance and energy.

Nandini Bhaskaran copy-edited the manuscript dazzlingly under duress.

Much of this book was written at Meher Pilgrim Retreat; Barr House, Matheran (where Francis Wacziarg has created an artist's haven managed with marvellous efficiency by Surendra Singh); and 815, Evelyn Avenue.

I am indebted to Swami Vignanananda, Founder, Yogalayam, Berkeley.

This book is for Sai Baba and for Meher Baba.

About the Author

Siddharth Dhanvant Shanghvi's first novel, *The Last Song of Dusk*, won the Betty Trask Award in the UK and the Premio Grinzane Cavour in Italy, and was nominated for the IMPAC Prize in Ireland. His second book, *The Lost Flamingoes of Bombay*, was shortlisted for the Man Asian Prize. *The Rabbit & the Squirrel*, with illustrations by Stina Wirsen, and *Loss*, essays on death and grief, are published by HarperCollins India as well. Shanghvi works and lives in a village in north Goa.

About the Author

HarperCollins *Publishers* India

At HarperCollins India, we believe in telling the best stories and finding the widest readership for our books in every format possible. We started publishing in 1992; a great deal has changed since then, but what has remained constant is the passion with which our authors write their books, the love with which readers receive them, and the sheer joy and excitement that we as publishers feel in being a part of the publishing process.

Over the years, we've had the pleasure of publishing some of the finest writing from the subcontinent and around the world, including several award-winning titles and some of the biggest bestsellers in India's publishing history. But nothing has meant more to us than the fact that millions of people have read the books we published, and that somewhere, a book of ours might have made a difference.

As we look to the future, we go back to that one word—a word which has been a driving force for us all these years.

Read.

Also by Siddharth Dhanvant Shanghvi

The Last Song of Dusk

The Rabbit and the Squirrel

Loss

THE LOST FLAMINGOES OF BOMBAY